A Penguin Special
The Sanctions Handbook

Roger Omond was born in East London, South Africa, in 1944. He was educated at Grey High School, Port Elizabeth, and Rhodes University, Grahamstown, where he graduated in history and politics. In 1967 he joined the *Daily Dispatch*, with Donald Woods as editor. He became successively political correspondent, head of the office in South Africa's first African 'homeland' of Transkei, features editor, leader writer and night editor. When he left the *Dispatch* in 1978 he was assistant editor. While in South Africa he wrote for the *New Statesman*, *Observer* and Gemini News Service. He joined the *Guardian* in 1978 and is now chief sub-editor in the foreign department. In 1985 he published *The Apartheid Handbook* (Pelican).

Dr Joseph Hanlon was correspondent in Mozambique for the BBC, the *Guardian* and various financial magazines from 1979 to 1985. He has written extensively on politics and economics, including: *Mozambique: The Revolution under Fire* (1984), *SADCC: Progress, Projects and Prospects* (1985), *Apartheid's Second Front* (Penguin, 1986) and *Beggar Your Neighbours* (1986).

Joseph Hanlon and Roger Omond

The Sanctions Handbook

Penguin Books

Penguin Books Ltd, Harmondsworth, Middlesex, England
Viking Penguin Inc., 40 West 23rd Street, New York, New York 10010, USA
Penguin Books Australia Ltd, Ringwood, Victoria, Australia
Penguin Books Canada Ltd, 2801 John Street, Markham, Ontario, Canada L3R 1B4
Penguin Books (NZ) Ltd, 182–190 Wairau Road, Auckland 10, New Zealand

First published 1987

Filmset in Plantin

Made and printed in Great Britain by
Richard Clay Ltd, Bungay, Suffolk

Contents

Acknowledgements

Part 1

South African Pressclips, of the many sources of news about that country, has been the backbone of research for this book. *SA Pressclips* is a weekly digest of cuttings from South African newspapers sent on subscription by Barry Streek, 36 Woodside Road, Tamboerskloof, Cape Town. It is essential for keeping up to date with South Africa throughout the year. *SA Pressclips* also produced in late 1985 two supplements on disinvestment and sanctions which, together with the weekly digest, proved invaluable. The Institute of Race Relations' annual *Surveys of Race Relations* are, as always, essential.

The BBC's *Summary of World Broadcasts*, which daily monitors Southern African radio and television and news agencies, provided ready access to news from that part of the continent.

The House of Commons Foreign Affairs Committee Sixth Report, with all the evidence given to it, brings together a mass of opinion on South Africa – some of it debatable, but all interesting and much of it useful in researching this book. Dan van der Vat of the *Guardian* pointed me towards a number of sources, particularly American ones. Joseph Hanlon, author of the second half of this book, was helpful, especially about South Africa's neighbours.

Geraldine Cooke and, until he left Penguin, Martin Soames, were both encouraging during the months when this book was being thought through. Geraldine deserves much credit for seeing the project to fruition.

Annie Pike, who copy-edited the book, did as excellent a job as she did before on *The Apartheid Handbook*.

Finally, thanks again to my wife, Mary, for all the help during the months when the book was being conceived, researched and written.

Roger Omond

Part 2

Part 2 of this book is partly based on research funded by:

War on Want
Inter Pares
Sadruddin Aga Khan
Broederlijk Delen
Nationaal Centrum voor Ontwikkelingssamenwerking

The book would not have been possible without information and help supplied by many people. I would like to thank Teresa Smart, Richard Moorsom, Peter Robbins, Abdul Minty, Mike Terry, Brian Bolton, Donald Roy, Pam Smith, David Wield, Ruth Jacobson, Diane Lambert, Sue Ward, Jenny Rossiter, John Saul, Signe Arnfred, E. S. Reddy, Catharina Breedeveld, An Snoeks, Jim Cason, Tim Smith, Ken Zinn, Harold Lewis, Rei Maeda, Øystein Gudim, Elizabeth Schmidt, U. Albrecht, Walter Sauer, Juha Rekola, Thierry Verhelst, Jos Deraedt, Michael Keating, Steve Godfrey, Britta Dörp, Louise Asmal, Simon Sapper, Stuart Bell, Tamme Hansma, Richard Fifield, Ann Woodall, Kristoffer Leonardson, Trevor Richards, and Marion Wallace.

Joseph Hanlon

Introduction

The moral argument against sanctions, the British Prime Minister, Margaret Thatcher, said in mid-1986, has been won. It was a typically resolute approach. It was also wrong. Few international problems have aroused so much passion as South Africa's policy of apartheid, and of the many 'solutions' put forward as a way of ending apartheid, that of sanctions has generated more heat than light. The moral arguments for and against sanctions have not been widely aired: rather a series of declamatory statements have been presented as arguments. In this debate there are few agnostics. Support for sanctions has become almost a litmus test of 'morality': the anti-sanctions lobby is automatically regarded as being in favour of apartheid and repression.

Yet this is a false argument. Supporters of sanctions do not always have morality on their side. But neither do opponents – as the South African government, Mrs Thatcher and President Ronald Reagan of the United States would like to claim. Sanctions can be an international gesture; their effects cannot be quantified. And that, primarily, is what a large part of the argument on sanctions is about.

Proponents of sanctions say that instituting international boycotts and disinvestment will send a message to the white voters of South Africa that apartheid puts them beyond the world's moral pale. Sanctions hearten the disenfranchised black majority, making them aware that they are not forgotten. They will also make apartheid too expensive to maintain and force change upon the country. It is also hoped that sanctions will push whites to the conference table and thus avoid a South African bloodbath.

Opponents of sanctions often argue the converse. International campaigns of this kind, they say, will simply drive the whites back into the laager, slow the 'reform' programme of President P. W. Botha, affect South Africa's blacks, and its neighbouring black states, more than the whites, and stunt economic growth which, it is said, will bring political liberalization.

Many of those arguments, too, are debatable. The whites, it could be said, are already in a laager of their own creation. President Botha's 'reform' policies appear to have ground to a halt already – before serious international sanctions have had time to bite. South Africa's blacks are already suffering under apartheid and a worsening economy. Many of their leaders have said that they are prepared to suffer more if apartheid can be brought to an end through sanctions. The country's black-ruled neighbours have been destabilized through deliberate South African policy already and, in threatening that the effect of sanctions will be to hit first states like Zimbabwe, Zambia, Lesotho, Swaziland, Botswana and Mozambique, the Pretoria government is both blackmailing these nations and imposing its own sanctions – which it professes to oppose as a matter of high principle.

The further argument that an influx of capital will lead to political liberalization – an argument much favoured by South African liberal capitalists – is not borne out by history. The 1960s, once the country had recovered from the effects of Sharpeville, were years of economic boom. Yet this was the period of, arguably, the greatest political repression in South Africa's history and when the dreams of classical apartheid ideologues were being implemented at vast cost in human misery. There is no political or economic law that dictates an expanding economy will go hand in hand with greater rights for blacks.

It is often said, in the words of President Reagan, that sanctions will 'hurt the very people we are trying to help' – the blacks of South Africa. They are often the forgotten people in the international and South African arguments about sanctions. Often, both sides have some interest in ignoring them, for their opinions on the matter could, and sometimes do, prove inconvenient. If there are lies, damned lies and statistics, in the black South African context there are lies, damned lies and public opinion surveys on black attitudes to sanctions. There have been at least half a dozen polls – and each provides some ammunition for one or other of the lobbies. Depending on which survey is quoted, black South Africans either support sanctions by a margin of 75 to 25 per cent – or oppose sanctions by a similar, if not identical, majority. And depending on who is regarded as the authentic voice of black South Africa – the African National Congress or Chief Gatsha Buthelezi, for example – statements can be conjured up to support either option.

The issue of sanctions imposes dilemmas on black South Africans. Few if any have any truck with apartheid: the days when various

Uncle Toms could be produced by government ministers to sing the praises of separate development have long gone. Indeed, any black who repeated the tunes of the 1950s and 1960s would rather embarrass Pretoria as it energetically tries to project its 'reformist' images. Yet apartheid's fiercest foes know that sanctions will indeed probably hit the black constituency earlier and harder than the white. The whites, too, are generally better cushioned: higher-paying jobs with greater skills and adaptability, a benign government made more so by its acute awareness that loss of employment could mean loss of votes. Social welfare benefits are usually better for whites than blacks. It is a white-orientated society – not surprisingly, as the franchise is restricted to those with paler-than-black skins, and power, economic and political, remains very definitely in the hands of those classified under the Population Registration Act as white.

So the black politician or trade unionist calling for sanctions faces severe problems. To what extent will fellow-blacks welcome sanctions? Will the loss of another black income, however paltry by white or Western standards, really make any difference to the apartheid state? Will the newly unemployed black, possibly threatened with deportation to an impoverished 'homeland', support the politician or trade unionist who has demanded of the world that it impose sanctions? Will the withdrawal programme not merely allow white South African capitalists to pick up lucrative factories and businesses at bargain basement prices? And will that capitalist be as sensitive to the needs of the black worker as some foreign firms have been? Is not the best policy of the politician and union leader to call for sanctions, in the hope of frightening Pretoria into making real concessions, while at the same time secretly hoping that no sanctions will actually be imposed?

And who does, in fact, have the moral right to decide what sanctions should be imposed? The university student protester at Berkeley or the London School of Economics? The Chairman of the board of General Motors? One hundred members of the United States Senate? The British Prime Minister weekending at Chequers? Or the underpaid factory worker living in a matchbox house in Soweto?

And does the South African government, unrepresentative of at least 73 per cent of the population (more if it is considered that the elections for the Coloured and Indian chambers of Parliament attracted a poll of about 17 per cent of eligible voters), have any right to oppose sanctions? White concern for the black underdog has, to put it mildly, not been at the top of the political agenda. The sudden concern for the sufferings that blacks will encounter if sanctions are imposed rings a little hollow – as does the 'moral humbug' (to use Bishop Desmond Tutu's memorable phrase) of Mrs Thatcher and President Reagan.

What is clear is that sanctions have been implemented, are being implemented and will be implemented whatever the pros and cons. 'Sanctions' has become a buzz-word, a neat solution for the world community to express its outrage at apartheid, often at minimal cost. The pressure for sanctions, Mrs Thatcher and President Reagan notwithstanding, has grown almost unstoppable. It will gain momentum, whatever the truth about its effects may be.

Indeed, a range of sanctions have already been imposed against South Africa – oil and arms embargoes, financial boycotts and corporation withdrawals. In one sense the oil embargo has 'failed', in that it is so leaky that South Africa is able to obtain all the fuel it needs. But in another sense it 'worked', in that the oil and financial boycotts combined brought about the first talks between white business leaders and the African National Congress. Similarly, sanctions against Rhodesia in the 1960s and 1970s 'worked', in that the white minority government agreed to hand over power to the majority sooner than if sanctions had not been imposed. Yet they 'failed', in that it took nearly a decade before they had any serious impact.

Sanctions are adopted as a weapon of last resort, when persuasion has failed and military action is out of the question. Sanctions are not a quick and easy solution; even tight sanctions will require several years to have an impact.

The main purpose of sanctions is not to punish white South Africa for the sins of apartheid, but rather to push it to the conference table to negotiate a hand-over of power to bring about majority rule and 'one person one vote'. The second purpose is to weaken the ability of the white minority to suppress the black majority.

Clearly arms and oil embargoes play a role in restricting the flow of vital goods to the South African military. But continued sanctions-busting is assured. Past experience of sanctions against other states, as well as consideration of the South African economy, points to South Africa's exports – fruit and vegetables, textiles, coal, and other minerals – as the prime target. These can be cut off, and if this is done, Pretoria will not have the money to pay for sanctions-busting imports.

Even if sanctions cannot be made watertight, they can at least make it difficult for South Africa to import and export. And difficulty means money – high commissions paid to the sanctions-busters. This is a kind of 'apartheid tax' on South Africa's foreign trade. And as that tax is pushed steadily higher by the wave of sanctions, South Africa will find that it has less and less money to pay for imports. Yet the South African economy is critically dependent on imports for fuel, machinery, arms, industrial raw materials and luxury goods. If sanctions push the apartheid tax high enough, the Pretoria government will no longer have enough money to pay for the war and to fund white luxury consumption. The war will come first and white life-styles will be hit. Most white South Africans will begin to rethink their positions only when they no longer benefit from apartheid – and that will take several years of tight sanctions. Only then will genuine negotiation be possible.

Even sanctions may not head off the apocalypse. Perhaps too many whites will decide that it is better for them and their families to die than to give up the privileges and power of apartheid. But apartheid is still so beneficial that most whites have yet to consider their position. Few have looked closely at neighbouring Botswana and Zimbabwe, so they do not realize that there are countries with majority rule which are prosperous and where white people still play a role. Perhaps sanctions will increase the pressure enough for more whites to begin to rethink.

It will be a long haul, and it will not be free. There will be some unpleasant side-effects in the countries imposing sanctions. A few people will lose jobs. Some products will become more expensive. But people will discover that claims that South African minerals are essential to the West are, in fact, a myth. The West can do without South Africa – and if sanctions fail and the inevitable widespread and violent revolution ensues, the West may be forced to do without South Africa in any case.

In Part 1 of this book Roger Omond looks at the political arguments for and against sanctions, while in Part 2 Joseph Hanlon considers how they can be imposed so as to be most effective. Sanctions are being imposed by a wide variety of bodies – national governments, private companies, local councils, pension funds, pressure groups. And a huge range of sanctions are available. The book ends with a directory of more than 50 sanctions, with details of who has imposed them and a discussion of their importance and problems. It is an array of possible actions in a long and difficult campaign.

Majority rule for South Africa is inevitable. Sanctions could speed the end of apartheid and cut short the bloodshed.

Terminology

Although English is spoken in South Africa, Britain and the United States, many of the terms used in this book are subject to confusing differences of usage between countries. Furthermore apartheid has brought about its own vocabulary. Thus it is useful to define a few terms here.

Sanctions will be used in the broadest possible way to mean all non-military actions intended to bring about the end of apartheid. This includes economic, financial and trade boycotts as well as corporate withdrawals. And it will include actions like boycotts and disinvestment aimed at transnational corporations linked with South Africa.

When a company pulls out of South Africa, this will be called *withdrawal*. When a shareholder (normally a pension fund) sells shares in a company because of its South African links, this will be called *disinvestment*. (Confusingly, in South Africa and the USA 'disinvestment' is sometimes used for withdrawal and 'divestment' for sale of shares. We shall not use the terms in this way, but they do often occur in quotations.)

South Africa has imposed a set of racial classifications and terminology which are considered objectionable by most of the people so classified. In general, all those not classified as white consider themselves *black*, as in, for example, Black Consciousness, a movement that includes people the state classifies into three separate groups. 'Black' is used in this sense throughout the book, to mean all people not classified as white. The state now uses 'black' to refer only to the majority it once called 'natives' and then 'Bantu'; it does not use 'African' for this group because in the Afrikaans language 'Afrikaner' simply means African, and Afrikaners are clearly 'white'. To avoid confusion, when forced to discuss the three subject race-groups, we shall refer to them as 'Coloured', 'Indian', and 'African'.

Joseph Hanlon and Roger Omond

Part 1

Why Sanctions?

by Roger Omond

1 *Black Leaders*

Black political groups in South Africa have long urged the world to take economic measures against apartheid. In 1959, when it was still a legal organization, the African National Congress welcomed moves then being made to boycott South African goods. At the same time it urged its members to intensify their boycott inside the country of 'Nationalist products'[1] – a campaign that, in the mid-1980s, was extended by a number of black communities to white-run shops. The Pan-Africanist Congress, formed in 1959 as a breakaway from the ANC, has also long called for sanctions. A third important group, the Black People's Convention (which included Africans, Coloureds and Asians and was also later banned), in 1972 rejected the involvement of foreign investors in the 'exploitative economic system' and urged those investors to 'disengage'.[2]

More mainstream politicians have also indicated support for disinvestment. David Curry, then Deputy Leader of the Labour Party, the most prominent 'Coloured' party, in 1972 endorsed the principle of 'disengagement' because of poor wages paid to blacks.[3] The following year Sonny Leon, then Leader of the party but later to be dismissed, said that he would maintain his calls for foreigners not to invest in South Africa.[4]

But not all black politicians have agreed with this line. Bishop Alpheus Zulu said in 1972, after returning from a World Council of Churches conference that had withdrawn investments from South Africa, that an improvement in blacks' economic situation could only be brought about by increased investment.[5] Chief Gatsha Buthelezi of KwaZulu, who in the 1980s emerged as the most vocal black opponent of sanctions, said in 1971 that it was a 'fallacy' to think that disengagement would help the situation. 'Those who are contemplating withdrawal would do better by remaining involved and improving the conditions of employment of black people,' he said.[6] This view was supported by M. T. Moerane, Editor of the *World* newspaper, who said that foreign investors should be agents for 'positive change'.[7]

Chief Buthelezi and another homeland leader were used in a series of advertisements placed by the white-run Trust Bank in 1973 opposing sanctions. He and Chief Lucas Mangope of Bophuthatswana, and Lucy Mvubelo of the largely black National Union of Clothing Workers all said that sanctions would be harmful to the country's blacks.[8]

Amid this disagreement among black leaders in the 1970s, much of the conventional wisdom was that foreign investors should stay. There was, however, widespread concern that overseas companies were badly underpaying their black workers, but it was thought that 'responsible' management could have beneficial effects, both economic and political.

In the 1980s the debate has become louder, particularly among those black leaders who support sanctions. This has happened despite a battery of laws that equate support for sanctions with 'economic sabotage' – the 1956 Official Secrets Act and the Riotous Assemblies Act of the same year, the 1962 Sabotage Act, and the 1982 Internal Security Act among others.[9] There have, however, been few prosecutions as calls for sanctions have increased. One of the few is Dr Allan Boesak, President of the World Alliance of Reformed Churches and a patron of the United Democratic Front (UDF). In September 1986 he was charged with subversion for allegedly advocating disinvestment and a consumer and school boycott. If found guilty, he could be jailed for 20 years. The case has been adjourned.[10] The charging of Dr Boesak came five weeks after the Minister of Manpower, Piet du Plessis, told the National Party's federal congress in Durban that calls for sanctions were considered to verge on high treason. He singled out particularly Bishop Desmond Tutu, the 1985 Nobel Peace Prize winner and Anglican Archbishop of Cape Town.[11]

Bishop Tutu, with his high-profile international image, has been perhaps the most vocal black champion of sanctions, albeit with some initial caution. In January 1985 he called for a campaign of 'persuasive pressure' in which foreign companies would attach 'reformist' conditions to their investments for a test period of 18 months to two years. Reforms that should be demanded included abolition of migrant labour, the ending of the pass laws, trade union rights for all and investment in black education and training. 'If these reforms are not implemented within the time limit, then the pressure must become punitive and economic sanctions should be imposed,' he said. Economic pressure, he added, was 'our last chance to avert a bloodbath'. He warned, however, that he might reassess his views on disinvestment within less than two years.[12]

He did. In December that year he said he would start campaigning for sanctions by April 1986 unless there were fundamental changes to apartheid, the State of Emergency then in force was lifted and soldiers were removed from black townships. On 20 March 1986 the Bishop said he would call for sanctions by the end of the month unless the government made real moves to dismantle apartheid, release jailed black leaders and start negotiations with them.[13]

There were, predictably, no moves by the government to meet Bishop Tutu's conditions. On 2 April 1986 he urged sanctions: 'Our land is burning and bleeding and so I call on the international community to apply punitive sanctions against this government,' he told a press conference in Johannesburg. All his attempts to persuade the government to remove apartheid had failed. Sanctions should be 'effective' and 'immediate', but he declined to say what kind of sanctions he would welcome. The decision was up to individual governments. But another run on South African currency, as in August 1985 after President P. W. Botha dashed hopes of major and quick political reforms, would be welcome. This would be relatively painless. 'We face a catastrophe in this land and only the action of the international community by applying pressure can save us,' the Bishop said.

Bishop Tutu also dealt firmly with the argument, much favoured by Mrs Thatcher, President Reagan and the South African government, that sanctions would mostly hurt blacks. 'I hope that most who use this argument would just drop it quietly and stop being so hypocritical. It is amazing how everybody has become so solicitous for blacks and become such wonderful altruists. It is remarkable that in South Africa the most vehement in their concern for blacks have been whites.'[14]

Bishop Tutu's call, not surprisingly, attracted criticism. Representatives of white business and industry opposed him, the Federated Chamber of Industries saying piously that constraint and responsibility were needed by all South African leaders if conflict and human tragedy were to be minimized. The Association of Chambers of Commerce (Assocom) said that 'a growing economy remains an essential condition for evolutionary reform' and that foreign participation was vital to economic performance.[15]

South Africa's state-controlled broadcasting service also reacted, accusing the Bishop of aligning himself 'still more closely with the forces of revolution'. It added that he was 'evidently completely indifferent to the miseries that would be inflicted on the mass of blacks'.[16] A few days later the S A B C returned to the attack, saying that the Bishop had no mandate to campaign for sanctions.[17]

The Bishop's call aroused other passions. The U D F and the pro-Black Consciousness Azanian People's Organization welcomed his stand. Mrs Helen Suzman of the Progressive Federal Party opposed sanctions because of the 'horrendous' effect on unemployment in South Africa, which has no social security safety-net. But if sanctions were imposed, she said, 'the blame rests entirely on P. W. Botha and his government for failing to honour their undertaking to dismantle apartheid'. The leader of the Herstigte Nasionale Party, Jaap Marais, accused the Bishop of 'declaring war in the name of God' and called on the government to take action against him.[18]

Bishop Tutu was not to be silenced. On 11 April 1986 he said on American television that if other countries did not help South Africa's blacks through sanctions, 'we will still become free, but almost certainly it would have to be through a violent overthrow which we are trying to avert'.[19]

The Bishop's call dominated the leader columns of most South African newspapers. Like the S A B C, *Die Burger,* official organ of the ruling National Party in the Cape Province, questioned who had given Bishop Tutu a mandate. So did another government-supporting paper, *Die Transvaler.* The *Natal Mercury,* a right-wing but generally anti-apartheid English-language newspaper, said the Bishop had a 'morbid fascination with violence'. *Business Day* added that sanctions could only succeed if violence was a part of the package. The *Citizen* said that he had 'a callous disregard for the well-being of black people' – a criticism that the Bishop had anticipated with his comment about 'altruists' concerned with black welfare.[20]

Bishop Tutu, having crossed the divide between threatening to call for sanctions and actually doing so, continued his campaign throughout the rest of 1986. In May of that year, after Britain and the U S A had blocked United Nations moves for sanctions, he returned to his attack on the 'altruists' he had previously criticized. 'I am no longer impressed,' he said at a religious festival in Wales, 'by the wonderful rhetoric we get from Britain and America about their so-called abhorrence of apartheid.' Ordinary people should make it clear that they would not tolerate governments who collaborated with apartheid.[21] In July in Nairobi he again said that unless sanctions were imposed South Africa was 'for the birds'.[22] The next month in Kingston, Jamaica, the Bishop warned that the West's refusal to impose sanctions could damage relations with a future black government.[23]

As Bishop Tutu continued to spread the word about sanctions – in Japan and China (which particularly annoyed Pretoria) among other places – the government stepped up its attacks. The Bureau for Information provided news agencies in South Africa with an English translation of an editorial in the *Beeld* newspaper which pointed out that, under the State of Emergency, encouraging sanctions or disinvestment was an offence subject to a maximum fine of R20,000 or ten years' imprisonment. Bishop Tutu's plea for sanctions 'in Red China of all places', *Beeld* said, 'could become an important test of the state's desire to maintain its own law. There cannot be one law for Tutu as an internationally known figure and another for lesser people.'[24]

A few days later Manpower Minister Du Plessis weighed in again: South Africa's patience with the Bishop was 'wearing thin'. Apart from the veiled warning, Du Plessis countered with other arguments against the Bishop's campaign: 'Sanctions are more easily imposed than lifted . . . they do incalculable damage to the very people they are supposed to help . . . They could irrevocably harm the country's economy and bring in their wake despair and the ghastly prospect of poverty and starvation and adversely affect the already dire unemployment situation.'[25]

Bishop Tutu also used his enthronement as Archbishop of Cape Town – the highest position in the Anglican Church in South Africa – in September 1986 to raise the sanctions issue. The onus was on those who did not want sanctions 'to provide us with a viable, non-violent strategy to force the dismantling of apartheid,' he said. 'I do not want sanctions. I know that those who advocate sanctions don't want them either. I told the State President as much. I said if you were to lift the State of Emergency, remove the troops from our townships, release political prisoners and all detainees, un-ban our political organizations and then sit down with the authentic representatives of every section of our community to negotiate a new constitution for one undivided South Africa, then for what it's worth, I would say to the world: "Put your sanctions plans on hold."'

But, he added, 'I am not sure that the government wants real change which would mean an entirely new dispensation, with a new disposition of political power and a greater sharing of the good things so abundant in South Africa . . .'[26]

Not all Anglicans have been pleased with their Archbishop's pronouncements. In May 1986 St Margaret's Church near Pretoria cut off funds to its diocese until Bishop Tutu 'ceases campaigning for disinvestment and takes up the role of a religious leader'.[27] The Registrar of the conservative Church of England in South Africa said in August 1986 that 'many' people had joined it from the Anglican Church because of Bishop Tutu. Senior Anglicans countered, however, that the reaction of some conservative whites was expected and that other congregations had increased.[28]

Bishop Tutu tried to counter some of the accusations made against him shortly before his enthronement. His call for sanctions did not necessarily reflect the position of the Anglican Church, which, if anything, was opposed to sanctions. 'When I speak, I speak as Desmond Tutu,' he said.[29]

The Bishop, of course, was not the only black African to call for sanctions. Many others have done so, including that other turbulent priest, Allan Boesak. He has been supported by the United Democratic Front which he helped found. The organization has, however, sometimes been more cautious than Bishop Tutu or Dr Boesak. The Acting Publicity Secretary, Murphy Morobe, said in December 1985 that it could not support the call for disinvestment because of legislation that made such calls a criminal offence. But while 'the State, its apologists and imperialist friends have been straining at the leash, trying to show how blacks will suffer when foreign capital is withdrawn', none of the liberation movements had opposed disinvestment, and 'neither have any of the credible leaders of our people joined a queue to propagate the merits of foreign investment in our country'. Mr Morobe said that the UDF demanded the right (currently denied by South African law) for all to discuss the issue freely, adding: 'Until then the assumption must be that the majority of our people support the disinvestment call.'[30] In 1986 the UDF Transvaal Vice-President, Ismail Mohammed, told the former West German Chancellor Willy Brandt that there was a mood among blacks in favour of sanctions. 'We asked him to impress on the Kohl government that the long-term economic interests of Germany stem with aligning them to those who are struggling for change.'[31]

The UDF's caution is understandable: much government and Security Police work has gone into trying to discredit and break the organization through disinformation, detentions, trials of many leaders, and, in late 1986, the declaration that the UDF was prohibited from receiving overseas funds. Overt support for sanctions might well have provided the government with a strong case for successful prosecution of the UDF.

In October 1986 the organization came out more strongly when it hailed the US Congressional overriding of President Reagan's veto of a package of sanctions. It called the decision 'a breakthrough for all those forces who have seen through the fraud of Botha's so-called reforms and the protectionist postures of the Reagan Administration'.[32]

Some of the black arguments for sanctions go largely unheard in South Africa. One reason is because they are put by the banned ANC. Its president, Oliver Tambo, spelled out the case in August 1986 shortly after the Commonwealth mini-summit on sanctions in London. In a broadcast on Addis Ababa Radio Freedom he tackled many of the arguments deployed against sanctions by, among others, Mrs Thatcher, at the summit. He dealt at length with the proposition that blacks would suffer most if sanctions were imposed:

This argument came in the first instance not from the oppressed, because it was the oppressed who called for sanctions . . . Those who were resisting the sanctions . . . came out with a very cheap argument that . . . this is going to hurt the very people we want to help. I think some of the slave-owners advanced the same argument about the emancipation of slaves. They said: 'You want to free the slaves; what is going to happen to them? They will die without us; we are helping them.'

. . . It is the multinationals who are quick to advance this argument because it is the multinationals who are going to lose their profits when once the sanctions begin to bite . . . The multinationals are reluctant anyway to hate the system which yields them such profits . . .

We are involved in a life and death struggle. As a result of that life and death struggle, we sacrifice . . . It is our lives that we are sacrificing, that we are ready to sacrifice.

Sanctions will not kill us. It is the apartheid system that is killing . . . Even sacrifice as a result of sanctions does not involve death which we get from the apartheid system. If sanctions will not kill us, sanctions will help us to kill the system that kills us . . .

If people today are facing bullets, no one should fear that if the apartheid system was attacked, those people would be dead . . . Unemployment runs into millions as far as Africans are concerned; part of that is precisely the apartheid system itself. So it is nothing new to be out of work. What would be new if sanctions were employed is that the white supporters of the regime would be thrown out of work because firms would close down . . .

The government does not care if Africans lose their jobs by the million, but the regime would care if whites lost their jobs by the thousands or even by the hundreds. If hundreds were thrown out of work as a result of sanctions, they would want to do something about it . . .[33]

Another view of sanctions has been given, at some peril, by Winnie Mandela, wife of the imprisoned ANC leader Nelson Mandela and a leader in her own right. Interviewed by Radio Havana in July 1986, she sketched some of the background:

From the beginning, we were a peaceful people. Up until the Sixties the African National Congress had not revolted against its oppressors . . . We tolerated the worst insult that a human being can endure – the insult to the human dignity, one of the most basic violations of human rights.

But it is obvious that the regime was not willing to change that policy. However, it is also obvious that we could not bear the humiliation of living oppressed by the racist minority any longer. Therefore we decided to take the unavoidable road of the armed struggle . . .

We do not see any choice for a peaceful solution other than the application of measures which strangle the regime economically and isolate it completely.

Let the foreign companies not be an obstacle in our struggle. Let them not finance the bloodshed. Let them not finance the armaments with which the regime kills us every day. Each time that we bury one of our dead, each time we pick up our brothers fallen on the streets, we know that the main allies of the bloodshed are the governments of the United States and Great Britain.

I do not think that at this point there is a better choice than economic sanctions against the regime. But they should all be compulsory. In this way the racist minority will be forced to kneel down.

The drop of the rand, the national currency, was a telling lesson for our oppressors. For the first time we saw the white South Africans react against the country's oppression, simply because their pockets were affected . . .[34]

The hope that sanctions will avert a 'bloodbath' in South Africa is often used. On the eve of the Commonwealth mini-summit, the ANC's director of international affairs, Johnny Makatini, told Radio Freedom that 'this is the opportunity to call on the British Government to join those countries which, in line with the position of the ANC, are calling for the immediate imposition of sanctions in order to avert that situation which could even result in a racial conflagration beyond the borders of South Africa and threaten world peace . . . Those opposed to violence must join the ANC in the call for sanctions.'

By opposing sanctions, Mr Makatini said, 'the British Government is taking a position that is contrary to what the founding fathers of the UN prescribed in the question of sanctions. What was prescribed . . . as an instrument to bring about peace wherever peace was threatened was . . . the imposition of sanctions.' [35]

After the Commonwealth mini-summit had decided on some sanctions (with Mrs Thatcher dissenting from nearly all of them) the ANC turned again to some of her arguments. One was that neighbouring countries would be hard hit. Radio Freedom commented:

For the leaders of Zambia and Zimbabwe especially, whose economies depend heavily on Pretoria's, their decision . . . shows how much concerned they are about the volcanic situation . . . These leaders know that as long as the genocidal and aggressive apartheid regime exists, their countries will never develop and they will never know peace. President Kaunda (of Zambia) and Prime Minister Mugabe (of Zimbabwe) know very well that Botha and his henchmen will retaliate viciously against them because of their courageous position. But because they themselves are freedom fighters, they too have been to exile, they have seen their people being killed by colonizers, they have witnessed apartheid aggression, they have suffered under a colonial yoke for years . . . they can see that the end of the apartheid system has commenced. They know that we are going to bring down that regime sooner rather than later. They have decided to suffer side by side with us . . . [36]

The British government's opposition to sanctions was strongly criticized in these and other Radio Freedom broadcasts. Mr Tambo put it even more bluntly when he saw the British Foreign Secretary, Sir Geoffrey Howe, in September 1986. Its policies, Mr Tambo said, together with those of the USA, were reinforcing white minority rule in South Africa.[37] This was expanded in another Radio Freedom broadcast the following month by Thabo Mbeki, the ANC's Head of Publicity and Information, who criticized Mrs Thatcher, President Reagan and Chancellor Kohl of West Germany for resisting sanctions. 'They do not want to weaken their ally,' he said. 'They want the apartheid regime strong so that it can defend the apartheid system and protect what they see as Western interests in South Africa and in southern Africa as a whole.'

But, he went on, 'the people in these Western countries have themselves come to understand what the apartheid system represents [and] . . . their own obligation to act . . . to ensure that their voice is heard

. . . the American people are not in fact represented by Reagan on the question of apartheid . . . It is clear that even in a country like Great Britain there is a very strong mass popular opinion in favour of sanctions.'

In the same broadcast the ANC turned to individual sanctions: 'People in the western countries are talking about people's actions . . . it is not necessary to wait for government to impose sanctions by law . . . the people themselves can act.'[38]

The ANC's view of sanctions was also explained to the House of Commons Foreign Affairs Committee in October 1985 and June 1986. Giving evidence in October, Mr Tambo stressed the peaceful nature of sanctions: the primary aim was to 'make the process of transition through struggle as limited as possible in terms of the scale of the conflict'. Sanctions 'would operate to weaken the system and make it less capable of resisting our struggle and encourage an early resolution of the problem, without us having to draw on everything we can to bring it down'.[39]

Mr Mbeki, son of the jailed ANC activist Govan Mbeki and regarded as one of the rising stars of the new generation of leaders, followed this up in his later evidence in June 1986. Sanctions had been shown to work:

When the banks, acting possibly purely out of commercial considerations, decided they were not going to extend loans to South Africa, clearly the South African regime almost went into a panic. They began even to float the idea of the release of Mandela each time negotiations were due with the international creditor banks . . .

. . . It is perfectly clear that it is finally penetrating into the heads of a lot of white South Africans that there is a crisis, a crisis that needs to be solved. The cost of the maintenance of the apartheid system is rising and, therefore, they are saying there must surely be a way out of this . . .

The important thing is to act now; for the United States, this country, the EEC, Japan and the main trading partners of South Africa, to impose sanctions against this regime. That would generate, from even within white South Africa itself, very many forces which . . . would say: 'But we can't stand by and allow this country to be destroyed, when we ourselves have already said this apartheid thing is dead. Botha has said so. So what is it that we are protecting?' . . .

. . . I am sure there would be increased unemployment, businesses closing down, all of those things . . . but the political result of it would be that many white people who are already saying, 'But is it really necessary that we continue with this system?', would say the price has now become too high . . .

It is in our interests to ensure that the South African economy is as little destroyed as possible, because clearly a new South Africa must address very many serious problems ... If we have to conduct an armed struggle over an extended period of time the economy will be destroyed in a physical sense ... The imposition of comprehensive mandatory sanctions ... is the most effective way to ensure the non-destruction of that economy.[40]

Mr Tambo, in his October evidence, said also that sanctions would affect whites who would lose their jobs. '... Blacks will see that as weakening a system that dominates them ... It is not that we want sanctions so that our people can be out of work; we say that we want our sanctions so that apartheid can end ... We are ready to make any sacrifice – it is not suffering, it is sacrifice – in order to see this sytem ended.'[41]

Sanctions were not, however, a substitute for the ANC's struggle: 'So we will continue, we will certainly embark on massive strike actions, we will do all the things that we can and must do for our own freedom, but sanctions are additional and sanctions alone would not bring about any results. We have to be involved in the two pressures from inside and from outside.'[42]

The ANC, seen both inside and outside South Africa as the senior and most effective liberation movement, is not the only black political organization to have called for sanctions. The PAC has long also called for sanctions. While saying that the 'internal factor' – the dis-possessed, exploited and oppressed people – would be the decisive factor, 'international support and solidarity are an important com-plementary factor'. It 'expected' Mrs Thatcher and President Reagan to reaffirm their 'reactionary' positions on sanctions.[43]

The South-West African People's Organization (SWAPO) has also made its position on sanctions clear. Reacting in September 1986 to what it termed the EEC's 'paltry and inadequate' package of sanctions – which were not made applicable to Namibia itself – it said that sanctions were not aimed at the geographic area of South Africa but at the government itself. Namibia could be used as a conduit for new European investment in South Africa, thus further encouraging Pretoria to continue its illegal occupation of Namibia:

The selfsame regime occupies Namibia, illegally defying the clear wishes of the Namibian people and numerous resolutions of the United Nations Security Council and General Assembly. This includes UN Security Council Resolution 435 (1978) which has received the apparent support of all member states of the EEC.

Are the EEC saying to the Namibian people that they find South Africa's

apartheid system in Namibia acceptable, its draconian laws and the character-
istic detentions, torture and murders of Namibians acceptable? Are they telling
us that South Africa's intransigence over the implementation of UN Security
Council Resolution 435 ought simply to be accommodated? . . .
    . . . We believe that sanctions imposed against the South African regime
must also apply to South Africa-occupied Namibia and that they should be
made comprehensive and mandatory.[44]

The Black Consciousness grouping, the National Forum, is strongly
in favour of sanctions. One of its former leaders, Saths Cooper, was
one of nine people charged in 1975 with, among other things, having
'unlawfully, and with intent to endanger the maintenance of law and
order in South Africa, conspired to discourage foreign investment and
[calling] upon foreign investors to disengage from this economy'. He
and the others were jailed for between five and six years, although not
on this particular charge.

The National Forum, whose most important affiliate is the Azanian
People's Organization (AZAPO), is regarded as a successor to the
Black Consciousness groups started by Steve Biko and others in the
1960s and 1970s. In late 1985, Mr Cooper stated its position:

The NF believes in anti-imperialism and anti-collaboration with the ruling
class and all its allies. The NF can't support investment in this country particularly because that means support for the status quo, because it gives unconditional licence to a minority government to repress the majority of the
people, to cordon off townships with the armed forces, to exile people to
barren so-called homelands, condemning people to starve in these areas . . .
investment definitely is not intended for the benefit of the majority of the
people. It is intended to exploit the cheap labour and gain quick returns for the
multinational companies.

Mr Cooper said that it was not true that the government was more
concerned about blacks suffering if foreign companies pulled out:
'The government will suffer more if disinvestment takes place because
of the loans from abroad to the South African government and its
agencies.' Investment enabled the government to spend more money
on budgets like defence. He also criticized the law that makes it illegal
to advocate corporate withdrawal and disinvestment: 'This
government is saying that there is no option to follow other than
violence. It is saying in fact to the Tutus and others that non-violent
methods cannot succeed.'[45]

Unemployment, Mr Cooper said in July 1985, would increase if
there was widespread disinvestment – but 'since already there is a

huge unemployment figure of around two million at present and increasing, this is not going to greatly affect black people because black
people are already suffering ... If investors pull out there would be
immediately a job slump and underemployment increase. But in the
long term it will even out and force the South African government to
make major concessions and that means real change.'[46]

The Black Consciousness view of sanctions has moved some distance
in ten years – a reflection of how the entire debate has progressed. In
the mid-1970s the prevailing view was spelled out by Steve Biko
during the trial of Mr Cooper and other members of the South African
Students' Organization and the Black People's Convention. Foreign
investment was not rejected by SASO as such, Mr Biko told the
court: 'We wanted foreign investors to help in the build-up of the
humanity of the blacks, to give them opportunity for training in
technical spheres, to recognize to some extent trade union work within
the firms, to give the blacks positions of responsibility within the
firms, in a sense to encourage humanity amongst blacks who are
employed by them, negating the whole effect of apartheid on blacks in
this country.' But if the firms did not do that 'they are in a sense
selling out on us and they might as well get out'.

There was, at that time, Mr Biko said, no desire to weaken the
South African economy or to create wide-scale unemployment. But
SASO rejected the efforts of people like Chief Gatsha Buthelezi of
KwaZulu and President Lennox Sebe of the Ciskei, who claimed to
speak on behalf of blacks, to encourage investment.*

* For the source of the quotes from Steve Biko used in this section, and for a
fuller explanation of the Black Consciousness view of disinvestment in the
mid-1970s, see *The Testimony of Steve Biko*, ed. Millard Arnold (Panther,
1979); published in the United States as *Steve Biko: Black Consciousness in
South Africa* (Random House, 1978).

2 Trade Unions

The dilemma that black trade union leaders face over sanctions was summed up by the General Secretary of a large federation: 'If I stand up in public and call for disinvestment, our members at Leyland would kill me.'[1]

On the one hand, the black unions want, as urgently as any political leaders, the removal of apartheid; on the other their job is to protect their members. Sanctions and job security are said to be mutually exclusive. Yet a number of unions, some of whose members would probably lose their jobs, have called for some form of corporate withdrawal or disinvestment. These calls have increased as unions have felt themselves more powerful, as black opinion appears to have swung in favour of sanctions, and as the whole debate has become more of an issue. The key phrase in the unions' contribution to the debate has been 'conditional disinvestment'.

The Council of Unions of South Africa, which favours Black Consciousness, called in March 1985 for 'selective disinvestment . . . in effect endorsing the legislation [then] before the United States Congress'. CUSA's General Secretary, Piroshaw Camay, said: 'Apartheid is a crime against humanity and the majority of people are racially oppressed. Under these circumstances we would consider a call for total disinvestment, but we don't think this would work.' The freeze on new investment, he said then, would be a control mechanism to be maintained as long as apartheid remained in force, but with the incentive that it would be removed once apartheid was eliminated. (Just how investment would be turned back on again once apartheid was ended is a key question used in argument by a number of liberal capitalists in South Africa who argue against sanctions.)

Mr Camay did not deny that foreign companies in South Africa had played a role in improving the welfare of their workers and setting an example to local firms, but said that workers were demanding fundamental change, not just the desegregation of canteens and toilets at their factories: 'What we are demanding of companies that stay in

South Africa is that they get involved in pressurizing the government into fundamental change.'[2]

Later in 1985, a CUSA activist said: 'Extra suffering is worthwhile, if the suffering is understood by the people, if it is chosen by them to achieve something. If the suffering is caused by somebody else without the workers' understanding, then it will have a negative effect.'[3] This is a dilemma that trade unionists are still trying to sort out: are workers prepared to suffer? Are they prepared to suffer if the pressure for disinvestment is made, say, in Washington or London rather than Soweto? How much suffering – or 'sacrifice', as the ANC's Oliver Tambo calls it – will or can be endured? And, most crucially, will disinvestment/sanctions indeed lead to the ending of apartheid?

These questions have been, and are being, faced by all unions. One of the then largest union groupings, the Federation of South African Trade Unions (FOSATU), which at its height had about 110,000 members, said in March 1985 that there should be pressure on the government, but that it was not convinced that disinvestment would bring about the desired change. Primary pressure for change should be generated inside the country, said the General Secretary, Joe Foster. It was Mr Foster who warned that Leyland workers would 'kill' him if he called publicly for disinvestment.[4]

Later that year FOSATU came out with a stronger line. One of its leaders, Alec Erwin, said that the vast majority of people supported disinvestment because they would back anything that would bring pressure to bear on the government: 'Whether a company stays or leaves is not the issue. Our economy and society are in crisis and unless drastic changes are made we are in an untenable position.' Using a number of arguments made by the pro-sanctions lobby, but careful not to say outright what his position was, Mr Erwin added: 'People are suffering on a massive scale. They are hungry, unemployed, very angry and very bitter. The impact one company can make is very small . . . A company can pay people the earth, but that is not going to change South Africa. We need to change the government before we will get anywhere.'[5]

Simple dislike of apartheid has been suggested to explain black worker support for some kind of sanctions. Jack Bloom, writing in the Johannesburg *Sunday Times* in September 1985 after completing a thesis on black attitudes to disinvestment, said: 'Emotionally . . . the hearts of many blacks are with overseas campaigners [for disinvestment]

... Such is the polarization of our politics that blacks often base opinions in obverse reaction to that of their white compatriots. Intense pleasure is derived from just about any perceived rebuff to the South African Government, while at its most blunt one can observe that when white South Africa cheers, black South Africa jeers.'[6]

As the sanctions issue became livelier, several unions and union groupings appeared more prepared to come out in favour instead of hedging their bets. In October 1986 CUSA and another Black Consciousness grouping, the Azanian Confederation of Trade Unions (AZACTU), combined to form a new federation, the second biggest next to the Confederation of South African Trade Unions (COSATU). The CUSA–AZACTU Federation is an amalgam of 23 unions with a paid-up membership of 248,000 and 420,000 signed-up members, compared to a claimed membership of 700,000 for COSATU. At the launch conference of CUSA–AZACTU, a resolution was passed saying it was 'committed to a full sanctions programme for as long as the racist capitalist minority regime exists'. It condemned foreign investment in South Africa as representing 'a further perpetuation of exploitation and oppression' and asserted that 'its continued presence in our country is not in the interests of the working class'. The new Federation believes in 'the principle of worker control . . . to build a non-exploitative democratic society based on the leadership of the working class'. Unlike COSATU, which has a number of whites in key positions, the CUSA–AZACTU Federation is committed to 'black working class leadership'.[7]

COSATU was formed at the beginning of December 1985. It immediately gave, in the words of its President, Elijah Barayi, 'full support' to disinvestment.[8] 'If the government remains intransigent, then this pressure will have to be increased,' he said. In resolutions released at a press conference COSATU said that foreign and South African multinational corporations exploited workers in southern Africa 'by reaping huge profits and exporting them to Europe and America'.[9]

Some COSATU affiliates have been vocal about sanctions, notably the National Union of Miners (NUM). In July 1986 two leaders of the union appeared at the British National Union of Mineworkers conference to seek support for sanctions. Both the General Secretary, Cyril Ramaphosa, and the President, James Motlatsi, rejected Mrs Thatcher's argument that black people alone would suffer under sanctions. 'If Mrs Thatcher is so sympathetic to working people, why is she planning to close so many pits in Britain?' Mr Motlatsi asked.[10] It was a theme to be repeated at the German Social Democratic Party conference in Nuremberg the following month: It was strange, Mr Ramaphosa said, that politicians like Chancellor Kohl, President Reagan and Mrs Thatcher showed so much concern about black unemployment in South Africa, their excuse for not imposing sanctions, when they had done so little for workers in their own countries.[11] The German, British and American leaders displayed a 'very serious lack of understanding of world political history' in believing that apartheid could be reformed. 'Apartheid is not about blacks being allowed to use the same toilets as whites,' Mr Ramaphosa said. 'Apartheid is an affront to humanity and democracy and must be destroyed. It is the fascism of the 1980s.'[12]

Later in 1986 the NUM became involved in a dispute with the Chamber of Mines, the employers' organization, over sanctions and the gold-mining industry. Mr Motlatsi was said to have called in a British television interview for sanctions that would directly affect the gold-mining industry, adding that limited sanctions that let the gold mines off the hook would be of no use. The Chamber demanded clarification; the NUM responded that it had a responsibility to defend the interests of its members at all levels, economic and political. For this reason the union had consistently called for international economic pressure against the government. The Chamber, the NUM said, supported the government on a number of issues and was an ally in maintaining key institutions of apartheid such as hostels (where miners live in single-sex accommodation) and the migrant labour system.

The Chamber accused the NUM of making contradictory statements 'supporting sanctions while in the same breath threatening to strike if men are retrenched as a result of the implementation of sanctions':

The union must accept responsibility for the consequences that will inevitably flow from such action.

The industry employs 600,000 black workers with three million dependants and supports a large service industry. If even a small percentage of these workers lost their jobs, this would have a disastrous impact on black employment in southern Africa and on the rural areas in particular which rely substantially on the flow of income from the mining sector.[13]

Union ambivalence towards sanctions/disinvestment was evident in late 1986 when General Motors in Detroit sold its operations to a South African consortium. The union response was to strike – not on the principle of the deal (which the government would have loved dearly) but on the way it was carried out and the implications for workers.

GM's plant is in Port Elizabeth, once known, together with neighbouring Uitenhage, as the Detroit of South Africa. Two other motor giants were there: Ford and Volkswagen. Together they employed 17,500 workers. By mid-1986 this had been whittled down to 8,000 through a combination of the recession and the phased withdrawal of Ford to the Transvaal.[14] The largest union in Port Elizabeth, the National Automobile and Allied Workers' Union (NAAWU) estimated that for every worker in the auto industry who lost a job, three were made unemployed in the adjacent components industry. In July 1986 it was estimated that if GM, which employed 3,500 workers, closed down another 84,000 people would be made destitute.

Unemployment in Port Elizabeth is high: a university study in mid-1985 found that 56 per cent of blacks were without work. A year later, with Ford's withdrawal under way, it was believed to be running at 60 per cent – probably the highest in urban South Africa. The city was unable to attract new industry, partly because of the government's policy of decentralization, which favoured areas closer to the black homelands such as East London (once derided by the people of Port Elizabeth as a sleepy tourist centre). Other industry was weaned away. But it was close enough to the desperately poor homelands of the Transkei and Ciskei to attract tens of thousands of refugees. Huge slums have mushroomed.

Port Elizabeth is also a highly politicized city: historically it has always been a centre with strong support for the ANC. The UDF has found it a natural area for activity. The Security Police there have long had a reputation for brutality: this is where Steve Biko suffered the fatal injuries in detention that caused his death. Under the State of Emergency, Port Elizabeth and the surrounding Eastern Cape have experienced some of the country's toughest repression.

Into this climate came the news that GM in Detroit was selling. Black unions, as part of what is sometimes described as the broad opposition to the government, are loth to oppose international pressure on apartheid. But they are also there to protect members' jobs which could be jeopardized by sanctions. In mid-1986 NAAWU itself was in the process of canvassing all its members on sanctions. It has never been a particularly vocal supporter of sanctions, largely because multinationals such as GM, Volkswagen and Ford were its best-organized factories. In addition, the State of Emergency severely restricted debate on the issue. But NAAWU is an affiliate of COSATU, which favours 'all forms of international pressure on the government – including disinvestment or the threat of disinvestment'. COSATU also seeks to 'ensure that the social wealth of South Africa remains the property of the people of South Africa for the benefit of all'. This has been interpreted by many workers as advocating greater worker control over all investment, foreign or South African.[15]

NAAWU's response to the GM move was to declare a strike. It demanded one month's severance pay for every year of service, repayment of employee and company contributions to the pension and group life funds, and two representatives on the board of the company that was to take over GM.[16] The regional secretary of NAAWU, Les Kettledas, said the action was not aimed at preventing the Americans from leaving. 'The action is aimed at the Americans in that they have been operating in this country for years, they have exploited the apartheid situation and they've been making profits for at least 55 of the 60 years that they have been in the country . . . They cannot just leave without the workers getting at least some reward for their contribution.'[17]

Further, NAAWU had not been consulted about the decision to sell. Had Detroit 'advised and consulted its workers' before announcing withdrawal, NAAWU's lawyers argued, that strike would not have happened. The union feared that assets the workers had built up could be transferred out of the country overnight. There were no guarantees that the 'new' company would make a profit. If it failed, it would mean liquidation – with no payout for the workers. Nor was there any guarantee that the new company would continue operations with the same work force and conditions as before – conditions that NAAWU had painfully established over the years, aided, perhaps, by Detroit's awareness of the 'hassle factor' that would be created if it was too harsh with black workers.

Maintenance of jobs and conditions was not NAAWU's sole worry. With unemployment so high in Port Elizabeth there was always the danger that scab labour would be offered employment. Management responded to the strike by going to court. It won a 'rule nisi' against NAAWU and others to show cause why it should not be declared that they were instigating, inciting or conducting an unlawful strike.[18] Management also dismissed 567 workers involved in a sit-in at the factory and called police to remove them.[19] The company advertised for replacements: the response was so great that it stopped taking applications by noon on the day the advertisements appeared.[20] A few days later police were called in after alleged acts of 'intimidation' when strikers argued with strike-breakers employed by the new management.[21]

A day later the strike appeared to be collapsing. Management said that only 219 out of about 1,200 strikers had failed to return to work after being given a deadline of 9 a.m. on 18 November. In addition, 400 of the 567 sacked for the sit-in had applied for re-employment and were being interviewed. Management said that whether they got their jobs back would depend only on whether it could be proved that as individuals they had taken part in intimidation or violence.[22]

GM in Detroit appears to have come out of this episode relatively free of the stigma of collaboration with apartheid in some eyes, but not in the view of many activists. It still has a continued investment in South Africa, albeit not a controlling interest. The major cost was about $100 million to clear GM South Africa's existing debts. But franchise agreements will ensure that GM vehicles continue to be produced in the country. GM South Africa got the business at what President Reagan referred to as a 'fire-sale price'; it is no longer bound by the Sullivan Code of equal pay for equal work; nor is it forbidden to sell its vehicles to the state. The tactics of the management of GM South Africa in calling in police wielding rifles and sjamboks do not bode well for the future of industrial relations.[23] (See also Chapter 27, pp. 267–9).

In contrast to what GM workers regarded as a withdrawal sleight-of-hand, Eastman-Kodak announced in late November 1986 that it was selling its assets in South Africa and barring the export of any of its products to the country.[24]

3 Blacks Against Sanctions

The most vocal black opponent of sanctions is Chief Gatsha Buthelezi, Chief Minister of KwaZulu and President of the Inkatha 'cultural' movement. There are, however, others – from the Southern African Bus and Taxi Association to various 'independent' homeland leaders. One of the more surprising is Percy Qoboza, former Editor of the *World* newspaper and now Associate Editor of *City Press*. The *World*, regarded by the government as a dangerously radical newspaper, was banned, together with a range of Black Consciousness organizations on 19 October 1977 and Mr Qoboza detained without trial for nearly five months.

In June 1985, addressing a lunch organized by the South Africa– British Trade Association, Mr Qoboza came out strongly against disinvestment. There was no consensus among blacks on the issue: it evoked just as much passion in this community as in others, he said. Disinvestment might be regarded by some as the only alternative to violent change, but it would in fact create economic chaos and be the recipe for a full-scale bloody revolution. Multinational companies should show their commitment to the creation of a just society in South Africa. The black struggle for political power was not in itself enough – the resources to make life meaningful were needed.[1]

Mr Qoboza's views have been echoed by two homeland leaders who have attracted widespread criticism for their suppression of dissent in their 'countries'. The two, Chief George Matanzima, Prime Minister of Transkei, and Chief Lennox Sebe, President of Ciskei, also have very little time for each other, both wishing to claim leadership of the Xhosa people who live in the two homelands. In July 1986, Chief Matanzima announced that Anglican Church leaders in Transkei were to be investigated to determine whether they followed Bishop Tutu's ideas on sanctions. The Bishop, he said, was 'trotting the globe preaching disinvestment', knowing very well that his fellow-blacks would suffer. The 'prophets of doom' who believed in disinvestment were not interested in the plight of black people living in South Africa, he added.[2]

President Sebe said in September 1986 that punitive sanctions would drastically reduce employment opportunities and drive many thousands of people in South Africa and its neighbouring states to poverty. 'This is the remedy the world at large has prescribed to cure the ills which currently prevail in South Africa,' he said, adding that his government had never been a supporter of the 'abhorrent practice' of apartheid:

We are an interdependent society, and while there are defined boundaries for South Africa and its independent states, there are so many issues that can only effectively be dealt with on a community basis. We have never advocated economic suicide and would appeal to those in positions of power throughout the world to think again and abandon their sanctions campaign and prevent the bringing about of economic collapse leading to further suffering, hardship, disorder and violence.[3]

Not surprisingly, sanctions have also been criticized by black businessmen – that class of people whom the government, ideally, would like to get on its side as a buffer against what it regards as 'radicals'. Perhaps more surprisingly, the black business view of sanctions appears to be changing under pressure of events and opinion. The traditional opposition to sanctions has been expressed by P. G. Gumede, Vice-President of the National African Federated Chamber of Commerce (NAFCOC) and President of the Inyanda Chamber of Commerce and Industry. In the latter capacity he said in April 1985 that 'if there is anything which should unite South Africans across the colour line it is the issue of sanctions'. Disinvestment would be disastrous for all. It would be difficult for blacks to accept that the pressure of disinvestment would be to their benefit. It was foreign companies that had pioneered desirable labour reforms and blacks were usually the first to be affected by retrenchment.[4]

A year later, he was expressing the same opinions: sanctions would delay reform, leave thousands of blacks jobless and weaken the strength of the business sector. 'Most' blacks, he said, thought the free enterprise system should not only be retained but should also be protected at all costs. 'Most' blacks rejected ANC dogma because it was directly opposed to capitalism, which in turn presented the black middle class with the opportunity of raising itself.[5]

Less than six weeks later, however, NAFCOC appeared to be

changing its tune. Its President, Dr Sam Motsuenyane, said in July 1986 that his organization would reconsider its opposition to disinvestment. Many black organizations which had been in favour of conditional investment 12 months before were no longer committed to this: 'They are now instead advocating total disinvestment and the application of sanctions ... This sudden change ... follows a year of unabating conflict and violence.' NAFCOC, said Dr Motsuenyane, had supported for many years a policy of 'conditional investment': this meant that it did not back investment which was geared to benefit the whites at the expense of blacks. The organization was now, however, encountering increasing pressure to align itself more with other black groups which had already declared themselves in favour of disinvestment and the policy would shortly be reviewed.[6]

Later the same month Dr Motsuenyane, reporting on talks with the British Foreign Secretary, Sir Geoffrey Howe, in Pretoria, said that 'if conditional investment does not help to bring about change, if there is no progress, we cannot maintain our current position'. Black businessmen would be most likely to lose if sanctions were implemented, but 'we are losing anyway'.[7]

The Coloured chamber in the tricameral Parliament, the House of Representatives, has called for a five-year moratorium on disinvestment. Introducing a motion in the House, Peter Hendrickse, son of the Labour Party leader who is one of the two black members of the Cabinet, asked for the moratorium because 'the government has said it is sincere about reform. Give us a chance, one could say a last chance, to bring about change peacefully.'[8]

Several lesser-known bodies have declared their opposition to sanctions. The Southern African Bus and Taxi Association (SABTA) President, James Ngcoya, said in September 1986 that 'changes in our country today need active and constructive support – it does not need the penalty of sanctions'.[9] A former mayor of a Port Elizabeth black township, Thamsanqa Linda, who was forced to flee the township for a beach-front hotel, surfaced in June 1986 to claim that he and other members of a group called Victims Against Terror had met 'leading members' of the British government to campaign against sanctions. 'Those who advocate sanctions want to promote the turmoil in the country,' he told South African television. Mr Linda and a fellow former councillor were described on television by another member of Victims Against Terror as 'moderates' with 'several million' followers.[10]

Another opponent of sanctions, also sometimes described as a moderate with several million followers – although with rather more justification than Mr Linda – is Chief Gatsha Buthelezi, Chief Minister of KwaZulu. He has used a number of forums to express his views: the House of Commons Foreign Affairs Committee, newspapers and magazines, political rallies, the launching of a trade union intended to rival more radical unions, and meetings with Western political leaders. Chief Buthelezi has been undoubtedly one of the South African government's strongest weapons against sanctions. Accompanying his opposition is a powerful ego and a desperate desire to carve himself out a strong political role in the transformation of South Africa.

Chief Buthelezi's attitude to disinvestment has not, however, always been as simplistic as it sometimes appears. In the mid-1970s he, in conjunction with the now banned Christian Institute, questioned the role of foreign investors if their sole aim was to benefit shareholders and white South Africa. Inside South Africa at that time this was considered a radical stand. Chief Buthelezi argued in 1978 that it was 'morally imperative' for American firms to 'remain active here and support us in our struggle . . . It's very important that your American companies, when they come here, do more than just invest. They must take an active role, not a passive one.'[11]

Aspects of this attitude were shared during the same period by the Black Consciousness movement. Steve Biko, giving evidence in a trial of fellow-leaders, said in 1976 that there were limitations that made it 'impossible for anybody intimately involved with the South African economy to withdraw at will'. A major theme of the campaign for foreign companies to withdraw from South Africa was to increase pressure on Pretoria. 'Putting pressure on foreign companies about their participation in this . . . immoral set-up was also calculated to make sure that the foreign governments also equally began to feel unhappy about the fact of the participation of their firms in this country and assist generally in building up pressure to make South Africa shift its attitudes gradually to a more acceptable stance.'[12] That, however, was before events showed that disinvestment was practicable. And Biko was trying to defend his colleagues against a charge of advocating boycotts – a criminal offence.

As sanctions have become a more live issue, Chief Buthelezi's attitude appears to have grown more conservative. At the same time he has become more prone to claim to be speaking on behalf of a vast constituency – whether it is his Inkatha movement, the South African Black Alliance (a short-lived movement which brought together Inkatha and, among others, the Coloured Labour Party), or blacks in general. The personal pronoun appears frequently in Chief Buthelezi's speeches and writings – 'I was born to occupy a leadership position,' he told the House of Commons Foreign Affairs Committee – as an adjunct to his supposed mandate:

It is in Soweto that I hold one of my annual rallies . . . up to 40,000 fill a soccer stadium to express their solidarity with Inkatha and encourage its leadership to continue on course . . . No year passes without my putting the disinvestment question before Inkatha's annual general conference . . . No year passes when I do not address mass meetings in different parts of the country – and every year tens of thousands of ordinary South Africans roar their disapproval of disinvestment as a strategy.[13]

One such recent rally where ordinary people were said to roar their disapproval of sanctions was on May Day 1986 at the launching of the United Workers' Union of South Africa (UWUSA), generally considered to be an Inkatha response to the formation of COSATU: an attempt by Chief Buthelezi to claim some trade union ground. The crowd attending was estimated at between 70,000 and 80,000 – the latter figure given by South African Radio, which said approvingly that each time Chief Buthelezi asked the crowd their feelings on sanctions, 'they roared their disapproval while waving placards which condemned Bishop Desmond Tutu for supporting the type of action which would deprive them of employment and food'.[14] Chief Buthelezi said that he had told leaders of the USA, Britain, Israel, West Germany and 'others too numerous to mention' that 'you as black South Africans have never given me a mandate to advocate sanctions and disinvestment . . . Judging by what happened in Rhodesia under Ian Smith, sanctions would not topple the present oppressive regime.'[15]

Limited sanctions could, however, 'send some messages' to President Botha, Chief Buthelezi told the House of Commons Foreign Affairs Committee in January 1986. But 'the pressure of EEC partial sanctions and President Reagan's partial sanctions are as far as you can go . . . I do not think you should overplay your hand in it, because then it would be destructive.' Saying again that he had addressed tens of thousands of people who had not called for sanctions, Chief Buthelezi added: 'I would challenge anyone who said that black people

wanted sanctions to go to the pass office in Johannesburg, to go to the
pass office in Cape Town, in Durban and other cities, and see how
many hundreds of black people are queueing up for jobs . . . they are
voting with their feet for more investment and for jobs.'

The KwaZulu leader also used an argument much favoured by
liberal white capitalists, that economic expansion will lead to political
liberalization. He told the Foreign Affairs Committee:

Whereas in the past the government did not allow blacks to perform certain
jobs . . . economic reality has caused it to fall away to the extent that participation by blacks in the trade union movement has come about and has increased
buying power, and mobility of blacks in the political field has increased
interdependence in the political field. If this is allowed to happen more
and more it will not be difficult to extend it to political interdependence. That
is why I say we need massive and sustained economic growth in South Africa
for the purpose of change; that is why I say sanctions cannot solve the problem
for us.[16]

. . . For liberation to have a meaning for the ordinary people, you must
improve the quality of their life. You cannot have a situation where you destroy
the economy of the country, because whoever runs the country will have
problems.[17]

Chief Buthelezi's reservations about sanctions also concern the
West. In a lengthy memorandum to the Foreign Affairs Committee, he
said he was 'very sceptical' on whether the West 'would come to the
rescue of more than a million citizens of independent states when the
crunch comes and South Africa decides to expel them as a retaliatory
act . . . I have not seen a single Western country do anything to the
rogue elephant, which the South African Defence Force has been,
when they have killed our brothers and sisters in countries such as
Lesotho, Mozambique, Angola and Botswana.'[18]

Another argument against sanctions was put to the Foreign Affairs
Committee in July 1986 by Dr Oscar Dhlomo, Secretary-General of
Inkatha and also Minister of Education and Culture in KwaZulu:

One wrong thing the West could do would be . . . to fail to differentiate
between apartheid as an evil system and South Africa as a country inhabited
by an oppressed black majority . . . Sanctions do not make that distinction. So
if you were going to claim that you were assisting the victims of apartheid by
imposing sanctions on South Africa you would be . . . acting as somebody
who bombs the cells in order to free the prisoners.[19]

Sanctions assume, Dr Dhlomo said, 'that if South Africa is strangled economically, then all of a sudden South Africa would change course and become a democracy and include the excluded majority. Now we are not sure, and is it fair to gamble with the lives of millions and millions of people when you are not even sure that the effect of sanctions is what we speculate it will be?' Rather there should be some kind of Marshall Aid plan 'targeted on the victims of apartheid ... geared to assisting black people to rise above apartheid and challenge it more competently and successfully'. [20]

Chief Buthelezi has also warned against sanctions on the grounds that they would strengthen right-wing Afrikanerdom – an argument also much favoured by 'verligte' Nationalists and white liberals. During the visit on behalf of the E E C of the British Foreign Secretary, Sir Geoffrey Howe, to South Africa in July 1986, he said: 'If by virtue of a combination of pressures the present cabinet is forced to make hasty concessions under duress, or to suspend its authority, the chances of a take-over government by the security forces, the right-wing parties, or both, is very great indeed.' [21]

Another homeland leader to oppose sanctions is Dr Cedric Phatudi, Chief Minister of the 'non-independent' homeland of Lebowa. In evidence to the Foreign Affairs Committee in July 1986 he, like Chief Buthelezi, claimed that 'a large majority of blacks in Southern Africa are strenuously opposed to punitive sanctions imposed on South Africa'. Apartheid was unwise, uneconomic and unproductive, but sanctions 'have never succeeded anywhere' and were 'a futile exercise by all standards'. Dr Phatudi criticized the clergy campaigning for sanctions:

Let us make efforts to kill apartheid and not kill a black man. Yet there are those who advocate measures that will kill a black man instead of apartheid ... We note that among the apostles for punitive sanctions on South Africa there are some of the leading clergy in our land. The clergy do not understand the problem at grassroots level, where people are already starving, deprived, humiliated and injured. The time has really come, in my humble opinion, for the clergy to impose 'fasting' on themselves. Then they will appreciate what hardships the ordinary mass of black people will suffer if punitive sanctions are imposed on South Africa.

Dr Phatudi went on to claim that 75 per cent of black opinion was against sanctions. So why, he was asked, were Bishop Tutu, Winnie Mandela, Oliver Tambo and the Frontline states saying that the blacks overwhelmingly wanted 'this destruction of their economy as the only way they can dismantle apartheid quickly'?

Dr Phatudi replied that he was Chairman of the Committee of Chief Ministers of the Non-independent Homelands. KwaZulu had 6 million people, Lebowa 4.5 million, Qwa-Qwa one million, GaZankulu 1.5 million, KaNgwane one million – 14 million followers of chief ministers who all opposed sanctions. Added to that were the National African Federation of Chambers of Commerce with a 'large following' and the Interdenominational African Ministers' Association, 'a very large body'. 'Add those together,' Dr Phatudi said. 'With due respect, Bishop Tutu is head of a church, and I am not sure of whether the church is behind him, but the church alone cannot match the figure I have given you . . . I am speaking now on behalf of millions of people.'

People in Britain underestimated 'the help that they give us in South Africa . . . It is really useful to us. A large majority of black people are earning their daily bread by working in your factories.' He pointed out also that 'the Outspan oranges which Britain is very fond of come from my part of the country'.

With Dr Phatudi giving evidence was a white, Dr J. H. Pretorius, Chairman of the Lebowa Development Corporation. Ian Mikardo said that Mr Botha had scrapped the pass laws soon after international banks had imposed sanctions by refusing to roll over the country's debts: 'If sanctions worked on that occasion, why do you not think they will work on every occasion?'

Dr Pretorius denied that the abolition of the pass laws was the result of sanctions: 'I do not for one moment say changes have taken place in South Africa because of sanctions.' The pass laws had been scrapped because of the support of Parliament and committees working on the laws. He was also confident that 'in a short period – I cannot say whether a month or two months – I think we will see big things happening'.[22]

4 *Opinion Polls*

Few questions arouse so much controversy as black opinion in South Africa. On the issue of sanctions, a number of public opinion surveys have been done – and the conclusions of virtually all are hotly debated. This is not surprising: the polls vary wildly in their results. Each side of the sanctions debate has used the poll or polls that suit it best, ignoring or denigrating others.

One survey widely quoted by opponents of sanctions to back up their case was conducted by Professor Lawrence Schlemmer of the University of Natal in mid-1984. He questioned 551 black factory workers in seven major industrial regions throughout the country, finding that 75 per cent opposed 'divestment' in questions requiring a choice between continued investment and withdrawal. The result, Professor Schlemmer said, exactly confirmed an earlier poll in Natal in 1979.[1]

This survey has been widely attacked, as Professor Schlemmer has acknowledged.[2] Two of his colleagues described it as biased, irresponsible and ambiguous, and said that its findings were based on questionable methodology. Professor Schlemmer retorted that his critics were 'intemperate and unscholarly'.[3] The Schlemmer poll has been cited frequently by the US State Department as evidence for the Reaganite view that blacks oppose sanctions – but one criticism of the survey has been that it was partly financed by the State Department. Other criticisms have been that the sample was small, that the people questioned were limited to direct employees of foreign companies, and, in a less-than-temperate article in the ANC magazine *Sechaba*, that Professor Schlemmer seemed 'to have relied on members of Buthelezi's increasingly terroristic organization, Inkatha, to conduct the survey'.[4]

A second survey, commissioned through Market Research Africa, of 1,000 blacks in eight metropolitan areas, found that 79 per cent rejected 'divestment' as a way 'to frighten the government into removing apartheid'. Nineteen per cent supported this option.[5]

A third poll was conducted by the government's Human Sciences

Research Council (HSRC) among black males in the Pretoria/ Witwatersrand/Vereeniging (PWV) area in July 1984, February 1985 and May 1985. The figures for respondents rejecting international boycotts of South Africa were 80.9 per cent, 54.3 per cent and 75.8 per cent. Those supporting boycotts were 13.8 per cent, 29.7 per cent and 20.8 per cent. Asked in February 1985 specifically about 'divestment', 67.3 per cent supported further foreign investment, while 24.6 per cent opposed it.[6]

Other surveys, however, have produced different figures. A London *Sunday Times* poll carried out by Mori/Markinor in August 1985 found that 77 per cent of 400 blacks polled in Johannesburg and Durban agreed that other countries were right to impose sanctions unless the government agreed to get rid of apartheid. Twenty-one per cent disagreed. Forty-eight per cent expected that they would suffer personally if sanctions were imposed while 46 per cent did not.[7]

A year later, however, the *Sunday Times* and Markinor carried out another poll which produced rather different results. This survey was among blacks in the countryside and showed that 34 per cent of those polled were against sanctions and 22 per cent in favour.[8]

According to the Schlemmer and the first *Sunday Times* polls, support for sanctions comes in a large measure from the young and educated. The *Sunday Times* found that it reached 84 per cent in the 25 to 34 age-group,[9] while Professor Schlemmer's survey showed support for disinvestment came from blacks with post-high-school qualifications: 46 per cent of what he calls 'this middle class elite'.[10] However, a detailed survey conducted by the Community Agency for Social Enquiry in association with the Institute for Black Research (CASE/IBR) in September 1985 disputes this description, saying that supporters of one or other form of disinvestment are more politically aware, but 'it would be a rather patronizing mistake to infer that they are therefore well-heeled'. There was little difference between those earning less than R 500 a month and those earning more in their attitude to free investment, nor between students, white-collar and blue-collar workers. Nor did responses differ greatly between the unemployed and those holding down jobs.

Most polls apparently asked an 'either/or' question: for or against sanctions/disinvestment. Evidence from the CASE/IBR survey appears to show, however, that the people being questioned appreciate the complexity of the issue – and that many support conditional disinvestment. This study has attracted widespread attention – and some (inevitable) criticism. CASE/IBR found that 73 per cent of metropolitan blacks favour one or other form of disinvestment and that 49 per cent favour conditional disinvestment. Mark Orkin has written up the survey in *The Struggle and the Future: What Black South Africans Really Think*.[11] Most of what follows comes from this book.

The main criticism of the CASE/IBR survey is that the questions were 'loaded'. The full question said:

A lot of foreign companies and banks, that is companies and banks from overseas, do business in South Africa. They lend money to the government or businessmen, or they run factories here. This is called foreign investment. People and groups in South Africa and overseas have different ideas about foreign investment. There are three main views. Which of the three views do you support most?

The first view encourages investment. This view says that foreign firms help South Africa to grow, so they should be encouraged to invest here freely. This view is supported by P. W. Botha and the Nationalist Government, by businessmen like Harry Oppenheimer, by Chief Mangosuthu Gatsha Buthelezi and Inkatha, and other homeland leaders.

The second view wants to limit or restrict investment. This view says that foreign firms should not be allowed to invest here unless they actively pressure the government to end apartheid, and recognize the trade unions chosen by the workers. This view is supported by Bishop Tutu, by the trade unions in FOSATU and CUSA, and by the SA Council of Churches.

The third view wants no investment. This view says that foreign firms only help to keep apartheid alive and exploit blacks, so foreign firms should not be allowed to remain here at all. This view is supported by the ANC and the PAC, AZAPO, many members of the UDF, and some trade unions.

The result was:

Encourage investment	26%
Limit investment	49%
No investment	24%
Don't know	1%

Orkin denies that this question, or any of the others, is loaded. He defends his approach as follows:

The customary style of attitude polls, which is to present abstract issues for consideration in isolation, effectively constitutes respondents as self-seeking and private individuals, and thereby tends to bias their answers towards the economistic, market-oriented answers which suit business or the capitalist state.

For better or worse, when citizens in a democracy go to the vote, issues are conceived in a context of parties and personalities. We wanted our survey to approximate to democratic political choice. So we sought to provide the context, using the vocabulary and examples by which the views were typically being characterized in everyday discussion.

The CASE/IBR survey also compared its findings with an earlier one by Professor Schlemmer in December 1984 which also drew on a general country-wide metropolitan sample:

Option	Schlemmer	CASE/IBR
Free investment	47%	26%
Conditional disinvestment	44%	49%
Total disinvestment	9%	24%

Orkin suggests that, as Bishop Tutu, FOSATU, CUSA and the South African Council of Churches came to back conditional disinvestment and attitudes polarized with mounting violence and the first State of Emergency, 'some blacks moved from the free investment into the conditional disinvestment position and some from the conditional disinvestment into the total disinvestment position'.

Just who would suffer in the event of sanctions is a live issue. Many opponents claim that blacks, inside South Africa and in the neighbouring states, would be the first to be hit. (In some ways the government's use of this argument is a self-serving and self-fulfilling prophecy: in late 1986, after the US Congress passed a sanctions Bill and overrode President Reagan's veto, the government ensured that foreign workers, particularly Mozambicans, were the first to be expelled.) Black opinion seems unclear. The first London *Sunday Times* poll found that 48 per cent expected they would suffer personally if sanctions were imposed, while 46 per cent did not.[12] The HSRC in February 1985 said that 61.3 per cent of black males believed they would be most affected by sanctions, while 9.5 per cent thought whites would be most affected.[13] The CASE/IBR survey asked whether the people polled would stand by or change their positions on disinvestment if they knew that relatively few, or many, blacks would suffer unemployment as a result. Twenty-six per cent felt disinvestment was worthwhile if few or many suffered unemployment; 25 per cent if few but not many jobs were lost; and 48 per cent said the sacrifice was not worthwhile if few *or* many jobs were sacrificed. Orkin concludes that many of the people polled 'are looking to conditional disinvestment for a strategy which could help to end apartheid while threatening their everyday livelihood as little as possible'.

One interesting side-aspect of the CASE/IBR study was the support – or lack of support – given to various black political leaders and groups. Nelson Mandela and the ANC received 31-per-cent support, Bishop Tutu 16 per cent, the UDF and various radical groups 14 per cent, Chief Buthelezi and Inkatha 8 per cent, the government and pro-investment lobbies also 8 per cent, while 'don't knows', others and 'no leader/organization' got 24 per cent. (This totals more than 100 per cent because of small rounding errors.) The surprise in all this, Orkin comments, is that Chief Buthelezi gained only 6 per cent and Inkatha 2 per cent. Looking at other surveys, while warning that the figures must be treated with caution, Orkin concludes that 'across the metropolitan areas of South Africa, Buthelezi has basically lost the battle for popular support and the decline in his showing can be expected to continue'. Some of Buthelezi's supporters also do not back him on free investment: a quarter want conditional disinvestment.

5 *Whites For Sanctions*

Relatively few white South Africans have come out in favour of sanctions. This is not too surprising: the law discourages such initiatives, the white standard of living is a powerful inducement not to rock the boat, and few actually believe that the path of sanctions is the right one to take. There are exceptions, notably Dr Beyers Naude, General Secretary of the South African Council of Churches, Sheena Duncan of the Black Sash, a predominantly white women's group concerned with civil liberties and problems facing blacks, and several religious organizations.

Dr Naude is a former minister of the Nederduitse Gereformeerde Kerk and a member of the secret Afrikaner Broederbond. Once a government supporter, he has moved across the political spectrum, suffering seven years as a banned person as a result. The anti-apartheid Christian Institute which he founded and led was also banned. In March 1976 the CI issued a statement with Chief Buthelezi saying that it was prepared to support investment in the homelands but not in the central economy. A few years earlier it had tried to develop a code of conduct for further investment in South Africa: full trade union rights, equal pay for equal work, the scrapping of job reservation (which defined some employment for whites only), and moves to provide the same fringe benefits for blacks as for whites. In the mid-1970s when the Sullivan and EEC codes were introduced, after publicity about poor – or starvation – wages being paid by foreign companies to black workers in South Africa, the CI welcomed them, not as alternatives to a moratorium on further investment but in the hope that they might improve the conduct of firms operating in South Africa. After the 1976 Soweto shootings, Dr Naude and the CI accepted the Black Consciousness condemnation of foreign investment, which, it thought, accurately reflected black opinion. The CI then also felt that foreign investment and its technology bolstered apartheid, whether that investment was in the central economy or the homelands.[1] Dr Naude was banned in the crackdown on Black

Consciousness movements in October 1979 and was able to take part in politics again only after the banning order was lifted in September 1984. A few months later he was elected General Secretary of the SACC in succession to Bishop Tutu.

The SACC has long attracted attention for its opposition to apartheid. In 1981 the government appointed the Eloff Commission to inquire into its activities – a commission widely regarded as conducting a witch-hunt. In February 1984 the Commission reported, claiming that many of the SACC's aims, activities, tactics and strategies were revolutionary, destabilizing, secretive and confrontationist.[2] It deplored what it called the covert support the SACC was giving to the overseas disinvestment campaign, adding that the Council feared adopting a formal resolution because of legal prohibitions. The SACC presidium, however, replied that it had never supported a disinvestment campaign. The Commission called for the creation of a specific offence of economic sabotage, to be written into the Internal Security Act. The then Minister of Law and Order, Louis le Grange, termed the SACC 'a left-wing political activist organization which clearly enjoys hardly any support in South Africa'. No decision would be taken at that stage on creating the offence of economic sabotage, but the SACC would be brought within the provisions of the Fund-Raising Act, which allows the government to prohibit the collection of funds by an organization.

More recently Dr Naude himself has urged that sanctions be imposed because 'most sections of South Africa's black community, backed by the churches, now see sanctions as the last viable, non-violent means of bringing about the end of apartheid and limiting further bloodshed and the threat of an open civil war.'[3] There was deep disappointment among blacks at the failure of the West to impose tougher sanctions, he said, applauding Denmark for being the first country to impose a total ban on trade with Pretoria and urging the USA, Britain and West Germany not to delay in taking stronger steps against the white minority regime.[4] Dr Naude has also said that fundamental change in South Africa would only come about through increasing economic and political pressure and by actions undertaken in the country.[5]

The Black Sash was formed as the Women's Defence of the Constitution League in May 1955 during the government's protracted attempts to remove Coloureds in the Cape Province from the common voters' roll.* Its members, until recently mostly white middle-class women, picketed cabinet ministers, wearing black sashes. In recent years it has grown more radical, while at the same time highlighting the fate of Africans moved from their homes under apartheid and helping Africans through the maze of apartheid legislation. In late 1985 its President, Sheena Duncan, came out in support of selective, strategic and properly monitored sanctions, which could, she said, stave off years of bloody violence. She, like others, pointed to the effect South Africa's continued violence and the threat of sanctions had had on businessmen in the country: 'They are now running around like scalded cats' after little previous activity.[6]

At least three South African churches have joined the call for economic pressure on South Africa – the Anglican, Catholic and Methodist. Together they represent more than 1.2 million whites and 4.8 million Africans, Coloureds and Indians.[7] Bishop Tutu, now the head of the Church of the Province (as the Anglicans are called officially) in his capacity as Archbishop of Cape Town, has attracted international attention over his calls for sanctions, although he has said that he speaks in a personal capacity. In October 1986 the Synod of the Anglican Diocese of Cape Town passed a resolution which was interpreted as implicit support for sanctions. It also demanded that the State of Emergency be lifted, Nelson Mandela released, and banned organizations made lawful again. The Archbishop of Canterbury, Dr Robert Runcie, head of the Anglican Church throughout the world, called for tougher sanctions after visiting South Africa for Bishop Tutu's enthronement in 1986. The church, he told Mrs Thatcher, had to 'support the movement to achieve equal rights for all by refusing to give economic support to the regime', although he did not believe that sanctions alone would effect a change of heart.[8]

The World Methodist Council has also called for sanctions 'to make possible a less violent resolution of the South African tragedy'. It called in July 1986 for Methodist organizations to withdraw their

---

* The government's efforts to take the Coloureds off the roll occupied much parliamentary, legal and public attention over a number of years. Attempts to deprive them of their common roll vote were defeated in the courts, and in the end, the government had to pass special legislation which (a) enlarged the Senate with government nominees so that it could get the two-thirds majority laid down by the Constitution in 1910, and (b) enlarged the Appeal Court, again with government nominees, so that its parliamentary victory would not be overturned.

funds from companies or banks with interests in South Africa, and urged governments to impose sanctions. An unspecified number of South Africans attending the conference in Nairobi were said to have abstained from voting on the resolution.[9]

It is the Catholic Church that has attracted the most criticism for its stand on sanctions. Relations between the Dutch Reformed Churches and the government on the one hand and the Catholic Church on the other have long been uneasy at best: the phrase 'Roomse gevaar' (Roman danger) was at one stage a theme of anti-Catholic propaganda. Official hostility to the Catholic Church was intensified when, in May 1986, the Catholic Bishops' Conference gave cautious approval to economic steps as 'the most effective of non-violent forms of pressure' against Pretoria: 'Economic pressure has been justifiably imposed to end apartheid . . . such pressure should continue and, if necessary, be intensified.' But the bishops added: 'Such intensified pressure can only be justified if applied in such a way as not to destroy the country's economic infrastructure and to reduce as far as possible any additional suffering to the oppressed through job loss.' Before the conference there had been some opposition to the expected statement: priests in the Durban archdiocese voted 35 to 6 against disinvestment. The bishops acknowledged that Catholics were not obliged to agree with their stance, but said they had given a lead which should be taken seriously. They could not give specific advice on how pressure could or should be applied, but would set up an advisory commission.[10]

The President of the Catholic Bishops' Conference, Archbishop Denis Hurley, termed the arguments for economic pressure 'something of a ritual'. He added: 'The measure of how bad you think apartheid is lies in whether you call for economic pressure. If you don't, it means you don't think the system is really evil. Of course, whether, having called for them, you actually want sanctions imposed is another story altogether.'[11]

6   *Whites Against Sanctions*

The paradox about white South African opposition to sanctions is that the arguments are aimed towards two opposite goals: the abolition of apartheid or its maintenance. Some of the points made by both sides are similar or identical, yet the end results they seek are irreconcilable. Probably the most coherent intellectual case against sanctions, where the aim is to end apartheid, is made by the former Leader of the Opposition, Frederik van Zyl Slabbert. Dr Slabbert is an Afrikaner, a former professor of sociology, an amateur who went into politics with some reluctance and rose quickly to lead the Progressive Federal Party. He created something of a sensation by resigning publicly and dramatically in February 1986, at least partly because the government had failed to live up to its promises of reform. His resignation was greeted with dismay by the government and the PFP, but the ANC hailed him as a 'new Voortekker' for quitting Parliament. He now heads a think-tank which he established trying to find common ground between black and white.

Dr Slabbert has spelled out his views on sanctions in his autobiography (*The Last White Parliament* – see Bibliography), in evidence to the House of Commons Foreign Affairs Committee and in innumerable speeches in South Africa and abroad. One of the first points he made to the Foreign Affairs Committee in November 1985 was that the sanctions debate had to a large extent developed its own momentum, becoming embroiled in the domestic politics of Britain and the USA 'almost independently of the internal situation in South Africa'.[1] Further, 'one's attitude towards sanctions is seen as a measure of one's opposition to apartheid'. In his autobiography he adds that the impact of special-interest lobbies 'is more effective domestically than on a foreign target area . . . [they] sustain a kind of moral climate against apartheid and racism rather than concretely managing to change any specific policy'.[2]

In his evidence to the Foreign Affairs Committee and in his autobiography Dr Slabbert lists a number of arguments for sanctions, giving his counter-arguments:

1. *Sanctions will weaken the apartheid economy.*

The economy in any country assists the government in pursuing its policies, but the economy is also the economy that improves the quality of life of everybody in that society, so to the extent that everyone is dependent on the economy it is true that it could strengthen the government. It could also improve the lot of those who have suffered as a result of the government's policies.

2. *Sanctions will bring the government to its senses.*

The evidence is overwhelmingly to the contrary ... the government tends to become more obstinate and more obdurate as a result of punitive, blunt external pressure or isolation ... The other side of the coin ... when it is considered, is done in tortuous logic which argues that this is necessary because it 'has to get worse so that it can become better'. The one clear case of a reasonably successful external embargo somehow fails to impress those who persist with this kind of strategy. Through Armscor, South Africa is now almost self-sufficient in supplying its own weaponry and is successfully exporting arms.* When I pointed out this anomaly to someone who had regularly drafted resolutions for international conferences in favour of an arms embargo against South Africa, he conceded that it did not make sense, but in the present 'moral climate' it would be 'suicide' not to support such resolutions. Somehow the means had become confused with the ends – the strategy had become the goal itself ...

... There are those in government who would say we have to be more sensitive and careful and think about the consequences for the economy, but there are also those who are arguing that if we cross a certain threshold and if they want to isolate the whites, if they want to adopt a kind of punitive approach, then there is the attitude of withdrawing, of becoming more obstinate, of saying, 'Let's batten down the hatches. Let's clamp down and hold what we have got.' ... If a threshold is crossed and the people in government actually go for the latter position, they can maintain a situation of stable

* See, however, Chapter 24, p. 222.

repression for a very long time at a great cost not only to blacks but to whites as well.

3. *Sanctions may increase black suffering, but this will bring about improved circumstances in the long term.*

This presupposes a stage in the South African conflict where that conflict will be resolved as a result of the application also of sanctions and will be resolved in such a way as to benefit the majority of people in that country. It is not quite clear to me how it is going to come about, unless one assumes that there will be some dramatic violent resolution of that conflict. I do not see this. I do not see any conventional revolutionary conclusion to that situation . . .

. . . The fallacious assumption [is] that if the South African Government is deprived of commodity Y it will then spend its money on commodity X which will be to the benefit of the blacks. For example, less money spent on defence will mean more money spent on black education. This is an absurd argument.

The most far-fetched argument in this vein is that blacks cannot suffer any more than they are at the moment and therefore concerted external action will increasingly isolate the South African Government and weaken it. Eventually this weakening process must be to the benefit of the majority. The other side of the argument is, of course, that things can get considerably worse without getting better at all, and that, relatively speaking, the South African Government can become stronger and even more coercive than it is at present.

4. *Sanctions will strengthen the resolve of the black majority.*

. . . In a situation of economic downturn, in a situation where you have increasing unemployment, it is unlikely that this would strengthen the resolve or the ability of the blacks to apply pressure on that situation . . .

. . . The next decade or so will see strategies for change focus on three particular areas: labour, education and constitutional development . . . As population increase and urbanization gather momentum . . . labour and education will inevitably become increasingly politicized the longer it takes for adequate constitutional channels to develop.

The ability of blacks to apply pressure through their labour organizations [if sanctions were applied] would also suffer in the long run. They would be less able to apply that pressure simply because of the substitutability of labour . . . Another consequence of economic growth and development has been increased industrialization and increased urbanization and . . . if one can talk about pressures coming to bear on the South African situation . . . it has been the result of the urban situation far more than the rural situation.

5. *Sanctions can punish those responsible for apartheid.*

This desire to punish is an understandable one, but I think one should draw a distinction between the desire to punish on the one hand and the ability to change the domestic situation on the other.

6. *Sanctions can be imposed and lifted depending on the situation.*

. . . A rather mechanistic view of the economic position in South Africa, as if one can turn the economy on and off at will; that, for example, one can now have a situation of withdrawal of foreign interests and foreign investments and then at some later stage one can encourage people to go back and invest there again. I do not think the economy works in that way, particularly if it is based on private enterprise. Investors assess their own interests on the way in which they can improve their own interests in terms of the domestic situation, and it is unlikely that they are going to come back just to show their approval for that society now that apartheid is no longer there . . .

. . . There is no such thing as a collective international business ethic concerning the domestic affairs of any foreign country. Business pursues profit, not morality. Even if some business firms are more sensitive to domestic pressure concerning foreign investments, there is abundant evidence that if there is profit to be made and for whatever reason some withdraw, others will take their place . . . I prefer a foreign company sensitive to domestic pressure concerning fair employment practices in another country than one which is not . . .

. . . In fact, if it is quite clear from available evidence that foreign governments and businesses are not going to act as prime movers in changing the domestic situation in South Africa, the morality of keeping alive the hope or fiction that they can play such a role is equally questionable.

Under questioning by members of the Foreign Affairs Committee, Dr Slabbert did point to one area where international boycott brought about changes – sport: *

The sports boycott did bring about changes in the internal situation in South Africa ... [Now] the changes that have come about as a result of the sporting boycott are regarded as cosmetic, regarded as not being very effective by those who were responsible for bringing it about, so in a sense the debate has shifted away from simply desegregating sport or promoting non-racial sport to, in fact, sporting authorities in the country now having to be responsible for bringing about changes in government policy, the argument being that you cannot have normal sport in an abnormal society ...

... You still have the Group Areas Act or the Population Registration Act. In other words the goals have been shifted as far as desegregating sport is concerned.

On sport, his predecessor, Colin Eglin, who took over again as Leader of the opposition PFP when Dr Slabbert resigned, told the Foreign Affairs Committee:

It was a specific boycott with a clear objective ... In a sense there was a reward available if that objective had been met. It was: Sportsmen, put your house in order and you will be readmitted to the world of sport. Seeing that in those terms, the sportsmen did not see it as a punitive exercise. They saw it as an exercise of putting things right in order to be able to be readmitted and in that sense they set about their task. Maybe they did not do it as completely as they should but they set about their task ... with very considerable success. But having attained that objective ... the goalposts were then shifted ... The result is that the sportsmen no longer see the boycott as a corrective measure to achieve an attainable objective. It is now seen as part of a general coercive punitive strategy in a situation in which they have no direct control ...

... It is important that, if pressures are perceived to be just coercive or punitive, there will be far less positive response than if they are seen to be an attempt to get a corrective action in order to achieve an attainable objective, after which there will be a reward for having achieved that objective.

Dr Slabbert drew a distinction between pressure and sanctions. The sporting boycott was 'punitive external pressure' but 'the other form of external pressure would be not punitive so much but a greater degree of involvement in pressure to bring about change in, for ex-

* See Chapter 14.

ample, black education, the level of black skills, industrial bargaining, black community development, diplomatic pressure – these would all be the kinds of external pressures that could be applied, and have been applied, in affecting the internal situation'.

The left-wing Labour MP, Ian Mikardo asked what forms of pressure, other than sanctions, could be applied. Dr Slabbert replied:

To assist in cultural, academic exchanges. If you can assist blacks in education that is a government-to-government pressure; it is also private-enterprise-to-private-enterprise pressure. The pressures that come about of, say, multi-nationals improving the quality of life and the working conditions of people there are a form of indirect pressure that builds up inside that situation . . . Diplomatic pressure, no doubt, can be brought about in the sense that you can say that if certain things do not happen you will withdraw or call back your representative.

The lack of business confidence in South Africa also had a role, Dr Slabbert indicated. Sanctions had not had an impact on firms like General Motors and IBM until very recently:

All of a sudden they have decided that the internal situation is no longer favourable for them to conduct their business . . . because of the rate of urbanization, the inability of the government to cope with the urbanization properly, the pressure on the government structures in order to try to maintain order and the assessment of these companies that there is not a sufficient degree of stability for them to carry on their business focuses the attention of a lot of people in South Africa, including the government, on looking for alternatives . . .

Mr Mikardo then asked a key question: 'So you accept that business opinion, business actions and maybe some selective sanctions as we understand them might be helpful, provided they are linked to the actual situation on the ground and produce the sort of results we have been talking about?'

Dr Slabbert replied diplomatically: 'I would say that any kind of pressure that promotes the situation of negotiation, of looking for alternatives, would be something that had to be considered, but that is not the same as saying sanctions as such.'

Dr Slabbert and Mr Eglin are not the only PFP Members of Parliament to have spoken out against sanctions and disinvestment. Perhaps the best-known opposition MP, Helen Suzman, who was her party's sole parliamentary representative from 1961 to 1974, has been talking and writing against sanctions almost since they became an issue. In April 1986, however, she warned the whites-only House of Assembly that she would drop her campaign unless the government made 'really positive steps to dismantle apartheid'. She had not changed her attitude to sanctions, but, 'I will not go on fighting for a lost cause unless the government gets off its butt and does away with apartheid ... Unless really positive steps are forthcoming from the government, action and not just rhetoric, repealing acts and not just appealing advertisements, I for one shall stop banging my head against a stone wall.'[3]

This theme that the government was in fact buttressing the arguments for sanctions has been taken up by other PFP members. Dr Alex Boraine, who quit Parliament with Dr Slabbert, said in January 1985 that the then Minister of Law and Order, Louis le Grange, had single-handedly done more to encourage disinvestment than any other person or group in South Africa or outside.[4] One of his more conservative colleagues, Philip Myburgh, said two months later that the government's inept handling of black unrest by 'blindly insisting on law and order at all costs' had contributed greatly to the disinvestment campaign.[5] Another MP, Jan van Eck, said in September 1986 that punitive sanctions could have a 'positive' effect – if they were aimed at the National Party government and its supporters. It would result in a small minority – two million out of 22 million people – being identified, isolated and punished.[6]

Mrs Suzman, using an argument often deployed by liberal capitalists in South Africa, has repeated that she thought disinvestment was 'self-defeating because it blunts the one weapon that blacks are able to use to insist that their demands be accommodated – the power to withdraw skilled labour' in a powerful economy increasingly dependent on black labour. Echoing Dr Slabbert, she also said that if the withdrawal of foreign investment limited economic expansion so that budgetary planners had to decide whether to increase spending on the army or black schooling, then the army would have first claim: 'If white survival is in the balance, I have no doubt which priority the government will settle for.'[7]

She has also rejected the argument that blacks would not care if there was mass unemployment through sanctions and disinvestment: 'I am at the receiving end of many requests from recent job losers for assistance in obtaining jobs, and I say that blacks who don't care are those whose jobs are not endangered or who have never had a job to lose.'

Mrs Suzman believes that American and European firms should accelerate efforts to uplift black participation in the South African economy. All firms not adhering to the Sullivan and EEC codes of conduct for black employees should have penalties imposed on them:

The West should raise its voice long and hard against apartheid in general and in particular against any outrageous actions by the South African government ... I have no doubt that protest by Western envoys helped to un-ban people such as Beyers Naude and was instrumental in freezing forced removals as at Crossroads.

The South African government is more sensitive than one thinks. It does not enjoy being a pariah. It would like to be welcomed back into the Western community of nations. But not at any cost. Rather you should aim at attainable objectives than adopt measures that could reduce the country to economic chaos, with totally unpredictable consequences.[8]

The PFP's opposition to sanctions reflects the constituency it represents: in Dr Slabbert's words, 'predominantly urban-based, middle to upper middle class, English-speaking ... about 3- to 6-per-cent Afrikaans-speaking support'. Its support among the electorate has varied between 17 and 20 per cent and it has 27 Members of Parliament. The PFP, and Dr Slabbert in particular, campaigned vigorously against the new constitution introduced by President Botha in 1984. It could not, however, persuade all its followers to vote 'no' in the referendum that preceded its introduction: one survey showed that seven of them voted 'yes' for every five that voted 'no'. The mainly English-speaking areas of Natal and the Border had the largest 'yes' majorities, and Mr Botha won his referendum by 65.95 to 33.53 per cent. With the collapse of the New Republic Party (formerly the United Party, which was defeated in the 1948 election by the Nationalists and declined steadily afterwards), the PFP is, in many seats, the only opposition and many of the people who vote for it are undoubtedly more conservative than the party's manifesto. In the white South African context, too, the 'predominantly urban-based, middle to upper middle class English-speaking' voters are more likely to be in industry and commerce – so sanctions would probably affect their profits. Sanctions would also hit multi-nationals like the Anglo American Corporation whose former chairman, Harry Oppenheimer, is a vocal opponent of disinvestment.

Another famous South African liberal has added his voice to those opposing sanctions. Alan Paton is the author of *Cry the Beloved*

Country and former National President of the Liberal Party, which disbanded itself in 1968 rather than obey government legislation to confine its membership to one racial group only. Mr Paton, writing in June 1985, opposed disinvestment on moral grounds:

Those who will pay most grievously for disinvestment will be the black workers of South Africa.

I take very seriously the teachings of the Gospels, in particular the parables about giving drink to the thirsty and food to the hungry. It seems to me that Jesus attached supreme – indeed sacred – significance to such actions. Therefore I will not help to cause any such suffering to any black person.

I am told that this is a simplistic understanding of the teachings of the Gospels. Let it be so. That is the way I choose to understand them. I am also told that I am ignoring the views of those black South Africans who support disinvestment. Most of these black South Africans will not be the ones to suffer hunger and thirst. Many of them are sophisticated, highly educated, safely placed. I also know sophisticated and highly educated black men and women who will have nothing to do with disinvestment. I choose to associate myself with them . . .

. . . My conscience would not allow me to support disinvestment. For I must ask myself – and my readers who are concerned to do what is right – how long must the suffering it would cause go on before the desired end is achieved? A month? Two months? A year? Five or ten years perhaps?[9]

Mr Oppenheimer, often regarded as the paymaster of the PFP, also opposes sanctions, not surprisingly. He disputes the contention of some proponents of sanctions that the conditions of blacks have worsened. In June 1985 he wrote:

Particularly over the last five years or so – roughly the period covered by the Reagan policy of constructive engagement – change towards the dismantling of apartheid has been proceeding at an increasing rate. Naturally it is not to be expected that these new developments should satisfy those who continue to suffer from the grave injustices which remain . . . On the contrary it is only natural that the changes that have been effected should be denounced as being merely 'cosmetic' and that the chink of light that has appeared at the end of a seemingly endless tunnel should sharpen blacks' determination to emerge into the full light of freedom – not in some distant future but now . . .

The elimination of apartheid is . . . not going to be easy and will only be possible as a result of a process that will take time. Now at what point in that process would the advocates of sanctions and boycotts consider that their objective has been reached and that sanctions and boycotts should be abandoned? It is not an easy question. And it is surely extremely naive to think that sanctions could be switched on and off in accordance with a flexible policy genuinely aimed at building a just society in South Africa. It surely cannot be honestly maintained that sanctions should continue until racial discrimination in all its aspects has been eliminated. Such an ideal state of affairs has not been reached anywhere in the world. No society is entirely just and it seems that no one is able or willing to define what changes are necessary for South Africa to become an acceptable member of the community of nations.

Mr Oppenheimer, like Dr Slabbert, supported 'direct pressure' in 'particular circumstances':

... the general moral condemnation of South Africa is in itself an important sanction ... Campaigns to bring pressure for the elimination of discrimination in particular spheres – the performing arts for example – may well be effective provided their objectives are limited and clearly defined ...

If the necessary level of investment and the skills associated with it are not made available, industrial growth will decline, racial conflict will sharpen, the laager mentality among whites will become stronger, real earnings will stagnate and eventually fall, unemployment will increase, and the flow of blacks to the towns, which all the apartheid laws could not put a stop to, will for lack of available jobs gradually grow less and perhaps eventually come to an end.

That may not be what the disinvestment lobby aims at. But nevertheless it is the logical outcome of the policy they pursue. And if they were to succeed in isolating South Africa economically they would have done more to implement the apartheid policy than all the South African government could manage by its influx control and pass laws. The rigid application of the apartheid policy also would have led to misery, despair and eventual revolution in South Africa and that is why it is now being abandoned. Effective economic sanctions would lead to the same end by a different route.

Mr Oppenheimer added that businessmen, for 'common humanity and enlightened self-interest', should give time and money 'to work for an open, free, stable society in which no one is deprived by law or custom from making the best use of his or her talents'. They should also prod the government to do what 'it knows to be necessary and right'.[10]

Mr Oppenheimer's successor at Anglo American, Gavin Relly, is also an outspoken opponent of sanctions. His public affairs adviser, Michael Spicer, warned in October 1986 that the issue of sanctions was distracting potential mediators in South Africa: 'Black trade unionists, faced by the spectre of sanctions becoming a reality, increasingly take the position that business has a duty to keep workers in employment. The business community's response is that it can only do this if sanctions are avoided or evaded. The considerable energy that will go into this stand-off will inevitably be lost in the search for political solutions.'[11]

Mr Relly himself has said that sanctions could lead to 'revolution and tyranny ... a tyranny of people, whether they were white or black, who were determined to come on top of the dung heap ... It would not be a reform process. It would be a revolutionary process.'[12] British and American business executives, he said on another occasion, 'face an awesome responsibility. Many have made good profits in South Africa for decades. But, faced with lean times and a host of pressures, they are attracted to the easy option of withdrawal, especially if the ignorance, mischief-making and mythology underlying those pressures are ignored.'[13]

A host of other liberal capitalists have spoken against sanctions. Next to Messrs Oppenheimer and Relly, the most prominent is probably Tony Bloom, Chairman of the Premier Group, one of the five largest industrial companies in South Africa. Mr Bloom's financial acumen should be better than his political prophecies, however: in June 1985 he said that 'the prospects of reform within South Africa seem to be reaching unprecedented heights'.[14] Two months later Mr Botha gave his 'Rubicon' speech in Durban which effectively said there would be little further change. Mr Bloom, like Mr Oppenheimer, urges multi-nationals to stay in South Africa and not to give way to pressure. Multi-nationals should 'lead by example, not isolate by withdrawal', he said: 'It is too important from the point of view of their long-term strategic interests – too important as a fundamental question of principle – and too important from the point of view of the lives and hopes of their employees and their families in South Africa, of whom there are hundreds of thousands.'[15]

Using an argument that was once a favourite of the government but which is heard less frequently today, Mr Bloom argued that South Africa is 'geographically crucial to the West, as a huge percentage of the crude oil and strategic mineral imports of Western Europe and the United States are transported around the Cape sea routes'. He added, however, that 'South Africans must not deceive themselves with comforting thoughts about strategic geography and resources into believing that severe moral and political differences can be ignored'.[16]

7　*The Right-wing Threat*

One favourite argument of opponents of sanctions and disinvestment is that these forms of action foster the growth of right-wing Afrikanerdom. At its most apocalyptic, this position postulates the rapid fall in popularity of P. W. Botha's 'reformist' government; a number of defections by National Party MPs to the two right-wing parties, the Conservative Party and the even more fanatical Herstigte Nasionale Party; white right-wing violence against blacks, encouraged by the neo-Nazi Afrikaner Weerstandsbeweging (AWB); and a mistimed general election in which the Right sweeps to power. Armageddon results.

It is an argument which the government itself is not loth to use. The question is posed: the present administration may not be perfect, but what is the alternative? Government ministers use the Right as an excuse for not moving further and faster away from classical apartheid: the *volk* cannot be hurried. Mr Botha has to take the prejudices of his constituency into account. Sanctions and disinvestment will hit working-class Afrikaners before the 'middle to upper middle class English-speaking' whites who are in the PFP's natural constituency. Sanctions will drive the Afrikaners back into the laager. The government will lose faith in reform if the outside world, and blacks in the country, do not give it credit for what it has done.

This is the line taken by the South Africa Foundation when putting their case against sanctions to the House of Commons Foreign Affairs Committee. The Right, it said, was the 'important exception' to agreement in South Africa and abroad that apartheid was an 'anachronism'. The Right's support 'appears to be growing' and 'any government strategy for the future has to aim at containing rather than accommodating this element'.[1] In evidence to the Committee, the Vice-President of the Foundation, L. G. Abrahamse, said that Mr Botha, in trying to 'find a means of accommodating all the other constituent members of the South African community', had done what was considered inconceivable – 'he has actually torn asunder the solidarity of Afrikanerdom'. Mr Botha had 'created and precipitated a right-wing counter-action which is not insignificant in the South African scene. No man would embark on that and deliberately break that solidarity if in fact he was indulging in a cosmetic exercise. Why sacrifice your main power strength unless you are sincere in your efforts, although your efforts may not necessarily be appreciated either in terms of what you have achieved to date . . .?'[2]

Mr Abrahamse is less than totally accurate, however. The first right-wing breakaway from the National Party took place not under Mr Botha but in 1969, when B. J. Vorster was Prime Minister. It was then that a group of extremists under the former Minister of Posts and Telegraphs, Albert Hertzog, and the present leader of the HNP, Jaap Marais, were forced out and established their party. The HNP did not win a parliamentary seat until 1985, but it did establish a focus for right-wing dissent. Further, to the left of the National Party (if only marginally on occasions) was the United Party, now called the New Republic Party, which always had a relatively strong, although steadily declining, Afrikaner vote. The PFP, too, has siphoned off a small percentage of Afrikaner support, and about a dozen of its 27 MPs are Afrikaans-speaking.

The argument that the Right presents a threat to Mr Botha and his party can be persuasively presented. But how true is it? Dr Slabbert, Afrikaner, politician and sociologist, is less than convinced. In his autobiography he says that Mr Botha himself did not see the Right as a serious electoral threat: 'That was certainly quite evident in the conversations I had with him on the issue . . . All the right-wing parties combined have never polled higher than 17 per cent of white voter support and in the most recent poll they have slipped to 15.5 per cent . . . How then can that percentage of electoral support be distributed over 84 seats to win control of the House of Assembly? It is obvious nonsense.'[3]

In November 1985 Dr Slabbert told the Foreign Affairs Committee that the previous six months had been the most favourable for the Right to win by-elections, yet they had only scraped home in one at Sasolburg, where the HNP won its first seat since its establishment in 1969. Since then other by-elections have been held: at one of the most recent, Klip River in Natal, the HNP was beaten by a majority of 1,000 more than the National Party had hoped for.[4]

There have been hopes – or fears – that the HNP and Conservative Party might unite to present the voters with a single party of the

Right. Despite a number of talks, there has been no merger and in October 1986 the HNP made it clear that this was not an immediate prospect. There have, however, been informal agreements in some by-elections that one or other party would step down so as not to split the right-wing vote, and the HNP has also said it favours cooperation with the CP in a general election.[5]

One issue that apparently divides the HNP and CP is their attitudes towards the Afrikaner Weerstandsbeweging (AWB). Jaap Marais of the HNP has accused the AWB of causing 'division and paralysis' in right-wing politics and of being 'a political party wearing a mask'. HNP members are not allowed to join the AWB.[6] The CP leader, Dr Andries Treurnicht, on the other hand gave formal blessing to the AWB and its 'vigilante' offshoot, Brandwag, in March 1986. After discussions between the two organizations aimed at forging stronger links among right-wing groups, Dr Treurnicht said: 'We are satisfied that the Brandwag is not militant and will operate totally within the law.'[7]

The AWB gained international notoriety in May 1986 when it prevented the Foreign Minister, Pik Botha, from addressing a National Party meeting in Pietersburg, Transvaal. The AWB took over the meeting and police eventually fired teargas after fighting broke out between NP and AWB supporters. The police were accused by a Cabinet minister of not acting quickly and decisively, and there have been a number of claims that many policemen support one or other of the far-right groups. Replying to allegations that the AWB was trying to infiltrate the police, one of its leaders said: 'Nonsense. One cannot infiltrate one's own allies.'[8] A former security policeman and feared interrogator, Colonel Arthur Cronwright, was reported in July 1986 to be ready to train children, some as young as 10, to handle guns 'to support their parents in terror attacks'.[9] The AWB's leader, Eugene Terreblanche, said a few days later that Colonel Cronwright had been suspended as leader of the Brandwag branch: 'He has no right to make press statements or talk on behalf of the AWB,' Mr Terreblanche said, but added that this did not detract from the right of parents to train their children in self-defence.[10]

Mr Terreblanche himself has a sanguine view of sanctions. God had made sure, he said in June 1986, that South Africa could never be boycotted. God had endowed the Afrikaner with the world's richest country:

The Americans, though first to set foot on the moon, cannot take off in a single aircraft without the chrome and platinum they get from South Africa ... If sanctions and boycotts could succeed they would effectively have been applied the day Dr Verwoerd stepped out of the Commonwealth and formed a republic. The world today is just as powerless against us now as in the past – in fact we are much stronger. Our only trouble is that we have a spineless government who have become part of the international money giants ... Our only hope is to get rid of the government and all they represent ... Should the Botha government either capitulate or also decide to run in the event of a black revolution, the AWB will take South Africa back by force.[11]

The AWB serves a useful function for the National Party, Dr Slabbert believes. A Cabinet minister told him: 'Come election time all we do is show Eugene Terreblanche giving his Nazi salute on TV and your voters will flock to our tables in the northern suburbs of Johannesburg' (the affluent English-speaking area where the PFP holds several seats).[12]

The argument that sanctions will strengthen the white Right achieves its purpose if it holds off the threatened sanctions. It also provides a convenient excuse for whites to do nothing concrete in helping to end apartheid. For the other side of the argument is that Mr Botha is determined to move at his own pace and at nobody else's: if he is pushed too far and too fast, the logic goes, he will stand still or retreat. That line of thought also provides a handy rationale for continued repression. Dr Slabbert summarized the idea thus: 'Coercion and reform go hand in hand; a measure of instability is a symptom of successful reform.'* The logic demands that pressures, internal or external, be minimized so that the reform process can be implemented. So sanctions, as an external pressure, must be resisted by supposed liberals who want 'evolution not revolution'.

This whole thesis begs the question of whether 'reform' comes anywhere close to providing the outlines of a solution for South Africa. In the eyes of the majority of blacks, and most of the world, it does not. It also predicates that more reform is on the way – and that this reform could be stopped by sanctions.

The theme that sanctions will slow or halt reform has been taken up by, among others, South African radio, Gavin Relly of the Anglo American Corporation, and Dr Chester Crocker, the US Assistant Secretary of State for Africa and architect of President Reagan's

* For a fuller discussion on this theme, see article by the present author, 'Divisions in the Laager', in *Marxism Today*, August 1986.

policy of 'constructive engagement' towards Pretoria. Dr Crocker told a Congressional committee in March 1986 that white South Africans would resist reform for as long as they felt threatened. 'On the other hand,' he said, 'there is no question that, for as long as it exists, apartheid will be the principal source of conflict and instability, creating opportunities for outside intervention' – most likely from Soviet bloc countries.[13] Mr Relly said in October 1986 that sanctions would 'contribute to revolution rather than assist evolution. It really is in the interests of all South Africa's neighbours that the South African economy remains healthy and does not atrophy to an economic wasteland.'[14]

South African radio has sometimes adopted an air of injured innocence. In August 1986 a commentary claimed that while the sanctions movement had not stood still, nor had South Africans:

They are at present engaged in the most momentous political change and constitutional reform of modern times.

The fact that, while change has been taking place at an unprecedented pace, the sanctions steamroller has thundered on, underlines the fact that those who are orchestrating the sanctions campaign will not stop until all their political demands are met – and those demands are more than South Africans can reasonably be expected to accept. Indeed it is clear that the momentum of sanctions will be slowed only if there is total capitulation by South Africa to demands that most would find totally unacceptable. Against that background, the only possible commitment is to continue on the often difficult but only realistic road of meaningful and purposeful reform.[15]

A fortnight later the radio returned to the same theme after the US Senate accepted a package of sanctions and shortly before the EEC was due to meet to consider its sanctions. It said that 'harsh sanctions are hardly appropriate in the face of the positive and meaningful action that continues to be taken on the road of reform'.[16]

As further American sanctions began to look inevitable in late 1986, government ministers complained that little or no account was being taken of its reforms. The Foreign Minister, Pik Botha, said on two occasions in late May and early June 1986 that the West was not interested in the achievement of democracy in South Africa but only in the handing over of power to the ANC for reasons of economic convenience. The country could expect more sanctions because countries abroad did not understand that South Africa wanted to negotiate peacefully on a new constitution in terms of which all communities would be protected. 'The West does not care if South Africa is governed by a tyrannic system,' he said – apparently missing the point that many Western countries see the present government as approximating to that description – 'as long as it can obtain essential minerals and does not have to grapple with the complexities of the country.'[17]

In August 1986, after the Commonwealth mini-summit had agreed on a package of sanctions, Mr Botha returned to the same theme during a press conference:

We have come to the conclusion that it does not matter what reforms we introduce because the world is not interested in reforms and in the upliftment of black people in this country and better living conditions and more rights for black people. It does not matter what we do short of giving in . . . to the instigators of violence . . . Our options are clear. Either we capitulate under pressure, only to be confronted with more pressure until we are destroyed . . . or we say: 'So far and no further . . . Do what you like.' It is not us who did not want to remove apartheid. It is not us who did not want to negotiate.[18]

At a lower level, the Deputy Minister of Information, Louis Nel, who was dismissed a few months later, said just before the opening of Parliament that the government 'remains committed to reform and to expand negotiations with black leaders'.[19]

The question of what, if any, further reform lies ahead is one of the crucial aspects of the sanctions debate. It is also one that the government has failed to spell out. Great things had been promised by nods, winks and hints in August 1985, but Mr Botha's 'Rubicon' speech in Durban dashed any hopes of major changes. A year later a federal congress of the National Party was called to meet in Durban: initially there was speculation that Mr Botha might announce new reforms. This soon died down. Opening the congress, Mr Botha stuck with generalities sprinkled with Afrikaner Nationalist code language:

The onslaughts against us alone are in shrill contrast to the reality of our striving, and that with which we are busy – the broadening of freedom and democracy in our country. The venom can come over us like a tidal wave, and wash over us, but we remain in a land of minorities . . . Political freedom in a country with a multi-cultural composition and history must come about in an evolutionary manner by a parallel process of both power-sharing and division of power. Unique solutions have to be sought through power-sharing and division of political power. Division of power provides for differentiation, power-sharing provides for cooperation and community interests . . .
    . . . I told the international community a year ago that if by apartheid is

meant political domination by any one community of any other, or the exclusion of any community from the political decision-making process, or the injustice or inequality in the opportunities for any community, or racial discrimination and impairment of human dignity, then the South African government shares in the rejection of that concept. First we were attacked because of so-called petty apartheid. Now grand apartheid gets the blame. And it is neither of the two under present day circumstances. It is the peaceful coexistence of a diversity of cultures . . .

Later in his speech, Mr Botha became tougher:

Negotiation, for the National Party government, does not mean the abdication of the rights of the white man in his own fatherland . . . We are irrevocably committed to dialogue as part of the process of participation in our democratic institutions. Dialogue must, however, not lead to the endangering of the self-determination of the groups and the communities in our multi-cultural country. I will have no part in that . . .

. . . We do not desire sanctions, but if sanctions must come in order that our freedom, our justice, must be maintained, we will survive it. We will not just survive; we will come out stronger in the end.[20]

8 Sanctions and the Economy

Just what effect sanctions will have on the South African economy is one of the major questions in the debate. Some, like President Botha, claim that 'we will not just survive, we will come out stronger in the end.'[1] His Foreign Minister, Pik Botha, addressing a political meeting, has said: 'The sooner sanctions come the better ... We will show the world that we will not be made soft.'[2] That kind of bluster, for which both Bothas under stress are notorious, is countered by other arguments also used by the government – including the two Bothas – that sanctions will cause large-scale unemployment both inside South Africa and in its neighbouring states.

A University of the Witwatersrand sociologist, Duncan Innes, trying to look into the future in the immediate aftermath of the US and EEC sanctions, concluded that 'South Africa is unlikely to suffer a major economic decline in the near future. In fact, the level of economic activity may improve.'[3] One stimulus would be the potential for an improved price for gold, platinum and other metals of which South Africa is a major world supplier:

Each $10 increase in the gold price alone earns the South African economy an extra $200 million, so a major improvement in the gold price to, say, $500 [from $400] would provide a powerful boost to the ailing economy ... An irony of the sanctions campaign is that the more it promotes crisis conditions inside South Africa, the more likely it is to push up the price of gold and platinum: South Africa produces 60 per cent of the West's gold and 80 per cent of its platinum. Intensification of crisis in South Africa thus leads to panic in the world metal markets and a rush for gold and platinum which pushes up their prices. The more pessimistic the West's perception of the crisis, the higher the metals' price – which thereby reduces the severity of the crisis.[4]

The West is highly unlikely to ban imports of gold and platinum, Innes argues, 'because without South African supplies industrialized nations could not meet their own needs. Were the West to be starved of gold there would be major disruptions to its financial and monetary systems; disruptions which would in turn reverberate through the international economy. Catch 22: the West does not want to include gold in the sanctions because it is too important to its economies; but by excluding gold, the effect of sanctions is crucially diminished.'[5]

The economic upswing is also likely to be boosted by the effect of sanctions on local business activity: 'As imports decline, local companies and entrepreneurs will probably move to fill the import gap. Government spending is also likely to increase, providing a further important boost.' But Innes believes that jobs will be lost by some export industries and inflation is likely to remain high, providing

... a fertile breeding ground for social disorder, particularly among the hardest-hit black section of the community, but also among so-called poor whites. Such conditions feed political resistance to government policies from both left and right, encouraging political ferment across the spectrum ... Should the sanctions campaign gain ground, as seems likely at present, South Africans can expect gradual but serious inroads on their economic life ... This economic war of attrition may take decades to achieve its goal of forcing the government to enter serious negotiations. But combined with a deteriorating political situation and escalating violence, it will get there in the end.[6]

The government's view is rather different. It has echoes of two former Prime Ministers, both now rather out of favour in top circles: Hendrik Verwoerd (1958–66) and B. J. Vorster (1966–78). Dr Verwoerd is supposed to have said that his people would prefer to be 'poor and white rather than rich and mixed'. More recently, a government official told the American Investor Responsibility Research Centre that white South Africans would 'ride bicycles and eat mealie pap' before giving in to economic pressure to concede universal suffrage.[7] In June 1986 Pik Botha warned that South Africa would have to accept 'poverty and a lowering of standards' in dealing with a 'sick' Western world.[8] The other part of the defiance harks back to 1977 when Mr Vorster fought and won a general election based largely on his challenge to the West, and to President Carter in particular, to 'do your damndest'.[9] The National Party won 66 per cent of the vote and 135 of the 165 seats in the House of Assembly. Mr Vorster's successor, P. W. Botha, anticipated further sanctions after he declared a State of Emergency in June 1986: 'If we are forced to go it alone, then so be it ... The world must take note and never forget that we are not a nation of weaklings.'[10]

Rather less bellicose noises have come from other government ministers, particularly the Minister of Finance, Barend du Plessis. Protective measures would have to be introduced if substantial sanctions were implemented, he said in August 1986. These would be necessary for the country to balance its trade account and overall balance of payments: 'A country that is not permitted to export can obviously not continue to import . . .' Any erosion of the current account surplus because of sanctions against exports would reduce South Africa's capacity to service its foreign debt. 'This will obviously have to be taken into account in future negotiations with creditors for any further redemption of capital.'[11]

This seemed to some observers to be a hint that South Africa could default on its debts. A month before, however, Mr Du Plessis had moved swiftly to dampen speculation that this was a policy option being considered by Pretoria. The speculation had been raised by testimony of the then South African Ambassador to London, Dr Denis Worrall, to the House of Commons Foreign Affairs Committee. Agreeing with a British MP that sanctions would have 'a very major effect' on the South African economy, Dr Worrall added:

If there were sanctions on the scale indicated by the EPG,* South Africa certainly would consider not paying its international loans, which would be all Mexico and a few other countries would need as a precedent, and it would bring down the whole Western financial system. I am not saying this is a consideration at the moment; I must stress that. But if you put South Africa in an extreme situation, that kind of thing might apply.[12]

A few days later Mr Du Plessis said that Dr Worrall 'intended no threat' but was merely making a statement of fact.

Threat or not, Dr Worrall's statement raised eyebrows, particularly in view of the 1985 bank loan crisis. South Africa then froze repayment on most of its $24 billion foreign debt when banks, concerned about the country's stability and under pressure from the sanctions/disinvestment lobby, withdrew credit lines. Under a rescheduling agreement made with creditors in early 1986, South Africa said it would repay about 5 per cent of the frozen debt before June

* The so-called Eminent Persons Group was established by the Commonwealth in a last effort – spearheaded by Britain – to avoid sanctions. The group visited South Africa several times attempting to negotiate some kind of peaceful resolution to apartheid. Predictably, it failed. For the group's full report, see *Mission to South Africa: The Commonwealth Report*, Penguin, 1986.

1987. After Dr Worrall's statement to the Foreign Affairs Committee, foreign bankers warned that South Africa's ability to roll over its foreign debt might be endangered. One banker said: 'This is not the right time to issue threats. South Africa's foreign debt is a very sensitive issue. South Africa needs to build up its credibility in the world financial markets and the Worrall statement will not help.' Another said: 'Foreign bankers may be tempted to pre-empt non-payment and call up their dollars as credit lines mature.'[13] Mr Du Plessis admitted that South Africa had debt-repaying problems when he told the federal congress of the National Party in August 1986 that 'we must continue to seek, through negotiation, the cooperation of overseas bankers to roll over as much as possible of their existing loans to South African banks and other institutions in the private sector instead of immediate repayment'.[14]

Foreign debts continue to worry the government. In October 1986 both Mr Du Plessis and the Governor of the Reserve Bank, Gerhard de Kock, spoke out. Dr De Kock, in Washington for the annual meeting of the International Monetary Fund and the World Bank, said that he hoped South Africa had 'picked up some points for our promptness' in repaying $3 billion in the previous 20 months. South Africa was under some pressure from the commercial banks to speed up its repayments because of the improvement in the country's balance of payments as a result of the oil price fall and the rise in the gold price. But South Africa was resisting this until it was clear that gold would remain strong. The country wanted to wait until April 1987 before discussing faster debt repayment, Dr De Kock said. He added that he did not believe that 'one more push' would make Pretoria adopt policies acceptable to the rest of the world: 'We are not Iran under the Shah or the Philippines under Marcos ... We are slowly bleeding, but it is so slow that we can keep on bleeding for many years.'[15]

In the same month Mr Du Plessis said that South Africa wanted to honour all its international financial commitments and would keep to the agreement with banks. But he refused to say what effect mounting sanctions would have on Pretoria's willingness to continue payment from 1987 onwards.[16]

Apart from its foreign debt worries, South Africa has taken some publicly declared action to counter sanctions – and, more likely than not, other measures have been implemented without publicity. On the propaganda level, South African radio has beaten a drum that sounds remarkably similar to the noises made by white Rhodesia after UDI in November 1965. The country's adversaries, the radio said in August 1986, 'must expect the same determination, ingenuity and endurance with which South Africa has responded to great challenges in the past'.[17] President Botha urged his Cabinet to ensure that all levels of government gave preference to locally manufactured goods.[18] Self-sufficiency and sacrifice have been demanded:

If it is expected of us to forego essential manufactured products, let us manufacture them ourselves. If it is expected of us to forego essential agricultural products, let us cultivate enough so that we can also export. If it is expected of us to forego other essential goods which we cannot manufacture or build, let us obtain it by exploiting the self-interest of others . . . Let us dedicate ourselves anew to an era in which 'South Africa first' is our motto.[19]

More concrete steps have been taken than patriotic appeals. 'Literally thousands' of [unspecified] items had been stockpiled for more than a decade to safeguard the economy, the Manpower Minister, Piet du Plessis, said in August 1986: 'The government has learned from experience how vital it is to safeguard sources of supply. Thorough provision has been made, including the protection of the flow of technology and know-how, of a large variety of products . . . Trade can be conventional or unconventional. That is being planned by a counter-trade committee in the Department of Trade and Industries, which is also dealing with barter agreements.'[20]

A more junior minister, the Deputy Minister of Finance, Kent Durr, has also spoken of stockpiling, while declining to specify the items apart from oil: 'We can produce almost anything, and if it is a very important strategic item . . . produce it locally even if it was not cost effective.' Asked whether the state would become involved in sanctions-busting, he said it would have a role 'to help, to facilitate trade', but private companies 'are well able to look after themselves . . . they know precisely what they should be doing'.[21]

Parliament prepared to lend a hand when, in September 1986, it agreed to set up a joint select committee, with the white, Coloured and Indian houses represented. It will investigate the implication for the economy of existing and possible future sanctions and boycotts, the adequacy or otherwise of steps taken to deal with them, and further steps to be taken.[22] Findings will be published 'to the extent that the committee deems appropriate and subject to considerations of South Africa's national interests'.

One of the government's first measures to counter sanctions after the package of US and EEC measures were agreed was to impose a news black-out on all shipping using Durban, the main port. The ban prohibits naming ships that dock and giving information on imports and exports. Keeping ships' names secret would 'prevent reprisals and possible boycotting of shipping companies', according to the government, and would also make it easier for South African shuttle ships to load from vessels anchored at sea. Durban is South Africa's busiest harbour, handling 20 million tons of cargo a year.[23]

The Durban ban, after some confusion, was extended to other ports. Similar curbs were imposed on some trade figures: statistics from the Commissioner for Customs and Excise were reduced from a four-page document to a single line. This secretive approach, in a country where official information is often sparse, was not universally welcomed. Mike Perry, author of a paper on the challenge of sanctions, told a Johannesburg newspaper that 'we should be publicizing the goods we are buying from our top four supplier nations. If we start hiding what we buy, we will be seriously reducing our negotiating power. For example, we should make sure that the automobile trade unions in Germany know how much South Africa purchases in motor vehicle parts to encourage them to work against sanctions on German exports to South Africa.'[24]

From August 1986, when the Commonwealth summit agreed on a package of sanctions, a number of measures or plans were announced to combat them. The first came the day after the summit when Pik Botha said stricter border controls, import licences and levies on neighbouring states would be considered when sanctions became a reality. He claimed also, in an argument that was to be heard more frequently, that some states were encouraging sanctions through jealousy and to boost their own economies at black South Africans' expense: 'Australia may employ thousands of whites in their coal mines, robbing thousands of South Africa's blacks of their jobs,' he said. 'Australia stands to gain in every respect from the sanctions decision. It will be interesting to see how Prime Minister Bob Hawke will explain the morality of that.'[25] Mr Durr used the same argument: countries applying punitive measures were doing it 'primarily to serve their own best economic interests' – the protection of industries and jobs in those countries in a difficult economic climate. Australia was vying for the same export markets for coal, iron ore and agricultural products, while in the USA the Democratic Party's sanctions Bill concentrated on coal, steel and uranium. These industries would be the greatest beneficiaries of sanctions because they were in direct competition with South Africa.[26]

In September President Botha announced an economic conference to be attended by leading South Africans to plan a development strategy.[27] In the event, when the meeting took place, it did not focus specifically on sanctions-busting measures. Several of the country's top business leaders, including Gavin Relly of Anglo American, did not attend the summit with President Botha – supposedly because of 'prior engagements'. However, some sources claimed that their opposition to government policies led Mr Botha to withdraw their invitations. Big business, as both opponents and supporters of sanctions have noted, has become more critical of government as pressure for sanctions has increased. In March 1985 six business associations, representing the employers of 80 per cent of workers in South Africa, urged the government to give 'visible expression' to reform to avert sanctions. The government's response was one of irritation: one senior minister, Gerrit Viljoen, told them he appreciated their concern, but South Africa should implement reform for domestic not external reasons. In June 1986 President Botha, responding to another approach from the Federated Chamber of Industries, told it to mind its own business and stay out of politics.

While business and government were assessing the likely impact of sanctions, the South African Broadcasting Corporation was keeping up the propaganda, highlighting optimistic comments. Dr Fred du Plessis, of Sanlam, one of the country's largest insurance companies, was reported to have said that the US Congress sanctions were 'a positive challenge to stimulate economic activity', while the chief economist of the Trust Bank, Ulrich Joubert, believed import replacement could provide 'the necessary boost for getting the long-awaited economic upswing under way'.[28] A few months earlier, echoing President Botha, the radio had commented that the country would suffer short-term setbacks if sanctions were introduced, 'but such steps will lead to it becoming even more independent and self-sufficient, and in the long term it will emerge stronger than ever'.[29]

While a stronger South Africa was being promised, money was flowing out of the country on the eve of the Commonwealth, EEC and US sanctions. In August 1986 figures released by the Receiver of Revenue, the country's tax authority, showed a big increase in the non-residents' securities tax (NRST) of 15 per cent. Dividend payments overseas jumped 41 per cent between the year ending March 1985 and March 1986 (R2,312 million against R1,640 million). In the three months ending June 1986 – when the campaign for sanctions was reaching new heights – overseas dividends were 58.2 per cent higher than the previous year (R827 million against R520 million).

Higher gold-mining dividends were said to account for part of the increase, but it was also possible, according to stockbrokers, that subsidiaries of foreign firms were maximizing dividend payments to get funds out of the country. Higher white emigration also accounted for some of the increase, as migrants can receive dividends from investments left behind.[30] In the first seven months of 1986, South Africa lost nearly as many professional people as for the whole of 1975: 1,432 versus 1,659. Emigrants like these would have been likely to be shareholders. Also in the first seven months of 1986 there was a net loss of 4,138 residents compared to a net gain of 5,954 for the corresponding period of 1985.[31]

Tourism, an important source of foreign currency, was also down: 349,027 for the first half of 1986 against 417,128 in the first half of 1985.[32] This led the South African Tourist Board to 'work purposefully on a strategy to counter the adverse effects' of sanctions. In August 1986 the Board's Chief Director said the strategy included developing the 'domestic scope to its full potential'. Among the initiatives planned was the establishment of a tourism board for blacks and Coloureds. It was also intended to market South Africa as an international congress venue.[33]

Business leaders were now embarking on jet-setting public relations trips abroad in (usually vain) efforts to prevent sanctions. People such as Raymond Ackerman, a large retail magnate, Tony Bloom of Premier Holdings, and Mike Rosholt of the huge Barlow Rand group, made tours, particularly to Britain and America. Mr Ackerman claimed in July 1986 that South African businessmen contributed 'in no small way' to Mrs Thatcher's and President Reagan's rejection of sanctions.[34] In September, on the eve of the EEC's decision on sanctions, the country's coal, steel and engineering industries combined to mount an anti-sanctions advertising campaign in the British press. The advertisements warned that sanctions would increase unemployment, poverty and racial polarization.[35]

Confusion abounds and points are made for political purposes about the effects of sanctions/disinvestment: truth is often in the eye of the beholder. This was well illustrated in the middle of 1986 – before the

Commonwealth, EEC and US announced their sanctions measures, and before there was an increased exodus of American firms. Speaking in Frankfurt, West Germany, in June, the Minister of Finance, Barend du Plessis, said that South Africa needed foreign investment to reach and maintain an annual average growth rate of 5.5 per cent. 'From our own resources we can provide for 3.5 per cent growth,' he told business editors. 'But we need foreign investment for the other 1.5 per cent.'[36] This was challenged by Professor Brian Kantor of the University of Cape Town's School of Economics, who asserted that the economy could grow much faster than Mr Du Plessis believed, and without foreign investment: 'If we want economic growth we can demand that the government does the simple things to encourage growth – which is largely to remove government as an influence on economic action.' What he appeared to be saying was that labour should not be subject to government controls; since the industrial council system was designed to protect established labour from low-wage competition, deregulation should boost growth.[37]

In September 1986 the authoritative Economist Intelligence Unit of London warned that South Africa's growth rate would be a mere 3.3 per cent – lower than the 3.5 per cent Mr Du Plessis claimed could be met by South African capital. Six months before it had calculated the growth rate at 4.2 per cent for 1986–90, but had later revised it downwards because of growing sanctions threats and already existing boycotts as well as the 'increasingly evident effects of the political situation on international and domestic confidence'. Growth prospects were beginning to suffer through lack of external capital, but consumer attitudes 'have also been changing, with an apparent reluctance to engage in long-term commitments, evidenced in sluggish sales of durable goods and new housing'. But the 'political discount' on the exchange rate of the rand had made South African goods increasingly competitive on international markets, despite the effects of sanctions and the threat of more to come.[38] The South African Reserve Bank in August 1986 readjusted its predicted real growth rate for 1986: down from 2 per cent to 1.5 per cent.[39]

The extent to which foreign capital has been leaving South Africa was reported by the Reserve Bank Governor, Gerhard de Kock, also in August 1986. He said mildly that 'outflows of short-term capital remained high in the second quarter of 1986', while long-term outflows 'continued to be recorded in the first half of 1986 as foreign loans falling due perforce had to be repaid without new loans commonly being made available'. In all, R2.6 billion left South Africa in the first half of 1986; of this R556 million was short-term capital. For the first time in many years there was a net outflow of capital from public corporations (R110 million). This contrasted with a gain of R817 million in 1985 as a whole.[40]

The Bank also reported that real gross domestic fixed income and real remuneration per worker continued to decline at an increasing rate and inflation stood at an officially estimated 17 per cent. Dr De Kock said that 'events such as the social unrest, the State of Emergency and intensified threats of disinvestment and economic sanctions have brought about a deterioration in overseas perceptions', and such factors had 'contributed to the sluggish conditions that have prevailed in the economy'.[41] But there would, it appeared, be little attempt by the Reserve Bank to persuade the government to change the policies that were resulting in a sluggish economy: 'Any formula for the restoration of confidence and prosperity must include the government's programmes for maintaining law and order and for comprehensive further political and constitutional reform,' said Dr De Kock.[42]

Further official figures showed the reliance of the economy on exports. In September 1986 the South African Transport Services (formerly known as the Ministry of Transport) revealed that export shipments through the country's main ports were running at up to nine times the level of imports.[43] Although the figures included trans-shipments of local cargoes from one port to another, these were so small (only 175,000 tons in July) that the extent to which imports were lagging could still be seen clearly:

Month	Imports (tons)	Exports (tons)
April	872,000	6.8 million
May	926,000	8.1 million
June	856,000	5.8 million
July	970,000	7.2 million

These government figures also give some indication of the secrecy surrounding imports and exports. In July 1986 seaborne mineral imports, including trans-shipments, totalled 194,000 tons, of which nearly half (94,000 tons) was listed as classified information under 'other mineral products'. Of the 1.5 million tons of mineral exports, 1.3 million tons was classified. A further indication that official figures often hide more than they reveal has been given by the Johannesburg business consultant Michael Perry, who said in October 1986 that '54 per cent of our export trade is semi-clandestine, meaning no data is available on the country of origin'.[44] Leading exports for July in tonnage terms included fruit, vegetable and grain products (581,000 tons), timber and paper products (597,000) and base metals (617,000). Imports included fruit, vegetable and grain products (160,000), chemicals, plastics and rubber (190,000), and vehicles, aircraft and spares (89,000).[45]

One worry for the government about sanctions is the possibility of a ban on farm produce: white farmers have traditionally been a bulwark of the National Party, although their importance has declined with increasing white urbanization. Fruit-growing would be a major sufferer if this form of sanction were imposed. Exports are estimated to be worth R500 million a year. In August 1986 the General Manager of the Deciduous Fruit Board, Louis Kriel, said that two thirds would be hit by full-scale sanctions. About 85 per cent of exports go to the EEC and the rest to 24 countries in the Far East and North America. The fruit sector is the biggest employer in the Cape Province, accounting for 250,000 jobs – 95 per cent of them African and Coloured – in farming, canning and producing dried fruit. Mr Kriel also ascribed some pressure for sanctions to the competition factor: Australia and New Zealand stood to gain, but the Cape's main fruit competitor was Chile, which was unlikely to press any country in the world to impose sanctions, whatever the profit to its fruit exports. But if the Cape was shut out, even in a small way, the consequences would be serious, according to Mr Kriel.[46]

The Cape is also the country's wine-producing area. But, despite its image, it does not figure largely in the world wine and spirit market. Nevertheless any sanctions would hit KWV, the cooperative of 6,000 growers in the Western Cape. Wine and spirit exports rose 33 per cent to R18.9 million from 1984 to 1985. Britain was the biggest growth market and KWV aimed to more than double table-wine exports there to reach 120,000 cases in 1986.[47] But three months after these figures were given publicly by KWV's Chief Director of Marketing, Kobus van Niekerk, he declined to give statistics on exports: 'We don't think it would be in our interests.'[48]

One hidden irony of the whole sanctions/disinvestment debate is the fact that some of the strongest South African critics of these tactics are themselves disinvesting in their home country. As the pressure for disinvestment increases, there could well be moves to send South African investment overseas back to source. There that repatriated money could be used to create jobs, fuel the economy and try to ensure that the government carries out its 'reform policies' – exactly the tasks that opponents of disinvestment/sanctions say need to be performed by foreign capital.*

This has already happened to one South African businessman, Raymond Ackerman, head of the Pick 'n' Pay supermarket group. He is probably one of the most, if not *the* most, vociferous business critics of apartheid – yet in early 1985 he was forced by Australian trade unions to withdraw from starting 'hypermarkets' there on his South African pattern. Mr Ackerman, in trying to diversify his interests to Australia, was doing what many other South African capitalists have done: trying to find an alternative profit base. His Pick 'n' Pay stores have been hit by several strikes, and boycotts by blacks of his and other white-owned businesses have in the past drastically affected profits.

Mr Ackerman is not alone, of course. Some mining houses have had extensive overseas interests for years. Recently, however, there have been several instances of large South African groups moving abroad. Barlow Rand has spent R 550 million in Britain acquiring the animal food and industrial group, J. Bibby & Sons, on the basis that this acquisition would 'provide Barlow's with a springboard for significant international operations'. Liberty Life, a large insurance firm, acquired Britain's seventh biggest property development firm, Capital and Counties, for an investment of R 800 million. This purchase was described as 'a major step forward in the development of Liberty Life's international strategies that should be of considerable long-term benefit to the group'.

In addition to these two firms there are Anglo American, the largest foreign investor in the United States according to 1984 figures, and Rembrandt, which virtually controls the world tobacco markets through Philip Morris. Firms like these, the *Weekly Mail* commented, 'are skilled at hiding direct South African links and take over existing foreign businesses rather than, like Pick 'n Pay, exporting a boldly packaged, identifiably South African product'. The paper continued:

* This section is based largely on an article in the *Weekly Mail* of 18 April 1986. To a large extent the issue has been ignored by South African newspapers.

Barlow's and Liberty Life have good-sounding reasons for going international – if you are a shareholder. But are they being patriotic? What about the millions of unemployed in South Africa who don't have jobs, we are told, because there is not enough foreign investment? Why should foreigners risk their money here while South African businesses are investing large sums abroad? . . .

. . . Critics of disinvestment surely have a clear duty now to send South African overseas investment back to South Africa. They would give real bite to the policy of 'constructive engagement'.

. . . Apartheid is dead. It no longer provides Liberty Life and Barlow Rand with as good a return on capital as it used to. The companies show the extent of their commitment to a post-apartheid economic system in South Africa by making vast investments abroad. At the same time they are among the strongest critics of disinvestment.

There is a contradiction but no mystery. They want to have their cake overseas and eat someone else's here in South Africa.

Perhaps these companies are just reading the writing on the wall. A constant theme of African National Congress propaganda in the past few years has been that it will 'remember our friends', whether individual companies or governments. South African critics of disinvestment like Barlow Rand and Liberty Life are unlikely to be regarded as 'friends' if the ANC comes to power. Further, although the ANC favours a mixed economy, large-scale nationalization is probably inevitable. Thirdly, the attitude of young black South Africans has been, and is, turning increasingly in a socialist direction. In the 1985 CASE/IBR opinion survey on what blacks thought of disinvestment and sanctions,* respondents were asked:

Suppose South Africa had the government of your choice. There are two main patterns how it should organize people's work and the ownership of factories and businesses. Which view do you most support?
- The capitalist pattern, in which businesses are owned and run by private businessmen for their own profit.
- The socialist pattern, in which workers have a say in the running of businesses, and share in the ownership of profits.

More than three quarters of the respondents, 77 per cent, favoured the socialist vision and 22 per cent the capitalist – although it must be said that this question, like some of the others, has attracted criticism for being loaded. Even taking this into account, it is significant that CASE/IBR found that 'the distribution of opinion holds roughly

* See Chapter 4.

constant across the categories of age, education, sex and language and even across the different political tendencies'. The survey found that even among Chief Buthelezi's urban followers, 70 per cent favoured socialism – while Buthelezi himself has lately been vocal in his support of the private enterprise system.

This support for socialism is perhaps not surprising in a country where capitalism has become equated with apartheid and where many opponents of the government have been branded 'communists'. It will mean more pressure on an ANC government to nationalize – perhaps without compensation or with what the firms would regard as inadequate compensation – large capitalist institutions. To that extent, the firms which have sought to remove some of their base from South Africa could be said to be taking the financial equivalent of the 'chicken run' that has meant such a large increase in the flow of emigrants from South Africa. It may also reflect these companies' fears that disinvestment will lead to a siege economy in which removing money from the country will be made much more difficult.

9 Sanctions and Jobs

One of the main arguments about sanctions has concerned its effect on employment – both in South Africa and abroad. To summarize briefly, opponents of sanctions say that economic measures against Pretoria would cause job losses among black South Africans ('the very people we want to help', in President Reagan's phrase) and in the countries imposing sanctions. According to this view neither prospect should be encouraged. Proponents of sanctions say that black South Africans are prepared to endure higher unemployment if sanctions help to end apartheid. Any job losses in countries imposing sanctions would usually be made up in other ways – perhaps through increased trade with South Africa's black-ruled neighbours – and that, in any case, to allow jobs to depend on apartheid is immoral.

Much in dispute in this argument is the extent of unemployment that will be caused by sanctions and disinvestment.* The conventional wisdom is that black South Africans will be hit first and hardest. Part of this assumption has been challenged by Mark Orkin in his book on black public opinion, *The Struggle and the Future*.† Orkin points out that 'much foreign investment, especially that of large transnational corporations, uses capital-intensive techniques, so that jobs have not been created that would have been had the production been undertaken by smaller local concerns. Moreover, the presence of transnationals then obliges other local concerns to be similarly capital-intensive in order to compete.'[1] Further, Orkin says that US-controlled firms have a white-to-African employee ratio of 1:1, compared to 1:3 in manufacturing and 1:9 in mining for South African-controlled firms. Overall, the ratio of white to African employees among all foreign firms is 1:2 – 'in other words, foreign companies tend to have a much higher proportion of whites than local companies [reflecting] the overwhelmingly skill-based nature of their operations'.[2] Orkin continues:

* See also Chapter 25, pp. 229–37.
† See Chapter 4.

Unemployment, nationally, is presently [April 1986] running at 5 per cent for whites, compared to 25 per cent for blacks. Now suppose that all directly-owned American companies were to withdraw overnight. When categorized by race, their employees comprise more than 3 per cent of the total white workforce, but less than 1 per cent of the black. So white unemployment would rise from 5 to 8 per cent, i.e. an increase of some 60 per cent, whereas black unemployment would rise from 25 to 26 per cent, an increase of only 4 per cent.

Obviously, our supposition has been very crude: in some cases blacks might be laid off more readily than whites; in others, a local company taking over might have a more labour-intensive approach; and there would be ripple effects. However, it establishes the point that white South Africans would experience the impact of disinvestment more heavily than blacks as regards the percentage increases in prevailing unemployment.[3]

This is not a popular, or undisputed, position. Largely for political purposes – because black unemployment can be used to gain sympathy – white politicians and business leaders have all tended to play up the negative effects, as they see them, of sanctions and disinvestment on black jobs. Just how many jobs, black and/or white, would be lost depends on who is doing the calculations, and how heavy sanctions and disinvestment are assumed to be.

In June 1986 the Production Management Institute gave a figure of more than 1.1 million as a top estimate. It said that if boycotts on South African exports were 20-per-cent effective, the chain reactions would put about 90,000 whites and 343,000 blacks out of work. If export boycotts spread to become 50-per-cent effective, the toll would rise to 1.1 million, causing 'inconceivable hardship', as about R 2,600 million would be wiped off the combined incomes of black and white workers.[4]

Another estimate of a million put out of work if total trade sanctions were imposed was made in July 1986 by Professor Piet Nel of the University of South Africa's Bureau of Market Research. Of these, 84 per cent would be black. 'Already 1.7 million blacks are unemployed or underemployed,' the Johannesburg *Sunday Times* said in reporting Professor Nel's study. 'If another 600,000 were laid off, 31.9 per cent of all economically active blacks would be out of work.' The survey was based on more than 3,300 companies employing 52 per cent of all job-holders.[5]

The Federated Chamber of Industries (FCI), which has lobbied both against disinvestment/sanctions and for more government 'reform', said in October 1986 that mandatory United Nations sanctions could lead to 1.34 million unemployed in five years. Gross Domestic Product would decline by about 6 per cent a year and nearly 20 per cent of South Africans would lose their jobs.[6]

The Afrikaanse Handelsinstituut (AHI) Chairman, Christie Kuun, said in the same month that if sanctions against exports were only 20-per-cent successful, white unemployment would rise by 120,000 and black unemployment by 430,000. The personal income of whites would decline by R520 million and that of blacks by R470 million.[7] These figures differ from those of the Production Management Institute (see above), although it postulated the same level of efficiency for sanctions.

There has been another estimate of unemployment in the event of comprehensive sanctions. The South Africa Foundation, in a memorandum to the House of Commons Foreign Affairs Committee, said that an extensive, but unnamed, survey of business attitudes 'has shown that sanctions [undefined] will lead to a loss of over 600,000 jobs for black workers'.[8]

In October 1986 economic analysts said that at least 45,000 people, 'most' of them black, would lose their jobs as a direct result of the US Congress's overriding President Reagan's veto of the sanctions Bill.[9]

If there is sometimes little agreement on how much unemployment would be caused by varying degrees of sanctions, there is naturally even less on how this would break down in individual categories of jobs. Looking specifically at the US sanctions package, economic analysts said that 'thousands' of Cape families, most of them Coloured, would be affected by the import ban on rock lobsters.[10]

Widely differing figures have been given relating to the effects of sanctions on the South African fruit industry. In June 1986 the EEC decided to impose sanctions in three months if certain demands were not met: this was immediately followed by a warning about the effects that blacks would suffer. The South African Embassy in Bonn said that more than one million people depended on the fruit industry in the Cape, which produced 90 per cent of the country's fresh fruit. Of the 442,000 people directly employed, 413,000 were African or Coloured.[11] Different figures were given less than two months later: the authoritative *Financial Mail* said that only 250,000 jobs were in fruit farming, canning and producing dried fruit. Of these, 95 per cent, i.e. 237,500, were African and Coloured. These figures were confirmed by the Deciduous Fruit Board's General Manager, Louis Kriel.[12]

Tourism is another victim of the country's poor public image. The South African Tourist Board told the Economic Affairs Committee of the President's Council in September 1985 that between 5,000 and 30,000 workers in hotels and tourist-related industries had lost their jobs as a result of the decline in the number of foreign visitors. Ninety per cent of those employed were African, Indian and Coloured, and up to half were unskilled or semi-skilled, it said.[13]

The country's mining industry – particularly coal – has been among those most worried about the likely effects of sanctions. Again, the cost has been differently forecast and most took a 'worst case' view in the run-up to the decisions by the Commonwealth, EEC, USA and Japan to impose sanctions in mid to late 1986. In the event, the 'worst case' did not fully materialize: the Commonwealth decided on a coal ban – except for Britain which refused to go along with the plan, the EEC exempted coal from its embargo, and Japan also did not mention coal. The USA, however, did include coal.

Coal-mining is one of the country's most vulnerable industrial sectors: 44 million tons was exported in 1985, worth R3.14 billion in foreign exchange. The EEC was estimated to have taken 22 million tons and Japan 8.5 million tons – two thirds of the total exports and a pointer to the relief felt by colliery owners when the EEC and Japan exempted coal from their bans. In the EEC countries, Britain is said to import about £45 million worth of South African coal a year – sixth in the EEC league – but two major users, the Central Electricity Generating Board and British Coal, ban its use. Before the sanctions decisions were announced the Chamber of Mines claimed that 35 per cent of the 110,000 people employed in the coal industry, of whom 95,000 are black, could lose their jobs if all foreign markets were lost through sanctions.[14] The chamber also criticized the black National Union of Miners (NUM) for supporting sanctions, saying that the policy was inexplicable, since their own members would be affected. The Chamber said that black jobs had more than doubled in the coal industry since 1971 and real wages had risen by more than 300 per cent in the same period.[15]

The iron and steel industries also predicted job losses in the event of sanctions. The EEC ban on iron and steel announced in September 1986 was said to be worth R1 billion. The Steel and Engineering

Industries Federation (SEIFSA) said shortly before the EEC decision was announced that a total of 93,000 jobs stood to be lost if successful metal and coal sanctions were imposed.[16]

The second half of the employment argument concerns those countries imposing sanctions. Here, too, the concern is sometimes more with making political points than with strict accuracy. The main contention is sometimes the converse of Pretoria's claim that specific countries – Australia is often mentioned – favour sanctions only because they could then sell in the world market place without South African competition. The aim is, crudely, to frighten off potential proponents of sanctions with horror stories about resulting unemployment at home if they dare to press for economic measures. At a slightly more sophisticated level, the argument is much favoured by Mrs Thatcher: British jobs should not be lost for the sake of 'immoral' and 'unworkable' sanctions.

With Mrs Thatcher in the forefront of this argument and given the scale of British investment in South Africa relative to the size of its economy, much attention has been paid to the effects of sanctions/disinvestment on that country's already huge unemployment figures. The highest estimate has been 250,000; more common figures settle at around 120,000. But the difference between the two suggests that a fair amount of politics is being played. The suggestion that a quarter of a million more Britons could be out of work if disinvestment took place was displayed prominently in the government's *South African Digest*, a weekly summary published by the Department of Information of carefully selected news items and newspaper editorials which rarely reflect badly on Pretoria. The idea was taken from an article which appeared in *Southern African Fact Sheet* in May 1986 and quoted a study by the Institute for Economic Studies in Britain, in conjunction with the École Supérieure de Commerce in France and the Fachhochschule in West Germany. 'A total boycott would cost Western countries 500,000 jobs,' it said. 'This can be regarded as a conservative estimate.' Britain would be worst hit 'where 250,000 jobs depend on South African trade . . . In West Germany about 130,000 people would be out of work immediately if sanctions were imposed on South Africa . . . Other countries that would be affected include the Netherlands, which has 28 ships exclusively plying the South African route. Large sectors of Swedish industry would come to a standstill if there were a total boycott of South Africa, according to

Mr Bengt-Erik Nilsson, an executive of the War Contingency, Strategical and Psychological Authority in Sweden.'[17] Raymond Ackerman has also said that 500,000 jobs could go in the West, 250,000 of them in Britain, if a total boycott were imposed.[18]

But this seems very high. And, as the report of the House of Commons Foreign Affairs Committee makes clear, 'H M Government have implicitly admitted that precise estimates of the numbers of jobs involved cannot be relied on.'[19] Before the Committee reached that conclusion, the Foreign Secretary, Sir Geoffrey Howe, was asked for his estimate of the cost to Britain of total economic sanctions. He replied: 'Our best estimate of the number of UK jobs that could be jeopardized by sanctions imposed at this end is about 120,000 jobs. That could be increased, of course – or would be increased – if South Africa were to retaliate.'[20] Also giving evidence, the Chairman of the British Industry Committee on South Africa, Sir Leslie Smith, said that total economic sanctions would damage the interests of 'a number' of major British companies 'not disastrously but considerably'.[21] Asked specifically about job loss if all British–South African trade was cut off, he admitted that 'there are no accurate figures available'. His organization thought that 'something in the order of 50,000 jobs are at risk if the visible export trade was cut off'. Another '70,000 jobs we estimate would come from the invisible income we get from South Africa, which includes financial services, insurance, etc. . . . It does not seem to us to be an unreasonable estimate to say that there are 120,000 jobs involving an income of nearly £4,000 million a year.'[22]

The Foreign Affairs Committee sought 'more detailed guidance' from the Foreign Office on how 'the much-quoted figure of 120,000 jobs' was calculated. The Foreign Office conceded that 'the calculation of the effect of any interruption in our economic relations with South Africa must necessarily be imprecise' and added:

There can be no doubt that a significant number of jobs, particularly in the engineering, transport equipment and chemical sectors, are dependent on our visible and invisible trade with South Africa . . . It is clear that, even if only partial sanctions were applied, there are few measures which would not have an adverse effect on one sector or another or which would not help to erode the UK's advantage in the market . . . We have more to lose than our competitors . . . The banning of South African imports could also cause considerable problems . . . This too could in turn have implications for employment in a wide range of industries in the U K.[23]

The Foreign Affairs Committee expressed no surprise in its conclusions at the Foreign Office's refusal 'to put any precise figures on the number of jobs actually at risk'. It commented:

The calculations on which the much-quoted figure of 120,000 jobs seems to be based entirely reflect the assumption that no other changes in the UK's trading arrangements would result from the United Kingdom's failure to impose sanctions, and on crude estimations of the number of jobs involved in the production of the United Kingdom's goods for export, and services to export, to South Africa . . .

. . . There are, in any case, other estimates, produced according to equally valid criteria, which suggest that the direct job implications of sanctions for the United Kingdom are of an altogether lower order. The Fabian Society, for instance, which made use of the Cambridge Economic Model in its calculations, suggests that job losses in the UK as a result of total trade and economic sanctions would not exceed 26,000 in the worst year after the imposition of sanctions, and would have fallen to 4,500 by year four.[*][24]

There would be losses, the Committee agreed, but it apparently declined to give a firm estimate.

In the midst of all the arguments about sanctions and disinvestment, the question is sometimes asked: Why don't black South Africans take their own sanctions by refusing to work? Pik Botha made the point at the National Party's Federal Congress in Durban in August 1986: 'Let those blacks who allegedly want suffering set a personal example. They don't even need sanctions imposed from abroad. They can achieve the same results by resigning their jobs here – by giving up their income here and thus set an example to those who are called upon to sacrifice.'[25]

A similar point was put to the ANC's Oliver Tambo when he gave evidence to the House of Commons Foreign Affairs Committee in October 1985. MP Jim Lester asked him: 'Is not the most effective sanction that you can employ the internal withdrawal of labour? I was in Soweto in 1975 when Soweto did not go to work for three days and Johannesburg totally closed down. That is surely something within your control and that is something you can organize within the country without the external pressure, if people feel as strongly as you suggest they do.'

Mr Tambo replied: 'No, we do not conceive of sanctions as a

* See also Chapter 25, p. 233.

substitute for our own struggle and our own sacrifices; it is additional. So we will continue, we will certainly embark on massive strike actions, we will do all the things that we can and must do for our own freedom, but sanctions are additional and sanctions alone would not bring about any results. We have to be involved in the two pressures from inside and outside.'[26]

The question, not unnaturally, is rather more complicated than Mr Botha's simplistic propaganda point. The law is heavily weighted against this kind of mass action by, among others, the Intimidation Act, the Internal Security Act and the Unlawful Organizations Act, all of which have sections with heavy penalties that could and would be used against people inside South Africa attempting such a course of action. This proposition also assumes, in the words of historian Tom Lodge, discussing the PAC's anti-pass campaign that led to the Sharpeville massacre, 'by defining South African oppression in terms of race and psychology . . . a uniformity of African political behaviour which [is] naively idealist'. Such a concerted, united and lengthy work boycott would require massive organization. The leaders would certainly be detained without trial and probably charged. It is questionable whether that kind of organization exists today. Certainly there was little unity in the PAC's campaign in 1960 and the ANC opposed it. The history of the post-Sharpeville strike indicates that the government would not allow any prolonged 'stay-away' to continue.[27] Since then there have been a number of strikes called for specific purposes, some successful and others less so. Organizational difficulties and tactical differences between various groups make it unlikely that this kind of internal sanction would succeed. Massive unemployment, too, would be a complicating factor, as the strike at General Motors in Port Elizabeth in late 1986 showed.*

* See Chapter 2.

South Africa's attacks on its neighbours

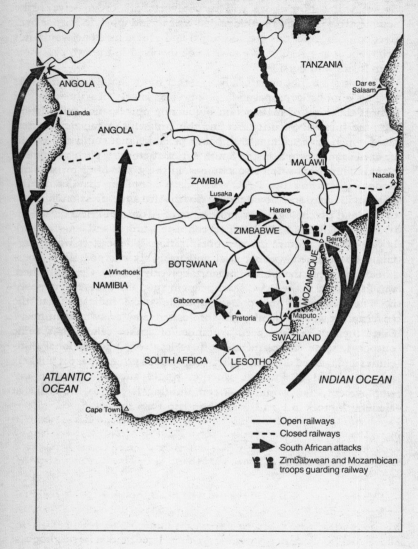

Open railways
Closed railways
South African attacks
Zimbabwean and Mozambican troops guarding railway

The issues of apartheid, sanctions and jobs involve not only black South Africa but also Pretoria's neighbouring majority-ruled states. Those states have a complex and ambivalent relationship with South Africa. They are vociferously opposed to apartheid (and have themselves largely eliminated racial discrimination). Partly because of these factors, they have come under heavy attack from South Africa. Yet they retain important economic links with that country.

In 1980 the nine majority-ruled states of the region formed SADCC, the Southern African Development Coordination Conference, with the joint goals of cooperating to promote economic development and reducing economic dependence on South Africa.

'Southern Africa is dependent on the Republic of South Africa as a focus of transport and communication, as an exporter of goods and services, and as an importer of goods and cheap labour,' admitted SADDC in *Southern Africa: Toward Economic Liberation* (a Declaration by the Governments of Independent States of Southern Africa made at Lusaka on 1 April 1980). But it went on to argue:

This dependence is not a natural phenomenon nor is it simply the result of a free market economy. The nine states . . . were, in varying degrees, deliberately incorporated – by metropolitan powers, colonial rulers, and large corporations – into the colonial and sub-colonial structures centring in general on the Republic of South Africa. The development of national economies as balanced units, let alone the welfare of the people of southern Africa, played no part in the economic integration strategy. Not surprisingly, therefore, southern Africa is fragmented, grossly exploited, and subject to economic manipulation by outsiders.

The formation of SADDC was a threat to South Africa's regional hegemony, and it responded by attacking the neighbouring states. In his book *Apartheid's Second Front* (Penguin, 1986) Joseph Hanlon shows that South Africa is waging an undeclared war on its neighbours which has cost them more than £10,000 million and more than 100,000 lives since 1980. Military raids have been made into seven of the neighbouring states, and large-scale wars are being waged against Mozambique and Angola.

This war is intended to weaken the neighbours. One reason is to try to show that majority rule brings chaos, and thus justify the continuation of apartheid in South Africa. Another motive is to force neighbouring governments to mute their opposition to apartheid.

Yet a third reason is to make the neighbours hostages against sanctions. In part this is done by preventing the neighbouring states from breaking their economic links with South Africa, which in turn allows South Africa to argue that sanctions will hurt the neighbours. The starkest example involves railways. South Africa and rebel forces (such as Unita in Angola) supported by Pretoria have closed four of the seven railways which link the inland SADCC states with SADCC ports. This forces the inland states to ship goods through South African ports. South Africa tells the world that the neighbours are dependent on South Africa for transport, and thus will be hurt by sanctions.

South Africa makes continued use of its economic power. The Commonwealth Eminent Persons Group noted in its report that 'despite protestations to the contrary, South Africa not only believes in the principle of sanctions, but has consistently applied them to its neighbours. This economic coercion is largely covert, since the government likes to pretend to the world that it opposes economic boycotts. Clearly, it has no desire for the international community to follow suit. Nevertheless, the evidence is clear.'

Not surprisingly, this has led to confusing and sometimes contradictory statements by the neighbouring states on sanctions. SADCC has repeatedly called for mandatory economic sanctions against South Africa. But it has also argued that sanctions must be imposed first by South Africa's main trading partners in the developed world. Only then should the neighbours be expected to follow. As is noted in Chapter 27, some of the neighbours should be exempted completely.

The consensus in the neighbouring states is that sanctions will work. There will be a cost to the neighbours, but the cost of sanctions will be relatively small compared with the cost of destabilization. Peter Mmusi, Vice-President of Botswana and Chairman of SADCC's Council of Ministers, explained in his opening statement at the SADCC annual conference at Harare on 30 January 1986: 'We know sanctions will impose a hardship on us. We accept such hardship, as does a woman in labour, knowing that it will bring forth new hope.' In particular, SADCC has publicly stated (in the context of the Lagos Plan of Action, a report submitted to the Organization of African Unity in July 1985) that possible harm to its members should not be used as an excuse not to impose sanctions: 'Those who are concerned about the negative effects of sanctions on the neighbouring states should provide assistance to those states to minimize the impact.'

This view is broadly supported by the six SADCC members who also form the Frontline states – Angola, Botswana, Mozambique, Tanzania, Zambia and Zimbabwe. The Commonwealth Eminent Persons Group concluded in their report that 'countries whose economies are intertwined with that of South Africa, and who inevitably remain vulnerable, none the less regard the imposition of economic sanctions on South Africa as the sole remaining instrument for effective change ... Frontline leaders have repeatedly called on the international community to take just that course.'

The other three majority-ruled states – Lesotho, Malawi and Swaziland – have historically closer links with South Africa and have proved more ambivalent on sanctions.

The three smallest independent countries in the region – Botswana, Lesotho and Swaziland (BLS) – were incorporated in a customs union with South Africa before they were granted independence by Britain. Consequently they remain heavily integrated in the South African economy, and will have the most difficulties de-linking.

Botswana is unusual in that, despite its heavy economic dependence on South Africa, it also has some power. It is the region's major diamond producer, and production is controlled by De Beers, part of the Anglo American Corporation of South Africa. Diamonds have made Botswana relatively wealthy, while De Beers needs to retain control of Botswana diamonds to keep its international monopoly. Although South Africa would be unlikely to permit Botswana to cut its ties with De Beers, Botswana still has substantially more freedom to manoeuvre than Lesotho or Swaziland. For example, Botswana is a member of the Frontline states and hosts the headquarters of SADCC.

Its views were spelled out in August 1986 by its President, Dr Quett Masire, and in a radio commentary a fortnight later. Apartheid, he said, was 'immoral, inhuman ... unsustainable in natural law ...

impractical for the conduct of foreign relations . . . the sole cause of
conflict in South Africa . . . [and] also the sole reason for which South
Africa resorts to war against its neighbours in a vain attempt to coerce
them to accept it'.[1] But Botswana's links with South Africa were
economic, cultural and sociological: 'Its links with the outside world
are through South Africa . . . Botswana is landlocked and the nearest
ports are in South Africa . . . it is cheaper to use the South African
ports.' Pretoria, Dr Masire said, had attacked Botswana on three occasions without any provocation. A number of bombs originating from
South Africa had exploded in Botswana and he said that President
Botha had threatened to carry out more attacks.[2]

The radio commentary explained Botswana's attitude further, defending it against charges that the country was 'neutral, unsym-
pathetic, ambiguous, timid and contradictory':[3]

The survival of this nation is of paramount importance in the formulation of
any policy. After all, self-preservation is the first law of nature. We are satisfied
that our foreign policy . . . is clear enough to be appreciated by an average
Batswana who is, after all, the pillar of this government in terms of the power
of his vote.

Armchair critics of our foreign policy want us to do what they think is
correct. The government takes a number of relevant variables into account in
arriving at any foreign policy. Our foreign policy should be as it is: principled
and pragmatic, and having the best interests of Botswana at heart. We cannot
pretend to be what we are not, simply to meet the demands of those with
fertile imaginations. That is hypocrisy.[4]

More specifically, Dr Masire told a West German magazine in July
1986: 'We are vulnerable in the highest degree . . . Obviously we can't
prohibit the West from imposing sanctions on South Africa, and we
welcome every form of pressure on the apartheid regime. But the
people who would be hardest hit by a boycott and reprisal measures
by the South Africans are simply the blacks, the neighbouring states
like Botswana.'[5] The Agriculture Minister, Daniel Kwelagobe, said
the same month that Botswana should be prepared for South African
retaliation if sanctions were imposed: 'If carried out, it would make
life very difficult . . . but we must be prepared to face it.'[6]

Also in July 1986 Dr Masire said he was 'quoted out of context'
when he had said that Pretoria was applying selective sanctions by
withholding refrigerated trucks for beef and refusing to fill oil storage
tanks. A spokesman said that the President 'was merely referring to
past incidents and was not referring to anything happening currently'.[7]

South Africa also denied that it was applying sanctions: its relations with neighbouring states were based largely on economic considerations. But 'should the senseless sanctions campaign, which is currently enjoying so much attention, jeopardize our economic development, black Southern African states will consequently suffer'.[8]

Lesotho is totally surrounded by South Africa and has the least freedom to manoeuvre. Pretoria has supported an anti-government guerrilla force, the Lesotho Liberation Army, and the South African army has made raids into Lesotho, killing ANC members as well as Basotho people. Pretoria has frequently imposed economic sanctions, and in January 1986 it simply closed the borders and blockaded the country; by the end of the month a coup had overthrown Chief Jonathan and installed a government more sympathetic to South Africa.

Lesotho, having seen Pretoria's power in action, is as, if not more, wary of sanctions than Botswana. In addition, it has more citizens working in South Africa: about 140,000, of whom three quarters are in the mines. Their earnings, most of which are sent back to Lesotho, make up a substantial proportion of the country's foreign income, totalling about R187 million in 1984.[9] South African radio, commenting on the twentieth anniversary of Lesotho independence in October 1986, reminded the country that it had no mineral resources and that more than half the economically active adult population worked in South African mines, with thousands more on farms or in factories:

The money sent back to Lesotho by these migrant workers in South Africa finances 79 per cent of Lesotho's imports and constitutes 50 per cent of her GNP. The South African connection is also vital to Lesotho's budget, customs duties from South Africa representing more than 70 per cent of her total current revenue. South Africa also supplies 99 per cent of the electricity consumed in Lesotho, markets her main agricultural crops, and in many other ways underpins her economy. The imports of food and other essential commodities, work for more than half her adult males, the balancing of the budget, the strength of the GNP; all this and much more besides is being placed in jeopardy by the current sanctions moves in the Western world.[10]

Lesotho's Secretary for Labour, A. L. Thoahlane, remarked mildly in July 1986 after talks with South Africa on sanctions that 'should there be a decline in employment it will have an impact on us'.[11]

Lesotho hopes that if sanctions are applied, aid will come from the international community. 'They are the ones who are insisting on sanctions and we are placing the onus on them to see that we don't suffer,' said a spokesman for the office of the ruling Military Council, which took power after deposing the former Prime Minister, Chief Leabua Jonathan, in January 1986.[12] Like Botswana, Lesotho is trying to introduce measures that would make it less dependent on South Africa.

Lesotho's King Moshoeshoe II has been rather more militant than some members of the government. In August 1985 he told an SADDC summit:

Various sanctions against South Africa are but a reflection of international opprobrium against the policy of racial discrimination ... The effects of sanctions are very clear to us, and they will call for great sacrifices among our peoples. We cannot stand against the sanctions campaign; thus we call upon the rest of the world that, as it exercises what it feels to be a moral obligation, it should be cognizant that we are not a party to apartheid. We therefore strongly elicit the international community to increase moral support to SADDC states so as to cushion the indirect effects of sanctions to us.

Swaziland has an additional problem not shared by the other two BLS countries: it is sandwiched between South Africa and Mozambique. Refugees have fled to Swaziland from both countries: about 5,000 from Mozambique and 7,000 from South Africa according to the local representative of the United Nations High Commissioner for Refugees (UNHCR), Ahmed Farrah.[13] Swaziland has also been raided by armed gangs from South Africa who have killed or kidnapped ANC members and Swazis. Three of the former were shot dead in the capital of Mbabane in June 1986.[14] Compounding this, South African-backed rebels opposed to the Mozambique government have disrupted the railway line between Swaziland and the Mozambican port of Maputo, forcing the kingdom to rely on the longer and more expensive South African routes to carry its main exports of sugar and wood pulp. In addition, South Africa closed its border with Swaziland twice in 1984. Almost 80 per cent of Swaziland's imports come from South Africa,[15] although less than 25 per cent of its exports go there.

Swaziland's attitude to sanctions was summed up in August 1986 when the Prime Minister, Prince Bhekimpi, said that his country 'would be committing suicide' if it supported international measures against Pretoria. Like Lesotho, Swaziland hoped for international aid: Western nations should set up industries in the country to create job opportunities for Swazis who might be turned away from South Africa when sanctions were imposed.[16]

South Africa's Foreign Minister, Pik Botha, visited Swaziland in August 1986 to discuss sanctions and warned that if they were imposed, 'then it would have certain inevitable results, not only for the South African government, but for Swaziland, for Lesotho, for Botswana, for Zambia, for Zimbabwe, even further afield . . . If, for instance, we cannot export textile goods, then surely I have got to protect our textile manufacturers, and we would not be able, I think, to import freely textiles from other countries surrounding us any more. If we are to scale down on imports, then Swaziland and Lesotho and Botswana will get less income from the customs pool.' However, Mr Botha said, 'South Africa does not believe in sanctions.'[17]

Three of Pretoria's other neighbours, Zimbabwe, Zambia and
Mozambique have recently been in the forefront of countries calling
for punitive measures – in the full knowledge that they will suffer.
Indeed, South Africa has made a special point of telling them so,
apparently in the hope of frightening them off. If so, the attempt has
failed. In two of the countries, further, Pretoria is engaged in active
destabilization campaigns: supporting the MNR against the
government in Mozambique (and being accused of causing the death
of President Samora Machel in late 1986), and backing rebels opposed
to Prime Minister Robert Mugabe in Zimbabwe. In another Frontline
state, Angola, South Africa helps Dr Jonas Savimbi's Unita rebels and
has itself invaded the country on a number of occasions. Initially the
aim was to ensure that the MPLA did not come to power. When that
attempt failed, South Africa kept up the pressure, claiming that its
'hot pursuit' operations into Angola were to fight SWAPO guerrillas
operating against South African rule in Namibia.

Zambia, the oldest independent black-ruled state in Southern Africa,
is physically removed from South Africa (although it borders South
African-occupied Namibia), but still reliant on it to some extent. In
1985 South Africa supplied only 14.5 per cent of Zambia's imports,
but about 60 per cent of the country's total imports were transported
through South Africa. These included vital industrial machinery and
spare parts for Zambia's copper mines, and chemicals and fertilizers
for its agriculture. About a third of its exports, mainly copper, were
transported through South Africa. The other two thirds goes via the
Tazara railway to Dar es Salaam. But Zambia's alternative route to
the sea, the Benguela railway in Angola, has been cut by South African-
backed Unita rebels.[1]
   Despite this reliance on South Africa, Zambia's President Kenneth
Kaunda has been one of the African leaders saying that not to impose
sanctions is 'to invite disaster'.[2] Employing sanctions 'against the

apartheid system is the lesser of two evils', he told South African television in August 1986. 'We are saying abolish apartheid and all of us can work together. We will be stronger.'[3] Later the same month, opening the national council meeting of his ruling UNIP party in Lusaka, he questioned the opposition of countries like the USA, Britain, West Germany and France to sanctions.

They argue that these will not work but only hurt the black people and the neighbouring countries ... The question is: How then does one solve the problem in South Africa peacefully if peaceful means are being rejected? ... The Reagan Administration knows that sanctions work. It has applied them against Nicaragua, Libya and Cuba. Why then refuse sanctions ... against South Africa? The answer is [clear]. They care more about their interests in South Africa than about the plight of the black people ...

None of us in this region is preparing to invade South Africa. We mean no ill towards whites in South Africa, none at all. We mean well for all South Africans, because we want them to live together in peace, as brothers and sisters, and as nationals of one country. A free and democratic South Africa will be an important partner of development in this region. It will be richer than it is today, and it will be for the benefit of all South Africans and to all of us in this region ... We have always preferred dialogue ... The question is how to move towards the beginning of dialogue between black and white leaders in South Africa. The ball is therefore in Mr Botha's court.[4]

Mr Botha's government had by that stage already given notice to Zambia and the other Frontline states of its potential reaction to sanctions. On 4 August 1986 it introduced a customs clamp on all supplies going through South Africa to Zambia. A 'provisional payment', or cash deposit, was to be paid on all goods destined for Zambia. The full duty plus 25 per cent had to be paid in cash to South African Customs and Excise before the goods were released. On duty-free goods, a provisional payment of 25 per cent had to be put up. The deposits were to be repaid once a Zambian bill of entry was produced as proof the goods had reached their destination and that the duties had been paid.[5] The move was said by the Commissioner of Customs and Excise to be purely a customs matter to counter irregularities and fraud, although 'it could have political implications'.[6] Those political implications were spelled out with typical subtlety by Pik Botha: it would make countries calling for sanctions 'put their money where their mouth is'.[7]

South Africa's decision caused immediate alarm. The Executive Director of the South African Association of Freight Forwarders,

Allan Cowell, said there would be severe shortages in Zambia of petrol, wheat, clothing, tinned goods, 'you name it', within two to three weeks. Forwarding agents in South Africa were not prepared to put up thousands of rands for the provisional payment unless somebody provided the funds, as otherwise they would recover their money up to a year later, if at all. Zambia also had a problem because it lacked foreign exchange. The total amount of money tied up could be between R7 and R12 million, Mr Cowell said.[8] The situation was further complicated a week later when the Bank of Zambia banned credit and invoice letters from businessmen wanting to buy goods from South Africa. The measures included halting the processing of all applications for foreign currency for business exchanges with South Africa.[9] To add to the pressure on Zambia – and Zimbabwe – Customs and Excise introduced, a week after the provisional payments, searches of cargo trucks and trains to 'obtain a clear picture of goods transported through South Africa bound for foreign countries'.[10] This was ended on 27 August, with the Bureau for Information saying that the information gained since the introduction of the measure on 4 August was considered 'sufficient': 'It is public knowledge that the South African government needs the information if it is to lodge counter-measures against those countries for their pro-sanctions stand.' The Department of Foreign Affairs said that 'action could be taken again' if more information was required.[11]

Against this background, President Kaunda was reported to have softened his rhetoric calling for sanctions. He said that South Africa's reprisals 'will affect our economy very adversely indeed'. Zambia would not cut air links with South Africa as it would need to coordinate action with other Commonwealth states, the EEC and the USA. He added: 'We must proceed immediately to gear ourselves to effective measures . . . In doing so our nation will be called upon to be prepared to endure hardship.' The South African measures meant that 'we will have to suffer that much more. We have to thank the West for supporting apartheid.' But Zambia was not going to apply sanctions unilaterally: 'We can't do it piecemeal. It's a complicated affair. We want sanctions to succeed. It's not just a matter of a demonstration of hatred of apartheid.'[12]

While Zambia appeared to be toning down its rhetoric on sanctions in late 1986, Zimbabwe found itself in a worse situation than its northern neighbour. Its dependence on South Africa is greater: 90 per cent of its overseas trade goes through South African ports. In 1984 South Africa took 18.3 per cent of Zimbabwe's exports and supplied 19.3 per cent of its imports. Zimbabwe has to use South African ports because Beira in Mozambique can handle only 800,000 tons of the country's export–import volume of three million tons. The 'Beira corridor' is a top-priority SADCC project, and rehabilitation now underway means that it could handle nearly all of Zimbabwe's traffic by 1988. This would sharply reduce South Africa's economic power over Zimbabwe, and Pretoria wants to ensure that this does not happen. There have been frequent raids by the MNR and South African commandos on the railway, port and oil pipeline, and the line is kept open by 3,000 to 5,000 troops from Zimbabwe, at a cost of £500,000 a day. Because South Africa is expected to step up its attacks, there is now talk of an international force to protect the line, perhaps including Indian and Nigerian troops or aircraft.[13]

South Africa has frequently used its economic power by imposing sanctions against Zimbabwe and Zambia, most notably in 1981 when it disrupted goods to Zimbabwe and Zambia, and in 1982 when it disrupted fuel supplies to Zimbabwe.

As the Commonwealth mini-summit in London decided – with Britain opposing – on a package of sanctions, South Africa again imposed its own sanctions against Zimbabwe and Zambia: import licences, a levy on all goods destined for the two countries and stricter border controls. Mr Mugabe was defiant when he returned to Harare a few days later from the mini-summit: 'We may suffer for a while, but Zambia and Zimbabwe will not die,' he said. 'If we have to eat sadza [maize meal] without stew, we will do it' – an echo of UDI days when the then Rhodesian Minister of Agriculture, Lord Angus Graham, said in 1966 that Rhodesians would rather eat sadza than give in to sanctions.[14]

South Africa insisted its new measures were not an embargo on trade. The Minister of Trade and Industry, Dawie de Villiers, said it was 'an economic [measure] instituted to protect our foreign sources of supply'.[15] His department said that the decision to introduce the licensing system for exports from Zimbabwe would not be discriminatory: 'If you apply for a permit, you're going to get it ... We won't stop imports coming in. It will merely enable us to monitor the nature and volume of products from that country.'[16] The decision was, however, seen in Harare as a warning that South Africa 'could choke Zimbabwe to death if it chose'. The two economies are so closely linked that Zimbabwe's Finance Minister, Bernard Chidzero, described it in 1985 as 'an umbilical relationship'. But he also pointed out that South Africa earned valuable income from Zimbabwe: $110 million a year, about half from freight traffic and the rest in profits, dividends, interest and pensions. The inflow from South Africa to Zimbabwe was only about $15 million a year. In addition Zimbabwe owes South Africa about $133 million, a debt largely inherited from the years of U D I. South Africa also had heavy investments in Zimbabwe: about a quarter of Zimbabwe's capital stock is South African-owned and South African interests control most of Zimbabwe's mining and manufacturing sectors.[17] The other side of that coin was that searches of Zimbabwean exports would hit hardest the tobacco industry, which in 1985 earned £140 million from exports. One tobacco agent expected his profit to be halved by the South African restrictions.[18]

Pretoria also stepped up the propaganda war. In late August 1986 South African radio compared the state's relations with Zimbabwe and with Swaziland. Relations with the latter were 'marked by cordiality and friendship'; those with Zimbabwe were 'in absolute contrast'.[19] Much play was made, on the radio and in the other media, with the fact that, while Mr Mugabe 'was at the forefront of pleading for economic sanctions against South Africa', members of his government were signing a new trade agreement with Pretoria. The Zimbabweans, Pik Botha said, got 'important additions to the existing trade agreement which amounted to asking for preferential treatment of their goods'. Harare, he added, had deliberately decided to conceal news of the agreement until after the Non-Aligned Movement meeting in Zimbabwe. South Africa had consented to this, but 'we decided, in the light of current circumstances, to reveal it now'. The same day as Mr Botha made public the signing of the agreement, South Africa ended its 'statistical survey' of traffic heading for Zimbabwe and Zambia via the Beitbridge border-post.[20]

Mr Mugabe's lobbying for sanctions by the Commonwealth was preceded by a careful scheme to get support from the influential Confederation of Zimbabwe Industries. In early July 1986 Mr Mugabe urged the C Z I to 'voluntarily change their transport routes to the sea'. The next day the C Z I's annual congress adopted a resolution calling for comprehensive mandatory sanctions against South Africa. The resolution was submitted without warning and declared adopted by acclamation without discussion or dissent: this pre-empted a move by the government to introduce an identical resolution which, CZI leaders said, would have led to an acrimonious debate. Many white delegates were said to be angry at what they termed 'a course for economic disaster in Zimbabwe'. But CZI officials said that 'as it sinks in they will realize that change is coming to South Africa and they will have to adapt'.[21] The four major oil companies in Zimbabwe also indicated they would back the government in its efforts to secure alternative routes and sources if sanctions were applied to South Africa.[22] The South African raid in the heart of Harare on 19 May 1986 seems to have convinced many Zimbabwean businessmen that Pretoria is not on their side. White businessmen have established a private company, the Beira Corridor Group, to promote the use of Beira instead of South African ports.

Mr Mugabe also threatened to withhold profits and dividends from South African companies. This had been preceded in May 1984 by an attempt to improve the country's balance of payments by prohibiting all remittances for rents, dividends, interest payments and profits from leaving the country. The ban was partially lifted in 1985 to allow a percentage of dividends to be paid outside, provided the remainder was spent on government bonds. Pensions, alimony payments and approved expatriate wages had been exempt from the original ban, but Mr Mugabe's threat in August 1986 applied also to pensions.[23]

As hostility between South Africa and Zimbabwe increased, Mr Mugabe maintained his firm support for sanctions. Returning to Harare from the Commonwealth mini-summit in August 1986, he said his country would impose the full Commonwealth sanctions, including severing air links, which would extend to banning any international airline serving South Africa from overflying Zimbabwe. Zimbabwe air links with South Africa were the most profitable; Britain warned Zimbabwe that if British Airways flights through Zimbabwe to South Africa were banned, retaliation would follow against Air Zimbabwe flights to London. Cancellation of flights between South Africa and Zimbabwe would also hit tourism: 40 per cent of Zimbabwe's tourists come from the south.[24]

The Zimbabwean leader also strongly criticized Mrs Thatcher for not agreeing to the Commonwealth's total package of sanctions. 'I have given her up, written her off, as a bad case,' he said. '. . . She appears to be motivated by racism.'[25]

*

Mozambican reliance on South Africa is not as great as that of Zambia and Zimbabwe. Only 12 per cent of Mozambique's imports come from South Africa ($50 million in 1985). Mozambique does not use South Africa for any of its transport. Indeed, South Africa sends nearly 1 million tons per year of cargo through Maputo port, although as a result of South Africa's sanctions against Mozambique, this is only one tenth of the cargo sent by that route 15 years ago. Half of Maputo's electricity comes from South Africa. In 1986 about 60,000 Mozambicans were working legally in South Africa, mainly in the gold mines.

Pretoria opposes Mozambique's policies more strongly than those of Zambia and Zimbabwe: South African support for the MNR rebels is denied only by the government, with increasing lack of conviction. The death in late 1986 of Mozambique's President Samora Machel was widely blamed on South Africa, despite Pretoria's denials. Pretoria had only itself to blame for the accusations – even if it was wholly innocent. South Africa has bombed Maputo, the Mozambique capital; its agents have killed opponents of apartheid there; and it finances, trains and arms the MNR. Many observers concluded not only that the plane crash in which Machel died was not an accident but that it was a logical extension of South African destabilization.

On 16 March 1984 President Machel had been pressed into signing the Nkomati Accord with South Africa, an 'agreement on non-aggression and good neighbourliness'. It committed the signatories to settle their differences by peaceful means and forbade each country from being used as a base for acts of aggression against the other. Each had to undertake to eliminate bases, training centres, accommodation and transit facilities for elements hostile to the other. The immediate result in Mozambique was that a number of ANC personnel were forced to leave the country. On the South African side, some Defence Force personnel with MNR sympathies were transferred or dismissed. However, Pretoria admitted that it had made some 'technical violations' of the treaty. One of these violations was building a landing strip for the MNR; another was 'humanitarian' aid – all designed, it said, to encourage the MNR to negotiate with the Frelimo government.[26] MNR documents captured from the MNR headquarters in the Gorongosa mountains showed that the violations were more than technical. There had been massive arms shipments after Nkomati. The then Deputy Foreign Minister, Louis Nel, had visited the base three times since the Accord. MNR leaders were said to have been taken by South African submarine and plane for meetings with top South African ministers.

Mutual suspicion and hostility continued. It flared again in early October 1986 when six South African soldiers were injured in a landmine explosion near Mbuzini, close to the Mozambique and Swaziland borders. Mozambique was immediately blamed for allowing the ANC to operate from its territory. The South African Minister of Defence, General Magnus Malan, warned: 'President Machel has the Nkomati Accord in his hands. Nkomati and landmines cannot exist side by side. If President Machel chooses landmines, South Africa will react accordingly.'[27] South African radio followed up this broadside two days later with criticism of President Machel's statement at the Non-Aligned Movement meeting that Pretoria was trying to destroy Mozambique, adding that in 1986 'there have been at least 23 terrorist attacks in South Africa that were masterminded in Mozambique'.[28] A week later the radio, somewhat ironically, preached the virtue of compromise. Fighting between Frelimo and the MNR, it said, 'can achieve nothing but much more death and destruction . . . There can be only one solution to such a situation . . . It is time to give negotiation and peaceful coexistence a chance.'[29] The following day the radio said, after listing MNR successes, that 'the crunch, it would seem, is coming in Mozambique. The Soviet Union and her allies stand poised to use the turmoil in Mozambique as a pretext to rush in more weapons of war and more Communist bloc troops. The further destabilization and militarization of southern Africa needs to be resisted actively before Mozambique becomes another Afghanistan or Nicaragua.'[30] On 20 October President Machel was killed.

Amid all these accusations, Mozambique continued to call for sanctions against South Africa. The Security Minister, Colonel Sergio Vieira, in July 1986 rejected Western arguments that sanctions would hurt blacks and the Frontline states. Black South Africans were already suffering from repression, forced removals and killings. Countries like Mozambique were confronted by South African banditry.[31] Mozambique's Foreign Minister, Joaquim Chissano, who took over as President after Samora Machel's death, said the same month that the call for sanctions came from the South African people themselves: 'We in Mozambique cannot oppose sanctions, even if they do involve some difficulties for our economy.'[32] But Chissano has always stressed that 'sanctions ought to be effective. We in the Frontline states should not apply sanctions when they won't be effective. We would like to see those sanctions applied by those who can make them effective. The countries which have economic power in South Africa must take the lead ... Our countries have physical and geographic links with South Africa. European links are of a political and economic nature. So there is more flexibility there for those countries to impose sanctions.' (Mr Chissano, then Foreign Minister, was speaking at a press conference after the SADCC Conference in Maputo on 28 November 1980.)

Another of South Africa's 'neighbours' is Namibia, occupied by Pretoria in defiance of the United Nations. The South West African People's Organization (SWAPO), which has been fighting a guerrilla war against South African rule since the mid-1960s, favours sanctions against Pretoria as part of its strategy to win internationally accepted independence for Namibia. At present an interim administration rules the territory, with some powers still reserved by Pretoria. The South African government has been trying to 'sell' the 'internal settlement' as an acceptable basis for independence – so far without success.

The economies of Namibia and South Africa are so intertwined that all sanctions would affect Namibia. A Provisional Government spokesman said in August 1986 that application of sanctions to Namibia would be the 'cruellest' part of the campaign: 'We scrapped apartheid years ago; we have a predominantly black government; and our people are yearning for independence. Now we're going to be punished for white South Africa's sins.' He added that if EEC sanctions were imposed, this would hit the uranium, karakul sheep and fishing industries hardest, and wider sanctions would hurt the diamond and other mining sectors, which constitute more than 80 per cent of Namibia's exports and a third of GDP, while employing 15,000 blacks.[33] In September 1986 Namibia's Chamber of Commerce appealed for the territory to be excluded from sanctions: their imposition would force concentration on survival rather than independence, would polarize opposing radicals and create desperation. The international community, it said, should help to 'uplift the backward masses of our population'.[34] In fact, Namibia was exempted from EEC sanctions (see also Chapter 1, pp. 27–8, and Chapter 21, p. 198).

As opposition to apartheid has increased over the years and the pressure for sanctions has grown, South Africa has favoured two counter-arguments. The first has been: if South Africa is as bad as it is painted, why do hundreds of thousands of 'foreign' blacks flock to the country? The second has been a thinly veiled warning: if sanctions are imposed foreign blacks will be repatriated, on the grounds that charity begins at home.

Just how many foreign blacks are in the country is not known accurately. The most common estimate is 350,000 legal workers (excluding those from the 'independent' homelands of Transkei, Bophuthatswana, Venda and Ciskei, known as the TBVC states), supporting an estimated two million dependants throughout the region. The number of illegal workers has been put at between 1.2 and 1.3 million, which, if the same number of dependants per person were assumed, would mean they support between 6.84 and 7.41 million people.[35] However, other estimates have put the figure for illegal workers as low as 300,000 and as high as 2 million. In September 1986, using a figure of 249,921 legal foreign workers, Andre Wilsenach of the government-supporting Africa Institute estimated that they sent back R537.6 million a year during 1983–4.[36]

In 1985, as the US Senate was debating a sanctions Bill, South Africa's Deputy Minister of Foreign Affairs, Louis Nel, said it was not the government's intention to retaliate against neighbouring states if sanctions were imposed. But it was impossible for the USA to limit the measures to South Africa: 'Let's be frank. Our neighbours will suffer before we do.'[37]

As the threat of sanctions became more real, Pretoria stepped up its warnings that foreign blacks would be expelled. In June 1986, Pik Botha said that neighbouring states would be 'making a mistake' if they thought South Africa's infrastructure would continue to be made available to them, as further economic steps against the country might force the government to curtail or even end important services and cooperation.[38] The Minister of Manpower, Piet du Plessis, took the opportunity of a visit by a Lesotho labour delegation to say that the estimated 1.3 million illegal workers from neighbouring states were depriving unemployed South Africans of a livelihood. He said an estimated 703,000 people were unemployed at the end of March 1986, excluding the TBVC states. Strong action against illegal workers and their employers could be expected. 'Irresponsible' behaviour by legal foreign workers 'such as participation in illegal actions . . . will result in their repatriation and a reduction in their numbers'. Workers from foreign countries leading South African trade unions would be similarly treated should they incite workers to participate in illegal actions and advocate or support sanctions: 'No trade union leader in South Africa who advocates sanctions against the country and promotes the disruption of the South African economy can possibly have the interests of workers at heart.'[39] This was followed by a similar warning from the Director-General of the Department of Manpower a few days later. Indicating that the heat was on, South African radio weighed in as well: if what the 'international media and certain foreign politicians' said about South Africa was true, 'one would expect that not a single black person from anywhere in Africa would want to set foot in South Africa'. But there was not enough work in neighbouring states: 'With their relatively poor economies they are not able to support their workforce. In South Africa, however, there is work and food and a far higher standard of living. It is the only country on the African continent that has a black middle class . . .'[40]

Pik Botha had an ingenious explanation when he was interviewed by South African television in August 1986. Pretoria did not want to impose punitive measures, but 'it is a chain reaction of events, not started by us, but actually passed on to neighbouring states . . .'[41] The interview continued:

Q. At this stage is South Africa implementing economic sanctions against southern Africa?
A. Absolutely not. We are against sanctions and we trade with all countries. We would export to Russia as long as they signed and paid.
Q. Would it be in South Africa's interests to impose counter-boycotts?
A. Not a boycott as such. It is not our aim, it is not our plan, it is not our policy, but I repeat – take, for example, if coal sanctions are imposed and as a result thereof there is a decline in production and exports of coal. As a result the mine bosses would have to retrench 30, 40, 50,000 mineworkers or not renew their contracts. What do you do now then? You let those people go back to their countries. It is not a punitive measure against those unfortunate people. It is a necessary result of this blind, cynical, negative action against us. We do not have a choice.
Q. Sanctions by South Africa would be our final trump card. Would we ever play that final trump card?
A. I cannot go into that now . . .[42]

The campaign against foreign workers stepped up. In the *Sunday Times*, the country's biggest-selling newspaper, which often supports Mr Botha's *verligte* moves, unnamed health officials were quoted later in August 1986 as saying that foreign workers were carrying infectious diseases into South Africa and placing a 'huge' burden on state medical services. The health officials, the *Sunday Times* said, 'argue that if neighbouring states impose economic sanctions on South Africa, the government will have every justification for sending foreign workers home. In support of this view, officials have assembled evidence that contagious diseases such as AIDS, malaria and cholera are being carried by people from neighbouring states where preventative health services have all but collapsed.'[43]

A few days later the government issued a statement threatening to repatriate all foreign workers found to be carriers of the AIDS virus. The black National Union of Mineworkers (NUM) replied that this was no departure from the government's 'norm of exporting unemployment and disease to rural areas to get away from responsibility'. The NUM was involved in talks with the Chamber of Mines to try to find a solution. Blood tests had been conducted but these had been suspended as there was great resistance from workers. 'The NUM also strongly commends the Chamber's stance of dealing with the problem in a compassionate and humane manner rather than by dismissing these workers ... We don't see repatriation as a solution ...'[44]

In September 1986 the Department of Home Affairs announced that it would step up measures against the estimated 1.3 million workers and their employers contravening the Aliens Act (which controls admission to the country). Increased action was being taken to determine the location of aliens, the Department's Director-General, B. G. S. van Zyl, said. The Department was also considering more inspections which might result in more prosecutions of employers: the Act provides for fines of up to R5,000 or two years' imprisonment for a first conviction. It was emphasized, however, that the measures did not apply to citizens of the 'independent homelands', the TBVC states, who did not require a work permit under the Act.[45]

That was merely an initial step. On 8 October 1986 the Bureau for Information issued a news release by the ministers of Foreign Affairs, Manpower, Mineral and Energy Affairs, and Home Affairs:

[The ministers] hereby announce that a note has today been sent to the government of Mozambique intimating that the South African government has decided that no further recruitment of workers from Mozambique will be allowed as from today as a result of the activities of the ANC and SACP [South African Communist Party] who are responsible for the continuing deteriorating security situation on the common border with the RSA [Republic of South Africa], and who according to information in possession of the RSA government, as confirmed by recent incidents, are still operating from Mozambique.

Employers are thus requested to cease with immediate effect to recruit and employ any further Mozambican workers and to actively endeavour to employ South African workers. Workers whose work permits are still valid will be allowed to complete their period of service, after which they will have to return to Mozambique and will not be allowed to re-enter South Africa. Organized mining and agriculture have already been informed of this decision.[46]

Not surprisingly, South African radio backed up the claim that the ANC and SACP were rebuilding in Mozambique 'with the full knowledge of President Samora Machel's government'. Security spokesmen had said that the acting leader of the SACP and second-in-command of the ANC's military wing, Joe Slovo, had been seen in Maputo on a number of occasions since the beginning of 1986. A number of 'terrorists' who had been arrested in connection with attacks in the eastern Transvaal had infiltrated the country from Mozambique.[47]

The South African decision aroused immediate and widespread concern. Maputo radio termed it 'the prelude of a series of sanctions which the Pretoria regime had been applying against our economy'. Since independence in 1975 a number of sanctions had been imposed, it said. Soon after independence South Africa had decided to reduce the number of Mozambican miners working in South Africa from 150,000 to 40,000. Before independence, 60 per cent of the salaries of the Mozambican miners were paid in gold, but Pretoria had unilaterally ended this. South Africa was financing, training and sending 'armed bandits' [the Mozambican term for MNR guerrillas] into the country at an 'extremely high' economic cost. The MNR was targeting communications 'as a way of perpetuating the dependence on South Africa of Mozambique and the southern African countries . . . The measure announced today . . . is the continuation of destabilizing actions . . .'[48]

The Chamber of Mines was not very pleased either. Earlier it had warned of chaos if there was mass repatriation of Mozambicans. The figures showed why: In 1985 the Chamber's gold and coal mines employed 51,698.[49] On 31 July 1986 nearly 62,000 Mozambicans were employed. Mozambique stood to lose about R 200 million a year, according to the manager of the Maputo office recruiting for South African mines, Richard Yapp. In addition to the miners, it was reported that a number of Mozambicans working legally in agriculture would be affected by Pretoria's decision.[50]

The Chamber warned that a 70- to 80-year relationship with the people of Mozambique was being disrupted by the government.

Although it could not evaluate the security reasons for the decision, the Chamber hoped that negotiations between the two countries would lead to an early return of normal relationships. It regretted the government's move but welcomed the fact that the inevitable disruption to its operations would, to an extent, be cushioned by the decision that workers presently employed would be permitted to complete their contracts.[51]

The NUM was less mealy-mouthed. Cyril Ramaphosa, the union's General Secretary, said the decision was 'outrageous and unwarranted retaliatory action which the miners would not take lying down ... The government continues its policy of destabilization and aggression against neighbouring states. Mozambique and other countries in the area are part of a regional economy and have contributed to the wealth of South Africa.'[52]

The Progressive Federal Party said that South Africa should be 'trying to build up good economic relationships with neighbouring countries rather than politicizing Pretoria's problems ... The government is punishing the wrong people. All the workers currently employed in South Africa are being condemned by the actions of a minority.'[53]

Before the Pretoria decision had been announced, the UN High Commissioner for Refugees in Harare, Jean-Pierre Hocke, said that Southern Africa could become the world's next refugee disaster area. There were already 250,000 refugees in the area, mostly Angolans fleeing the war. If the 350,000 legal black foreign workers were expelled, Southern Africa could face a large-scale problem. This would worsen if illegal migrant workers were also thrown out, he said.[54]

The decision aroused international concern, too. Britain and other members of the EEC protested and expressed concern at reports that South Africa might be contemplating military action against Mozambique.[55] The International Labour Organization expressed its worry, said Mozambicans were being made to suffer for unjustified reasons, and promised it would offer Mozambique all possible technical assistance. It estimated that for the next 18 months up to 4,000 Mozambicans a month were likely to face repatriation.[56] In January 1987, however, a 'temporary' agreement was reached between the Chamber of Mines and the government, under which skilled and semi-skilled workers from Mozambique, and those unskilled with seven years' service, would be allowed to renew their contracts. A ban remains, though, on the recruitment of new workers.

More exact figures on the numbers of people then being expelled by

South Africa were given at the end of October 1986. The Director-General of Home Affairs, Gerries van Zyl, also denied that the operation was directed at blacks: there were many illegal white workers in the country, he said. In 1985 more than 24,000 black workers were repatriated. From the beginning of 1986 to the end of August, about 22,000 illegal workers had been repatriated: 13,000 to Mozambique, 5,000 to Botswana, 2,000 to Zimbabwe, 1,500 to Lesotho, 400 to Swaziland, 22 to Malawi, three to Tanzania and one to Zambia. Repatriation of illegal workers had been going on for years, with an annual average of between 1,500 and 1,800 for the last few years. But the Mozambican miners were not illegal workers and were not involved in this operation.[57]

One reason given for the crackdown on illegal workers – which Mr van Zyl denied was a crackdown – was that illegal workers were depriving South Africans of jobs at great cost to the Unemployment Insurance Fund which provides limited compensation to the unemployed.* According to the Department of Manpower in April 1986, the UIF paid out R219 million in unemployment benefits in 1985, compared to R105 million in 1984. The number of people paid rose from 186,125 to 304,905.[58] In the first quarter of 1986, UIF benefits increased by 25 per cent compared with the same period of 1985. The government has also allocated about R695 million in 1985 and 1986 in work creation and training projects. About 500,000 people were employed and/or trained in the same period.[59] In October 1986 it was announced that the unemployment relief scheme would be extended for five years.[60]

The exact extent of unemployment is unknown, mainly because government figures for blacks are unreliable. In September 1986 two University of the Witwatersrand academics estimated that the total could be as high as six million people – almost 12 times as high as the government's most recent official figures of 533,000: 'The aggregated results of . . . surveys show on average that more than 25 per cent of the total population, or 48 per cent of the economically active population, is unemployed.'[61] Another academic, Professor Wynand Pienaar, of the University of South Africa, said in May 1986 that about 80 per cent of blacks between the ages of 18 and 26 had no jobs.[62] In March 1986 86,000 whites were unemployed and looking for full-time work – up from 48,000 in March 1986, according to one estimate.[63] In

* See also Chapter 9 on jobs.

a country whose economy has for long been built on the theory and practice of whites being at the top of the labour heap, it was reported in July 1986 that white casual labourers were being seen doing manual work for the first time since the 1930s.[64]

The academic boycott of South African universities has proceeded in fits and starts since the 1950s when the government legislated to segregate higher education. The issue is one of the more complex of all the arguments about contact with South Africa, for the mainly white English-speaking universities there are regarded generally as intellectual, and sometimes physical, centres of opposition to apartheid. These universities are now increasingly mixed, with a much higher number of African, Coloured and Indian students attending than in 1959 when the mis-named Extension of University Education Act was passed. This legislation provided for the establishment of university colleges for 'non-white persons' and gave the Minister of Education the power to prohibit blacks from attending 'white' universities.[1] These new 'tribal colleges' were strictly controlled by government-supporting appointees, regulations were oppressive, the teaching staff often below standard and academic standards said to be low. Through the years more university colleges were established and proportionately fewer blacks were given permission to attend the 'white' universities: in 1960, for example, seven Africans who wanted to study engineering at the University of the Witwatersrand were refused because the Minister of Bantu Education saw 'no prospects of employment for qualified Bantu engineers'.[2]

It was partly in response to university apartheid that the academic boycott began. Support has been sporadic. Proponents of the boycott tried to ensure that academics, mainly in Britain and the United States, did not take up posts at South African universities or accept visiting lectureships. Some moves have also been made to refuse to recognize South African degrees and to refuse South African academics posts abroad. In 1986, for example, Trinity College and University College in Dublin severed all formal links with South African universities. The boycott has been, however, far less than watertight and as higher education budgets began to shrink, particularly in Britain, posts in South Africa began to look more attractive. In addition, a number of university personnel regarded the boycott as a negation of academic freedom. Further, many specialists in African affairs found research in southern Africa important.

Opposition to the academic boycott was summed up by Professor Richard Rorty, of the University of Virginia, in late 1986 on a visit to South Africa: 'Academics must keep contacts between universities going and that seems well worth doing just for its own sake,' he said. Universities 'tend to wither and decay' if they are not in touch with scholars in the rest of the world. U S academics viewed South African universities as 'centres of resistance to the regime' and foreign opponents of the government needed to visit to 'show their solidarity. Academics agree with black students [in the USA] that it is a vicious and cruel government but they think the universities are one of the few islands of free discussion.'[3]

The whole controversy, which arouses considerable passions, was encapsulated in late 1986 with the visit to South Africa of Dr Conor Cruise O'Brien, a former Irish Cabinet minister, former editor of the *Observer*, former Chairman of the Irish Anti-Apartheid Movement and present Deputy Chancellor of Trinity College, Dublin. The academic boycott has generally been opposed by South African university students and staff who regard it as, at best, misdirected. Professor David Welsh, head of the University of Cape Town's politics department, characterized it as 'not only destructive but also mindless'. Professor Welsh said that Dr O'Brien was to teach a course on siege societies: 'Like Dr O'Brien, I am quite unable to see how boycotting UCT contributes to the abolition of apartheid.'[4]

However, the publicity secretary of the pro-Black Consciousness Azanian Students' Organization (AZASO), Riaz Jawoodeen, said that AZASO used to support a total academic boycott, but now believed that only people who were actively supportive of the struggle should come to South Africa. Dr O'Brien was coming 'under the pretext that UCT is at the forefront of the struggle against apartheid. But the campus is a by-product. The campus as such, including the politics department, is not at the forefront of the struggle.'[5]

Dr O'Brien did go, despite the present Chairman of the Irish Anti-Apartheid Movement calling the trip 'an act of betrayal'. Dr O'Brien retorted: 'The boycott is silly and unjust. I am happy to break it.'[6] The academic boycott was 'good for a laugh' in Pretoria while opponents of apartheid were 'fiddling with Mickey Mouse stuff'. He conceded, however, when questioned by students at UCT, that a case could be made for a boycott by scientists whose research could benefit the Defence Force and police. The boycott would not help to end apartheid: 'What universities would be doing to themselves if they supported academic boycotts would be to put political blocks on intellectual communication.' Economic sanctions were necessary to put pressure on the government, 'but support for economic sanctions does not require specific measures against universities and scholars'. Asked why he was in South Africa when the ANC, with its proved mass support, had called for the academic boycott, Dr O'Brien said: 'I don't accept the right of these people to tell a free scholar where and what to teach. By sacrificing my own right to my own mind I would not be alleviating the suffering here.'[7]

Dr O'Brien got a rough reception at UCT and the University of the Witwatersrand when radical students disrupted lectures he was giving. The students objected to not being consulted about his visit and to his description of the academic boycott as 'Mickey Mouse stuff'.[8] The disruption was welcomed by the Anti-Apartheid Movement in London: 'It will be a good lesson to Dr O'Brien to learn that the academic boycott . . . has support in South Africa itself and is not something we are trying to impose from outside.'[9]

Both the Council and Senate of the UCT condemned the violence which led to the cancellation of Dr O'Brien's lectures. 'The university is against the denial of freedom of speech and assembly on the part of anyone,' the Council said, while recognizing the right of people to protest in a 'reasonable manner' against the presence and viewpoints of speakers. The Council also set up a committee of inquiry into the incident.[10] The Senate supported the Council, rejecting 'any actions aimed at further curtailing academic freedom', and saying that anybody wilfully disrupting teaching, research or examinations 'has forfeited the privileges of being a member of an academic community'.[11]

However, 81 UCT academics took a different line:

We dispute the definition of academic freedom . . . in which the notion of freedom of speech is divorced from the South African context and can be invoked against members of the university who challenge its traditions and authority . . . True academic freedom and freedom of speech . . . are inseparable from the establishment of fully democratic institutions in a free society. To this end we affirm the need to work for a fundamental restructuring of this university as an integral part of the broader democratic struggle. We commit ourselves to developing a position with progressive organizations on the complex tactical, strategic and political issues concerning the academic boy-cott.[12]

South African academics have tried to minimize the impact of the academic boycott by drawing up political guidelines which would point the way to a selective boycott of individuals and institutions. Professor Colin Gardiner of the University of Natal in Pietermaritz-burg said in August 1986: 'What we are trying to say to those abroad is that while we understand the reason for the boycott, we be-lieve they should distinguish between opponents of apartheid and others.'[13] The move came after three sociologists, including Natal University's Professor Lawrence Schlemmer,* were barred from a conference in New Delhi. The ANC intervened in the case of two other academics from the University of the Witwatersrand, with the result that they were allowed to participate.[14] The Association for Sociology in Southern Africa (ASSA) has tried to overcome its isolation in the face of the academic boycott by deciding to meet the ANC to re-establish contact with sociologists outside South Africa.[15]

The pros and cons of the academic boycott were extensively debated in late 1986 at the time of the World Archaeological Congress in Southampton.† Southampton City Council, the Anti-Apartheid Movement, the local students' union and the Association of University Teachers said that they would not accept South African scholars; financial support and accommodation would be withdrawn and demonstrations held. African countries threatened a boycott. The organizers, headed by Professor Peter Ucko of Southampton Univer-sity, then told the South Africans who had applied to attend that their presence would not be accepted. This did not please everybody: about 300 people out of several thousand said they would not attend as a result; there were resignations from the organizing bodies; and archaeology's supreme body, the International Union of Prehistoric and Protohistoric Sciences (IUPPS) withdrew support from the Southampton congress.

Who was right? Neal Ascherson argued in the *Observer* that many South African archaeologists were strong opponents of apartheid: 'In

* See Chapter 4 on opinion polls.

† The arguments for and against were summarized by Neal Ascherson in the *Observer* of 24 August and 14 September 1986, on which this section is largely based.

fact, their work has knocked away one of the ideological props of apartheid, by demonstrating that white settlement did not take place in a land inhabited only by a few Bushmen but that Bantu settlement in the region is at least 1,000 years old.' But Ascherson went on:

The injustice done to South African scholars has limits. Living in that country is still a matter of choice for a white scientist or professor, which is not the case of – for example – the Soviet Union. It is a choice with a price. From now on, a part of that price will be increasing exclusion from the world's academic communities ... There is no need piously to condemn those who choose to stay and work in that country, but neither is there any need to feel especially sorry for them.[16]

Dr O'Brien took issue. The 'disinvitation' to white South Africans was an odious and pointless form of apartheid by address rather than colour. 'A kind of intellectual mob' was trying to enforce the 'unjust and vindictive punishment of private individuals who neither serve the apartheid regime nor have the power to change it,' Dr O'Brien said.[17]

Ascherson conceded that the personal unfairness to South Africans who opposed apartheid was obvious. He asserted, however, that this was not the only consideration:

But there is a wider issue. Those who want a boycott are saying that they will not accept at international gatherings delegations, official or semi-official, representing areas of South African life which are connected with government or in some sense form part of the apartheid system. South African official research and education, denying knowledge and enlightenment to the majority of the population, are plainly such an area. That is not altered by the fact that within the system are large numbers of academics and students fighting to change and extend it. This does not mean that individuals ... should be prevented from meeting their colleagues in Europe or elsewhere. That would be idiotic as well as impossible ...

... The position of white liberals working within South Africa doesn't lack for irony. They know that pain and irony with more sophistication than we do. In politics it can be a matter of 'if you're not part of the solution, you're part of the problem'. Mrs Helen Suzman, founder of the Progressives, recently moved into the 'problem' zone when she opposed economic sanctions, while her colleagues Frederik van Zyl Slabbert and Alex Boraine left parliamentary politics to find a way into the solution.

With scientists and academics, that is too facile. But if they choose to stay and fight, in their own jobs and in their own country, there is a price to pay. This is not only the risk of dismissal or arrest. It is also that those abroad who want their struggle to succeed are laying on them an extra burden: that they cannot be invited to international meetings of their profession. That hurts, but it seems to me to be a hurt that goes with the job – like the hurt of ostracism for those who worked for a German occupation regime by day to conceal their work for the Resistance by night. It should not be understood as a real rejection. A South African exile I know commented: 'The onus should be on them. They should say to themselves: I won't go to this or that meeting, for it would mean representing South Africa.'

Ascherson concluded:

I believe . . . that the West will eventually be drawn into military intervention as South Africa's death struggles tear the continent apart. Sanctions, seen in that light, are an exercise. They are training the world to act towards South Africa in a coordinated way, getting the international community used to joint decisions and action. The crisis is coming, and if we have not learnt our drills for it in advance, God help us all.[18]

If the arguments for and against the academic boycott have been complex, then so too are those about the cultural boycott. This seeks to keep out of the country books, plays, films, music and any other entertainment. The reasoning is that this is a way to show solidarity – perhaps at a personal cost to the author, playwright, actor or musician – with the oppressed of South Africa. The ANC supports the cultural boycott on these grounds; others oppose it because, in the words of South African author Nadine Gordimer, 'a total boycott is unproductive in the struggle for liberation here'.[1]

The cultural boycott is even less quantifiable in its end results than economic sanctions and disinvestment. Proponents and opponents are reduced to having to speculate on the psychological effects on both black and white South Africans. A South African exile has said that the cultural boycott 'hammers down the self-perception of the boycotted . . . their image of themselves; their confidence in its cause; their sense of acceptability in the world'.[2] On the other hand the exiled South African writer Lewis Nkosi, now Professor of Literature at the University of Zambia, has said that the cultural boycott cannot attempt, like sanctions and disinvestment, to cripple the economy and so exert pressure on the regime to change: 'It is difficult to see how a state as powerful as South Africa can be brought down by a rhyming couplet.'[3] But Professor Nkosi goes on:

Music, especially popular music, is [an] area in which boycotts have hurt, if only because they create among white South Africans powerful feelings of resentment at their isolation; and hopefully some of this resentment may be directed at the regime itself or its hateful policy of apartheid . . . It is easy to see why Frank Sinatra or Stevie Wonder should not go to sing in South Africa. Apart from their skill with song, they actually take their *bodies* there. By so doing, they lend their immense prestige and glamour to the propaganda of those who wish to create an impression of a 'sunny South Africa'.[4]

The UN Centre against Apartheid, which monitors and blacklists entertainers who have performed in South Africa, claimed in early

1986 that there has been a 'significant decline' in performers going to South Africa and a consequent advance in efforts to impose the cultural boycott. New additions to the blacklist were almost matched by deletions made in return for pledges not to perform in South Africa again. In 1985 its blacklist contained nearly 500 names with 54 new additions and 51 deletions. Those on the list included James Fox, Anthony Newley, Frank Sinatra and Ray Charles. Deletions included Elton John, Cliff Richard, Barry Manilow, Julio Iglesias and Tina Turner.[5]

The arguments for and against serious plays are rather more complex. Nadine Gordimer has said that if writers have a conscience about their works being performed in South Africa, royalties could be donated to organizations fostering black theatre talent. Further, playwrights should insist on several conditions to their works being seen, approving performances 'only in theatres or other venues where all races may perform and attend, except in the case of segregated black or Coloured areas where laws other than those pertaining directly to the theatre or other venue prevent whites from attending along with blacks'. For example, plays should not be performed at all in small towns where open venues are not available. Ms Gordimer summed up her position: 'These are not half-way measures; they are principled but pragmatic means of ensuring that whatever may open people's minds may reach them – but that the white expense-account audience will not be the only one to enjoy this privilege.'[6]

The counter-argument is that the government knows that 'a satire running in a small theatre is not going to be seen by significant numbers of South Africans who count politically in terms of grassroots support for apartheid ... Yet it is this controlling minority of whites that is hardest hit psychologically by boycott, because boycotts make it impossible to pretend that what they are doing does not bother people elsewhere in the world.'[7] Against this, the newspaper *Business Day* editorialized in March 1986 that the cultural boycott 'combined with our xenophobic isolation over the past 40 or so years has made a material contribution to exacerbating the country's problems. South Africans at every level are inadequately aware of the concerns of ordinary people in other parts of the world ... Overseas the very people who should be at the forefront of opening wider our windows on the world have been doing the opposite.'[8]

One of the organizations blamed for this state of affairs by *Business Day* was Equity, the British actors' union. In April 1986 it held a referendum among its 32,000 members which resulted in a majority, among the 10 per cent who voted, forbidding members to work in South Africa.[9] The issue was taken to the High Court in July by a former Equity president, and the judge ruled that the union had exceeded its powers. One of those who gave evidence was Janet Suzman. Before the court case she had said that no trade union had the right to dictate the conscience of its members: 'I absolutely abhor apartheid, but I also detest political censure.' The judge said that Ms Suzman, a founder of the non-racial and anti-apartheid Market Theatre in Johannesburg, was the clearest example of an Equity member who would be adversely affected by a ban: she would not have been allowed to perform at the theatre's tenth anniversary celebrations.[10]

Another area of controversy in the cultural boycott is books. The Anti-Apartheid Movement says that while they support books being sent on demand, they draw a line when it comes to publishers making a commercial venture out of South Africa.[11] Publishers are coy about sales and profits from South Africa, but claim that they sell books there at least partly because 'freedom of information is essential'.[12]

Professor Nkosi asks: what kind of collaboration can books be supposed to enter in with Botha? 'Once produced they can travel anywhere in the world without their authors forming part of the infrastructure of their distribution or consumption . . . Book distributors cannot be said to control the interpretation of novels. Certainly it would be odd to withdraw *The Communist Manifesto* from the black townships under the illusion that one were thus harming the government . . .'[13]

The whole issue was encapsulated in November 1986 when there were plans to publish *Maus*, a book on the Holocaust by Art Spiegelman. Publishers André Deutsch and Penguin planned to sell the book in South Africa, but Mr Spiegelman deleted this clause in his contract, saying that *Maus* was 'an object lesson in the consequences of any compromise with fascism'. André Deutsch asked him to reconsider: 'It is morally wrong for publishers, who must fight censorship in all its forms, to ban their own books from South Africa . . . particularly when these books, such as your own, are themselves such powerful and convincing arguments against racism.' Such action would deprive liberals, particularly Jewish South Africans, of 'material they want and need'. Further, 'one is preventing cogent and rational argument against racist views from reaching the Afrikaners who might actually see the book and read it and might conceivably learn some-thing from it'. Mr Spiegelman replied, however, that he had to respect the ANC's request for a total cultural boycott. He also felt that the British book trade was more concerned about business than morals: more than £20 million worth of books were said to have been sold in South Africa in 1985.

It was the ANC that eventually broke the deadlock, reinforcing the view that there should not be hard-and-fast rules about books. They told Mr Spiegelman that they did see the significance of *Maus* and its relationship to their battle with racist oppression. The ANC was said to be arranging for a publisher inside South Africa to publish it there; all profits would go to the ANC. 'My book's message,' Mr Spiegelman then said, 'might be heard in South Africa without moral misgivings on my part.'[14]

14 Sport

The one undoubted success of sanctions and boycotts against South Africa has been in sport. Apartheid in this field, the government claims, has been eliminated, and there are complaints from Pretoria and a number of sportspeople that the country has not been allowed back into international competition. There has even been a warning by senior Cabinet minister Gerrit Viljoen that if boycotts are continued there could be a backlash against multi-racial sport.[1]

A different view of apartheid and sport is held by a number of people in the country, most prominently by the South African Council on Sport (SACOS). Its President, Frank van der Horst, said in late 1984: 'We believe that international sport with South Africa can take place only if there is a non-racial society with non-racial sport.'[2] This is expressed also in the slogan: 'No normal sport in an abnormal society.' A further point is that there can be no real equality on the sports field while facilities for different races are so unequal. In 1984 a University of Potchefstroom study found that between R7.13 and R19.71 a head was spent on whites for sport in the various provinces, while the figure for Indians throughout the country was R3.61 and for Africans R0.82.[3] The government's Human Sciences Research Council found that white schools had 72 per cent of all school sports facilities. Whites owned 73 per cent of all athletic tracks, 83 per cent of swimming pools and 82 per cent of rugby fields.[4]

Moves towards desegregating sport began in the 1970s as the international boycott began to bite. The campaign was of the government's own making: in 1961 the then Prime Minister, Hendrik Verwoerd, banned Maoris from inclusion in visiting New Zealand rugby teams, and in 1968 his successor, B. J. Vorster, said that Basil D'Oliveira, a Coloured former South African, could not play as a member of the MCC team due to tour South Africa.[5] A prominent sports administrator later said that a long-serving Minister of Sport, Dr Piet Koornhof, had admitted that the government had made 'a grave mistake' in refusing to accept D'Oliveira.[6]

At that stage most sport was strictly segregated by custom or legislation. Among other pieces of legislation, the Natives (Urban Areas) Act, the Group Areas Act and the Reservation of Separate Amenities Act forced sporting segregation. In 1956 government policy, as laid down by the Minister of the Interior, was that whites and blacks should organize their sporting activities separately with no interracial competition in the country. Black organizations seeking international recognition should do so through the aegis of white associations.

In 1963 and 1964, after much confrontation had arisen, the government restated its policy: participation in international competition by mixed teams representing South Africa could in no circumstances be approved. If whites took part, they must do so as representatives of the whites of the country, and blacks would represent the blacks. Black sporting associations should develop alongside the white bodies – parallel development was one phrase used officially to describe apartheid – with the white executive committees coordinating the work of both and representing both in international organizations. It was this policy that led to the withdrawal of South Africa's invitation to take part in the 1964 Olympic Games – the start of growing international boycotts of South African sport.[7]

Partly to meet the objections of the International Olympic Committee, in 1967 Mr Vorster adopted what was described as a more flexible approach. If South Africa competed in the Games, each racial group could select its own representatives for different events. White and black sporting administrators would then meet to decide on the composition of the team. Those finally selected would form one contingent, wear the same uniform, march under the one South African flag and be accommodated together – conditions necessary to comply with Olympic regulations.[8]

The IOC then sent a fact-finding team to South Africa, concluding that some progress had been made towards selection based on merit, rather than race. After a postal vote of its members, the IOC invited South Africa to send a team to the 1968 Games in Mexico City. A strong boycott campaign, mainly from African and Asian countries, developed, and after another ballot the invitation was cancelled.[9] The official South African Yearbook adds drily: 'In 1970 recognition of the South African [Olympic] association was withdrawn by the International Olympic Committee for political reasons.'[10]

In Britain during this period Peter Hain was organizing the 'Stop the 70 Tour' campaign against a South African rugby tour, which focused much attention on the whole issue of sporting apartheid and sports links between South Africa and the outside world. At that stage, in the words of Progressive Federal Party MP Colin Eglin to the House of Commons Foreign Affairs Committee, 'it was a specific boycott with a clear objective and in a sense there was a reward available if the objective had been met. It was: sportsmen, put your house in order and you can be readmitted to the world of sport.'[11]

It was Dr Koornhof who began the gradual moves to desegregate sport, amid much confusion, talk of 'multi-national' as opposed to multi- or non-racial sport, threats against South African sportspeople who went further and faster than the government wanted at the time, and legislative confusion. It was during this period that the government's sports policy was described by Dr Slabbert as 'a centipede out of step with itself', and that one Cabinet minister, displaying a rare public flash of humour, confessed that he did not know what the sports policy was because 'I haven't talked to Dr Koornhof today'.

Despite the changes, South Africa was not welcomed back into international competition: the New Zealand rugby authorities, for example, under strong government pressure called off a tour by a South African rugby team planned for 1973.

From about 1971 to 1975, whites and blacks were allowed to compete against one another in 'open international' events – if two or more other countries were also competing – in all Olympic sports including soccer, and in tennis and golf. A tour by an overseas side was regarded as an 'international' but not an 'open international'. Multi-racial teams from countries which had 'traditional' sporting links could play against different races – but at separate matches at segregated venues: whites were not to be given permits to watch teams play against blacks, and vice versa. Multi-racial sport at club, provincial or national level was not permitted inside the country. South Africa would not send multi-racial teams abroad except for the Olympic Games, the Canada Cup golf competition and the Federation Cup and Davis Cup tennis competitions – if invitations were extended. There were to be no mixed trials for such teams, which would be regarded as South African: Springbok colours (national colours for sport) were still reserved exclusively for whites. In 1974 this policy was slightly relaxed: sporting bodies under international suspension could stage 'multi-national' events even if overseas teams were not competing.[12]

During this period international boycotts continued. During 1976 South Africa was suspended from the International Amateur Athletics Association, the International Football Federation and the International Softball Federation, and South Africans were prevented from taking part in the World Yachting Championships, the World Squash Championships and a polo tour of New Zealand.

In 1976 yet another 'new' sports policy was announced. Different races should belong to different clubs; inter-group competition would be allowed at all levels should the controlling bodies so decide, sometimes 'in consultation with the Minister'; each racial group should arrange its own sporting relations with other countries or sporting bodies and each should award its own badges and colours; and 'teams comprising members from all racial groups can represent South Africa and can be awarded colours which, if so desired, can incorporate the national flag or its colours'. Later in 1976 the Minister said that all South African teams taking part in international events would be selected on merit through racially mixed trials. All selected could play in Springbok colours or under the national flag.[13]

Still boycotts continued. During the Commonwealth Conference in June 1977 the Gleneagles Agreement was signed, denouncing all sporting ties with South Africa, and resolving to withhold funds from sport exchanges with South Africa, to apply sanctions to bodies defying this policy, to vote for the expulsion of racialist bodies from international sport federations and to refuse to host events in which South Africa participated. The same year South Africans were stopped from participating in, among others, the Women's World Bowls Championships, a women's international golf tournament in Colombia, the World Archery Championships in Australia, the World Motor Cycle Championships in Yugoslavia, the World Pentathlon Championships in the USA and the Davis Cup competition in Colombia.

In 1977, as this was going on, the four provincial National Party congresses agreed that, although racially mixed membership of sports clubs was not government policy, legislation to ban this should not be introduced. (In 1968 the government had said that even sport at club level between Africans on the one hand and Coloureds and Indians on the other should not be encouraged and would not be allowed in white areas.) A few months later the government said that, although it considered they should be segregated, clubs could decide who should and should not be allowed to join – but if abuses occurred legal curbs might be introduced. The following year, 1978, national or provincial sporting bodies could obtain annual permits for people of all races to attend sporting fixtures, if the owners of the stadium (usually local authorities) did not object. This was called 'inter-club status'. Later that year it was announced that clubs with 'inter-club status' could decide for themselves about inviting or accepting invitations from other race groups without applying for permits.[14]

Despite these developments there were few signs that the international campaign was letting up. One problem was that although there was more multi-racial sport, back in the clubhouses legal complications still existed. Permits were still needed to admit black club members to clubhouses situated in white areas. If clubs had liquor licences (and most white clubs did – often their main attraction), they could not serve refreshments, meals or alcohol to blacks unless in a segregated part of the premises. Nor could they admit blacks as guests.

In 1975 a new device had been found to get around classical apartheid in hotels: they could apply for 'international' status to serve and accommodate black guests. But there could not be any mixed dancing; swimming pools were restricted to bona fide guests, and 'men only' bars (of which there were many, both in hotels and sporting clubs) had to remain reserved for the population group that had previously been admitted.

It was not until 1978, with still little indication that this relaxation of pure apartheid was leading to any let-up in sporting boycotts, that it was realized that sports clubs too could apply for 'international' status. They would then be able to host visiting black players, officials and guests signed in by club members. Refreshments and alcohol could be offered. By the end of 1979, a total of 59 clubs had been granted 'international' status and nine had been refused.[15] But, as with hotels, there was to be no mixed dancing or swimming and access to bars might be restricted. There was a further complication: a legislative anomaly meant that under the Groups Areas Act blacks accepted as members of sports clubs – rather than as guests – were not entitled to refreshments, meals or alcohol.[16] In October 1979 the government announced that all sports activities were being dissociated from the Group Areas Act.[17]

As these legal complications were being sorted out, the campaign against South Africa carried on: during 1978 Canada said it would not issue visas to South Africans coming to attend sporting events; Fiji refused visas to golfers wanting to play in the World Amateur Championships; the Rhodesian National Football Association cancelled a tour of South Africa; and the exiled South African Non-Racial Olympic Committee announced it would campaign to isolate individual South African sportspeople.

The government then appointed, in 1978, an inquiry into sport to be carried out by the Human Sciences Research Council. It reported in 1980, recommending 'freedom of association and choice in sport' – the right for all to take part in, administer and watch the sport of their choice. There should be equality of opportunities regardless of race; sport should be 'de-politicized' as far as possible and various 'obnoxious' and 'humiliating' laws should be amended; the final decision on open school sport should be left to local bodies; and there should be equal financing of sports facilities.[18]

Yet the country's sporting isolation continued. The Commonwealth Games Federation resolved to end all sports links with South Africa and to expel any country that maintained them – thus strengthening the Gleneagles Agreement. On the other hand, a rebel cricket tour by Britons went ahead: when they returned they were banned from Test cricket for three years. There have been a number of other rebel tours in several sports: some were greeted with acclaim by white South Africans, others failed. In the words of one South African exile: 'When South Africa has to bribe sportsmen to go there it is humiliating and disheartening as well as expensive, and the first flush of triumphant defiance at breaking the boycott soon gives way to the realization that a burdensome precedent has been set which does not lift the main curtain of disapproval.'

By 1983 the government was saying that there was no racial discrimination in South African sport. Dr Koornhof said sports clubs should decide for themselves how they wished to deal with sport, but this should be 'within the framework of overall policy'. The right-wing Conservative Party claimed that by passing a law exempting whites from having to apply for permits to participate in sport in African areas, the National Party had become 'the instrument for gradually increasing integration in every sphere of life'.[19] Later that year Dr Viljoen told international rugby journalists on a special tour of South Africa to see the extent of desegregated sport that the government was not moving towards total integration in school sport. It was providing procedures whereby increased contact could take place.[20]

The government's official position is now that 'any sportsman or sportswoman in South Africa, irrespective of population group, may play for the same club or provincial or national team. The traditional Springbok colours, awarded to a representative national team, may be awarded to all team members. No permit or other legal permission is needed by any player to play on any sportsfield in South Africa or to join any club.' The Group Areas Act has been amended to abolish clauses concerning sport, the Black (Urban Areas) Consolidation Act amended to allow whites access to African townships (with some reserve powers to prohibit individuals), and the Liquor Act changed to allow clubs to decide for themselves whom they wish to serve.[21]

All these changes were made under international pressure. Had there not been this pressure it is doubtful whether the changes, which in terms of classical apartheid are major ones, would have been made at this rate. It belies the statement made by the former South African Ambassador to Britain, Dr Denis Worrall, that 'the anti-South African campaign [which] has been one of the best financed, orchestrated international campaigns of the second half of the century . . . has produced very little . . . The reason it has failed so dismally is that it does not appeal to, or take into account, the self-interest of the white South African.'[22] More accurate is the comment of the British Labour Party's foreign affairs expert, Denis Healey: 'The moves which are taking place – and some are not wholly cosmetic – have been in response to external pressure. The sports boycott has led to a great improvement in interracial sports in South Africa [which] would never have come about without it.'[23]

15 The British Debate: Those in Favour

Britain's ties with South Africa go back a long way. It, more than any other Western country, has the largest historical responsibility for a political system that allowed the policy of apartheid to develop. British involvement in the sub-continent began in 1795 when it occupied the Cape – then run by the Dutch – as part of a war against the French. This occupation lasted only eight years: the Cape was returned to the Dutch. Three years later, in 1806, the British invaded for a second time, again for mainly strategic reasons during the build-up to the Napoleonic wars. In 1814–15 they took formal possession.[1] Britain was to remain in South Africa as the colonial power, extending its responsibility over the entire country, until 1910 when the Union of South Africa was formed. In the eyes of some Afrikaners, South Africa only became 'free' much later: in 1926 when the Balfour Declaration said Britain and the Dominions were 'autonomous communities within the British Empire, equal in status', or, in the extreme view, in 1961 when Dr Verwoerd took South Africa out of the Commonwealth and it became a republic. From another point of view, Britain bears the responsibility for agreeing to the formation of the Union while refusing to insist that blacks be given equal status with whites.

Britain, apart from its historical political role as the former colonizing power, has an economic responsibility. According to figures given by the British Industry Committee on South Africa to the House of Commons Foreign Affairs Committee in July 1986, it has investments in South Africa worth £6,000 million – 40 to 45 per cent of all foreign investment there. This is 7 per cent of all British overseas investment. South Africa has investments worth £700 million in Britain, about 1.9 per cent of all foreign investments in Britain. Visible British exports to South Africa are worth about £1,010 million a year; in return visible South African exports to Britain are about £990 million a year.[2]

There are also cultural and family ties: about one third of the white population came originally from Britain. One of the two official languages is English. South Africa's parliamentary system, until abruptly changed by P. W. Botha, was based on the Westminster model. Much of its culture is of British origin.

These historical, political and economic ties have helped to ensure that South African issues are on Britain's political agenda – increasingly so as the pressure for sanctions and disinvestment has built up. The debate has been – and will be – fierce. What raises the temperature is that the British government (and particularly Mrs Thatcher) remains opposed to comprehensive mandatory sanctions against Pretoria. So, too, does most of British commerce and industry. Yet with the decision in November 1986 by Barclays Bank to sell its remaining shares in Barclays South Africa, it appears that withdrawal will take place regardless.

The political pressure for sanctions has been led by the Labour Party. Historically, this party has had a far closer affinity than the Conservative Party with black African – not only South African – leaders, although it was under Conservative government that many of Britain's African colonies gained independence. Labour's involvement in economic campaigns against apartheid goes back to at least 1960, when it, the Liberal Party and the Trade Union Congress (TUC) supported a boycott for the month of March. The left-wing *Tribune* journal, closely identified with the Tribune Group of Labour MPs, published a list of 40 products for shoppers to avoid, and similar lists were distributed among trade unionists and the public.[3]

Labour's record in office has, however, been criticized. In 1966 the British delegate to the UN, Lord Caradon, said that there were 'limitations' to what Britain could and could not do in regard to mandatory sanctions against South Africa.[4] In 1967 the then Foreign Secretary, George Brown, told the UN that Britain could not and would not contemplate an economic war with South Africa.[5] Later Labour governments also declined to press for mandatory sanctions, although the then Prime Minister, James Callaghan, indicated in 1979 that a number of 'hard decisions' would shortly have to be made about South Africa.

By 1986 the Labour Party was firmly committed to sanctions. Its front-bench spokesman on foreign affairs, Donald Anderson, said in May 1986 that the party was pledged 'to isolate South Africa internationally and promote effective action to hasten fundamental political change'. A Labour government would make the embargo on arms and military material complete and would 'support the enforcement of UN economic sanctions'. Pretoria would not be able to rely on a British government acting as a brake on pressure within the EEC and the Commonwealth. Britain would be in the vanguard working for sanctions.[6] In July the Labour leader, Neil Kinnock, re-emphasized this when he committed the next Labour government to leading the world by example towards imposing comprehensive economic sanctions. He said that as a minimum first step his government would enforce a total ban on imports of coal, iron, steel and uranium.[7]

During the Party's annual conference in October 1986, a motion calling for sanctions was carried unanimously. But a resolution demanding that a Labour government should provide arms and other material support to liberation movements was rejected.[8] Denis Healey, the Shadow Foreign Secretary, told the conference that there would be black majority government in South Africa within 15 years. 'But that will come about only after the most fearful bloodshed unless the struggle inside South Africa is supported by economic sanctions from outside.' Blacks in South Africa knew that sanctions would hurt them in the short term:

But they know too it is the only way of shortening the agony which is bound to grow worse until apartheid is overthrown . . . In the Labour Party we choose the side of freedom and democracy because it is in our own long-term interests, because we are ashamed to live in a Britain that is fast becoming known as a friend of racism and tyranny, but most of all because it is right. This is perhaps the last chance to show that Britain can be the friend of freedom.[9]

Mr Healey touched on one of the arguments about sanctions – that Britain would be on the wrong side – both in his conference speech and in his evidence three months earlier, in July 1986, to the House of Commons Foreign Affairs Committee. 'The unanimous view of my informants in South Africa, black and white, was that President Botha's current posture of defiance of the outside world and his statement that South Africa can "go it alone" is based on his conviction that in any case he would be protected from sanctions by President Reagan, Mrs Thatcher and Chancellor Kohl,' he told the committee. '. . . President Botha was right when he said . . . that the British government's position on sanctions is determined entirely by British commercial interests in South Africa.'[10] In his conference speech, Mr Healey remarked that the US Senate would vote in a few hours to override

President Reagan's veto of the sanctions Bill. That would leave only Britain and West Germany opposed to sanctions: 'In a year from now those governments will be in the dustbin of history.'[11]

Mr Healey told the Foreign Affairs Committee that another reason for sanctions was that 'South Africa is now a threat to peace and stability throughout Southern Africa. It has adopted a deliberate policy of destabilizing the independent black regimes which surround it.' If sanctions were imposed, 'you have an obligation to help the Frontline states to develop northern routes for their imports and exports, through Dar, and, of course, the eastern route through Beira'.[12]

Answering further questions, he said: 'I myself went to South Africa (in mid-1986) . . . believing there was something to be said for a gradual escalation of sanctions. But everyone I talked to there took a different view . . . they all thought you would have to have something very severe and sharp to begin with to have any chance of affecting the political situation . . . If one wanted something to happen fast, the best thing to do would be to cut South Africa's export earnings, to go for gold, diamonds and metals.'[13] Later he expanded on this: 'If the countries with large gold stocks used them to depress the gold price, it would have a massive impact on the South African economy . . .'[14] On the question of whether mandatory international sanctions would persuade Pretoria to change its policies, he said, 'I think they are more likely to than a few marginal measures.' Mr Healey was then asked how such sanctions could be enforced:

They would require unanimity in the Security Council . . . The most effective way of enforcing it would be a naval blockade . . . *Jane's Fighting Ships* said it would require about 30 frigates . . . If you wanted to operate a blockade and you had international support, as you would have through the Security Council, you would be able to assemble a force which would be able to blockade all the major ports, and the sort of things which could break the blockade, small ships sailing into small ports or dropping cargo on beaches, would be negligible . . . We needed five frigates for the Beira patrol [attempting to stop oil imports reaching Rhodesia during UDI] . . . This is something to be considered. I would not commit myself to it as an objective.

Secondly, there is satellite photography: ships coming in would be spotted. This is the technical side of operating mandatory sanctions. It would not be easy. South Africa has a large coastline, but it is possible. My own view is that the threat of action of this nature would produce changes, but without such a threat no changes will take place.[15]

British action against apartheid has also been led by the Trades Union Congress and local authorities, usually Labour-controlled ones. In 1959 Chief Albert Luthuli, then President of the ANC, called for a boycott of South Africa. About 20 local authorities responded, and about 10 imposed a permanent boycott. In 1981 a Sheffield City Council initiative led to the coordination of policy on purchasing and investment, library services, education and the like.[16]

The TUC role has included calling on Britain's leading 50 retailers to remove South African goods from their shelves: by December 1985 at least nine had agreed.[17] It has also warned that there is 'growing commercial logic' to back up the 'moral case' against economic links with South Africa. The TUC General Secretary, Norman Willis, launching a report on investment in South Africa, said that 'in the short term it makes no investment sense to tie up assets in an unstable economy that is running down fast. In the longer term, our economic interests will be gravely jeopardized by British companies having been identified with hostile British policies when a change in control comes'[18] – echoing points made by Mr Healey and warnings by the ANC that it will remember its friends on taking power.

Britain's Social Democratic Party, which has an electoral alliance with the Liberal Party, summarized its position in July 1986:

The SDP believes that sanctions would call the bluff of right-wing Afrikaners who have hitherto derided the threat. They would, secondly, have the effect of raising the morale of the oppressed while lowering the morale of the oppressor. And thirdly, effective sanctions would represent an unmistakable declaration to Pretoria that it must pursue real reform urgently. We believe that the pressure of sanctions could tilt the balance of argument within the white community and impel the government towards direct negotiations with black leaders.[19]

Among other sanctions the SDP called for were an EEC ban on South African coal, wine, fruit, vegetables and wool. Direct air links should be stopped so that people wanting to travel to and from South Africa would have to do so via neighbouring African capitals: 'This would impress upon white South Africans their isolation from the outside world. It would also, for the first time, tilt the balance of power away from Pretoria to the Frontline states and increase their security from South African aggression.' In addition the oil embargo should be tightened; vehicles made in Britain should not be sold to the South African government; export credit guarantees for British exports to South Africa should be stopped; there should be no new loans or credit or rolling over of existing credits; the EEC code of conduct should be tightened, all branches of South African banks in Britain and the EEC closed, and visas introduced for South African passport-holders; there should be a re-orientation of the British Embassy in South Africa towards establishing links with black leaders; and these measures should be sponsored by Britain in the UN with the aim of making them mandatory.[20]

The Church of England and the Roman Catholic Church in Britain have also supported boycotts. In July 1986 the Church of England Synod called on the government to impose 'effective economic sanctions' as, in the words of the Archbishop of Canterbury, Dr Robert Runcie, 'the only hope there is – however slender – of doing what we can in this country to stop the present bloodshed and prevent it becoming far greater'. Bishop Tutu sent a message saying that sanctions were the only way to stop a slide 'back to the dark ages'. Political negotiation had yielded nothing and there was no alternative. 'Please, please, stand by us,' Bishop Tutu concluded.[21]

His predecessor as Bishop of Johannesburg, the Right Reverend Timothy Bavin, now Bishop of Portsmouth, urged the Church to 'feel for the oppressor as well'. A Tory MP, Sir William van Straubenzee, recalled that apartheid was being carried out by Christians: 'We should bring these people to their knees in prayer, not in economic chaos.'[22] Two months later Dr Runcie, writing to Mrs Thatcher as President of the British Council of Churches, said the South African government's claim to be Christian was 'blasphemy against the gospel of God's equal care for all in creation and redemption'.[23]

The Catholic bishops of England and Wales recommended in May 1986 that the Church's adherents should not invest in South Africa and should boycott South African goods. Asking what foreign governments, business, public opinion, churches and other institutions could do 'to contribute to a path of change in South Africa involving the least possible violence', the bishops said that 'the overwhelming answer to this question given by black South Africans is: stop supporting apartheid'.[24]

The British opponents of sanctions are led by the Prime Minister, Mrs Thatcher. She has made the cause a personal crusade, in the teeth of strong pressure from the entire Commonwealth, a number of members of the EEC, virtually all members of the UN, and some members of the Conservative Party – including, to some extent, her two immediate predecessors.

Those two former leaders of the Conservative Party and Prime Ministers of Britain are Edward Heath and Lord Home. Their criticism, some of it muted, has been joined by an ex-Cabinet minister, Leon Brittan. Three Conservative MPs have formed a pressure group aimed at making Mrs Thatcher encourage Mr Botha to embark on reform. The somewhat clumsily named 'Conservatives for Fundamental Change in South Africa' believe that 'sadly our party tends to be regarded as being represented by those Conservative members who are most vocal on South African affairs, and who, by their words and deeds, give succour to the South African government and its apartheid policies'.[1] One of those, John Carlisle, termed the group 'instant experts [with] limited, scanty knowledge' and claimed that he was one of those 'who are desperately trying to see the dismantling of apartheid'.[2]

More heavyweight opposition to Mrs Thatcher's policies on South Africa has come from Mr Heath, Lord Home and Mr Brittan. Mr Heath, whose antipathy to Mrs Thatcher is well known and is returned in measure by Mrs Thatcher, said in July 1986 that he favoured taking action affecting South African trade, culminating, if necessary, in a blockade. He was careful not to criticize Mrs Thatcher or her Foreign Secretary, Sir Geoffrey Howe, who was on a mission to South Africa on behalf of the EEC at the time. But he said Britain was already imposing sanctions against South Africa. The key question was not whether there should be sanctions 'but how far should they go. If we are going further, then we have to take action which affects trade – I don't think there is any doubt about that at all. If one is going to follow this through to its logical conclusion then it does involve trade blockage; it does involve making arrangements for supplying the Frontline states; it does mean saying to South Africa: "If you are going to attack the Frontline states, if they want us to help, we are prepared to help."' He said that South Africans should be made aware that Britain was not prepared to support them in 'the extreme policies they are now pursuing'.[3]

Both Mr Heath and Lord Home – and opposition politicians like Mr Healey – regarded Mrs Thatcher's policies as threatening the Commonwealth. In a letter to *The Times* in August 1986, after the Commonwealth mini-summit, Lord Home subtly criticized Mrs Thatcher and some Commonwealth leaders: 'Voluntary sanctions as a means to achieve a political aim are at best peripheral and as full of holes as a sieve. Effective sanctions would need to be universal, mandatory and, in the case of South Africa, enforced by a naval blockade.'[4]

That coded criticism appeared to refer to Mrs Thatcher's opposition to mandatory sanctions and her acceptance, under pressure, of some selective sanctions. But Lord Home also criticized other countries:

All Commonwealth leaders should ponder deeply as to whether they really wish to turn the Commonwealth Secretariat into an executive instrument dealing in the political issues concerning its members ... Surely the role of the Commonwealth is to meet, to learn and then to act individually as each government thinks best, and not to try to lobby and pressurize one member or another to take action against its judgement. That was the concept of the Statute of Westminster and we would be wise to stick to it.[5]

Mr Brittan was less guarded when he spoke, also in July 1986. He said that Mrs Thatcher's refusal to countenance the sanctions weapon was closing the main option for forcing the South African government to compromise: 'Weapons need not always be used to be effective, but if their preferable deterrent effect is to be achieved, it must be clearly understood that the will and readiness to use them exists. So it is with sanctions. The world must know of our readiness to have recourse to stronger measures in the event of the failure of Sir Geoffrey's mission.'[6]

Sir Geoffrey's mission did fail. But Mrs Thatcher's views have changed only marginally. These views were expressed at length, and with passion, in an interview given to a political writer for the

Guardian, Hugo Young, in July 1986 – before the Commonwealth mini-summit, Sir Geoffrey's final failure in South Africa and the EEC meeting.

Mrs Thatcher had gone to South Africa when she was Secretary of State for Education and Science, before taking over as Conservative Party leader in 1975. She claimed to have seen both sides of South Africa: 'I've seen it on occasions when there's no apartheid, and I've seen it when there is apartheid.'[7] Her views on the subject were firm: 'I don't like apartheid. It's wrong. Let me make that clear. Apartheid is wrong. It has to go, and it's going.'

The Prime Minister believed in contact, dialogue and persuasion to speed apartheid on its way. She had received President Botha at Chequers, the Prime Minister's country residence, in 1985 and told him that forced removals of black communities were 'totally and utterly and particularly repugnant to us'. That meeting and subsequent correspondence had been fruitful, she said. 'Those things have been stopped now. Things are coming in the right direction. Naturally one wishes them to come faster.'

Sanctions would not work: 'South Africa has colossal internal resources. A colossal coastline. And whatever sanctions were put on, materials would get in and get out. There's no way you can blockade the whole South African coastline. No way.'

Was there no economic pressure that would have any effect? The banks which had pressed for the repayment of South Africa's debt had had some effect, Mrs Thatcher said. But the main influence was from people inside fighting apartheid – industry and some of the political parties.

Could and should governments add to that pressure? 'You're talking about economic pressure. I'm talking about how to bring about negotiations.' South Africa should never have been isolated. 'I think we should have had more contact. We would have influenced her more. She would have been able to see that multi-racial societies do work in other countries. They do, of course, have certain problems. We've seen the problems in Kenya and Uganda. But South Africa would have been much more influenced to come our way.' Even moderate blacks and whites, she felt, would react badly if they saw the West just hitting out at their country.

Was there no form of hostile pressure which was appropriate? 'There is no case in history that I know of where punitive, general economic sanctions have been effective to bring about internal change. That is what I believe. That is what the Labour Party in power believed. That is what most of Europe believes. That is what most Western industrialized countries believe. If that is what they believe, there is no point in trying to follow that route.'

Mrs Thatcher then attacked the morality of sanctions:

I must tell you I find nothing moral about people who come to me, worried about unemployment in this country, or about people who come to us to say we must do more to help Africa – particularly black Africans. I find nothing moral about them, sitting in comfortable circumstances, with good salaries, inflation-proof pensions, good jobs, saying that we, as a matter of morality, will put x hundred thousand black people out of work, knowing that this could lead to starvation, poverty and unemployment and even greater violence . . .

. . . That to me is immoral. I find it repugnant. We had it at the [European] Community meeting. Nice conference centre. Nice hotels. Good jobs. And you really tell me you'll move people around as if they're pawns on a chequerboard and say that's moral. To me it's immoral.

So how did she read the motives of black leaders like Bishop Tutu and many others who favoured sanctions? 'I don't have to read them. I can tell you there are many, many people in South Africa, black South Africans, who hope to goodness that economic sanctions will not be put on . . . You've heard Chief Buthelezi say it. He said it in this room [representing] seven million Zulus. He said it on the doorsteps of Downing Street. I've heard it, too, from some . . . other people here in this room.'

But Bishop Tutu, Nelson Mandela, the ANC and the UDF also represented a large segment of opinion which she rejected?

I totally reject it. Because I find it very difficult to know how they can turn around and say: 'Put our people into acute difficulty. They've got good jobs. They're looking after their children. But pursue a policy which can lead to children being hungry.' I find it very difficult indeed.

I sometimes get the map out and say look at it. Have you looked at how goods are going to get in and out of Zambia and Zimbabwe? Close Beitbridge and how are you going to do it? That's the maize route. When there was drought, that's the route through which maize went to keep people alive. I ask them: Have you looked at it? Have you looked at the poverty and hunger and starvation – just when we're after all trying to give things to Africa, to see she doesn't suffer in this way. I find it astonishing, utterly astonishing, that on the one hand we're doing everything to help Ethiopia, everything to relieve poverty and starvation, everything to get the right seeds, the right husbandry. And at the same time we're suggesting that you turn people who are in work out of work. And add to the problems you've already got. When people call that moral, I just gasp.

Then there was the question of the West's interest in certain raw materials:

Platinum comes in quantity from only two places, South Africa and the Soviet Union. Are people who say there's a moral question suggesting that the world supply of platinum should be put in charge of the Soviet Union? And there are other things. Your chemical chrome, your vanadium, and of course gold and diamonds. They would have a fantastic effect on the economy of the Soviet Union. To me it is absolutely absurd that people should be prepared to put increasing power into the hands of the Soviet Union on the grounds that they disapprove of apartheid in South Africa.

There was a desire to mark disapproval of apartheid through what she called 'signs and gestures'. Britain had therefore agreed to the EEC sanctions package in 1985. But 'the Commonwealth wanted more. And we did Krugerrands. And we put the extra gold coins in. And we've done no promotion of tourism. And various other things. But I don't know anyone in power in the Western world who calls for punitive sanctions.'

But were they not suggesting bigger gestures? 'All right. Suppose you start with fruit and vegetables. That would be 95,000 people, blacks and their families, out of work. Moral? Poof. Moral? No social security. Moral? Up would go the prices here. Some of it would be sold out of the coastline, through third countries, re-marked, and perhaps come in at a higher price. And the retaliation we could have to things we export to South Africa. What is moral about that?'

Did she object to the gestures designed to inconvenience South Africa in a minor way? 'We've gone along with the gestures and signals because I recognize that people want to do something more than words.' But she didn't really believe in them? 'I don't believe that punitive economic sanctions will bring about internal changes.' But she was not even keen on the gestures? 'I don't think the gestures are very effective. We withdrew our military attaché from South Africa. That means we don't get as much information as we should otherwise. Often you argue against the big things, the really damaging things that would cause unemployment. So you accept much smaller things, as we did.'

Mrs Thatcher was contemptuous of opposition politicians 'who took the same view as we do when they were in power, and voted in the United Nations the same way we did'. But had the situation not changed? Political upheaval had escalated hugely and the government was weaker. 'And apartheid has been reduced. There's practically no apartheid left in sport.' Due to a boycott? 'Well. Due to a boycott. Due partly to a boycott. Not economic sanctions. A political thing.'

The prohibition against mixed marriages had also gone, she said. 'As a matter of fact, I think it's the thing that signals the end of apartheid.' The pass laws were also going, Mrs Thatcher added, as were enforced removals and job reservation. And the Group Areas Act was 'starting to go'.

There were now 'many black people with professional qualifications and of considerable substance'. Their only problem was that they couldn't live where they wanted and couldn't take a proper part in government: 'Those are the things to which you've got to address your minds and your action. I think we've done quite well by persuasion, particularly in the last 18 months. But by non-economic ways. And we should go on that way.'

Mrs Thatcher's certitudes about sanctions have been echoed, sometimes in more sophisticated terms, by other ministers, particularly by Sir Geoffrey Howe as Foreign Secretary and by Baroness Young and Mrs Lynda Chalker, Ministers of State at the Foreign Office. All have been sent to a variety of capitals to repeat the British government's objections and the Foreign Office itself has issued a number of statements.

Sir Geoffrey said in June 1986 after EEC foreign ministers failed to agree on an immediate response to South Africa's State of Emergency that 'financial or economic trade boycotts have not been shown to work in the past. Our purpose must be to bring down apartheid and not the South African economy.'[8] At the end of July 1986, concluding another visit to South Africa, Sir Geoffrey warned that increasing sanctions by the Commonwealth, EEC and US, added to 'the self-inflicted economic costs imposed through the world market place on South Africa . . . is something that will make the solution of the problem more and not less difficult'.[9]

In September 1986 Sir Geoffrey told the UN General Assembly that the EEC members would 'keep up our effort . . . and do everything we can to promote urgent and peaceful change'.[10] The following month Sir Geoffrey had to reassure the Conservative Party Conference that the government was not being steam-rollered into sanctions. The party's right wing loudly applauded a delegate who attacked black African and other Commonwealth leaders pressing for sanctions: 'Some of the worst tin-pot dictators in recent history daring to lecture Mrs Thatcher on democracy and human rights ... If Britain's membership of the Commonwealth simply allows people to abuse our Foreign Secretary, is it a club we want to belong to any more?'[11]

Sir Geoffrey replied that the government would 'not be tutored by politicians from countries where democratic opposition is conspicuous only by its absence'. He condemned apartheid but said it was naive to think that a total trade ban would trigger the downfall of the Pretoria government: 'It would serve only to strengthen their resolve. It would cause millions of people to lose their jobs, blacks far more than whites.'[12]

Mrs Chalker had earlier defended the Commonwealth from attacks by right-wingers. Calling it 'a family of nations', she said in August 1986 that it, 'like any family, has its stresses and strains. But that family is one family. May it long remain.' This was the government's first response since the Commonwealth claimed after its mini-summit on South Africa that Mrs Thatcher was isolated and that Britain had lost the leadership of the Commonwealth. Mrs Thatcher had attracted wide attention before the mini-summit with a remark that was interpreted as a snub to the Commonwealth: 'If I were the odd one out and I were right, it wouldn't matter, would it?'[13]

Both Mrs Chalker and Baroness Young have emphasized the damage that sanctions would do to South Africa's neighbours. South African radio said in August 1986 that Baroness Young had given a 'warning' to Zambia and Zimbabwe that they could not expect any help in the event of South African retaliation against sanctions. This had 'called their bluff', the radio said.[14] A few days later Mrs Chalker said that Britain had to take into account the potential impact of sanctions on the neighbouring states when deciding on what measures to adopt: 'We must avoid a situation which would result in damaging economic warfare. That is why we are promoting the cause of dialogue.'[15]

Mrs Chalker was the first Conservative minister to meet the ANC when, in June 1986, she spoke to its President, Oliver Tambo, for 45 minutes. The meeting was a reversal of British government policy of no ministerial contact with the ANC until it renounced violence. The meeting was strongly criticized by right-wing Conservative MPs. Mr Tambo also broke new ground by addressing about 50 Conservative MPs who favour limited sanctions against South Africa.[16] A few days later Mr Healey met Mr Tambo in the British High Commissioner's residence in Lusaka, reflecting growing British acceptance of the ANC. Mr Tambo later met Sir Geoffrey himself, again to a chorus of disapproval from right-wing Conservatives.

Mrs Chalker's reflection of her government's position has caused anger in Africa. Zimbabwe's parliamentary Speaker, Didymus Mutasa, took the opportunity of a lunch in her honour in Harare in June 1986 to attack the West. Britain and the USA had earlier vetoed UN resolutions condemning South African raids against Zimbabwe, Zambia and Botswana – raids that finally signalled the end of the hope that the Commonwealth Eminent Persons Group would reach an agreement with Pretoria. The vetoes had been exercised because the resolutions called for mandatory sanctions. Mr Mutasa also expressed disappointment at British support of American air strikes against Libya: 'These activities of the West partly explain why the Eastern bloc looks like an angel in African eyes when compared to the evil machinations and acts of the West against African sovereignty and struggle for liberation ... Botha commits with impunity the worst crimes against humanity and continues to be a right-hand friend and ally of the West.' Mrs Chalker replied diplomatically that it showed the strength of British-Zimbabwe relations that the two could speak so frankly to each other. She said, 'We have told Botha in the strongest possible terms that the raids were indefensible.' She could not recall 'ever having spoken to a diplomat so stiffly' as in her reprimand to Pretoria's envoy. But 'what would mandatory sanctions do? I believe they would leave the Boers free to do what they want to the people of South Africa. There would be no further chance to intervene, to intercede or to negotiate. Sanctions close off an opportunity. With South African conduct bad now, what would it be like with all inhibitions, pressures and influences on them removed?'[17]

The Foreign Affairs Committee of the House of Commons was also worried about losing contact with Pretoria. In its report published at the end of July 1986 it recommended a 'carrot and stick' approach. There was an undoubted need for 'significant movement' from the South African government:

One approach which we have identified is to use the 'carrot' of positive measures and the prospect of substantial outside help in reversing South Africa's economic decline, in return for achieving real political progress. Another approach is to use the 'stick' of further negative measures on the South

African economy in an attempt to coerce the South African government.

We cannot be sure whether either will work. Things may have gone too far already. But we note the heavy international pressure on the UK to endorse the second, or negative, approach, even though its impact cannot be accurately forecast and may, in the view of some of our witnesses, be potentially counter-productive. Failing a positive and early response by the South African government to any alternative strategy, it is nevertheless likely that the industrialized countries, including the UK, will feel compelled to follow this course.[18]

The report was unanimous but gave no formal recommendations for the government to act.

The Foreign Office's views were set out in three papers: a memorandum to the Committee in December 1985, another in July 1986 and the government's formal response to the Committee's report in October 1986. All three, not surprisingly, opposed sanctions. The first memorandum used rather more formal language than the Committee's recommendation of a 'carrot and stick' approach: 'The government has for many years followed a policy of both restrictive and positive measures in regard to South Africa.' Restrictive measures included the following:

- The mandatory UN arms embargo of 1977.
- The Gleneagles agreement of 1977 discouraging sporting contact.
- The Luxemburg package of September 1985, which included measures already implemented by the government: not exporting or importing arms and para-military equipment, refusing military cooperation, not selling sensitive equipment to the police and armed forces, refusing to collaborate in South Africa's nuclear development, and refusing to sell oil.
- The government, with other members of the EEC, also agreed to discourage scientific or cultural events except where they contributed to ending apartheid or had no possible role in supporting it. It agreed to freeze contacts and agreements in sport and security, recalled its military attachés and refused accreditation to South African military attachés.
- The Commonwealth Heads of Government Accord in Nassau of October 1985 'drew on some aspects of the Luxemburg package' and included an additional ban on all new government loans to the South African government and its agencies, the ending of government funding for trade missions to South Africa and for

trade fairs in South Africa, and a ban on the direct import of Krugerrands. (A ban on all South African gold coins was introduced in May 1986.)

- At the Commonwealth mini-summit in London in August 1986, the government agreed to put voluntary bans on investment in South Africa and the promotion of tourism, and to accept any E E C decision to ban imported South African coal, iron and steel and gold coins.
- The Brussels meeting of the E E C in September 1986 agreed also to ban new investment in South Africa, imports of iron and steel – but not coal – and gold coins.[19]

In its memorandum of July 1986,[20] the Foreign Office argued against some of the measures included in Nassau. In effect the Foreign Office supported Mrs Thatcher's contention that sanctions are unworkable. A ban on air links 'would increase South Africa's isolation and further damage business confidence'; would cause losses to British Airways which 'could amount to several tens of millions of pounds'; and could lose British exports and tourism to Britain; if the ban was incomplete it would 'simply lead to the diversion of traffic' to other airlines still operating there.

A ban on new investment 'would in present circumstances have a limited effect on the South African economy', as 'little new investment is taking place'. A ban on reinvestment of profits earned in South Africa would be open to evasion and Pretoria might retaliate by banning the repatriation of profits.

A ban on importing agricultural products could make a 'significant' impact on the 1.25 million 'non-white' labourers, 'at least initially'. Perhaps significantly the Foreign Office did not back up the Prime Minister's contention (see p. 145) that a fruit and vegetable ban would mean '95,000 people, blacks and their families, out of work'. The Foreign Office added that South African losses could be reduced as trade patterns changed. It also said that policing the ban would be difficult, and that some seasonal shortages could be caused initially, though these, except for one particular type of maize, could be overcome, possibly at higher prices.

Termination of the double taxation agreement would allow South Africa to impose its higher tax rates on income allowed to go abroad: 'In the case of British companies in South Africa this would provide a net benefit to the South African exchequer.'

Termination of all government assistance to investment in, and trade with, South Africa through Overseas Trade Board services would damage the interests of small and medium-sized British exporters without being of much concern to Pretoria. A ban on new export credit 'if widely applied could have a significant impact on economic growth and development in South Africa'. It would be 'more costly than trading on credit and would leave less money for servicing of existing debt'. In addition 'large development projects would be difficult to fund with cash and might have to be cancelled'. As for British companies, many would not export without credit cover 'and important orders would be lost'.

A ban on all government procurement in South Africa was likely to be 'primarily symbolic'. But if Pretoria took retaliatory measures 'British companies could suffer the loss of some major contracts'.

Banning government contracts with majority-owned South African companies would be difficult because of the problem of identifying ownership: 'In view of the large number of U K companies with investments in South Africa, direct retaliation would be relatively easy . . .'

A ban on promoting tourism to South Africa could affect that country's $400 million earned in foreign exchange in 1985: 'In practice the present situation in South Africa would act as a more significant disincentive to tourism.' Some British tour companies could suffer and a proportion of Britain's £88 million earned from South African tourism in 1984 'could be at risk from any retaliation'.

The Foreign Office then moved to proposals agreed to in The Hague Communiqué. South Africa exported 3.5 million tonnes of raw steel in 1985, 10 per cent of which went to the E E C, including 2.4 per cent to Britain. If this was banned by the E E C, U S A and Japan, 'it would account for a substantial proportion of South Africa's total steel exports'. Roughly half the more than 70,000 workers in the industry were black, but the Foreign Office did not attempt to quantify job losses as a result of a ban. Evasion would be relatively easy for South Africa, 'albeit at a reduced profit'.

South Africa produced 170 million tons of coal in 1985, of which 25 per cent was exported. A ban would be 'a serious setback' for the industry and the large 'non-white' workforce of 95,000 'would bear the brunt of any cutbacks'. British imports were worth £40 million in 1985 and alternative sources could be found, 'albeit at a higher price'. In the event, however, although Mrs Thatcher had signalled that she would abide by any E E C ban on coal, the Community did not impose it; nor did Britain encourage the imposition of such a ban.

Even the severely limited sanctions introduced by the government have not, however, been fully applied. This was made clear in late 1986 in several reports, some highly critical of the government. In its July memorandum the Foreign Office had warned that Britain would face difficulties in policing and enforcing all but one of the measures proposed by the Commonwealth and the EEC. The ban on British export credits, which the government itself administers, was the sole exception.

Ironically, perhaps, the British government seemed at times more efficient in persuading – or, in one case, preventing – other states from applying sanctions than in successfully implementing its own sanctions. In March 1986 Britain was reported to have stopped Bermuda, site of the Nassau agreement, from imposing sanctions against South Africa. The Bermudan premier, John Swan, wanted to introduce additional sanctions, but Mrs Thatcher told him in a letter that this would go beyond the limited measures agreed at the Commonwealth conference. Sir Geoffrey told the House of Commons that it was 'perfectly rational' for Britain to prevent Bermuda, a British dependent territory, from doing this. Britain's relations with South Africa 'should be uniform' throughout its colonial territories, he said.[21]

In July 1986 the Anti-Apartheid Movement said the government had refused to implement even the limited measures agreed at Nassau. It called Mrs Thatcher's claim that Britain had done more than any other major Western power to fight apartheid 'a complete charade'. Military equipment and police computers were still getting through from Britain and sporting links were still stronger than with anywhere else in the Commonwealth. Britain, despite Mrs Thatcher's claim that its record in upholding the arms embargo was second to none, had failed to introduce controls and the government had sanctioned the sale of arms and military equipment to South Africa. Because the government itself defined what came within the embargo, it had allowed spare parts and vital strategic equipment such as a Plessey military radar system to get through.

Britain was also 'an important conduit for the world-wide distribution of South African para-military equipment'. The South African police and armed forces still received British computer equipment and there was substantial co-operation on military – particularly naval – intelligence. An international ban on the sale and export of nuclear technology and materials was not being fully honoured. There was no ban, 'just guidance', on the sale of oil. The government had admitted that it cannot control the sale of North Sea oil through third countries and there was trade between Britain and South Africa in petroleum products. Unlike some other countries, Britain had failed to implement the Gleneagles agreement by refusing to control the entry of South African sportspeople into the country.[22]

Cultural links, some British sources said, might even increase after the decision to 'discourage' them except where they could contribute to ending apartheid. These links were almost entirely with blacks, so it would be hard to imagine what cultural agreements might be affected.[23]

Even as the Commonwealth mini-summit decision was announced, Mrs Thatcher's own package – far less than the Commonwealth wanted – was being derided as token. The British package was to halt new investment; ban the import of coal, steel and Krugerrands; and impose a voluntary ban on promoting tourism. These measures became even more token when the EEC declined to ban coal imports from South Africa. Krugerrands were already covered by existing restrictions and new investment in South Africa had slowed to a trickle in recent years. It was estimated that the measures would affect only 2 to 3 per cent of the £2 billion trade between Britain and South Africa. Iron and steel imports to Britain were worth £33.6 million in 1985 – a small fraction of domestic needs that could easily be replaced because of world over-supply. Tourism to South Africa was unlikely to be seriously affected: as the Foreign Office pointed out, 'the present situation in South Africa would act as a more significant disincentive to tourism' than a ban on promotion.[24]

British investment in South Africa was still being actively promoted in October 1986. The Nassau agreement meant the end of government funding for trade missions to South Africa and for trade fairs in that country.[25] At the Commonwealth mini-summit, Mrs Thatcher was alone in refusing to go further by agreeing to 'the termination of all government assistance to investment in and trade with South Africa'.[26]

The Department of Trade and the Foreign Office were reported in October 1986 to be offering a wide range of assistance to companies in an attempt to boost their exports to South Africa. The Engineering Industries Association, planning a mission to South Africa, was told by the Department of Trade that the mission was 'unsupported', but that the British Overseas Trade Board remained free to provide assistance 'for business visitors to the market whether they go as individuals or as members of a group'. The British Embassy in Pretoria would 'be pleased to give any assistance they can to enable the mission to be a success'. The department also promised the association that it would investigate whether the Central Office of Information could provide further help.[27]

Later in October 1986 Mrs Chalker told the European Parliament that limited sanctions agreed by the EEC in September were not yet fully in force in Community countries. Legal problems blocked implementation of the ban on importing gold coins and the embargo on new investment. The banning of iron and steel came into effect on 27 September. Implementation of the outstanding elements of the EEC package rested on a dispute between Britain and France on the one hand and West Germany, Belgium, the Netherlands and Luxemburg on the other. Britain and France wanted the embargo on gold coins and investment introduced by each government and then coordinated by the EEC, while the other group wanted it introduced on a Community basis. It was estimated that the total EEC package would affect less than $500 million of South African exports to the Community, which totalled about $9 billion a year.[28]

The investment ban was less than complete in Britain. In October 1986 the Trade Secretary, Paul Channon, told the Commons that the ban was not intended to affect exports and so would exclude 'financial transactions and bank lending in support of normal trading activity'. Portfolio investment, unremitted profits and any investment in health and social development were also left out. The ban did cover new direct investment, including new acquisition of shares, and loan capital injections through inter-company and branch/head office accounts. Mr Channon said: 'Given the extent of existing UK investment in South Africa, wholehearted cooperation by British companies with the voluntary ban on new investment should have considerable impact.'[29] This seemed a rather optimistic view: as the Foreign Office pointed out in July 1986, 'little new investment is taking place at present'.[30]

The ban on the promotion of tourism also appeared less than watertight. The Employment Secretary, Lord Young, appealed in October 1986 to those directly involved in the travel business not to promote South Africa as a tourist destination. He has also asked the media not to carry advertisements or other material promoting South Africa as a destination for leisure travel.[31]

All this leakage is not particularly surprising. Responding to the House of Commons Foreign Affairs Committee report, the government's official observations said it recognized 'the strong sense of frustration and moral outrage caused by apartheid'. But it shared the Committee's view that 'this does not constitute a valid reason for taking action that is likely to have further damaging consequences for all South Africans including the black population'. It added: 'The Committee is right to question to what extent further sanctions would in fact be effective in achieving a negotiated peaceful settlement in South Africa.'[32]

The government re-stated its doubts about sanctions, among them 'the difficulty of identifying any precise historical comparison from which conclusions can be drawn' – as if any historical comparisons can be precise. The government was also 'very conscious of the difficulty of assessing black opinion' and concerned that 'more than most, the British government would bear a direct responsibility for the consequences of adopting a policy which might compel the black people of South Africa to endure even greater hardship'. Punitive economic measures could also 'include distortions in the economy which might affect the future economic prosperity of both South Africa and its neighbours'.

The government admitted that the decision of Western banks not to roll over South African debts in 1985 had had 'a considerable impact'. But 'the government are dubious whether it provided a pointer towards the possible long-term effects of more sustained financial sanctions against the Republic. They note that the banks' decision was the action of market forces, not of government directive, and so could not be dismissed by the South African government as arbitrary foreign interference. In any case, it is not clear that it has had any significant long-term influence on political decisions taken by the South African government.'[33]

South Africa has surfaced as a major political issue in the United
States only comparatively recently. In Pretoria, American concern
over apartheid has been regarded with irritation and anger for decades.
In 1960, for example, the then Foreign Minister called in the American
Ambassador to protest against a State Department statement deploring
the loss of life in the Sharpeville massacre. At that stage the State
Department said US policy was that it did 'not normally comment on
the internal affairs of governments with which it enjoys normal relations'.[1] Outside government, however, the American Committee
on Africa was laying the groundwork for sanctions and divestment. In
June 1960 the Committee arranged a conference, co-sponsored with a
range of other organizations including Americans for Democratic
Action, trade unions and the National Association for the Advancement of Coloured People, which urged Washington to stop buying
gold and strategic raw materials from South Africa if other sources
were available. The conference also called for a consumer boycott of
South African goods, urged dockworkers to refuse to unload these
goods, and attempted to dissuade businessmen from investing in the
country.[2] In 1964 Ford did not tender for four-wheel-drive vehicles
wanted by the South African government after the State Department
warned that export licences would be refused because the vehicles
could be converted into armoured cars. Pretoria then placed no orders
with Ford until 1967, when purchases were resumed.[3]

Interest in South Africa built up in the mid-1960s. President
Johnson made his one and only speech on Africa in May 1966, saying
that there was increasing awareness in Africa that government must
represent the true will of its citizens: 'This makes all the more repugnant the narrow and outmoded policy which in some parts of Africa
permits the few to rule at the expense of the many ... Just as we
are determined to remove the remnants of inequality from our own
midst, we are also with you – heart and soul – as you try to do the
same.'[4]

President Johnson's speech came, not entirely coincidentally, as Senator Robert Kennedy left for a widely acclaimed visit to South Africa. He was invited by the liberal National Union of South African Students whose President, Ian Robertson, was banned under the Suppression of Communism Act a month before the visit took place. Pretoria had indicated its displeasure by banning Mr Robertson; it added to this by refusing visas to 40 American journalists who had wanted to accompany Senator Kennedy, saying it would not allow the visit 'to be transformed into a publicity stunt . . . as a build-up for a future presidential election'.[5] Dr Verwoerd refused to see him or to allow other ministers to do so. Senator Kennedy did, however, see Chief Albert Luthuli and received a rapturous reception at universities throughout the country.[6] He was also mobbed in Soweto, where he flouted the law by quoting Chief Luthuli, a banned person. Senator Kennedy did not spell out any detailed proposals on U S policy towards South Africa.

In 1967 an event more embarrassing than the Kennedy visit took place when the American aircraft carrier Franklin D. Roosevelt asked for permission to call at Cape Town for refuelling and provisioning on its way back from Vietnam. Consent was given and arrangements made for a full programme of entertainment, apparently within the framework of apartheid, for the 3,800 people aboard, with separate functions for white and black sailors. But after the carrier had docked shore leave was cancelled after the Pentagon authorized leave only for those participating in organized integrated functions. The Pentagon ordered another vessel to abandon a visit to Durban and to go to Kenya instead. American warships were subsequently barred by Washington from calling at South African ports. The Minister of Foreign Affairs said there were important, unfortunate points of friction between the U S A and South Africa. 'We are trying to avoid these and concentrate on the many fields in which we have common interests.'[7]

U S policy during the Nixon years was summed up by the President in February 1970: 'There is no question of the United States condoning, or acquiescing in, the racial policies of the white-ruled regimes. The United States stands firmly for the principles of racial equality and self-determination.' The President went on to say, however, that the 1960s had shown there could be no quick solutions and progressive change could not be furthered by force.[8] Later the same year an official policy statement endorsed by President Nixon repeated

US commitment 'for fundamental human rights in Southern Africa', but stressed that the solution lay not in violence but in 'the constructive interplay of political, economic and social forces which will inevitably lead to changes'. The USA did not believe that 'cutting our ties with this rich, troubled land would advance the cause we pursue or help the majority of the people of that country'.[9] This was a policy of 'constructive engagement', though the phrase itself had not yet been coined.

By 1972 the Nixon Administration was reported to be showing greater sympathy towards Pretoria than its two predecessors. The outside world was 'witnessing with sober hope the suggestions of change ... Private companies, many of them American, are considering new ways to open opportunities for African workers. There is an imbalance between the needs of South Africa's active economy and her adherence to racial policies which deprive her of the growing pool of human talent which that economy requires. There is some hope in that anomaly,' the President said in February 1972.[10]

In April of that year *The New York Times* examined in detail changing US policy. It concluded that there was a tilt towards the whites of Southern Africa, with the deliberate expansion of contacts and communication. Small executive jets had been sold to South Africa and Boeing 707s to the Portuguese who were embroiled, amid much international hostility, in fighting colonial wars in Angola and Mozambique. The ban on importing Rhodesian chrome had been ended in defiance of the UN, where Washington had abstained or voted against resolutions on Southern Africa.[11]

In contrast the Democratic Party, with its 1972 presidential candidate, George McGovern, pledged to 'end US complicity' with Pretoria. A Democratic administration would abolish tax credit for US companies and subsidiaries paying tax in South Africa, withdraw South Africa's American sugar quota, press American companies in South Africa to take measures to achieve the fullest possible justice for their black employees, assign blacks at all levels of the US diplomatic and consular corps, support UN sanctions against Rhodesia (especially the ban on chrome imports), support UN assertions of control over Namibia, and end military aid to Portugal.[12] Also in the Democratic ranks, Charles Diggs, Chairman of the House of Representatives Subcommittee on Africa, pressed after a visit to South Africa for an end to South African gold sales to the International Monetary Fund and for American companies to improve black working conditions. Acting true to form, Pretoria said it would refuse entry to foreigners investigating the employment practices of overseas companies.[13]

In 1976 Jimmy Carter arrived on the scene as President. Mr Carter was to follow what Pretoria considered the most hostile policy towards South Africa ever made by a US president. Ironically, he had been secretly funded by South Africa in his campaign for the White House. This emerged during what was called the 'Muldergate' scandal when the Minister of Information, Connie Mulder, and key aides were implicated in mis-spending taxpayers' money. The Secretary of the Department of Information, Eschel Rhoodie, confessed later that 'we got very close to Carter long before he was even nominated for the presidency . . . He even appeared on TV with one of my information officers. We saw him quite often in Georgia and were later to help contribute secretly to his campaign funds through people fronting for us . . . I think Carter would have been far more hostile had he had no contact at all with South Africa or South Africans. I think you have to judge it by that yardstick in this instance.'[14]

Just how much more hostile President Carter might have got is a matter for speculation. Certainly Pretoria saw him as its most formidable opponent. The then Prime Minister, B. J. Vorster, said in August 1977 that the Administration was embarking on a course that would lead to chaos and anarchy in South Africa. The only difference between American pressure and communist revolution was one of method – 'strangulation with finesse' instead of 'death by brute force'.[15]

The Administration's policy was spelled out in May 1977 by the Vice-President, Walter Mondale, after talks in Vienna with Mr Vorster:

We cannot accept, let alone defend, governments that reject the basic principle of full human rights, economic opportunity and political participation for all of their people regardless of race . . . perpetuating an unjust system is the surest incentive to increase Russian influence and even racial war . . . without evident progress that provides full political participation and an end to discrimination, the press of international events would require us to take actions based on our policy and to the detriment of the constructive relations we would prefer with South Africa . . . We hope that South Africa will not rely on illusions that the United States will in the end intervene to save South Africa from the policies it is pursuing, for we will not do so . . . A failure to make progress will lead to a tragedy of human history.[16]

Four months later, in September 1977, Mr Vorster called a General

Election for 30 November. Among the reasons he gave was that certain governments and influential world organizations and people had arrogated to themselves the right to meddle in South Africa's internal affairs. They had also taken the view that they had the right to prescribe how the country should be governed. The government had spoken out very strongly against this and the time had come for the white electorate to add their voice to this protest. President Carter's 'meddling' was a strong theme of National Party electioneering. The party won 134 of the 165 seats in the House of Assembly – 82 per cent, the highest proportion ever gained by any single party in South Africa.[17]

But American policy was not to exclude South Africa or isolate it from the rest of the world. The American Ambassador to the UN, Andrew Young, who had become something of a bogeyman for many white South Africans, not least because he is black, said the USA wanted to help South Africa embark on a new course. The USA, Britain and France – the permanent Western members of the Security Council – agreed in November 1977, in the wake of the death in detention of Steve Biko and the banning of Black Consciousness organizations, to the imposition of a mandatory arms embargo on South Africa.[18]

Although the Carter Administration was not in favour of sanctions,
the former President later changed his mind. In August 1985, after
both the House of Representatives and the Senate had passed bills to
impose sanctions against South Africa, Mr Carter said he favoured
sanctions and urged President Reagan not to use his veto if the two
houses of Congress came up with an agreed measure.[1] Andrew
Young, now Mayor of Atlanta, has also come around to what he terms
'moderate' sanctions. In an open letter to Bishop Tutu, Mr Young
said that the sanctions likely to be imposed in late 1986 'will probably
seem totally inadequate'. But South Africa should 'recognize that
sanctions are effective only if they can be enforced and relaxed'.

He set considerable store by selective measures rather than a total
embargo: 'Sanctions must be seen as a tactic, not an end in themselves.
I have always feared that South Africa would actually get stronger and
more intransigent under an oil embargo. Nor are such sanctions likely
to be effective. Oil shipments are almost impossible to track, and there
would surely be leaks along the South African coast. As for total
economic sanctions, they would probably be honoured only in the
breach. They could be enforced only with an extensive naval blockade
that is unlikely.' Quoting the Rhodesian experience – but without
saying that most sanctions were broken through South Africa and
there is no equivalent neighbour now to help Pretoria – Mr Young
said that import substitution and widespread leaks had meant that
'sanctions hardly influenced their politics'. He then went on to outline
a kind of sanction he would favour:

Such would not be the case with an airline embargo against South Africa,
especially one that was also backed by the United Nations Security Council
and monitored by the International Civil Aeronautics Organization. Such an
embargo of air travel – all airlines – would force South Africans to get to know
their neighbours on a more equal footing and might strengthen their political

and social ties to Zimbabwe, Zambia, Botswana, Mozambique and even Lesotho, for they would drive or go by train to those neighbouring states in order to travel out into the world. Nor would any poor black citizens be hurt by such a sanction.

These sanctions are not as moderate as they seem. They would actually be more powerful than harsher measures because they would be enforceable. They could be monitored and ended whenever there was a reasonable response from Pretoria. It would be ideal if they were voted in the next few weeks but did not take effect until December, for that would give President Botha the chance to respond to the agenda put forward by President Reagan and the British Foreign Secretary.

It would also force white South Africans to cancel their Christmas travel plans and begin to face the consequences of their isolation from Europe and America. As you well know, most South African whites set considerable store by the way they can travel the entire world with the wealth derived from the exploitation of the land and people of their country. Closing the door to easy access to the pleasures, freedom and culture of the world would be a serious threat to this way of life.

Another black American Democrat, the Reverend Jesse Jackson, a presidential hopeful in 1984, came up with an unusual form of what he called sanctions during a tour of Frontline states in August 1986. Mr Jackson suggested 'a major summit meeting' between President Reagan and southern African leaders. 'Specifically we must look at apartheid in regional terms, not just local terms . . . We must use a multiple strategy approach, such as diplomatic ties with Angola, aid to Namibia. All are really sanctions against South Africa . . . '[2] Mr Jackson said also that apartheid was an extension of U S foreign policy. 'We are essentially a destabilizing force in that region. We have the option to be the hope of a free southern Africa and not to continuously misuse and abuse our power, and a great opportunity to be a force for good on that continent.'[3]

A host of other Democrats have joined the sanctions lobby. One is Senator Edward Kennedy, whose visit to South Africa in late 1984 sparked off massive controversy – not least between the United Democratic Front (which invited him) and the pro-Black Consciousness National Forum (which regarded him as a representative of 'American imperialism'). Senator Kennedy has made many statements on the issue of sanctions. In August 1985, for example, he said that Mr Botha's Rubicon speech had 'dashed all real hope that the South African government is ready to change its racist ways. Let us send a clear and unmistakable message that the time for constructive engagement with racism is over and that the time for firm American action against apartheid has come.'[4]

Mr Botha's Rubicon speech* also annoyed other members of Congress. The House Foreign Affairs Committee Chairman, Dante Fascell, said Mr Botha's approach was 'tragically more of the same' and that President Reagan should abandon his 'ineffective' policy of constructive engagement. Senator Lowell Weicker, a Republican advocate of a tougher line towards Pretoria, described the speech as 'a vacuous attempt to take the world's eye off the ball'. District of Columbia delegate Walter Fauntroy said: 'We now have no choice but to move ahead vigorously with sanctions.'[5]

In July 1986 Senator Kennedy said President Reagan's support for Pretoria negated U S pressure for reform:

Every time that he has been questioned about South Africa since taking office, President Reagan has defended the white minority regime . . . His statements of support have largely neutralized pressure for fundamental change by the State Department and Congress. And his apparent insensitivity to the legitimate grievances of the black majority will surely jeopardize American relations with any future black government. Pressure by the Administration for change in South Africa will not work until the President himself is on board.[6]

A Democratic presidential hopeful in 1984 – and in 1988 – Senator Gary Hart, urged President Reagan in July 1986 to demand immediate negotiations in South Africa for majority rule. If Pretoria refused, diplomatic relations should be suspended and sanctions imposed. These should include revoking South African Airways' landing rights and severing military ties.[7]

The Republican case for imposing sanctions was put in October 1986 by two senators just before the Senate voted to override President Reagan's veto of the agreed sanctions Bill. Richard Lugar, Chairman of the Foreign Relations Committee, and Nancy Kassebaum, Chairman of the sub-committee on African affairs, wrote in the *Washington Post* that they believed 'regretfully but firmly' that the veto should be overridden. It was essential to the U S A's long-term foreign interests throughout Africa:

We believe it is time to send a blunt message to President P. W. Botha's government . . . A vote to sustain the President's veto would be seen as support for the South African government's policies. Regardless of what the United States says or how many executive orders are issued we would be perceived as

* See Chapter 6, p. 64.

apologists for apartheid ... By themselves, sanctions, no matter how tough, cannot solve the problems of South Africa. While it is important to seek effective leverage in influencing events there, we must not become preoccupied with meting out punishment to the white minority government. We cannot impose an external solution, and we run a serious risk of total failure if we try.

The real policy goal is to help bring about peaceful change. What we seek are a society and a system that not only are more just in recognizing the rights of the black majority, but offer a more secure and more stable future for all South Africans. If this transformation is ever to occur in South Africa, we believe it is essential for us to resolve clearly and forcefully the issue of sanctions, which in the short term may have little effect on the status quo, and to focus our efforts on shaping a framework for what must replace apartheid and unilateral white power.

The two senators suggested that the USA, Britain and West Germany assemble a team of special, high-level envoys to begin talks with all South African groups. This diplomatic initiative should determine whether there was a basis for broad agreement on what follows apartheid. It should also provide the opportunity for black leaders to join in the debate about South Africa's future: 'We in the West must make every effort to provide a forum for the kind of dialogue that must be started in South Africa. It is a crucial first step in moving beyond the present stalemate and focusing attention not on the evils of apartheid, which are plain, or on sanctions, which can be debated forever, but on the true objective: peaceful, political change.'[8]

Not only politicians have joined the American debate about sanctions. So, too, have churches, trade unionists and – because the issue of South Africa has become a dramatic news story – the press. Among the latest churches to endorse limited sanctions have been American Catholic bishops, strongly influenced by the Southern African Bishops Conference which supported economic pressure against Pretoria.* The General Secretary of the US Catholic Conference, Monsignor Daniel Hoye, wrote to senators in August 1986 saying that sanctions should be imposed if 'significant progress against apartheid' was not made by January 1987: 'A policy of moral and political appeasement of those who promote and acquiesce in systematic discrimination would relegate us to the sidelines in the world-wide struggle for human rights.' Limited sanctions would allow room to enact more stringent measures later.[9]

Trade unions have played an increasing part in trying to persuade

* See Chapter 5.

American corporations to sell their South African interests. One of the biggest moves came in March 1986 when the American Federation of Labour–Congress of Industrial Organization (AFL–CIO) endorsed a consumer boycott of Shell to coincide with the twenty-sixth anniversary of Sharpeville. The AFL–CIO President, Lane Kirkland, said Shell had played a major role in supporting the apartheid system. He asked consumers to cut their Shell credit cards in half, sending one half back to the company and the other to the AFL–CIO. Shell called the accusations outrageous and unjust, claiming it did not discriminate against black workers, rejected apartheid as inhuman, and it said that it was exerting pressure to promote non-violent change.[10]

Thousands of column inches have been printed in editorials in American newspapers on sanctions. Much has been made of the morality of the issue by editors and columnists. Lou Cannon, for example, writing in the *Washington Post* in July 1986, questioned President Reagan's selective enthusiasm for sanctions: 'The president has eloquently declared that "freedom's fight is our fight". He is under no illusion that the Marxist governments in Nicaragua and Afghanistan will bargain away their power. He has employed economic sanctions against Libya, Poland and Nicaragua not because they could bring these governments down but because they make the moral case for freedom. The same case could be made for South Africa.'[11]

Haynes Johnson, another columnist, said in June 1986 that 'the question about US-imposed sanctions is not that they might hurt blacks. The question is how a great power claiming world moral leadership can continue to do business with a government that deserves condemnation and should be made to pay a price for actions outside the pale of acceptable human behaviour.'[12]

As pressure increased for the Senate to pass a sanctions Bill in July 1986, the *Washington Post* editorialized along much the same lines: 'The United States must be and must be seen to be enthusiastically on the side of black freedom rather than white privilege . . . America is a multiracial society that strives to ensure equal rights for all its citizens, and this impresses a moral stance on American policy toward South Africa.'[13]

Increased concern among politicians, trade unions, churches and the media about South Africa has been reflected, to some extent, in public opinion polls. A Louis Harris survey in 1978 found that by 46 to 26 per cent Americans thought that the USA and other countries should put pressure on South Africa to provide blacks with greater freedom and participation in government. More than half (51 to 24 per cent) supported a halt to arms sales; by 46 to 28 per cent they favoured U S companies putting pressure on Pretoria; by 42 to 33 per cent they supported a ban on new investment. However, by 51 to 21 per cent they rejected a halt to operations of U S companies in South Africa; and by the wide margin of 73 to 7 per cent they opposed any military action against South Africa. This Harris poll was largely confirmed by another one, a year later in 1979, by the Carnegie Endowment for International Peace.[14]

By February 1985 some attitudes were changing. A Business Week/Harris poll found then that by three to one Americans wanted U S companies to 'put pressure on the South African government to change its racial policies' – up from 46 per cent in favour in 1978. By 61 to 31 per cent they thought it would be against the interests of blacks employed by U S companies to close down their operations in South Africa. The percentage of those wanting the U S to press Pretoria to give more freedom to blacks was 68 per cent – up from 46 per cent in 1978. However, 54 per cent opposed the blocking of all new business investment – up from 33 per cent in 1978 – and 51 per cent were against the barring of new bank loans. Two thirds opposed ending all trade with South Africa. Also up was the percentage of those wanting U S businesses to be forced to close down their South African operations – 76 per cent in 1985 and 51 per cent in 1978. But almost two thirds were 'sympathetic' to recent protests at South African government offices in the U S A; and by 53 to 39 per cent respondents said it was 'immoral for the United States to support a government such as South Africa that oppresses blacks'. Yet 64 per cent said the U S 'must stay on good terms' with Pretoria because of South Africa's rich resources.[15]

Towards the end of 1985 a Media General/Associated Press poll found that 32 per cent favoured U S companies stopping investment or doing business with South Africa; 40 per cent opposed and 28 per cent were unsure. Half said withdrawal would hurt blacks and whites. Twenty-eight per cent said it was immoral to conduct business in South Africa.[16]

American public opinion may be confused about the right and proper
options to follow in South Africa. It is in good company. United
States multi-nationals operating in the country have faced all ways in
the controversy about their involvement in the South African economy
and apartheid. The standard line for some years was the one laid down
by Milton Friedman: the sole responsibility of business is to make
profits for its shareholders. That line became untenable after the
introduction in 1977 of the 'Sullivan Principles', a code which asked
U S companies in South Africa to desegregate facilities, pay equal
wages to blacks, improve job training and advancement and the quality
of their workers' lives. American multi-nationals, 178 of the 350 there
who are signatories to the code, then protested that these efforts were
helping blacks and that their efforts were a positive force for peaceful
change in South Africa.

That appeared to be the view of the Reverend Leon Sullivan, author
of the code, as recently as February 1985. Mr Sullivan, a member of
the board of General Motors and a veteran civil rights campaigner,
said then that the code had 'created a revolution in industrial race
relations for black workers, a revolution that has its own momentum'.
American factories that used to be segregated 'like in Mississippi'
were desegregated and the pattern was spreading to other companies.
The code was not designed to be a solution to apartheid, but was 'a
beginning and a process, an evolving process that is strengthened with
each step and with each phase'. Further, 'we need the disinvestment
campaign to keep pressure on the companies'.

Mr Sullivan, against the opposition of most of the companies
involved, wanted the code made mandatory so the firms would live
up to the principles. 'And if they don't, there should be embargoes
and sanctions and ultimately the loss of [American] government
contracts.'[1] Eighteen months later Mr Sullivan was seeking
pledges from large institutional investors to sell off $100 billion worth
of stock in U S firms doing business in South Africa if apartheid

was not abolished by 31 May 1987.[2] (See also Chapter 27, pp. 267–8.)

President Reagan took over some parts of the Sullivan Code in September 1985 when, to beat back a congressional sanctions Bill, he signed an executive order imposing some sanctions of his own. Under the order, American firms with 25 or more employees in South Africa had to comply with some of the Sullivan Principles, including desegregation of the workplace and equal pay for equal work. According to the State Department in March 1986 'most' companies were complying. Only four refused to say whether they were applying the measures, and 160 certified they were in compliance.[3]

Another view of the code has been put by Elizabeth Schmidt, a researcher into Southern Africa:

Signatories of the code control the most strategic sectors of the South African economy. Some of them bolster South Africa's nuclear capability; others help to run its military and police forces, prison system and general apartheid administration. Investment by signatory companies, together with the transfer of their technology and expertise, are buttressing Pretoria's programme of strategic self-sufficiency, helping the white minority regime to withstand the impact of any sanctions that might be imposed . . . [while] signatories argue that they provide blacks with jobs, they employ only 0.4 per cent of the African labour force in South Africa.

The Sullivan principles are not simply irrelevant to the struggle for freedom and justice. They are antagonistic to it. They disguise the true nature of American corporate involvement in South Africa. With their emphasis on community development and betterment projects, they divert attention from the real issues . . . The goal cannot be to make black life under apartheid more palatable but to abolish the system completely.

Ms Schmidt also questioned the extent of adherence to the code. One of the principles called for increasing the number of blacks in management and supervisory positions. More than eight years after the introduction of the code, figures showed that 95 per cent of managers were white and only 2 per cent African. Seventy-six per cent of workers being trained for sales and professional positions were white. The proportion of black employees training for such jobs had dropped by more than 50 per cent since 1984: 'In such a setting, principle three (equal pay for equal work) is an empty slogan. Where there is no equal work and none planned for the future, there will certainly be no equal pay.'[4]

A lot of money has been committed by American firms to improve pay and to improve the quality of life of their workers. There have also been political gestures, some of them under pressure from black unions. In February 1986 General Motors' local factory manager in Port Elizabeth announced that the company would give legal and financial help to any of its 1,800 black workers who defied beach apartheid – laws which segregate most South African beaches for use by one or other legally defined race group. Police and soldiers patrolled beach areas after GM's announcement. A month later the City Council voted to open all beaches under its jurisdiction to people of all races.[5]

More contentious has been the attitude of multi-nationals to black workers detained by police, either under states of emergency or the 'normal' security laws. Port Elizabeth was again one of the centres of controversy. GM, in mid-1986, refused to pay full wages to two detained employees, both members of the National Automobile and Allied Workers' Union (NAAWU). Instead it would pay half their gross earnings. This was rejected by the union. Another large motor company in the area, Volkswagen, owned by the West German multi-national, improved this to 75 per cent of detainees' wages and guaranteed their jobs for 180 days. The American Chamber of Commerce said it was up to individual member companies to use their discretion. At that stage 344 trade unionists were known to be in detention; a total of 2,735 had been detained by mid-August 1986 under the State of Emergency introduced in July that year. Later, however, both GM and Volkswagen agreed to pay 100 per cent of detained workers' wages.[6]

More controversial from the point of view of Pretoria and many whites is the question of multi-nationals paying the salaries of men called up for Defence Force duties. Most, if not all, firms have for years paid without question. The increasing presence of the Defence Force in black townships after the introduction of the State of Emergency in 1986 led, however, to some multi-nationals stopping the salaries of men called up for camps. Defence Force sources said: 'Many of these international companies are coming under pressure to leave, but they are making too much money. They believe they can defuse the situation by refusing to pay national servicemen and citizen force members.' There is no legal obligation to pay, but it is an offence to dismiss or retrench employees required to do military service.[7]

Late 1986 saw a rash of American and British firms deciding that they had to sell their South African interests. The three most important were General Motors, IBM and Barclays Bank. There were widespread expectations that, after these giants, many others would follow: the domino principle. Much of the reason for the three firms' decision was the 'hassle factor' – too much time was being taken up in fending off anti-apartheid activists for too little profit.

Rumours that G M would quit had been around for many months before the company finally decided on 20 October 1986 that enough was enough. The public statements of G M executives on the issue betrayed intense politicking – and differing views. In September 1985 G M South Africa got a new managing director, Bob White, who said: 'In the case of a multi-national company such as G M, it is often more important in terms of global strategy to be based in a country, despite financial loss, and G M has no plans to disinvest from South Africa at this point in time.'[8] Three months later the company gave the government-supporting newspaper *Die Burger* the same message: it had no plans to get out.

In May 1986 G M's Chairman in Detroit, Roger Smith, said the firm would resist calls on it to withdraw. At the same time, however, the company announced that it would stop selling vehicles to the South African military and police – but it would maintain business with other government departments. G M had not made military vehicles for a long time, but had sold cars and trucks to all government departments. Sales to the military and police in 1985 were said to be about 2,000 vehicles. The decision to stop sales to the military and police, Mr Smith said during debate at G M's annual meeting, came about as a result of pressure from the U S Commerce Department, as well as from shareholders. He added that he could foresee the possibility that the company might eventually be compelled to pull out of South Africa. But at that stage, publicly at least, Mr Smith was still protesting that he was against withdrawal as a way to end apartheid. 'I think the South African government is trying to move towards getting rid of apartheid . . . You've just got to give them a chance.'[9]

By mid-October 1986 the possibility of leaving was becoming a reality. However, Mr White pinned a notice on boards in the factory which said: 'I want to assure each employee that this company will be here next week, next month and next year.'[10] Three days later Mr Smith announced that G M South Africa would be sold to a group headed by local management. Detroit headquarters said that G M South Africa had 'been losing money for several years in a very difficult South African business climate and, with the current structure, we could not see our operations turning around in the near future'. G M

South Africa's sales in 1984 totalled $310 million while GM's world-wide revenue was more than $100 billion. The lack of progress in ending apartheid made operating there 'increasingly difficult'.

GM's move was interpreted as political. A motor industry analyst, Gary Glaser, commented in New York: 'They like to avoid resistance by consumers and investors in the United States to their continued involvement in South Africa. The decision was simply helped by the poor market conditions.'[11] Sales in South Africa had dropped since its last good year in 1981: in 1986 vehicle sales were expected to be 27,000 compared with 35,000 in 1985 and more than 44,000 in 1984.

The US State Department's reaction was predictable: the move would hurt black workers and the South African economy 'which has on the whole weakened the premises of apartheid', and would weaken US influence.[12] The NAACP took a different view: 'We think it is good for the elimination of apartheid and good for the image of America.'[13]

Within 24 hours South Africa got another shock: IBM, the world's biggest computer company, announced it was selling its South African subsidiary to local employees. 'The deteriorating political and economic situation in South Africa and between South Africa and its trading partners makes our action necessary,' IBM said. The company, which in 1985 pledged $15 million for black education, business development and legal reform programmes, said it would continue its social responsibility projects.[14] IBM sales in South Africa constituted 1 per cent of its world-wide market. One IBM dealer in America said: 'For 1 per cent of the sales, they don't need 99 per cent of the hassle.'[15] Like GM, IBM had denied in previous months that it had any thought of leaving South Africa.

The pull-out of GM and IBM was not greeted with wholehearted enthusiasm by proponents of withdrawal. They questioned whether the decisions had real meaning – or whether they were even permanent. Investment groups noted that the sale of South African subsidiaries still left the corporations free to sell their products there and, in some cases, to receive regular licensing payments. Workers, too, were unhappy, particularly at General Motors.* Even an opponent of withdrawal, Peter Duignan, of Stanford University's Hoover Institution in Palo Alto, California, said: 'It really doesn't mean much in the long term. It's just a silly game US companies are playing.' Sales would

* See Chapter 2.

hurt blacks while providing a windfall for white businessmen to buy the subsidiaries at bargain prices. He said also that there had been pull-outs before in the 1950s, after Sharpeville in 1960, and after Soweto in 1976 – but companies had later returned: 'Don't assume they are truly getting out.'[16]

Others thought that, whatever the 'silly game' being played, GM and IBM's withdrawal would put more pressure on US companies remaining. The Reverend Audrey Smock, head of the South Africa group of the Interfaith Centre on Corporate Responsibility, was one who was especially pleased at IBM's sale. The church group had specifically targeted the company, handing out 200,000 postcards for churchgoers to send to IBM calling for it to pull out of South Africa. Ms Smock said the idea that US companies could work for change in South Africa was a concept that had 'died years ago'. This was now being accepted by 'key members of the corporate community', and 'by the end of the year several other key investors will leave'. The Interfaith Centre had 12 companies listed that it saw as crucial to the South African economy. Since the list was begun in May 1985 three – GM, General Electric and IBM – had announced plans to pull out. Those still on the list included Mobil, Caltex (owned by Chevron and Texaco), Citicorp, and Ford, which has a 42-per-cent stake in the South African Motor Corporation.[17]

Ms Smock and many others pointed out that the withdrawal of GM, IBM and, before those two, Coca-Cola, did not mean their products would no longer be available in South Africa. There would be no complete break, as the multi-nationals would retain valuable licensing arrangements with their former subsidiaries. This, Ms Smock said, 'is a violation of the intent of withdrawal'.[18]

Only days before the GM and IBM pull-outs, another multinational, Royal Dutch/Shell, warned that it might join the exodus because of strong international pressure. The Chairman of Shell South Africa, John Wilson, said: 'If the bottom line of Royal Dutch/Shell is adversely affected internationally, the shareholders will have to reconsider their position in South Africa . . . [but] it would have to get really bad before shareholders decide to pull out.'[19] Two days before, Royal Dutch/Shell's senior Managing Director, Lo van Wachem, told senior executives around the world that apartheid was threatening a slide towards ungovernability and chaos. He urged Pretoria to release all political prisoners, end the ban on political organizations, stop detention without trial, 'and to begin the process of negotiation about the future with representatives of all South Africans ... Shell South Africa has firmly committed itself to doing all in its power to eradicate apartheid and to work for a better tomorrow, for all South Africans.'[20] Mr Wilson shortly afterwards told employees that Shell had adopted 'a more open political stance' to demonstrate its opposition to apartheid and that 'it is important that every member of staff realize that this company's survival depends on their commitment to the company's stance'. Mr Wilson's statement recalled the large advertisements in the press by the rival Mobil company – under severe pressure in the USA to withdraw – in which it spelled out its opposition to apartheid and desire for South Africa to move towards a non-racial society.[21]

20 The American Debate: President Reagan and Other Voices

Virtually no opponent of sanctions defends apartheid: their goal is always to move away from racism and towards a free, non-racial (or multi-racial) society. President Reagan, with Mrs Thatcher the strongest opponent of the use of economic pressure against South Africa, is no exception. But, as with Mrs Thatcher, his command of what is actually happening in that country is sometimes sketchy – or just plain wrong.

The President who gave South Africa a policy of 'constructive engagement' delivered a major speech on sanctions on 22 July 1986. This was five days after the House of Representatives voted to approve legislation requiring the withdrawal of all U S firms operating in South Africa within 180 days of the law being enacted, and imposing a trade embargo against South Africa except for key minerals needed by the American defence industry. Mr Reagan's speech was clearly designed to defeat or water down this legislation and to do the same with a Bill before the Senate.

He began with the almost obligatory attack on apartheid, 'the root cause of South Africa's disorder'.[1] America's view of apartheid was clear: 'Apartheid is morally wrong and politically unacceptable. The United States cannot maintain cordial relations with a government whose power rests upon the denial of rights to a majority of its people, based upon race.' But 'the primary victims of an economic boycott of South Africa would be the very people we seek to help. Most of the workers who would lose jobs because of sanctions would be black workers.'* The President quoted Alan Paton's declaration that he would do nothing to cause any suffering to any black person. † Further, 'Southern Africa is a single economic unit tied together by rails and roads'. Zaire, Zambia and Zimbabwe all depended on South African

---

* See, however, Chapter 9, pp. 86–7, for Mark Orkin's view that white unemployment would increase proportionately more than black unemployment.

† See Chapter 6.

ports. People from Botswana, Lesotho, Swaziland and Mozambique worked in South Africa's mines: 'Shut down those productive mines with sanctions and you have forced black mine-workers out of their jobs and forced their families back in their home countries back into destitution. I don't believe the American people want to do something like that.'

Mr Reagan then turned to business as a positive force, bringing from Europe and America ideas of social justice: 'If disinvestment is mandated, these progressive Western forces will depart and South African proprietors will inherit, at fire-sale prices, their farms and factories, plants and mines. How would this end apartheid? Our own experience teaches us that racial progress comes swiftest and easiest not during economic depression but in times of prosperity and growth. Our own history teaches us that capitalism is the natural enemy of such feudal institutions as apartheid.'

Later in his speech the President returned to the same theme: 'We need not a Western withdrawal but deeper involvement by the Western business community, as agents of change and progress and growth. The international business community needs not only to be supported in South Africa but [also] energized. We will be at work on that task. If we wish to foster the process of transformation, one of the best vehicles for change is through the involvement of black South Africans in business, job-related activities and labour unions.'

South Africa also mattered strategically: it was 'one of the most vital regions of the world. Around the Cape of Good Hope passes the oil of the Persian Gulf – which is indispensable to the industrial economies of Western Europe. Southern Africa and South Africa are a repository of many of the vital minerals – vanadium, manganese, chromium, platinum – for which the West has no other secure source of supply.' The Soviet Union knew the stakes: it had installed, using Cuban troops, 'a client regime' in Angola and was providing it with weapons to attack Unita, which he described as 'a black liberation movement which seeks for Angolans the same right to be represented in their government that black South Africans seek for themselves'.

Apartheid threatened American vital interests 'because it is drawing neighbouring states into the vortex of violence'. South African forces had struck into these states and 'the Soviet-armed guerrillas of the African National Congress – operating both within South Africa and from some neighbouring countries – have embarked upon new acts of

terrorism inside South Africa'. Both sides' behaviour was to be condemned. 'But South Africa cannot shift the blame for these problems
onto neighbouring states, especially when those neighbours take steps
to stop guerrilla actions from being mounted from their own territory.
If this rising hostility in southern Africa – between Pretoria and the
Frontline states – explodes, the Soviet Union will be the main bene-
ficiary. And the critical ocean corridor of South Africa, and the
strategic minerals of the region, would be at risk.'

Mr Reagan implicitly argued that sanctions could make South
Africans retreat into deeper isolation: 'As I urge Western nations to
maintain communications and involvement in South Africa, I urge
Mr Botha not to retreat into the laager, not to cut off contact with the
West. Americans and South Africans have never been enemies, and
we understand the apprehension and fear and concern of all of your
people. But an end to apartheid does not necessarily mean an end to
the social, economic and physical security of the white people in this
country they love and have sacrificed so much to build.'

The President had some harsh words for what he called 'the calculated terror by elements of the African National Congress'. The mining
of roads and bombings of public places was 'designed to bring about
further repression, the imposition of martial law, eventually creating
the conditions for racial war'. The 'necklacing' of blacks by fellow-
blacks was 'designed to terrorize blacks into ending all racial
co-operation – and to polarize South Africa as a prelude to a final,
climactic struggle for power.'* He added that although 'the South
African government has a right and responsibility to maintain order in
the face of terrorists . . . by its tactics the government is only accelerat-
ing the descent into blood-letting. Moderates are being trapped between the intimidation of radical youths and counter-gangs of vigi-
lantes.' The State of Emergency would 'bring South Africa neither
peace nor security'.

Then came the optimism: 'Behind the terrible television pictures
lies another truth: South Africa is a complex and diverse society in a
state of transition.' There had been dramatic change:

Black workers have been permitted to unionize, bargain collectively, and
build the strongest free trade union movement in all Africa. The infamous
pass laws have been ended, as have many of the laws denying blacks the right
to live, work and own property in South Africa's cities. Citizenship, wrongly

---

*Mr Reagan's sources for these statements were not cited.

stripped away, has been restored to nearly six million blacks. Segregation in universities and public facilities is being set aside. Social apartheid laws prohibiting interracial sex and marriage have been struck down. Indeed, it is because State President Botha has presided over these reforms that extremists have denounced him as a traitor.

Before the State of Emergency imposed in mid-1986 'there was a broad measure of freedom of speech, of the press and of religion. Indeed, it is hard to think of a single country in the Soviet bloc – or many in the United Nations – where political critics have the same freedom to be heard as did outspoken critics of the South African government.' But 'by Western standards South Africa still falls short, terribly short, on the scales of economic and social justice'.

Mr Reagan suggested a programme of 'progress towards political peace':

● A timetable for the elimination of apartheid laws should be set.
● All political prisoners should be released.
● Nelson Mandela should be released to participate in the country's political process.
● The government and its opponents should begin a dialogue about constructing a political system resting on the consent of the governed, in which the rights of majorities, minorities and individuals should be protected by law. The dialogue should be initiated by those with power and authority: the government.
● 'If post-apartheid South Africa is to remain the economic locomotive of southern Africa, its strong and developed economy must not be crippled. Therefore I urge the Congress – and the countries of Western Europe – to resist this emotional clamour for punitive sanctions.'

The President announced that the Secretary of State, George Shultz, had already begun intensive consultations with Western allies on ways to encourage internal negotiations. The USA fully supported the British Foreign Secretary's visit to South Africa. The leaders of the region should also 'join us in seeking a future Southern Africa where countries live in peace and cooperation'. Mr Shultz and the director of the Agency for International Development, Peter McPherson, would begin a study of the USA's assistance role in Southern Africa to see what could be done to expand the trade, private investment and transport prospects of South Africa's neighbours. Nearly a billion dollars had been provided in five years to those neighbours and in

1986 the USA hoped to provide $45 million to black South Africans.

Mr Reagan's speech was not greeted with unbounded enthusiasm. His comments on South Africa's freedoms and the breaking down of apartheid attracted particular criticism. Blacks might have been permitted to unionize, but thousands had been detained – both before and during the states of emergency. The pass laws had been abolished, but other legislation was often being used to control the movement of blacks. Citizenship had not been restored to six million blacks. There was still segregation at universities and in public places, albeit less than before. Sex apartheid laws had been abolished but affected only a handful of people.

The Reverend Jesse Jackson called the speech 'an apologetic statement for the terrorist regime in Pretoria'. There were widespread charges of double standards in relation to President Reagan's opposition to sanctions – Washington has sanctions in place against 20 countries. An influential black Congressman, William Gray, asked: 'How can sanctions hurt black South Africans when apartheid is killing them?' Bishop Tutu told the West to 'go to hell . . . Mr Botha must be feeling very thrilled that he has got such a wonderful public relations officer in the White House . . . It's an utter nonsense for him to refer to our freedom fighters, who tried over 50 years to use peaceful means, as being engaged in terroristic activities, when the South African government kills four-year-olds here and his government supports the contras in Nicaragua.'[2]

Criticism of Mr Reagan did not end there. In mid-August 1986 he gave a press conference in Chicago which was dominated by the sanctions issue.[3] The President sought to draw a distinction between the sanctions he has used against Poland and Nicaragua and those which others want against South Africa. The sanctions were justified against Nicaragua because it was seeking to export revolution while South Africa was not. Further, black South Africans were not being as severely oppressed as Nicaraguans were by the Sandinista regime. In the Polish case, sanctions were directed against the government and not the people or Solidarity.

Sanctions, Mr Reagan said, were being advocated by 'one group' that 'very definitely has been the most radical. And [it] wants the disruption that would come from massive unemployment and hunger and desperation of the people, because it is their belief that they could then rise out of all that disruption and seize control.' Asked if that included Bishop Tutu, Mr Reagan said it did not: 'I guess that was careless of me.' Responding to another question, he later identified the 'most radical' group as the ANC, which, he said, included communists. He acknowledged that Mr Shultz had had contacts with some members of the ANC, but said: 'The ones we're hearing from – that are making the statements – are members of the [South] African Communist Party. If you could do business with and separate out and get the solid citizens in the ANC to come forward on their own, that's just fine.'

Defending further his opposition to sanctions, Mr Reagan said that he was supported by 'some of the most prominent of the black leaders' in South Africa – Bishop Isaac Mokoena of the Reformed Independent Churches Association, who was the leader of 4.5 million Christians, and Chief Buthelezi. One of the black leaders had written him a 'statesmanlike and eloquent' letter saying he was impatient but approving of Mr Botha. The President also said that much of the violence in South Africa was being 'inflicted by blacks on blacks because of their own tribal separations'.

This press conference betrayed Mr Reagan's deep ignorance of events in South Africa, according to analysts generally opposed to his policies on Pretoria. Bill Johnston of the New York-based Episcopal Churchpeople for a Free Southern Africa said: 'He is a total ignoramus on South Africa. His whole understanding of the situation is absolutely flawed.' Jackie Wilson of the Washington Office on Africa referred to the President's comments that South Africa, unlike Nicaragua, was 'not seeking to impose their government on other surrounding countries'. Ms Wilson said Pretoria ruled Namibia in defiance of the UN and had launched military attacks on Angola, Zimbabwe, Zambia, Mozambique, Botswana and Lesotho. South Africa also backed guerrillas in Mozambique, Angola and Zimbabwe. 'Who are Reagan's advisers?' Ms Wilson asked. 'Who gave him a script so blatantly wrong?' Mr Reagan had said that the Sandinistas denied Nicaragua's people 'a pluralistic society, a democracy, free speech, freedom of the press and free labour unions'. Cecilie Counts of TransAfrica, which campaigns against apartheid, responded: 'There is nothing in the Nicaraguan constitution that denies the right of political participation to any groups or individuals on the basis of race, ethnicity or religion.'[4]

Other statements that Mr Reagan has made about South Africa have attracted criticism. In March 1981, interviewed by Walter Cronkite of CBS News, he said that the USA 'should be trying to be helpful' to South Africa, which was moving away from apartheid: 'Can we abandon a country that has stood beside us in every war we've fought . . .?' [5] But in fact many Afrikaners opposed South Africa's participation in both World Wars: former Prime Minister Hendrik Verwoerd, when a newspaper editor during the Second World War, was found by a judge to have made his paper 'a tool of the Nazis in South Africa'; former Prime Minister B. J. Vorster was interned in the 1940s for his alleged pro-Nazi sympathies; and a sabotage campaign against South Africa's participation in the war was launched by a number of Afrikaners.

President Reagan's dislike of sanctions against South Africa has been echoed many times by members of his Administration. Most follow the same lines: abhorrence of apartheid; caution that the USA does not have unlimited power in the region; stress that it does, however, have important interests there; warnings that if violence increases the Soviet Union will step in; emphasis that persuasion is better than condemnation and withdrawal; and hope that the South African government is changing and will change further if the USA, diplomatically and economically, maintains a positive presence. What is noteworthy about all the speeches, statements and evidence to Congressional committees is the repetition of these arguments: often the same phrases recur over months and years.

The principal architect of the policy of 'constructive engagement' is Dr Chester Crocker, Assistant Secretary of State for African Affairs. His background is as an academic specialist in Africa; before joining the Reagan Administration he was head of the African Studies Programme at Georgetown University's Centre for Strategic and International Studies. In September 1984, testifying to a sub-committee of the Senate Foreign Relations Committee, he rejected what he called 'pinpricks' against the South African government like restrictions on Krugerrand sales or on landing rights for South African Airways: 'Such moves are likely to become a show of impotence and to erode our influence with those we seek to persuade.' American policy was to 'open doors and build bridges – not the reverse . . . Recognizing that the cult of Afrikaner unity was hostile to serious reform, we moderated our public rhetoric in an effort to persuade the government there to respond to the realities of the South African situation itself . . .Today [1984] . . . we believe there is clear evidence of progress toward a more favourable climate for change.' He gave a cautious welcome to the South African constitution introduced at about the same time: the flaw was that

Africans were excluded, but 'it would be premature to dismiss the new willingness of the whites to support the concept of reform or the potential of the new constitution for stimulating further change . . . the departure of "whites only" politics may well prove to have a substantial effect on those who govern South Africa.'[6]

By 1986 Dr Crocker was still opposing sanctions and urging quiet diplomacy. U S influence, he conceded, was 'at the margins, but it is there and we're determined to use it'. He appeared less hopeful about reform than he had done in 1984: 'There is a mood of siege politics which de-emphasizes the external factor and strikes the apparent posture of being ready to go it alone and suffer the consequences' – a view that seemed to question the whole basis of any claimed success for 'constructive engagement'.[7]

One of the favourite arguments against sanctions – of President Reagan particularly – is that the West depends on South Africa's minerals. However, in September 1982, the Deputy Assistant Secretary of State for African Affairs, Frank Wisner, appeared to question the whole thesis:

Globally, South Africa is a highly industrialized country, but in overall terms of trade, it is not of crucial importance to any other industrialized country, nor is any other industrialized country of crucial importance to it. There is very little which is produced by South Africa which cannot be replaced, although at a price, by substituting some other commodity from elsewhere in the world, or through conservation, or by recycling existing stocks . . . what is important in our relationship is not some absolute dependence on each other, but rather a recognition that we each have something to offer the other – if only we can bring together our common interests. Whether we can do so will not be a function of geography, strategic minerals or metals but rather a compatibility of values and interests – social, political and economic.[8]

Another reason for the Administration opposing sanctions was said to be the need for South Africa's cooperation over Namibia. The then Secretary of State, Al Haig, told a Senate sub-committee in March 1982 that 'we have attempted to work somewhat differently with the government of South Africa than the preceding administration'. Mr Haig, notorious for his convoluted prose, continued:

I think in hindsight over this past year, when one considers that no progress was made in the preceding two years on that subject, none, despite our high level of rhetoric and condemnation against the issues you have asked about and as a result we have made great progress, substantial progress, and with a great

deal of cooperation from the government of South Africa, which is itself pre-
siding over a tightly balanced constituency which contained those who are
concerned about the things you and I are concerned about and those that are
opposed, and I think in recent weeks you have seen some manifestation of that
controversy.[9]

Two-and-a-half years later, Dr Crocker was still sounding optimistic. 'Today, after three years of active diplomacy with all the regional
states concerned and our allies, we are closer to the threshold of
Namibian independence than ever before.'[10] By 1987 there were still no
signs, despite all this optimism, that after six years of 'constructive
engagement' an internationally acceptable settlement for Namibia was
any closer.

Secretary of State Shultz, probably unwittingly, listed some of the
failures of 'constructive engagement' in April 1985. When the Reagan
Administration came into office in 1981, he said, it found Southern
Africa marked:
  'by growing racial tension in South Africa;
  'by escalating cross-border violence;
  'by Soviet and Cuban intervention in the region;
  'by stalled negotiations for the independence of Namibia . . .'[11]
  Plus ça change. . .
Mr Shultz went on to say that a 'peace-making role can only be
played by a power that has a working relationship and influence with
all the parties, including of course South Africa . . . There is now less
cross-border violence than there has been in 11 years. There has been
more reform in South Africa in the past four years than in the previous
30.'[12]

One intriguing aspect of the whole sanctions issue is why it became
so important to Americans. Until recently, South Africa, after all, was
a faraway country of which most Americans knew little and cared less.
The Louis Harris poll on American attitudes in 1978 found that 20 to
25 per cent of those questioned answered 'don't know'. This, said two
analysts, 'is only the visible tip of the iceberg. It is deceptively low
since many people are reluctant to say "I don't know." They answer
questions even when they have no firm opinion about the matter.'[13]
The increasing coverage of South Africa in the press and on television
has obviously focused more attention on South Africa and hardened
attitudes – one of the reasons why Pretoria banned TV crews and
print journalists from being in areas of unrest during the State of
Emergency. Foreign readers and viewers were often better informed

about South Africa than people inside the country – just as the outside world knew more about Pretoria's invasion of Angola in 1974 than did South Africans.

A persuasive analysis of the growing interest in South Africa among Americans has been offered by the *Guardian*'s former Washington correspondent, Harold Jackson.* The Reverend Jesse Jackson, a candidate for the Democratic Party's Presidential nomination, was one key figure. When his campaign started at the beginning of 1984, he made no mention of South Africa or apartheid. Nor, when he met the UN representatives of 50 African countries in New York, did he raise the South African issue. But it was during the many televised debates between the six Democratic runners that it started to emerge.

During one of the New York primary debates Mr Jackson, annoyed by the Chairman's intimation that the real battle was between Walter Mondale and Gary Hart, suddenly burst out: 'Why do neither of you ever talk about South Africa and what's going on down there?'

It caught Mondale and Hart completely on the hop so that they faltered in their strides. That of course had been the whole point but I really don't think it was planned. It seemed to be much more the instinctive reaction of an embattled populist politician . . .

From the New York primary onward, however, South Africa became one of the repeated themes of Mr Jackson's campaign rhetoric and his opponents were forced to respond. It didn't exactly become the burning issue of the Democratic campaign, but it was bubbling away gently through the rest of the primary season. It certainly became one of the platform issues on which Mr Jackson demanded – and got – concessions at the San Francisco convention, but it still didn't take off in the country at large and it certainly did not figure in the lopsided contest between Mondale and Reagan.

Bishop Tutu's award of the Nobel Peace Prize also helped to revive interest in South Africa. Then, on 23 November 1984 – weeks after Mr Reagan had been returned to the White House by the largest electoral college margin in history – the TransAfrica group run by Randall Robinson in Washington decided to picket the South African Embassy. November 23 was the day before Thanksgiving, when the whole of the USA shuts down, resulting in a slow news day. Harold Jackson describes what happened:

* The following section is based on an unpublished paper by Harold Jackson, 'Domestic Quirks in Foreign Affairs', dated February 1986.

. . . The District of Columbia's City Congressional Delegate, Walter Fauntroy, and a member of the Civil Rights Commission, Mary Berry . . . were among a number of people arrested by the local police that afternoon, and their detention generated headlines and broadcast coverage all over the country. It was about the only news event on an otherwise somnolent holiday.

There was an astonishing – and wholly unexpected – response. Apartheid, it became evident, had been the sleeping giant of the 1984 campaign, possibly because of the overwhelming nature of the Reagan victory. There were a lot of sore losers looking for an issue with which to beat the Administration – and the election had demonstrated starkly that the state of the economy was not it.

Within days, it seemed, Jane Fonda, Harry Belafonte, Mrs Coretta King and hundreds of other political activists were lining up to be arrested. Given the ethnic composition of Washington, which is 70 per cent black, not the least bizarre aspect of the nightly television pictures broadcast to the rest of the country was the sight of black policemen arresting other blacks for protesting against apartheid . . . Within a few weeks the number of arrests had exceeded 3,000.

Another significant factor was the changed nature of the Administration's opponents, which now included young conservatives who, only weeks before, had campaigned for Reaganism. Some of those elected were students at the time of the Civil Rights Movement of the 1960s: one, for example, who is well to the Right is Senator Mitch McConnell of Kentucky, whose response to the mounting furore was to co-sponsor a Bill calling for sanctions. In the House, a group of conservative Republicans debated among themselves and then warned the South African Ambassador they would all vote for sanctions unless quicker action was taken to dismantle apartheid. Harold Jackson sums up the situation:

The black electorate, of course, is almost solidly Democratic and is unlikely to form any part of the natural constituency of the Republican Right so there is natural political antipathy between the two groups. But we now seem to have reached the point in America where racial discrimination has burst from the ideological boundaries. Only a lunatic fringe is left to argue the case for segregation. So the practice of apartheid is instinctively abhorrent right across the political spectrum in the United States.

The Administration became more and more isolated in trying to argue the case for 'constructive engagement'. The whole nature of the debate shifted. The White House had to abandon blanket opposition to any sanctions. Then Wall Street, under pressure from their customers to stop investing in South Africa, and with the rand losing value in the wake of township violence, started refusing South Africa more loans. This caught the Administration in a flanking movement, and support for existing policy crumbled further. In addition, Mr Reagan needed the Republican leadership in Congress for the final stages of the Budget battle – and most of them supported the sanctions Bill. The President, who had earlier threatened to veto any sanctions legislation, was forced into a position of signing the executive order imposing mild sanctions. A year later, faced with a Congress more determined than ever to impose sanctions, President Reagan did veto stronger legislation – but his veto was overridden in what was termed the biggest foreign policy defeat of the Reagan presidency. 'Constructive engagement' was dead.

Conclusion

As 1986, the year when sanctions began to dominate the debate about South Africa, ended, P. W. Botha announced a whites-only election. It was fought largely – at least from the National Party side – on the issue of outside 'interference' in what Pretoria regards as the country's 'internal affairs'. The theme echoed the 1977 election when the then Prime Minister, B. J. Vorster, challenged the West: 'Do your damnedest.' There was, however, some unease about this approach, with at least one government-supporting newspaper questioning whether it was appropriate to an election 10 years later.

The essentially negative electioneering of damning 'enemies' had its obvious attractions in getting votes. It also pointed to the dangers that 'liberal' politicians and businessmen had warned about: that white South Africa could well retreat further into the laager when faced with sanctions rather than face, at least for the present, the challenge of change.

It poses, too, a further question for the world community. What is to be done about South Africa in the next few years? In the short term, sanctions, combined with the guerrilla war, seem unlikely to affect the country sufficiently to force the whites to the negotiating table and the abolition of apartheid. World impatience at the pace of change – if any – will grow; so, perhaps, will a feeling of hopelessness. In those circumstances, committed states, groups and individuals will presumably demand increasing sanctions. But another response, from those not so committed to sanctions, could be to point to the failure of economic measures taken and to try to shrug off further responsibility for trying to end apartheid.

The black internal response will also be interesting. Presuming that the international campaign will lead to some job losses, black unions are likely to come under pressure from their members to tone down their calls for sanctions. At the same time, however, the demands of more radical blacks for further measures against Pretoria will grow. The unions in the two main federations, COSATU and CUSA–

AZACTU, see themselves very much as part of the liberation struggle yet will face countervailing pressures – not least from the government, determined to restrict their political role.

In the white community, the election having delivered the expected triumph for Mr Botha, pressures will also be at work. A worsening economy, sanctions and withdrawals will have a momentum of their own. Businessmen can be expected to press for more rapid 'reforms' as profits and markets shrink. Whether the government takes any notice will depend on the state of the National Party as a whole, the confidence or otherwise of institutions like the State Security Council that it can handle the entire situation, and the succession to Mr Botha's administration. On the basis of past experience, it seems unlikely that the government will bow to the calls of business and the Progressive Federal Party for faster reforms: the entire thrust of the government's policy, particularly since the introduction of the new Constitution, has been that it and it alone will determine the pace of change.

Sanctions *per se,* therefore, do not seem to have the potential for immediate change – and nor do their informed adherents expect them to. But, they argue, this strategy has more long-term potential. That is still to be seen. What it certainly does do is to demonstrate world condemnation of apartheid. Both these elements are spelled out in Part 2 of the book by Joseph Hanlon, who shows what sanctions have been taken and can be taken, and what their effects have been and are likely to be.

Part 2

Which Sanctions?

by Joseph Hanlon

21 *The Only Available Weapon*

I shall not argue that the economic ostracism of South Africa is desirable from every point of view. But I have little doubt that it represents our only chance of a relatively peaceful transition from the present unacceptable type of rule to a system of government which gives us all our rightful voice. The alternative . . . [is that] violence, rioting, and counter-rioting will become the order of the day. It can only deteriorate into disorder and ultimate disaster.

The economic boycott of South Africa will entail undoubted hardship for Africans. We do not doubt that. But if it is a method which shortens the day of bloodshed, the suffering to us will be a price we are willing to pay. In any case, we suffer already, our children are undernourished, and on a small scale (so far) we die at the whim of a policeman.[1]

The Nobel Peace Prize winner Chief Albert Luthuli made that prophetic statement in early 1960. Since then the situation *has* deteriorated, and deaths at the whim of a policeman or soldier are no longer on a small scale.

For more than a decade Chief Luthuli's call for sanctions was rejected or ignored in the West. Since the massacre of schoolchildren in Soweto in 1976, however, the issue of sanctions has been taken more seriously. As the first half of this book has shown, there remains substantial debate. Nevertheless agreement with Luthuli is growing: despite their obvious difficulties, sanctions seem to be the only means available to outsiders to push for a relatively less violent transition in South Africa.

Since black South Africans first called for sanctions more than 25 years ago, no alternative strategy has emerged. Talk has proved fruitless. A stream of diplomats and statesmen have visited South Africa in an effort to convince the government there of the necessity for change. But the white minority has shown itself unwilling to listen, and prepared to make only token changes without outside pressure. The apartheid system remains intact and the idea of 'one person one vote' remains anathema.

In early 1986 the Commonwealth sent an Eminent Persons Group

(EPG) to encourage 'political dialogue' in South Africa, with the goal of 'dismantling apartheid and erecting the structures of democracy'. The Co-Chairmen were Malcolm Fraser, a former Prime Minister of Australia, and General Olusegun Obasanjo, former head of government in Nigeria. The British nominee to the EPG was Lord Barber, Chairman of Standard Chartered Bank; a Standard associate is now the largest bank in South Africa, and Lord Barber would have been expected to be sympathetic to the present South African government. Yet, after six months of intensive work in South Africa and talks with all sides, the EPG unanimously concluded 'that while the government claims to be ready to negotiate, it is in truth not yet prepared to negotiate fundamental change, nor to countenance the creation of genuine democratic structures, nor to face the prospect of the end of white domination and white power in the foreseeable future. Its programme of reform does not end apartheid, but seeks to give it a less inhuman face. Its quest is power-sharing, but without surrendering overall white control.'[2]

Nor is this attitude confined to the government. The view of the self-proclaimed 'liberal' South African business community was expressed clearly by Sir Michael Edwardes, Chairman of Chloride and former Chairman of British Leyland. A South African living in Britain, Sir Michael returned to his homeland in late 1985 for a conference on how to encourage new international investment in South Africa. He told the conference his message was that renewed world confidence in South Africa 'could be achieved by sensible representation but without the trauma of "one man one vote"'.[3] In other words, a South African who has become one of Britain's most influential businessmen was telling his old colleagues that they could pacify the outside world with 'sensible representation' for black people that still ensured the continuation of white minority rule. Would Sir Michael have been prepared to give a speech in London suggesting that Britain end the 'trauma of "one man one vote"'?

Meanwhile, the victims of apartheid have made clear that they want majority rule, not power-sharing. And they have stepped up their demands for sanctions to help them overthrow apartheid. Although there remains some opposition, most black people inside South Africa have come to agree with Luthuli – sanctions will hurt, but they are worth the price if they help to end apartheid (see Chapter 1). For example, the President of the South African National Union of Mineworkers, James Motlatsi, has called for sanctions to ban the purchase of South African coal, and for trade unions to refuse to handle coal imported from South Africa.[4] A successful coal embargo would put some of Motlatsi's members out of work, but it would also hit the South African government hard; to Motlatsi, putting pressure on white South Africa clearly takes priority.

'We are suffering already. To end it, we will support sanctions, even if we have to take on additional suffering,' explains Archbishop Desmond Tutu. 'To whom is the international community willing to listen? To the victims and their spokesmen, or the perpetrators of apartheid and those who benefit from it?'[5]

In the neighbouring states, the view is the same. Sanctions – and South African retaliation – will hurt. But those leaders are convinced that sanctions will help to end apartheid. They also believe peace will not come to the region until apartheid ends. The cost of destabilization is already so high that the cost of sanctions is a proportionately small price to pay for ending apartheid.

With the victims of apartheid issuing ever louder calls for sanctions, and with the obvious failure of the US policy of 'constructive engagement' and other attempts to talk to South Africa, reluctant governments throughout the world are coming to realize that it is essential to put pressure on the white minority regime. Thus there is a growing acceptance that:

Sanctions may not be the perfect weapon but no others are available.

Few people would oppose the very concept of sanctions and other economic embargoes. Who, for example, would sell arms to their enemy during a war? The NATO countries have all agreed not to sell sophisticated weapons and other technology to the socialist bloc. And sanctions are an important part of international relations. In recent years Britain has imposed sanctions on Southern Rhodesia, Uganda, Libya and Argentina; the USA has imposed sanctions on Poland, Libya, Iran, Cuba, Nicaragua and a variety of other states; and South Africa has imposed sanctions on its neighbours, particularly Mozambique and Lesotho. The question is not about sanctions *per se*, but rather whether sanctions are appropriate against South Africa to end apartheid.

If sanctions are the chosen weapon, then internationally accepted, comprehensive, mandatory sanctions must be the most effective form of that weapon. This is because South Africa is so dependent on foreign trade and support that the white minority government could not survive for very long if it was totally isolated. The reality, however, is that resistance to sanctions remains strong, particularly by those countries and interests which have extensive financial links with South Africa. Furthermore, some degree of sanctions-busting is inevitable.

Thus, instead of effective and comprehensive international sanctions, we see a rising tide of individual actions taken by a remarkably wide range of agencies: the United Nations, the EEC, the Commonwealth, national governments, individual government departments, local councils, trade unions, pressure groups, and so on. This half of *The Sanctions Handbook* will look at how sanctions can most effectively be applied to add to that rising tide.

The word 'sanctions' is used here in the widest possible sense to cover *all* possible actions against the Pretoria government. This includes all withdrawals and breaking of links, economic sanctions and embargoes, diplomatic actions, and cultural and other boycotts. It also includes campaigns and secondary actions such as disinvestment intended to pressure others to take action against South Africa. And it includes positive measures such as codes of conduct, aid to South Africans fighting apartheid, and support for the Frontline states.

The rest of this chapter will deal with actions which have already been taken. This second part of the book will also look at some of the arguments against sanctions: that they don't work (Chapter 22), and that they hurt the wrong people (Chapters 25-7).

Individual sanctions, on their own, will not end apartheid and bring about 'one person one vote'. Thus it is essential to understand the role of sanctions, to set realistic goals and to introduce sanctions in the most effective ways (Chapters 23 and 24), and to make sure sanctions work as intended (Chapter 28).

In the light of this analysis, we then look at what different groups can do (Chapter 29). The book ends with a directory of more than 50 different actions which have been proposed or have already been taken. Each is assessed in terms of its prospects and problems, with a list of countries and groups which have already carried out the action.

Internationally agreed embargoes

While the debate about the merits of using sanctions against South Africa continues, it is clear that the mood has changed. All over the world, governments, organizations and individuals are already trying to put pressure on the Pretoria government to abandon apartheid and concede 'one person one vote'.

This pressure has already had some limited effects. But it is just a beginning. And as Britain's Foreign Minister, Sir Geoffrey Howe, commented, 'We are not facing a Jericho situation.' One trumpet blast will not bring down the walls of apartheid.[6] Rather, sanctions are a long and difficult attempt to undermine those walls – each sanction and boycott removes a bit more earth from beneath them.

Although no one sanction has been imposed on South Africa by the entire world, there are a group of measures which have been agreed by various international bodies and which have already had an impact on the RSA (Republic of South Africa):

- *Military*: Bans on the supply of arms and some other military equipment to RSA, on the purchase of arms from RSA, and on cooperation with the RSA military and police.
- *Oil*: Ban on the supply of crude oil to RSA.
- *Sport and culture*: Blocking visits of teams, athletes and performers to RSA, and of RSA sportspeople and performers abroad.
- *Capital flows*: Prohibitions on new loans to and investments in RSA.
- *Trade*: Limited bans on the import of a few RSA goods, particularly gold coins, fruit, coal, iron and steel, plus various restrictions on trade promotion.
- *Technology*: Restrictions on new support for the RSA nuclear industry and on the sale of some computers to the RSA military and police.
- *Air links*: Bans on South African Airways landing in or flying over some countries, and on national airlines flying to RSA.

International actions

The United Nations

The UN is the obvious forum for imposing sanctions, but the position there is complex. The General Assembly, where each nation has one vote, can pass resolutions, but under the UN Charter these are not binding on members. The only method of imposing mandatory sanctions that is internationally accepted is under Articles 37–42 of the UN Charter, which give the Security Council the right to impose binding sanctions. But in the Security Council each of the five 'big powers' (China, USA, USSR, UK and France) has the right of veto, so nothing can be passed without at least the tacit agreement of all five.

The Security Council has only once agreed mandatory sanctions against South Africa. Resolution 418 of 1977 instituted the mandatory ban on the sale to South Africa of 'arms and related materials of all types, including . . . weapons and ammunition, military vehicles and equipment, paramilitary police equipment, and spare parts'. Also banned were new licences and equipment and supplies for manufacturing such equipment. This *arms embargo* remains in force, and has had some effect in limiting South Africa's military capacity. But the ban has numerous loopholes (discussed in Chapter 28 and item 2.2 of the Directory of Sanctions) and is broken by a few states, notably Israel.

Vetoes by the big powers have prevented the UN from imposing any other mandatory bans. But in 1984 the Security Council 'requested' member states to refrain from importing arms, ammunition and military vehicles from South Africa (Resolution 558). And in 1985 (Resolution 569) it 'urged' member states to: (1) suspend new investment and export loan guarantees; (2) prohibit the sale of RSA gold coins; (3) restrict cultural and sporting contacts; (4) prohibit new contracts in the nuclear field; and (5) prohibit sales of computer equipment that may be used by the RSA army and police. Both lists are generally, but not completely, honoured by the international community.

The United Nations General Assembly has passed a number of resolutions, but under the Charter these cannot be binding on member states. It has repeatedly labelled apartheid a 'crime against humanity', and 'reaffirmed its conviction that the imposition of comprehensive and mandatory sanctions by the Security Council . . . is the most appropriate, effective, and peaceful means by which the international community can assist the legitimate struggle of the oppressed people of South Africa'. The General Assembly has called on individual member states to impose 'sports, cultural, academic, consumer, tourism, and other boycotts of South Africa', as well as banning oil sales, further investment and loans, and nuclear and military collaboration.[7] A Special Committee Against Apartheid was established to monitor and promote these, and the *sports and cultural boycotts* have become among the most widespread and effective.

The UN has also acted on Namibia, which is illegally occupied by South Africa. Decree No. 1 For the Protection of the Natural Resources of Namibia states that no person or corporation may mine, process, export, or sell 'any natural resource, whether animal or mineral', from Namibia without the consent of the UN Council for Namibia. 'Any produce, animal, mineral or other natural resource' from Namibia which has been produced without permission of the UN Council for Namibia 'may be seized and shall be forfeited'. Any ship or vehicle carrying the product can also be seized. The Decree was approved by the General Assembly on 13 December 1974, and is believed to be binding on all UN members because it arose out of a Security Council decision on the Council for Namibia. Nothing has ever been seized and the legal status of the Decree remains untested (although a court action is expected in the Netherlands in 1987). In effect Decree No. 1 calls for an almost total ban on Namibian exports, but it has never been applied.

The oil exporters

The other important international embargo is the *oil boycott*. In 1973 most oil-exporting countries agreed to boycott South Africa. Iran did not, however, and continued to supply South Africa until 1979, when the Shah was overthrown and Iran joined the boycott. Virtually all oil exporters now have an official ban on the sale of crude oil to South Africa, but the embargo is still being broken. (Chapter 22 looks at the oil embargo in detail.)

The Commonwealth

In the Gleneagles Declaration of 1977, Commonwealth members committed themselves to 'taking every practical step to discourage contact or competition by the nationals with sporting organizations, teams or sportsmen from South Africa'. (See also Chapter 14, p. 131.)

In October 1985 Commonwealth members agreed to bans on: (1) new government loans to the RSA government and its agencies; (2) import of Krugerrands (gold coins); (3) government funding of trade missions to RSA and participation in trade fairs in RSA; (4) sale of computer equipment which could be used by the military, police or other security forces; (5) new contracts for the sale of nuclear materials or technology; (6) oil sales; (7) import of arms and paramilitary equipment from South Africa; (8) all military cooperation. Member states also agreed to 'discourage' cultural and scientific contacts.

In August 1986 seven Commonwealth heads of government met to consider the failure of the EPG mission to South Africa. All but Britain agreed to recommend to member governments an end to the following kinds of involvement with South Africa: (1) air links; (2) new investment and re-investment of profits; (3) import of agricultural products, uranium, coal, iron and steel; (4) double taxation agreements (see item 6.5 of Directory of Sanctions for explanation); (5) government assistance to investment and trade; (6) government buying in RSA; (7) government contracts with majority-owned RSA companies; (8) promotion of tourism to RSA; (9) new bank loans to both public and private sectors; and (10) consular facilities in RSA for RSA nationals.

The EEC

In 1977 the EEC adopted a voluntary Code of Conduct for firms from the member states with branches or subsidiaries in RSA. Then in September 1985 and September 1986 the Community imposed two sets of very limited sanctions. They included bans on: (1) purchase of RSA arms and paramilitary equipment; (2) military cooperation; (3) new South African military attachés in Europe and all European military attachés in RSA; (4) oil for RSA; (5) 'sensitive equipment' for RSA military and police; (6) new nuclear collaboration; (7) imports of RSA gold coins, iron and steel; and (8) new investment in RSA. Cultural and scientific links are to be 'discouraged'. Curiously, the EEC sanctions do not apply to Namibia, despite UN Decree No. 1. By contrast, virtually all other international measures apply to both RSA and RSA-occupied Namibia.

The Nordic states

Denmark, Finland, Iceland, Norway, and Sweden have acted together to ban: (1) the import of arms and Krugerrands; (2) new nuclear contracts; (3) export of computer equipment that may be used by police or armed forces; (4) government procurement from RSA; (5)

government support for trade promotion; and (6) commercial air services to RSA. They also 'discourage' new investment, loans, leasing, and transfer of patents and manufacturing licences. All Nordic countries require visas for South Africans and these are never granted for participation in sports, cultural activities or trade promotion.

National actions

Most countries of the world have no official links with South Africa. The socialist bloc and most Third World countries have cut their links, or never established them in the first place (although some covert trade still occurs).

Three countries which had significant trade with Pretoria have severed links. India was the first to take action when it banned trade with South Africa in 1946 – losing 5.5 per cent of its exports at the time. Virtually all South African-made goods are banned from India, nor can South African ports be used to ship goods to India. In 1954 India broke off all diplomatic relations with Pretoria. South African planes are not allowed to overfly India.

More recently, in 1986, Denmark banned all trade with South Africa, including the import of any South African goods and services and the transport of oil to South Africa on Danish-owned ships. Finland's Transport Workers' Union (AKT) has imposed a total ban on trade with South Africa; this has been given tacit approval by the government and trade has fallen to 4 per cent of former levels.

But the most important countries have taken the smallest steps. South Africa's four biggest trading partners, West Germany, Britain, Japan and the USA, have taken lesser measures. West Germany only follows the limited EEC measures, while Britain accepts the EEC measures plus the 1985 (but not the 1986) set of Commonwealth measures.

Officially, Japan goes further than the main European countries. It has: (1) banned direct investment in RSA since 1968; (2) restricted diplomatic links; (3) restricted sports, cultural and educational links; (4) prohibited the sale of computers to the RSA military or police; (5) banned the sale of nuclear technology; (6) banned the import of gold coins, iron and steel; (7) stopped issuing tourist visas to South Africans; and (8) banned air links with RSA and prohibited government officials from flying on South African Airways (SAA). Nevertheless indirect investment and technology transfer are allowed; trade with

RSA is increasing, and Japanese firms may be filling some gaps caused by sanctions imposed by other states.

In October 1986 the US Congress overrode the veto of President Ronald Reagan to impose the strongest sanctions of the big four. They include bans on: (1) new public and private loans and investments; (2) imports of RSA agricultural products, uranium, coal, textiles, iron, steel, gold coins, arms, ammunition and military vehicles; (3) direct or indirect imports from RSA state-owned firms; (4) exports of crude oil, petroleum products and nuclear technology; (5) exports of computers, software and services to the RSA military, police, or any agency involved in the administration of apartheid; (6) landing rights for SAA and US air carriers serving RSA; (7) US government agencies' buying goods and services from RSA parastatals (see p. 303 for definition), and promoting trade and tourism; (8) military cooperation (except intelligence); and (9) the double taxation agreement (see Directory of Sanctions, item 6.5).

Switzerland, South Africa's sixth largest trading partner and a likely route for sanctions-busting, imposes no restrictions on trade with the apartheid state.

Private actions

Literally thousands of companies, councils, universities, trade unions and other organizations have taken some form of action against South Africa. In 1985 the major western banks temporarily refused to renew their loans to South Africa, provoking a major economic crisis. Nearly 200 US, British and other foreign companies have withdrawn from South Africa since 1980, while many others have reduced their involvement in South Africa.

Another area of activity has centred on the transport and sale of South African goods. In the United States and Europe many stores have stopped selling South African goods, particularly fruit and clothing, after campaigns by anti-apartheid organizations. Hundreds of local councils, government departments, hospitals, universities and other bodies have placed some restrictions on the use or purchase of South African goods. The most common action is probably to ban South African fruit from canteens and cafeterias. Others include banning goods made in South Africa, such as clothing and vehicles, and withholding facilities such as halls and sportsgrounds from people who have broken the sports or cultural boycotts.

Trade unions have played a key role. The Irish Distributive and Administrative Trade Union (IDATU) agreed at its 1984 conference to boycott South African goods. After representations from IDATU many shops stopped selling South African goods. But a long strike against Dunne's Stores was triggered when an IDATU member at the check-out was suspended for refusing to handle a South African grapefruit; this finally resulted in a government ban on South African fruit and vegetables.

Library staff in Britain and Australia have refused to process requests for information from South Africa. Staff at the British Library pointed to requests for two articles, entitled 'The cat as an effective punishment' and 'Flogging and nerves', and said they were no longer prepared to assist the brutality of the South African regime.[8]

Trade unions have also played an important role in monitoring sanctions-busting. As well as sometimes refusing to handle RSA cargoes, seamen have exposed arms and oil shipments to South Africa. Indeed, it has been trade unions and non-governmental organizations like the Shipping Research Bureau, rather than governments, which have done the most to expose sanctions-busting.

Bringing pressure

Because individuals can rarely take direct action against South Africa, much pressure group activity has been to push governments, companies and other organizations to take action.

Consumer boycotts are of growing importance. The most successful has been a 17-year-long campaign against Barclays Bank in Britain, which partly withdrew from South Africa in late 1986. It had been a target because its subsidiary, Barclays National, was until 1985 South Africa's largest bank. Barclays was also one of the biggest lenders to South Africa. And, as the *Guardian* commented, there was 'no British company more closely identified with South Africa than Barclays Bank'.[9] Barclays was seen as a strong backer of the South African government, and it had publicly adopted a policy of 'constructive engagement' with the government. But an intensive campaign by the Anti-Apartheid Movement, End Loans to Southern Africa, and the National Union of Students was so successful that Barclays' share of the student market fell from 27 per cent in 1983 to 17 per cent in 1985.[10] Local councils, charities, Oxford colleges and other organizations and individuals closed accounts with an annual turnover of

£7 billion. During the first 10 months of 1986 Barclays' shares fell 15 per cent in comparison with British bank shares as a whole, in large part because of its involvement in South Africa, with all the attendant bad publicity and disinvestment pressure, plus the increased risk. The day the withdrawal was announced, Barclays' share price soared.[11] Undoubtedly the boycott campaign has hurt Barclays. Chris Ball, the Chairman of Barclays South Africa, said simply that Barclays UK were withdrawing 'because they are under political pressure'. Clearly that pressure was not coming from the British government.[12] In practice it seems that a key factor was that Barclays wanted to expand into the USA and knew that it would face an even more intense boycott there.

Other boycott campaigns have also succeeded. The US information system group Bell & Howell publicly said it was withdrawing from South Africa because of a fear of disinvestment and boycotts of its products,[13] and such fears are surely behind the withdrawal of consumer giants such as Coca-Cola. The Swedish firm Esselte also withdrew from South Africa when faced with a boycott.

Currently, the biggest international campaign is against Royal Dutch/Shell, one of the most important international oil companies operating in South Africa (and thus helping to break the oil embargo). Shell is also a major exporter of South African coal. The campaign has been strongest in the Netherlands and the United States, but has been spreading to other countries as well. Where picketing of Shell petrol stations in the USA has been active, sales have dropped by 15 per cent or more, and several petrol station operators have switched to other suppliers. So far, Shell has responded to the boycott campaign by pledging to 'continue to invest heavily' in South Africa.[14] But Barclays said similar things until a year before it withdrew.

Linked with boycotts and shareholder pressure for withdrawal, there are growing campaigns urging shareholders to sell their shares in companies doing business in South Africa. This action is known as 'disinvestment' in the UK and 'divestment' in the USA. (I will use 'disinvestment'. Confusingly, in the USA and South Africa 'disinvestment' is sometimes used for a company pulling out of South Africa. I will call that 'withdrawal'.) There was a spate of disinvestment in 1977 after the Soweto massacres, but the movement only gained real momentum after 1983. By mid-1986 more than £150,000 million ($230 billion) in US investment funds had some restrictions on involvement with South Africa,[15] and at least £12 billion ($18 billion) in shares in companies with South African links had been or were being sold. Churches, universities, trade unions and state and local governments have been the most active disinvesters.

'There is no case in history that I know of where punitive, general economic sanctions have been effective to bring about internal change.' So says the British Prime Minister, Margaret Thatcher.[1]

'Total nonsense' is the reply of businesspeople who have experienced sanctions in Rhodesia and South Africa. Academics say the same thing. A recent study, *Economic Sanctions Reconsidered*,[2] examined 103 cases of economic sanctions and found that 36 per cent were 'successful'. Among the successes cited were British/UN sanctions against Southern Rhodesia, British sanctions against Argentina (imposed by Mrs Thatcher herself) and South African sanctions against Lesotho. Among the failures was the US boycott of Cuba.

In this chapter we will look more closely at Rhodesia. It is the only case to date of comprehensive, mandatory economic sanctions imposed by the United Nations. And there are some political, economic and geographical similarities to the position now in South Africa. We will also consider the current oil embargo against South Africa.

Ending UDI in Rhodesia

In an effort to prevent majority rule, the white Rhodesian government of Ian Smith issued its Unilateral Declaration of Independence (UDI) on 11 November 1965. Two weeks later the UN Security Council called for voluntary sanctions. In December 1966 it imposed partial mandatory sanctions, covering 60 per cent of Rhodesian exports and 15 per cent of imports. Then in May 1968 the Security Council imposed comprehensive mandatory sanctions, which banned all imports, exports, air links and diplomatic links.

The goal of sanctions was to end UDI and bring about majority rule through 'one person one vote'. There was a long and bitter liberation war, but the goal was achieved. In 1979 in negotiations at Lancaster House in London, the Smith government agreed to elections. It then handed over power to the victorious ZANU–PF under the leadership of Robert Mugabe. The question is: what role did sanctions play in achieving the goal?

At first, sanctions hit hard. In 1966, exports fell 38 per cent and the government imposed tight currency controls, cutting imports by 30 per cent. The economy stagnated between 1966 and 1968. But from 1969 to 1974 there was an economic boom, with GDP (Gross Domestic Product) per capita rising 34 per cent in just six years. However, 1975-9 saw an even faster collapse, with GDP per capita crashing back to the 1968 level in only five years.[3] After 1975, white living standards were hit for the first time, and whites began to leave Rhodesia in large numbers.

The initial crisis was caused by the effect of sanctions on exports, particularly tobacco and sugar. Rhodesian tobacco is distinctive and clearly identifiable, so sales plummeted. By 1969, 300 million pounds of tobacco were stockpiled – virtually the entire production since UDI.

But from 1969 the economy recovered and began to grow rapidly. Agriculture was transformed to cut production of tobacco and increase that of wheat and other food crops. Rhodesia was already the second most industrialized country in the region (after South Africa) and a major import substitution programme caused a rapid expansion of industry. Industrialists proved unexpectedly inventive in using local raw materials and making items which had been imported.

It was this boom which seemed to make such a nonsense of sanctions. How was it possible? A key factor was the removal of competition from imported goods, which allowed the expansion of local firms, even though they often made more expensive but poorer quality items. In addition, at the time of UDI 25 per cent of industrial capacity was unused, and capacity use rose to a remarkable 97.5 per cent by 1973.

Economic expansion was also spurred by tight government control of the economy. Agricultural and industrial transformation were heavily subsidized. Import licences were never issued for goods which could be produced locally. Furthermore, sanctions at first created surplus liquidity inside Rhodesia, releasing funds for investment. Britain had frozen Rhodesian assets and excluded Rhodesia from the Sterling area, cutting it off from most foreign credits. Rhodesia retaliated by repudiating its £108 million debts in London and to the World Bank, and by blocking outflows of dividends and profits. This yielded an immediate net profit of £4 million in 1966, and similar amounts for several years. South Africa made a vital £275 million of new investment over the first decade of UDI.[4]

Much of this industrialization and import substitution proved important and useful to the independent Zimbabwe. Indeed, Rhodesia is an excellent example of how heavy government involvement and strict control of imports can spur industrialization in an under-developed country – precisely the opposite of the normal free market prescription of the IMF.

But it was widespread sanctions-busting which really made the boom possible. Rhodesia's two most important neighbours, South Africa and Portuguese-ruled Mozambique, refused to impose sanctions. British oil companies broke sanctions, allegedly with the knowledge of the British government.[5] The United States, under the Byrd amendment, purchased Rhodesian chrome and other minerals from 1972 to 1977. In 1979 Donald Losman, then a visiting professor at the US Army War College, wrote: 'It must also be stressed that Rhodesia would have been unable to survive sanctions without enormous gaps in its enforcement. A truly universal embargo, one without loopholes, would have brought quick capitulation.'[6]

By the early 1970s, it was widely believed that sanctions had failed and that Rhodesia was an 'economic miracle'. In practice, by the mid-1970s Rhodesia had run out of easy import substitutions, while surplus industrial capacity had been used up, so industrial growth reached a natural plateau. Meanwhile, the long-term impacts of sanctions were beginning to show. And 1973–5 saw a number of changes, both domestically and internationally, which totally changed the position and which a sanctions-buffeted economy found impossible to adjust to.

The economic collapse in the third phase of sanctions can be attributed to five factors:

1. The rapidly growing guerrilla war put an additional strain on the economy.
2. Enforcement of sanctions improved. The Zambia border was closed in 1973 and the Mozambique border in 1976. The US stopped importing Rhodesian chromium in 1977. Other measures were also taken.
3. The 1973 oil price rise increased the cost of fuel to Rhodesia, while the subsequent international recession reduced demand for its sanctions-busting mineral exports.
4. Previously hidden effects of sanctions were taking their toll. In

particular, the lack of foreign capital, technology and machinery meant that equipment was wearing out and could not be replaced.
5. South Africa put pressure on Rhodesia to settle.

The long-term impact of sanctions was huge. Eddie Cross, who was chief economist for the Rhodesian Agricultural Marketing Authority from 1975 until 1980, and who is now head of Zimbabwe's Cold Storage Commission, estimated that over the 15-year period the Rhodesian economy lost 38 per cent of potential exports, worth R$3,600 million. Of this, R$1,080 million was lost tobacco exports, while another R$1,100 million was accounted for by commissions and discounts of up to 20 per cent that had to be given to the sanctions-busters.[7] On top of this, Rhodesia had to pay a similar 15- to 20-per-cent sanctions commission on imports, and it had to pay higher trans-port costs once it could no longer use Mozambique. Thus even the expansion during the second phase (1969–74) was much smaller than it might have been had it not been for sanctions. Without sanctions, Cross estimates that per capita income in 1979 would have been 42 per cent higher than it actually was. Thus, despite the apparent success in weathering the storm, sanctions hit the Rhodesian economy hard.

And Rhodesia was much more susceptible to the outside pressures that came in the mid-1970s. Sanctions-busting was only profitable when there was a high demand for Rhodesian exports; the world recession cut the demand for minerals, which could only be sold – if at all – with much higher commissions. The election of Jimmy Carter as US President brought a much more positive American attitude toward Southern Africa. One aspect was the repeal of the 'Byrd amendment', which had permitted the USA to import Rhodesian chromium in violation of the UN embargo. This was followed up by very tight US import rules, under which all chrome ore and ferro-chrome was analysed on arrival in the USA, and all imported steel required a certificate saying that tests had been done to show that no Rhodesian ferro-chrome had been used. By 1977 Rhodesia could not export chrome anywhere, and production came to a virtual standstill. The beginning of sanctions against South Africa also had an effect – the Arab oil embargo reduced supplies to South Africa, which in turn reduced those to Rhodesia, and petrol rationing was re-introduced in Rhodesia in 1974.

Ultimately, the real impact of sanctions was financial. Except for some capital goods, Rhodesia could find almost anything it wanted –

at a price. But it did not have the money to buy, both because of the fall in exports and because it was cut off from international borrowing. The biggest constraint on development projects, new industrialization, and eventually even repair and rehabilitation, proved to be the lack of foreign exchange.

The effect of sanctions, however, cannot be separated from those of the growing war, which was costing R$1 million per day by 1979. Foreign revenues fell below the levels needed to fund the war and also pay for raw materials and consumer goods, and the economy was plunged into a depression.

Furthermore there were growing shortages of skilled white staff. White men were having to spend more time fighting the war. This was just when they were also having to spend more time applying the string and chewing gum to keep the machinery running that could not be replaced because of sanctions.

Thus, sanctions on their own did not bring about majority rule, but they played a key role in bringing the war and the bloodshed to an early end.

Right up to the Lancaster House conference Rhodesians kept up the fiction that the boom of the early 1970s was continuing and that they were successfully beating sanctions. Indeed, the early 1970s boom plus the late 1970s bluster has convinced many people who should know better that sanctions really were a failure. But those same 'Rhodesians' now tell a very different story. One prominent business-man heavily involved in sanctions-busting commented that by the late 1970s 'we were running out of domestic revenue and foreign exchange, in addition to which the permanent call-up was wrecking what was left of the economy'. Because of sanctions, Rhodesia could no longer finance the war: 'I imagine that if we had been able to continue our economic strength, the political side would have continued the war longer.'[8]

The final irony of UDI is the role played by South Africa. There is a consensus of all commentators that without sanctions-busting, Ian Smith would have been forced to capitulate much earlier. South Africa played a central role, particularly after Mozambican independence and the closure of the Zambian and Mozambican borders meant that South Africa provided the only access to the sea. But independence in Mozambique and the growing war in Rhodesia led the South African government to conclude that majority rule in Rhodesia was essential for the survival of white rule in South Africa. Pretoria confidently assumed that Bishop Abel Muzorewa would win an election, and put pressure on the Smith government to negotiate, and disrupted cargo and financial flows to Rhodesia. It had the power to do this precisely because international sanctions had cut off all other routes in and out of Rhodesia. Eddie Cross comments: 'The key element in the process leading up to the successful Lancaster House talks and the subsequent transfer of power to "majority rule", and in due course to Robert Mugabe's government, was South African economic sanctions against the Rhodesian government.'

The oil embargo against South Africa

South Africa has no petroleum reserves and must import all its crude oil. Thus oil seemed an obvious target for a boycott. In 1973 most oil exporters agreed to stop sales to Pretoria, but Iran under the Shah continued to sell to South Africa. The fall of the Shah hit South Africa hard, and State President P. W. Botha admitted that at one point (probably in 1979) 'we had enough oil for only one week'.

Clearly, an effective oil embargo in the late 1970s could have brought South Africa to its knees. Instead, sanctions-busting was widespread enough for South Africa never to run out of oil. Since then, South Africa has opened three 'Sasol' plants which produce oil from coal, and can satisfy about one-third of domestic needs. Sanctions-busting is sufficiently easy for South Africa to have built up a reserve equivalent to several years' fuel imports. Estimates vary, but it seems clear that if South Africa imposed some rationing and stepped up the production of methanol and fuel from Sasol, it could ride out much tighter sanctions for some years.[9] Thus, in a narrow sense, the oil embargo has failed.

But in a broader sense the oil embargo has been a success. This is because sanctions-busting has not been cheap. Sasol produces the world's dearest oil, which is why the process is not used anywhere else. Sasol oil costs $75 per barrel, which is between two and seven times the cost of crude oil on the world market in recent years.[10] In addition, South Africa pays substantial commissions to the sanctions-busters. Other costs include those for maintaining a large stockpile – both actual costs and the interest lost on the large amount of money tied up in stored oil. P. W. Botha himself admitted that it cost South Africa R 22,000 million to break the embargo between 1973 and 1984.[11] This is roughly $25 billion (at the exchange rates of the period), or $2 billion a year.

The cost of sanctions-busting puts a huge strain on the economy – $2 billion is roughly 10 per cent of South Africa's exports. As P. W. Botha said, 'just think what we could have done if we had that R 22 billion today . . . But we had to spend it because we couldn't bring our motor cars and our diesel locomotives to a standstill as our economic life would have collapsed. We paid a price, which we are still suffering from today.'

Botha's audience knew just how high the price had been. On 1 September 1985 South Africa had announced that it was freezing repayments on most of its foreign debt, becoming the first major country in the world to default. That debt was $24 billion, almost exactly the cost of breaking the oil embargo!

The debt crisis was a direct result of apartheid and the growing revolution and repression inside South Africa. The banks had become increasingly nervous, and as South African loans came up for renewal, they were 'rolled over' for ever shorter periods of time. By the time of default, $14 billion was owed in short-term loans due to be repaid in the next year. Meanwhile, the growing and vociferous anti-apartheid movement in the USA was putting strong pressure on the banks, and by mid-1985 several key banks announced they would not renew their short-term credits. South Africa was unable to pay up.

For some days there was economic chaos. The government had to call a temporary halt to stock exchange and foreign exchange dealings. The Rand collapsed to its lowest ever rate against the dollar – $0.34, compared to $0.90 just two years before. The business community was particularly shocked.

Two weeks later, on 13 September 1985, some of South Africa's top businessmen flew to Zambia for their first ever talks with the banned African National Congress. They included Gavin Relly, Chairman of the Anglo American Corporation, South Africa's largest company.

Thus the oil embargo forced South Africa to run up an excessive foreign debt which it could not pay, while anti-apartheid pressure in the United States caused banks there to call in South African loans. The result was the first talks with genuine black leaders. It was just a tiny first step. But who can doubt that, in an unexpected way, the oil embargo has worked, and that *existing sanctions against South Africa have already succeeded in provoking the first talks*.

Finally, it is worth noting the interaction between sanctions. During the 1985 financial crisis, South Africa apparently cut its oil purchases in order to save foreign exchange, and instead ran down its oil reserves.

Then in February 1986 the creditor banks agreed an unexpectedly easy repayment schedule. In exchange for paying a slightly higher interest rate, South Africa was permitted to roll over its debts without making any political concessions or changes to apartheid. Released from immediate pressure to repay, and with a falling world oil price, South Africa made massive (R2 billion, £633 million) oil purchases in the first half of 1986, effectively rebuilding its oil reserve. Thus it is evident that South Africa can withstand either oil or financial sanctions, but would have much more serious trouble surviving both. By renegotiating the debt on such generous terms, the bankers helped Pretoria break the oil embargo.

23 Prospects for Success

It is nonsense to assume that 'one more push' will force the South African government to adopt policies more acceptable to the rest of the world, commented the governor of the Reserve Bank of South Africa, Dr Gerhard de Kock: 'We are not Iran under the Shah or the Philippines under Marcos.'[1]

Like Sir Geoffrey Howe's remark that 'We are not in a Jericho situation', Dr de Kock's assessment is at least partly correct – apartheid will not crumble under the weight of just a few more sanctions. It would surely collapse under widely enforced, comprehensive, mandatory sanctions. But this remains unlikely in the near future because of the views of the main Western governments, and also because of the likelihood of widespread sanctions-busting. So the question becomes: what are the prospects that sanctions would be effective against South Africa?

To assess this, we need to compare examples of past sanctions with the specific conditions of South Africa. It is dangerous to assume that the examples of other countries, particularly Rhodesia, can be simply transferred to South Africa. But it is also foolish to ignore the lessons of history.

From the examples of sanctions against Rhodesia, Cuba,[2] and other states, it is possible to pick out several key elements:

1. Importance of foreign trade.
2. Strength of the economy and the state of industrialization.
3. External support.
4. Sanctions-busting.
5. State of the world economy.
6. Internal opposition or support.

We will look at each of these areas in turn.

Foreign trade, economic strength, and industrialization

It is obviously harder to make sanctions work against an economy which is relatively self-sufficient. With South Africa, there are two conflicting aspects: it is an open economy highly dependent on foreign trade, but it is also moderately strong and industrialized.

South Africa is usually classed as a 'newly industrializing country' (NIC) along with Brazil, India, etc. By using a system of high tariffs and other restrictions it has protected national industry from foreign competition and promoted local production of a wide range of consumer goods and equipment. This has been encouraged by the government, in part because of the fear that sanctions are inevitable, and does make South Africa better able to withstand these. Also, if comprehensive sanctions were imposed, there might be a boom of innovation and expansion of production as occurred in Rhodesia after 1968.

Such a boom, and the general ability to resist sanctions, are constrained by two important factors. First, South Africa has passed the easy early phase of import substitution which fuelled the boom in Rhodesia: anything that can be easily made in South Africa is already being made there. Second, South Africa remains highly dependent on foreign trade: imports average 26 per cent of GDP and exports 30 per cent. This compares with 25 per cent and 22 per cent for the UK and 9 per cent and 6 per cent for the USA. The reality is that most of South Africa's new industries are still dependent on imports for some inputs. For example, cars must have two thirds local content, measured by weight. This means that most of the lightweight but more expensive and sophisticated components are still imported. In addition, the machinery and heavy equipment for industrialization is almost all imported; according to the most recent statistics, 45 per cent of all capital goods and complex manufactures come from abroad.[3] Furthermore, South Africa is highly dependent on foreign capital and technology, particularly from transnational companies (TNCs), for its industrial developments. Finally, to pay the high costs of imports, South Africa must export a significant share of its production. But its manufactured goods are often not competitive on the world market, so it is dependent on exports of primary products: minerals and fruit.

External support

It follows that South Africa's ability to evade sanctions will be central to the survival of the white government. One lesson of history is the importance of a 'big brother' – a larger, more developed state which will accept the target's exports and provide key inputs, possibly serving as an intermediary for re-labelling and swaps. The USSR served as Cuba's big brother, making a nonsense of US sanctions. South Africa played that role for Rhodesia; indeed, as we saw in the previous chapter, its decision to stop doing so was an important factor in forcing Ian Smith to negotiate.

But who would be South Africa's 'South Africa'? The South African economy was roughly ten times the size of the Rhodesian economy. Israel and Taiwan, which are also excluded by much of the international community, have already shown their willingness to help, but they have economies of only similar size to that of South Africa. They cannot provide or camouflage high volumes of imports and exports. So there are no obvious candidates for a 'big brother' for South Africa, and this will make sanctions evasions very much harder.

Sanctions-busting

The lack of a 'big brother' puts much more stress on straightforward sanctions-busting. South Africa's ability to evade the oil and arms embargoes shows what can be done. And both the South African government and the large private companies have already established a wide range of front companies in several countries. South Africa should be able to buy almost anything it wants, but at a high price. In terms of exports, it would be difficult to stop the sale of gold, diamonds and platinum. But most of South Africa's other exports are high-volume items like fruit and coal which would be impossible to conceal and could thus be reasonably easy to stop. The absence of a 'big brother' will raise the cost of sanctions-busting imports and make it harder to export bulk commodities. Thus the cost of sanctions-busting becomes one of the most important factors. And we have already seen how the Pretoria government had serious difficulty in 1985 coping with oil and financial sanctions at the same time.

The world economy

The Rhodesian experience points to the importance of the state of the world economy. During an international depression the demand for minerals declines and there is less advantage in using sanctions-busting products – unless the producer cuts the price to such a low level that it gains little from the sale. At present the world economy is so depressed that demand is very low for virtually all of the things South Africa produces (except gold and platinum). Thus sanctions imposed now would be much more likely to succeed than those imposed during a boom.

Internal opposition

One of the stark differences between Cuba and Rhodesia was the attitude of the population. Fidel Castro enjoys wide popular support, and the people joined with him to fight sanctions. Ian Smith, supported only by a tiny white minority, was able to continue until, from 1975, he faced an ever more costly revolution by the black majority. Castro, with popular support, held out; Smith, with the people against him, was forced to capitulate. On this point, South Africa is like mid-1970s Rhodesia, with a growing revolution making increasing claims on both human and financial resources. The majority of the people will act in ways that reinforce the impact of sanctions, rather than fighting against them.

It is possible to draw up a kind of balance sheet. The factors making it easier to survive sanctions include a developed and relatively autonomous industry, plus the proven ability to break sanctions. The factors making it harder to survive sanctions include a continued heavy trade dependence, the lack of a 'big brother', the likely high cost of sanctions-busting, the present world recession, and the opposition of the black majority.

Pretoria is worried

Eddie Cross, comparing the experience of Rhodesian sanctions with the possibility of those against South Africa, comments: 'Sanctions have the capacity really to damage the South African economy. In a sense they are more vulnerable than Rhodesia ever was, because they are so much more sophisticated, so much more dependent on access to technology, so much more dependent upon the exports of sophisticated products. It's difficult to hide a commodity which is made in South Africa, partly because they are so big.'[4]

And the *Financial Times*[5] commented that 'few people believe the Afrikaner business leaders' claims that sanctions can be countered by self-reliance which, in turn, will lead to a business boom. Nor, in the face of rising emigration, do many people really believe patriotic assertions that divestment and the departure of foreign firms will release a flood of local talent to develop domestic alternatives to foreign products.'

It is clear that the South Africans themselves are very worried about the possibility of sanctions. Gerhard de Kock, Governor of the South African Reserve Bank, comments: 'The tendency in some circles for people almost to welcome a siege economy, to me seems senseless. If we have to go into a siege economy we will have to make the best of a bad situation, but it is still a bad situation.'[6]

Finance Minister Barend du Plessis stresses that South Africa cannot cut down on its imports: 'Our analyses have shown that 80 per cent of our imports are absolutely essential goods.'[7] Both Liberty Life and Standard Bank have stressed that the openness of the South African economy means it simply cannot 'go it alone'.[8]

The South African Federated Chamber of Industries commissioned a computer model of the effect of sanctions.[9] It concluded that 'sanctions can damage the South African economy rather more seriously than appears to be generally perceived both inside and outside South Africa'. The study considered one scenario in which sanctions would not be very effective and 'substantial leakages will occur'; some mineral exports would be lost, as well as about 60 per cent of textile and agricultural exports. This is enough to cause GDP to decline by 3 per cent per year, causing a decrease in employment of 685,343 in five years. The second scenario assumes mandatory UN sanctions cutting 80 per cent of all South African exports, except for gold, diamonds, platinum, vanadium, and chromium which it was assumed would still be sold. This causes a 6-per-cent annual drop in GDP and throws 1.1 million people out of work in five years.

A different study by the Production Management Institute came to similar conclusions.[10] If boycotts of South African exports were only 20-per-cent effective, it would still throw 423,000 people out of work; if boycotts were effective it would cost 1.1 million jobs. And the Institute points out that one fifth of those thrown out of work would be white.

Finally, the media have been worried about the impact of specific sanctions. The *Daily News* (27 June 1986) said that a European ban on South African fruit would be a 'mortal blow'. The *Star* (23 August 1985) warned that an 'arms sales ban could hit S A where it really hurts'. It is essential for South Africa to sell some of the arms it produces in order to pay for its massively expensive efforts to become more self-sufficient in arms production, the newspaper explained. The *Star* (15 June 1986) also warned about 'the vulnerability of several key industries to blockages in the flow of imports from overseas suppliers'. It pointed out that 42 per cent of all machinery, especially for mines and factories, is imported. Similarly, 29 per cent of transport equipment comes from outside South Africa. If boycotts of sales of machinery to South Africa were even partly effective, there would be substantial loss of jobs on South African mines and farms, the *Star* warned.

Raising the cost

One point which arises very clearly from an analysis of sanctions and South African trade is the importance of foreign exchange. In 1979 Donald Losman commented that 'the major limiting aspect of sanctions in the Rhodesian case seems to lie in the reduction of export revenues. Imports have been obtainable, despite sanctions, as long as the foreign exchange has been available.'[11] Rhodesian businessmen confirmed this. South African experience and advance planning suggest this will be true there as well. Thus three objectives of sanctions should be: raising the price of imports, preventing the sale of exports, and halting other financial flows.

Robin Renwick in his study *Economic Sanctions* comes to a similar conclusion from a different direction:[12] 'Embargoes on imports from a target country, except in the case of scarce commodities (e.g. certain minerals), have tended to be more effective than a prohibition on exports to them as a natural function of the intense competition for export markets.'

A second point that arises from looking at past sanctions is the importance of being serious about them. As Renwick notes, sanctions will succeed 'only to the extent that sufficient real pressure is exerted to give the target regime a serious incentive to negotiate. Token or "mild" sanctions are liable to produce a reverse political effect . . . without exerting any real pressure.'

Professor K. K. Prah of the National University of Lesotho put it another way: 'Sanctions are rather like antibiotics. If not taken in the right dose, but rather administered weakly, they cause the bacteria to develop resistance and become even more difficult to eradicate.'[13]

Thus we can conclude that sanctions against South Africa will face serious difficulties, and will not work quickly. But if imposed correctly, they stand a good chance of helping to end apartheid.

Because sanctions are such a complex and long-term weapon, it is essential that the goals be very clear. The ultimate political objectives are reasonably clear: an end to apartheid; independence in Namibia; and democracy in South Africa and Namibia with 'one person one vote'. [1]

But since sanctions on their own will not accomplish this, it is important to clarify what role they can play.

Conflicts usually end at the conference table, but what happens at that conference can range from merely the signing of a surrender to genuine negotiations between two sides which still have the power to inflict substantial damage on each other. Negotiations by definition involve concessions by both sides.

One question for South Africa is the stage at which negotiations take place. Majority rule is inevitable, but what will the hand-over of power be like? Will it be as in Mozambique, where the colonial power (Portugal) fought until it was so totally defeated that it could only negotiate the minor details of withdrawal, and where embittered whites destroyed cattle and machinery rather than allow them to fall into black hands? Or will it be like Rhodesia, where the white minority began talking soon enough to be able to guarantee a place for itself in post-independence Zimbabwe?

Sanctions will be successful if, as in Rhodesia, they shorten the time before genuine negotiations begin. Surprised foreign visitors report that despite massacres like Sharpeville and Soweto, and the oppression, there remains a high degree of good-will in the black community and a willingness to allow whites an important role in a non-racial South Africa, just as happened in Zimbabwe. The Commonwealth Eminent Persons Group stressed the 'quality' of South Africa's black leaders: 'Their idealism, their genuine sense of non-racialism, and their readiness not only to forget but to forgive, compel admiration.' The EGP also stressed the willingness of ANC leaders Oliver Tambo and Nelson Mandela to create 'genuine democratic structures [which] would still give the whites a feeling of security and participation'.[2] Thus, if negotiations begin reasonably soon, whites will probably be able to retain many of their economic privileges, even though they will have to give up their political privileges.

Early negotiations must reduce the bloodshed and destruction, and prevent the destruction of South Africa's industrial base that could occur if there were a prolonged liberation war. One thing which makes South Africa so different from other African states is the importance in the struggle of organized black workers. This means that much of the fighting will be urban rather than rural, and could lead to destruction of the mines, factories, and railways. As ANC information head Thabo Mbeki told the British House of Commons Foreign Affairs Committee: 'It is in our interests to ensure that the South African economy is as little destroyed as possible [but] if we have to conduct an armed struggle over an extended period of time the economy will be destroyed in a physical sense.'[3] Indeed, business leaders already report widespread industrial sabotage by black workers,[4] and this can only increase.

Finally, there is an implicit goal in any sanctions campaign: to preempt revolutionary change. At the Lancaster House talks, Rhodesia's white minority was forced to give up political power. But it still had enough military strength to negotiate major economic concessions, in particular the blocking of nationalization. This made radical economic changes in Zimbabwe much more difficult and means that transnational companies and white Zimbabweans still dominate the economy. If genuine negotiations take place in South Africa, and if, as expected, the black majority will not permit the watering down of 'one person one vote', then concessions will have to be on the economic front.

Indeed, it is important to distinguish between the demands of Afrikaner farmers (who may have more interest in white supremacy) and those of white monopoly capital (which wants to protect its investments). The interests of the latter will surely win out in the end. And if the ANC were offered 'one person one vote', but told that the price was a guarantee not to nationalize Anglo American, it seems hard to believe that the ANC would not agree; it would be too hard to justify continued fighting if the essential political goals had been won.

A central point about negotiations, however, is that both sides must want to talk. This means that enough of the white minority must come to accept that it is in its own interests to hand over political power. Clearly it does not think so yet, and is unlikely to while it retains its privileged and often luxurious life-style. The reality is that despite limited sanctions and increased requirements for military service, most whites still benefit from apartheid – they fear change and see no possible gain from it.

In part, this is also because South African censorship prevents most whites from discovering what the alternatives might be – for example that majority rule has worked well in neighbouring Botswana and Zimbabwe and that whites there still have a privileged position. Similarly, whites are shielded from the views of the genuine black leaders inside, from the reconciliation policies of the African National Congress, and from world opinion in general. For example, restrictions imposed in January 1987 make it illegal for newspapers even to 'explain . . . any action, policy, or strategy' of a banned organization such as the ANC. Whites know little of what goes on in the black townships. They hear only the government views that 'trouble' in black areas is organized by outside agitators, and that South Africa is facing a communist 'total onslaught orchestrated in Moscow'. Majority rule, they are told, can only mean chaos and the end of 'Christian civilization' as they know it. And yet, until recently, South African censorship was not total. In a limited way, newspapers printed some alternative views. The problem is that white South Africa does not want to hear – and will not want to hear so long as apartheid remains so beneficial.

Thus an important role for sanctions is to put enough pressure on the white community for apartheid to be seen as harmful rather than beneficial to *whites*. This, in turn, may cause some rethinking and more openness to alternatives, and thus to negotiations.

The other side of the coin is that the white minority still believes that armed force can control the black majority and prevent majority rule. A corollary of this is the acceptance of continued killings and brutalization of black people, perhaps indefinitely, in an attempt to cow the majority into submission. Thus negotiations are only possible when the white minority no longer feels that military victory is certain. So sanctions must also weaken South Africa militarily.

In Rhodesia after 1975, the joint effect of the liberation war and sanctions was to make it impossible to maintain white living standards and at the same time to fight the war. Once this was clear, the white minority caved in and went to Lancaster House. In retrospect, it is obvious that tighter sanctions against Rhodesia would have ended the war much sooner, reaching a similar outcome with less bloodshed. But it is also true that the war ended sooner than it would have without sanctions, and the white minority capitulated before the industrial and transport infrastructure was destroyed by the fighting. The hope is that this will also happen in South Africa.

There is a sorry possibility, however, that the whites will continue to fight their losing battle until they are finally defeated. Most of the blood which is shed is black people's blood, often that of unarmed civilians standing up to (or running away from) heavily armed soldiers and police. Even if sanctions do not bring about early negotiations, they will significantly reduce the bloodshed and suffering if they limit the military and economic power of the white regime.

Thus we can say that there are two overlapping strategic goals for sanctions:

1. *To convince white South Africans that it is in their own interests to negotiate a prompt and peaceful handover of power to the majority.*
2. *To reduce the ability of the white minority to suppress the black majority.*

In the remainder of this chapter we will look at three tactical objectives for sanctions as ways of reaching these strategic goals.

Denial of essential items

The most obvious tactical objective of sanctions is to deny essential goods to South Africa. The international arms and oil embargoes fit into this category. Although South Africa has its own arms industry, there are few weapons which can be produced without imported parts and technology. Indeed, South Africa still imports nearly all its handguns (a relatively simple piece of technology, by arms industry standards), because local firms proved unable to make a pistol that was safe for the user.[5] Similarly, South Africa produces oil from coal in its Sasol plants, but it still imports more than half its needs. Thus the South African war machine is totally dependent on imported items.

Computers, electronics and other high-technology items are also not produced in South Africa, and are essential to the modernization of industry there. Modern machine tools, a key to the arms industry, are also all imported. Licences and other forms of technology transfer are also important, because South Africa has relatively little indigenous research and development. Denying these to South Africa would hinder the government's ability to oppress the black majority, and would also make it more difficult for South Africa to adapt its industry to be more self-sufficient.

Pressure on companies to withdraw from South Africa also falls partly into this category, because the presence of TNCs ensures a high level of technical support – both for new technology and for maintenance and repair of older equipment.

It is also important to deny skilled people to South Africa. By its very nature the apartheid system ensures that few blacks receive adequate education and training. Consequently South Africa is always short of skilled workers. Traditionally this gap has been filled by white outsiders who either emigrate to South Africa or are sent by parent TNCs. For example, in October 1985 Barclays tried to recruit 150 white British computer staff for South Africa; the advertisements promised salaries of up to £50,000 and 'a lifestyle of your dreams'. The availability of foreign specialists permits South Africa to continue with the dual education system that discriminates against blacks, while at the same time such outsiders are supporting the apartheid machine which oppresses the black majority. The shortage of skilled people was an important factor in the eventual effectiveness of Rhodesian sanctions, and will also be so in South Africa. The Governor of the South African Reserve Bank, Gerhard de Kock, has warned that the shortage of skilled labour will be one of the biggest constraints for a South Africa faced by sanctions.[6]

Economic strain and the 'apartheid tax'

Blocking the sale of essential items could bring South Africa to a standstill. But, as has already been stressed, there are too many people prepared to bust sanctions to make this a practical option. One lesson of Rhodesia and other targets of sanctions is the importance of controlling and restricting foreign currency, so that the target cannot afford to buy those essential items even if they are on offer.

Thus a second tactical objective is to put pressure on the economy and deny it hard currency. This is a broader, shot-gun approach which has two problems. First, it will also hurt the black majority, both in general terms and specifically as jobs are lost. But that majority has made clear it is prepared to accept this small additional suffering in order to speed the end of the much greater suffering of apartheid.

Second, squeezing the economy inevitably means some damage to the productive base, and thus that the black majority will inherit a weaker economy. Again, their reply is that if a strong economy is only used to oppress, then it is better to inherit a weakened economy than never to gain majority rule. Also, the Rhodesian example showed that the weakness is largely due to worn-out machinery which because of sanctions could not be repaired or replaced, and that this can be done relatively easily once sanctions are lifted. Furthermore, the economic damage caused by an extended liberation war would be vastly greater than the increased wear and tear caused by sanctions.

On the other hand, the only obvious way to put pressure on the white minority is to lower their living standards, and this will require strong and effective sanctions. Indeed, sanctions will work only if they put enough pressure on the economy to make the present government unable to fund the war and satisfy white consumption demands.

The most important way to squeeze the South African economy is to cut its access to foreign currency. South Africa is already in such a crisis that the Rand is of little use outside South Africa; payments for essential imports must be made in United States dollars, sterling, or some other hard currency.

There are three ways in which pressure can be applied to cut the flows of foreign exchange to South Africa:

- The most obvious way is to end loans and investments, and to prevent re-investment of profits so as to force companies in South Africa to withdraw as much money as possible.
- Exports can be blocked, and thus foreign currency earnings. As we have already seen, this is generally easier than blocking imports to South Africa. And if South Africa cannot sell, it cannot buy.
- Although sanctions-busting cannot be stopped, at least it can be made more expensive by imposing what is effectively an 'apartheid tax' on imports, exports, and locally made goods. Rhodesia paid commission of 15 to 20 per cent on all its sanctions-busting imports and exports. South Africa already pays a sanctions surcharge of 50 to 100 per cent on oil, as well as paying a higher price for goods made locally by inefficient industry forced to strive for excessive self-sufficiency. The present partial embargo on coal is forcing South Africa to sell at below the world market price, and thus earn

less. The best way to increase the level of the 'apartheid tax' is to strengthen sanctions enforcement, so that sanctions-busters demand higher and higher commissions.

Hitting white morale

The first strategic goal of sanctions is to convince white South Africans that it is in their interests to end apartheid. Any sanctions which increase the 'apartheid tax' or which deny South Africa important inputs will hurt white life-styles and military capacity, and thus affect white morale. And it is useful to add non-economic sanctions which also have this effect. In general these are measures which isolate South Africa culturally and politically.

It must be remembered that many white South Africans think of themselves as an outpost of Europe in a hostile and savage continent. Until recently they also assumed that their white supremacist ideas had at least the tacit support of their distant European cousins. It is the various boycotts, especially of sportspeople, that has made the average white South African understand that apartheid really is unacceptable in Europe and America.

South Africa is a sports-mad country. Participation in the Olympics and other foreign competitions as well as visits by touring teams were always important. When this was cut off, it hit many whites in a direct way that no other sanction could. And one thing which struck me, as a journalist in Southern Africa and thus a regular reader of the South African press, was the massive publicity given to any visiting sanctions-busting team, no matter how minor. These visits were taken as proof that the rest of the world had not really abandoned South Africa. Runner Zola Budd's defection to England was headline news, and again brought home to a shocked South Africa just how isolated it had become. When she was allowed to compete, however, there was a vicarious pleasure that a South African was again in international sport, even at the price of changing her passport.

The cultural boycott has a similar effect. White South Africa is very dependent on foreign films, TV programmes, and entertainers. The inability to hire top-class international performers is now admitted in the press.[7] The ban on *Dallas*, South Africa's most popular TV programme, was particularly traumatic. The TV critic of the *Cape Times*, Marian Thamm, remarked: 'The coming end of *Dallas* has shattered our complacency. People are not concerned about the cultural boycott as such, because they are not concerned about culture. But American soaps are different.'[8] The South African *Weekly Mail* (14 August 1986) put it another way: the cultural boycott has succeeded in 'making South Africans feel like lepers'.

Scientific and academic boycotts are more controversial. As well as the central political point about isolating white South Africa, they also have a practical reason: many researchers work for institutes and study groups which directly or indirectly serve the government, for example with weapons development or the administration of the bantustan system. It is important to deny them international academic support that might indirectly aid the government in administering and supporting the apartheid system.

Many white scientists, even some who work for agencies closely linked to the apartheid system, see themselves as liberal and progressive and argue that they should be exempted from boycotts. The reality, however, is that few would support 'one person one vote' *now*, as distinct from some time in the future when blacks are 'ready'. At the same time, they continue to benefit economically from the apartheid system, and tend not to bite the hand that feeds them. Such pseudo-liberals are as much a target of sanctions as any other part of the white community.

The issue of academic freedom is often raised with respect to the boycott, and there have been heated debates. During one such controversy in Britain in 1986, columnist Neal Ascherson made the essential point, when he argued that scientists and academics can leave South Africa, just as they fled from Nazi Germany and other oppressive regimes. 'But if they choose to stay and fight, in their own jobs and in their own country, there is a price to pay.' This is not only the risk of dismissal or arrest, but also of temporary ostracism.[9] (See also Chapter 12, pp. 121–3.)

In addition to the sports, cultural and academic boycotts, there are a variety of other actions which serve to isolate white South Africa. These include bans on air links and tourism, which also have some financial impact but which are mainly intended to make it more difficult for people to travel to and from South Africa. Various diplomatic measures also fall into this category: the breaking or restricting of diplomatic relations, the prohibition of certain attachés, and the requirement that South Africans obtain visas.

Some of these bans also have a practical effect. Embassy staff are often members of security agencies spying on and attacking refugees, or helping to destabilize countries. For example, the staff of the South African trade mission in Harare conducted a campaign of anonymous anti-government leaflets and letters.[10] Visiting businessmen are often sanctions-busting. Scientific and military attachés gather useful information. But the real goals of such bans are political – to stress that the South African government does not have the same legitimacy as other governments throughout the world, and to make white South Africans *feel* like global outcasts.

Thus the tactical objective of this class of boycotts is to disabuse white South Africans of any remaining belief that they have support abroad, and to bring home to them constantly that South Africa is a pariah state. This, it is hoped, will cause some people to re-think their position, and also in parallel with economic measures, further undercut white morale.

'Effective economic measures'

In its report,[11] the Commonwealth Eminent Persons Group (EPG) made clear its belief that sanctions were necessary and would work:

We are convinced that the South African government is concerned about the adoption of effective economic measures against it. If it comes to the conclusion that it would always remain protected from such measures, the process of change in South Africa is unlikely to increase in momentum and the descent into violence would be accelerated. In these circumstances, the cost in lives may have to be counted in millions . . .

The question in front of Heads of Government in our view is clear. It is not whether such measures will compel change; it is already the case that their absence, and Pretoria's belief that they need not be feared, defers change. Is the Commonwealth to stand by and allow the cycle of violence to spiral? Or will it take concerted action of an effective kind? Such action may be the last opportunity to avert what could be the worst bloodbath since the Second World War.

As the EPG argues, sanctions must be 'effective'; a gentle slap on the wrist will not help. On the other hand, it is not intended that sanctions should be punitive. The point is not to punish white South Africa for apartheid, but rather to force it to the conference table. Thus sanctions should be considered in light of the tactical objectives, and in terms of their ability to put pressure on white South Africa.

Inevitably, sanctions will have repercussions inside and outside South Africa. Opponents say the side-effects will be so serious as to make sanctions impossible. In practice this is not true, as has already been shown, or will be demonstrated in the next three chapters. The most significant claims are:

- Sanctions will cost hundreds of thousands of jobs in Europe, Japan and the USA. Indeed, sanctions *will* cost jobs, but many less than the critics claim; meanwhile, apartheid is already costing large numbers of jobs in Europe, Japan, and the USA (see pp. 229 ff. and 236 below).
- Disinvestment (sales of shares in RSA-linked companies) by pension funds would reduce the value of pensions. In fact, just the opposite is true (see pp. 237 ff. below).
- The West is dependent on South African minerals and industry would grind to a halt without them. In fact, all South African minerals but two can be replaced with little difficulty. One of those two is chromium, which can also be replaced, albeit at slightly increased cost due to the need for substitutes and modifications in steel-making processes. The second is platinum, which presents the biggest problem. Without South African supplies prices would rise sharply, but there is enough platinum for essential industrial and environmental uses. However, it might be necessary for governments to control the distribution of platinum and encourage the development of 'lean burn' car engines which use less platinum catalyst to clean up exhausts. It might also be reasonable to exempt platinum from sanction because its inclusion might not actually hurt South Africa. (Minerals are dealt with in detail in Chapter 26, pp. 243 ff.)
- Sanctions will hurt black people in Southern Africa so badly that it is better that they be left to suffer from apartheid. Clearly sanctions *will* hurt black people, both inside South Africa and in the neigh-

bouring states. But white South Africans will be the main victims, because they are most dependent on imports. Also black people have made clear they are prepared to add still more suffering to the present burden, because they see sanctions as a way of speeding the essential end of apartheid (see Chapter 1 and Chapter 27). In practice, Lesotho should not be expected to impose sanctions, and assistance should be given to the Frontline states, which will suffer from South African retaliation.

- Codes of conduct are better than sanctions because they improve the lot of black workers. In practice, that improvement is limited, and codes have been no help in ending apartheid (see Chapter 27).
- If just a few countries or companies impose sanctions, there will be no effect because others will take their place. In large part this is not true, although it partly depends on the effectiveness of sanctions enforcement (see Chapter 27.)

How many jobs at risk?

If comprehensive sanctions are imposed, workers in Europe, Japan, and North America might lose jobs if they work with imports from South Africa, or if they produce goods for export to South Africa. Quite rightly, job loss is a highly emotive issue. Opponents of sanctions bandy about ridiculous and totally unexplained numbers and it is essential to be precise in our numbers and definitions.

We will use three different terms to discuss jobs. First, jobs *at risk* are those of people who now do jobs related to South African imports or exports, and who might possibly not have work if trade with South Africa were ended. Second, there is the much smaller number of people who would actually be made *redundant* if South African trade ended. Third, there is the overall *job loss or gain* if sanctions were imposed – that is: would the total number of unemployed people increase or decrease?

To see the difference, consider British imports of South African apples. Workers at a fruit wholesaler who do nothing but handle South African apples would find their jobs 'at risk'. But would they be made redundant? That depends on the wholesaler. If the firm buys local apples instead, then the workers still have apples to handle, and no one is made redundant (even though their jobs were technically 'at risk'). If not, then some other wholesaler will sell more British apples, and will have to hire more workers. Some are made redundant and an equal number are hired – there are redundancies, but no overall job gain or loss. Finally, growing apples in Britain creates jobs for farmworkers. Thus there is an overall net gain of jobs; because of sanctions, in this one sector at least, more people would be in work.

There are several reasons why a job being 'at risk' often does not mean someone will be thrown out of work. South Africa represents a tiny proportion of exports for all countries. For both Britain and West Germany, South Africa accounts for just over 1 per cent of total exports. Far from being the key market it once was, South Africa is now only Britain's seventeenth most important export market; 20 years ago it was number three. Similarly, for most firms South Africa represents a small proportion of foreign sales and an even tinier proportion of total sales.

One of the striking features of a detailed company-by-company study by Barbara Rogers and Brian Bolton was that in many firms just one or two jobs, or sometimes even half a job, were at risk. In reality there would not be an identifiable man or woman in the firm who did only work for South Africa; so no person would lose a job. In the normal ebb and flow of export contracts and workers, these tiny effects would never be noticed.

Indeed, this seems to be true even for the big firms. Newspaper surveys of major British companies with significant South African trade showed they foresaw few job losses: ICI, one of the biggest chemical exporters to South Africa, said that 'the effect on jobs would not be that immediate'; Metal Box saw 'no impact' on jobs; BL/Rover said job loss would 'not be very great'; and so on.[1]

Finally, there is always substantial fluctuation in trade; companies will win a contract with South Africa one year, Nigeria the next, and so on. For example, when Rogers and Bolton did their study, Rolls Royce was a major exporter to South Africa and they estimated that 356 jobs would be at risk. But by 1986 Rolls Royce were saying that their order book with South Africa was 'very small' and that few jobs were at risk. This is true throughout the engineering sector, which dominates trade to South Africa. If companies are not able to bid for South African contracts they will pursue business elsewhere and will win at least some alternative contracts. Thus not all these jobs will be lost.

It is worth noting that exactly this happened in 1979, when the Iranian revolution suddenly cut off British exports of £500 million a year, roughly two thirds of the present value of UK exports to South Africa. Yet there were no massive redundancies.

This is also confirmed by a very detailed study of Canadian industry, which showed that 897 jobs were 'at risk' if sanctions were imposed against South Africa, but that implementing full sanctions would only put 381 people out of work.[2]

With the definitions clarified, we will consider separately the effects of cutting off imports and exports. A key factor in both, however, is re-orientation of trade: to what extent will other countries supply those goods now obtained from South Africa, and buy those goods and services now sold to South Africa?

Sanctions preventing the purchase of South African goods will cause harm only if those goods cannot be obtained elsewhere – if people are thrown out of work because essential raw materials are no longer available. In practice, nearly everything South Africa produces is also made, mined or grown in a wide variety of other countries. This is even true of minerals, as will be shown in the next chapter. There would be some disruption – for example, it might be necessary to use aluminium in some cases instead of stainless steel, and at certain seasons of the year it might not be possible to make a direct substitution for South African fruit. Nevertheless, these disruptions would be minor. Some jobs would be at risk and there might be a small number of redundancies, but overall there would be no job loss due to lost imports from South Africa.

On the other hand, cutting off goods from South Africa would create a substantial number of jobs – meaning a large overall gain. For example, the world glut of textiles, iron, steel and coal means that miners, steelworkers and others have been laid off in all the industrialized countries – in part because of competing low-price imports from South Africa. Indeed, there has been a flight of industry from Europe, Japan and the USA to South Africa, where wages are lower and where (until recently) draconian laws ensured a docile workforce.

The automotive industry has moved production to South Africa. The Ford P100 pick-up, which became the best-selling pick-up in Britain in 1983 and 1984, is imported from South Africa. The P100 could have been produced in Europe – indeed, its successor will be (a decision that at least partly reflects trade union and other anti-apartheid pressure). Other car-makers are producing parts at their South African subsidiaries and sending them to Europe for inclusion in cars there.

Similarly, the British Steel Corporation has sharply cut back production. In doing so, in 1981 it sold almost an entire South Wales steel plant to Iscor, the South African Iron and Steel Corporation. Iscor also hired redundant British steelworkers.[3] Iscor exported steel to the UK until the EEC ban, and still competes with Britain on the world market.

Fruit is a striking example. The EEC has paid subsidies which have encouraged the grubbing-up of 150,000 hectares of orchards, while encouraging imports of South African fruit. Furthermore, before the entry of Spain and Portugal into the EEC, South African oranges paid a lower duty than oranges from those Mediterranean countries. In 1982 the EEC agreed to import 120,000 tonnes of South African apples at the same time that it was destroying apples from a bumper European crop.[4] Importing South African apples is particularly bizarre, because apples can be kept in cold storage for one year, which means that South African apples compete with European ones in greengrocers throughout the year. South African competition is blatantly unfair, because farm-workers are paid at starvation levels; indeed, many are in prison labour gangs hired out to farmers, or are prisoners given parole to work on farms. Not surprisingly, with low wages and low EEC duties, South African fruit is often cheaper than that produced in the EEC.

Southern Europe produces citrus fruit which can substitute for South African Cape oranges. Britain, France and Spain could grow more apples. Australia, New Zealand and Zimbabwe are alternative southern hemisphere suppliers of fruit and vegetables, and the United States could be a more important supplier to Europe.

Thus if South African goods were cut off by sanctions, thousands of people in Europe, North America and Japan could get back into work. To some extent this is already happening. For example, when Denmark and France banned South African coal, Canadian mines picked up some of the contracts.[5]

No detailed studies have been done to quantify this, although estimates suggest that local production in Europe of coal and fruit now imported from South Africa would create up to 24,000 jobs.[6] The 1986 US ban on its much smaller coal and agricultural imports was expected to create about 2,000 jobs. Bans on iron, steel and textile imports from South Africa should also create significant numbers of jobs. So the conclusion is that cutting off goods from South Africa would create tens of thousands of new jobs outside South Africa and thus produce a substantial overall gain in jobs.

On the other hand, it seems obvious that cutting exports to South Africa must have some cost: what will happen to people now producing goods for sale to South Africa?

First, consider the UK in detail. A wide range of figures have been bandied about. In House of Commons statements Prime Minister Margaret Thatcher and various government ministers have given figures of 50,000, 120,000 and 150,000 jobs at risk in Britain. Surprisingly, these figures seem to have been plucked from the air, and no one can back them up with calculations. Indeed, the only source seems to be the UK South Africa Trade Association (UKSATA), an organization dedicated to supporting trade and opposing sanctions, and thus hardly neutral. UKSATA has pushed a figure of 250,000 jobs, which is composed of 180,000 due to lost UK imports from South Africa, and 70,000 due to lost UK exports to South Africa. The first is total nonsense – no jobs will be lost if Britain stops buying South African goods. However, the 70,000 cannot be dismissed totally out of hand. In a detailed study of possible job loss, Richard Moorsom[7] found that the UKSATA figure was based on incorrect 1977 data. Correcting the errors in the trade data and updating the estimate for the much smaller level of 1985 trade, he found a forecast of 40,000 jobs to be lost. This 40,000 should be taken as a *maximum* in any discussion, as it is effectively the figure put forward by the main opponents of sanctions.

In fact, several detailed studies have been done for Britain, both on an industry-by-industry basis and using the Cambridge economic model.[8]

Donald Roy used the Cambridge economic model to look at the effect of sanctions. He worked with 1984 trade data and made two sensible assumptions: that full sanctions would also cut off profits and dividends normally repatriated from South Africa, and that other markets could be found for half of the exports previously sent to South Africa. The result was that overall job loss reaches a peak of 26,500 two years after sanctions are imposed, and then quickly falls to a total loss of only 4,500 by the fourth year as new jobs are created, for example in mechanical engineering and textiles.[9] Roy finds the biggest losses in electrical engineering (3,000 in the second year, rising to a total of 6,500 in the fourth year). He also finds significant initial losses in the service sector (12,500 in the second year, but dropping to 4,000 by the fourth year because many new service jobs will be created as a result of the impact of sanctions).

Two studies looked more closely at industry. Both assume all sales to South Africa are lost, and thus their results should be halved to fit with the Donald Roy figures. One by Bernard Rivers and Martin

Bailey looked at key industrial sectors. Their method applied to 1985 data gives an estimate of 28,000 jobs to be lost if full trade sanctions are imposed and all exports to RSA lost. Half that figure (14,000) is strikingly close to the number of industrial jobs Roy predicts would be lost by the second year after sanctions.

The other is the company-by-company analysis by Barbara Rogers and Brian Bolton referred to on p. 230. Using 1977 data they point to a few significant job losses, such as 60 people at Pilkington Glass, more than 200 at NEI and GEC, and more than 200 at Plessey. They also look at many of the backward linkages – that is, at the suppliers of these big companies. Applying their method to 1985 data, the total job loss would be only 10,000.

There is reason to think that the Rogers and Bolton method of looking at individual firms is more accurate than the more aggregated methods of Roy and Rivers / Bailey. Exports to South Africa are mostly made by the most capital-intensive sectors of industry, and thus tend to involve fewer jobs than industry averages would indicate. And if, as expected, some of the big companies like Pilkington and GEC won other orders, the number would be even lower.

All of this combines to suggest that, at worst, in the second year after sanctions were imposed, the total UK job loss would be between 10,000 and 25,000 and that this would decrease after two years as the economy adapted. British exports account for one eighth of South Africa's imports. We could therefore estimate that the total short-term job loss, world wide, would be eight times that of the UK, namely 80,000 to 200,000. This is hardly a small number – but the world-wide total is clearly less than the opponents of sanctions claim for Britain alone. Perhaps half of these jobs (40,000 to 100,000) would be lost in Europe, but it has already been shown that simply cutting off coal and agricultural imports from South Africa could create 24,000 new jobs.

Thus these figures should be taken as an estimate of the number of jobs 'at risk', rather than of the much smaller number that would actually be lost. If the figures can be extrapolated to other countries on the basis of the value of their exports to South Africa (see Table 7), this would imply jobs 'at risk' as follows: United States and West Germany, between 11,000 and 35,000 each; Japan, 8,000 to 21,000; Italy and France, 3,000 to 9,000 each; Switzerland, Belgium, and Netherlands, 1,500 to 4,000 each; Australia, Canada, Sweden, Brazil, Norway, Spain and Austria, 500 to 2,500 each.

Detailed studies have been done of Canada and Norway, and these can be used to test this rough-and-ready extrapolation. On the basis of UK data, it is suggested that Canada and Norway have between 500 and 2,500 jobs 'at risk'. In fact, the Canadian study showed only 897 jobs 'at risk', with only 381 people actually put out of work. A study by the Norwegian trade union movement showed 1,600 jobs 'at risk', most of which could be saved through a programme of government restructuring grants. These two studies show that the estimates made here are not far out of line, although perhaps on the high side.

What this means is that relatively few identifiable people will actually be thrown out of work if comprehensive sanctions are imposed against South Africa. Most of the jobs 'at risk' are jobs which would be created if companies won contracts with South Africa, as they might be expected to do if trade continued as before. Thus the real cost of sanctions will be borne by some thousands of people in the dole-queues who will not find work. This cannot be ignored, but must be placed in the context of lengthening dole-queues caused by government economic policy in several countries. Furthermore, stopping imports from South Africa and encouraging exports to South Africa's neighbours would be effective ways of taking similar numbers of people off the dole. Finally, as Donald Roy showed, the economy will adjust to provide almost as many jobs after three or four years.

There are exceptions. Each country has one or two companies which are more heavily dependent on South African trade: GEC in Britain, Daimler Benz in Germany, ELKEM in Norway, etc. By concentrating heavily on their links with the apartheid state, they have put at risk both their own long-term profits and the jobs of many of their workers.

The conclusion of these estimates is that in those countries now selling to South Africa, if that trade were curtailed and if alternative markets could not be found, then several thousand people could be put out of work and some thousands of other jobs might not be created. But when job losses are balanced against possible job gains, the total number of jobs 'at risk', world wide, must be substantially less than 100,000.

Finally, three other points should be made about these figures. First, if a revolution does take place in South Africa and if it involves significant economic disruption, these export sales will be lost in any case, as happened with Iran.

Second, it has always been accepted that moral and political considerations may limit jobs. Sanctions against Cuba, Argentina and Libya all cost jobs. Similarly, the blanket ban on military and high-technology sales to socialist countries costs thousands of jobs. Indeed, the US National Academy of Sciences estimated that the US Defense Department ban on strategic exports to socialist countries costs the US economy 188,000 jobs. In just one case in the UK, when the USA forced the British computer company Systime to obey US sanctions against socialist and Arab countries, the firm was forced to sack nearly 1,000 workers.[10] And no one would argue that child pornography should be accepted simply because it provides jobs for photographers. It can be harsh, but we do already limit job opportunities on moral and political grounds – the question is only whether apartheid is such a ground. A strong argument can be made that when a government imposes sanctions it should also provide compensation in the few cases where people would be put out of work. At the same time, unions at companies still heavily involved in South Africa may want to put pressure on their bosses to look for other markets – for example, to stop wasting time on still more trade missions to South Africa and try to sell elsewhere instead.

Third, export jobs have already been lost because of apartheid, through South African attacks on the neighbouring states. It is estimated that South African destabilization of its neighbours has cost them £10 billion ($15 billion) since 1980.[11] Roughly one third of this money would have been spent on imports. Thus, as a direct result of South African destabilization, Mozambique, Angola, Zimbabwe, Malawi and Zambia have been able to import fewer goods from Europe, the United States and Japan. If similar sorts of calculations are made as for the sanctions predictions, it would appear that this has cost at least 30,000 jobs world wide.[12] If majority rule came to South Africa, destabilization would end immediately and the neighbouring states could increase their imports. Ending apartheid would bring back these jobs.

Thus the job position is as follows. Apartheid has already cost tens of thousands of jobs in the industrialized countries, both through unfair competition and by destroying export markets in South Africa's neighbours. The critics of sanctions shed crocodile tears over possible job losses if sanctions are imposed, yet they seem curiously unconcerned about jobs already lost. The transnational corporations have shown far more concern for short-term profits in South Africa than for job creation, in Europe or South Africa. Indeed, sanctions would immediately create some jobs because of the need to replace goods from South Africa. Ending apartheid would create more jobs by increasing the market in the neighbouring states. On the other hand, sanctions would result in some people being put out of work, although far fewer than the opponents of sanctions claim. This is a necessary cost of ending apartheid; just as the black people of Southern Africa see the cost of sanctions as an investment in removing the higher cost of apartheid, so Europe, Japan and North America must accept these limited job losses as their share of the burden. Consequently, any sanctions package should include some support for companies to re-orient their exports, and compensation for people who are genuinely thrown out of work due to lost sales to South Africa which cannot be replaced by exports elsewhere.

The Trades Union Congress, whose role is to safeguard British workers, argues that if sanctions are imposed against South Africa, 'the overall jobs impact in the UK would be minimal'. And it warns 'that jobs will be lost on a much greater scale if the situation degenerates into civil war, as will probably happen if sanctions are not applied'.[13]

Disinvestment and the value of our pensions

Disinvestment and divestment are the sale of shares in companies doing business in or with South Africa. The purpose is to put pressure on those companies to cease their activities in South Africa, and it is clear that disinvestment and shareholder action campaigns have been an important factor in the decision of several major companies to withdraw. Such campaigns obviously have a high moral profile, since many people feel it is unacceptable to profit from apartheid.

Naturally, individuals can choose to sell their shares in South African-linked companies. And they can choose to invest only in unit trusts (mutual funds) that do not purchase such shares. But most large holdings are by pension funds, insurance companies, foundations, university endowments, etc. They are administered by universities, local and state governments and various boards of trustees. Disinvestment campaigns have been directed at trying to force such funds to sell their South African-linked shares.

Many funds have disinvested, at least partially, but many more claim that they are not permitted to do so. Their argument is that fund trustees are required to act in the best financial interests of the future recipients of pensions, and are not permitted to make 'political' decisions.

In both the United States and Britain, the rules for pension and charity fund trustees are governed by a mix of laws and court rulings intended to protect the beneficiaries of these funds. In her book *Socially Responsible Investment*,[14] Sue Ward summarizes the legal responsibilities of someone acting in a fiduciary role (that is, a position of trust). They must:

- Act in the best interests of the trust's beneficiaries and put personal views to one side.[15]
- Act as a 'reasonable and prudent person' and look for the best rate of return possible, consistent with limiting the amount of risk.[16]
- Achieve a reasonable spread of investments.[17]
- Not turn down a good investment for non-financial reasons, although non-financial grounds can be used to choose between equally good investments.
- Take the advice of financial advisers unless they have reasons which a reasonable and prudent person would support.

The issue was defined in a key case in Britain relating to the National Coal Board Pension Fund. Although South Africa was not an issue in the case, disinvestment was already being widely discussed and was mentioned by the judge, Sir Robert Megarry, in his ruling.[18] He stressed that trustees must act 'so as to yield the best return for the beneficiaries, judged in relation to risk . . . In considering what investments to make the trustees must put to one side their own personal interests and views. Trustees . . . may be firmly opposed to any investment in South Africa or other countries, or they may object to any form of investment in companies concerned with alcohol, tobacco, armaments, or many other such things. In the conduct of their own affairs, of course, they are free to abstain from making any such investments. Yet under a trust, if investments of this type could be more beneficial to the beneficiaries than other investments, the trustees must not refrain from making the investments.'

The phrase 'more beneficial' is key. Megarry stressed that if trustees did use social and political criteria, and 'if the investment in fact made is equally beneficial to the beneficiaries, then criticism would be difficult to sustain in practice, whatever the position in theory. But if the investment in fact made is less beneficial, then both in theory and in practice the trustees would normally be open to criticism.'

Thus, assuming no differences in risk, disinvestment is *acceptable* so long as there is no loss, and *essential* if it would be likely to be profitable. The remarkable fact is that in both the United States and Britain companies not involved in South Africa perform better than those which have investments, subsidiaries or staff in the apartheid state.[19] These differences are significant. Various studies have shown that over the past five to ten years, money invested in companies not involved in South Africa would have earned between one eighth and three quarters more than money invested in similar companies involved in South Africa.[20] This means that pension and other funds which have failed to disinvest are earning significantly less. So it would seem that trustees who fail to disinvest, and thus earn less, may be, in Megarry's words, 'open to criticism'.

As well as pure financial grounds, there are sometimes other legal constraints which should put pressure on trustees to disinvest. For example, under Section 71 of the 1976 Race Relations Act, local authorities in Britain have a *duty* to promote equality and good race relations. Profiting from apartheid will clearly be offensive to black people living in the local authority area, and thus disinvestment promotes good race relations locally.[21]

The responsibility of fund trustees is not simply to earn the maximum benefit. They are expected to have a long-term view and to invest with minimum risk and maximum diversification of investment. In general, it is the biggest and most established companies which are involved in South Africa, while smaller companies have stayed out. But investment managers have tended to select larger companies at least partly on grounds of diversification and low risk.

Companies without South African links do better not simply because they avoid apartheid, but also because of the well-known 'small company effect': on average, small companies perform better on the stock market than bigger ones. Eliminating the bigger, more established and more diversified companies from a portfolio because of their South African links means not investing in many household names which seem to be safe for pension funds. The common assumption is that precisely because they *are* big, the household names are better managed, more profitable and less risky. In fact, 'all the research shows that small companies outperform big companies, on a risk-adjusted basis,' explains Stephen Lee, a Lecturer in Finance at the City of London Polytechnic.

There is one problem, however. Because such companies are smaller, fewer of their shares are traded. In finance jargon, they are less 'liquid'; it will take longer to buy or sell a larger holding in a small firm. This is only a problem for a fund which may need to make large payments at short notice; the average pension fund knows several years in advance what its outgoings will be, so it is not affected.[22]

Excluding the South Africa-invested (SAI) household names from the portfolio creates two other problems. First, it significantly reduces the pool of available investments. In Britain only one third of the companies in the Financial Times All Share Index are SAI, but they account for two thirds of the total market value.[23] Second, excluding SAI firms means that it is difficult to find investments in certain industrial sectors such as electronics, chemicals and oils.

Traditional fund managers and advisers argue that all of these points would make a fund that avoided SAI more risky and less diversified. In fact, this is not true. Despite the fact that eliminating SAI firms takes away a large chunk of the market, there are still more than enough companies in which to invest.[24] Diversification is hard to define, and it is simple laziness on the part of an investment adviser or manager to say that it means placing a proportion of the money in each industrial sector. Many advisers claim, for example, that British funds cannot disinvest from both BP and Shell because of their relative importance both in the market as a whole and their dominance of the oil sector.

As in many other areas, computers have now entered portfolio planning with a vengeance. What is known as Modern Portfolio Theory applies sophisticated mathematical techniques to ensure that volatility and other risks are kept to an acceptable level, and that the portfolio is suitably diversified. Stephen Lee, who has looked at this issue, says that with Modern Portfolio Theory it is 'simply false' to say that risk will be increased or performance decreased by not investing in the biggest companies, or by avoiding an entire sector like oil. The point about risk is not to avoid it, but to balance it. Lee cites the textbook example of umbrella and sunglasses factories; each is risky because it is dependent on the weather, but if you own both the risks cancel out. The job of a fund manager is not to take the easy way out and simply spread the money around, but to balance the risks intelligently.

The now accepted view was put by Blake Grossman and William Sharple in the prestigious *Financial Analysts Journal* (July–August 1986): 'A representative, highly diversified South Africa-free strategy can provide a slightly higher expected return with the same risk but considerably less liquidity (because of its concentration on small stocks).'

As all share analysts and salespeople stress, past performance cannot be used as a guide to the future. Just because SAI shares have performed more poorly for the past decade, we cannot be sure they will in the future. Indeed, analysts suggest that the share prices of companies heavily involved in South Africa are already trading at somewhat below the value of comparable non-SAI firms. For example, in 1986, before it withdrew from South Africa, the price of Barclays Bank shares had fallen 15 per cent below the average of bank shares. This 'risk discount' is due partly to the collapse of the Rand and of the South African economy, which has sharply cut profits from South Africa. But it is also because profits from South Africa in the near future are now considered so risky that they tend to be totally ignored by share analysts.

Clearly, fund managers who failed to heed the warnings about SAI shares served their beneficiaries badly. But can they now argue that the worst is over, that the losses have already been made and the 'risk discount' already compensates for South African involvement?

Probably not. The yield of a share is the combination of any capital gain (increase in price) plus any earnings. But the price is in turn based both on present earnings and expected future earnings. It would appear that investors have pushed SAI share prices down far enough to ignore South African profits in the near future, but they still assume that companies with investments in South Africa will make profits from them some day. This is a dangerous assumption on two grounds. First, a revolution could lead to the destruction of those assets, or to the nationalization of firms which did not withdraw and were thus seen to support the apartheid regime. Second, there is a clear danger that the present South African government will restrict repatriation of profits and dividends, and perhaps even of licence and other fees. Indeed, government officials have threatened to nationalize foreign companies in retaliation for sanctions.[25] Thus the political risk of remaining in South Africa is still high, and investors should avoid firms with South African investments. For those firms which have no direct investments but which still sell to South Africa, it would seem that the risk has not been discounted so far; sanctions or a revolution will hurt their sales, and thus their profits and share prices.

Finally, there is the issue of the herd instinct of the market. Despite their much vaunted research and computer facilities, most fund managers look to the climate of City and Wall Street opinion and follow the rest of the herd. If the herd goes off a company or an entire sector, the price falls sharply, independent of fundamentals. So far, disinvestment *per se* does not seem to have affected individual share prices. But as more funds disinvest and impose restrictions[26] on SAI shares, this will limit the market, which must eventually depress the price. And when enough people start to sell, there will be a herd effect against SAI shares. At that point, funds which still hold SAI shares will find them sharply devalued and thus virtually unsaleable. As the disinvestment campaign gains momentum it will hit SAI share prices, and those managers who lag behind will lose money. It therefore seems clear that investment in South African-linked firms is both less profitable and more risky. Thus:

A prudent person would not invest in South African-linked shares. Fund managers and advisers should disinvest, in the direct financial interests of their beneficiaries.

Naturally, some conservative and oldfashioned financial advisers will disagree. They still assume that white rule will continue in South Africa, and the profits will continue to flow and even return to their higher historic levels. They will also take the easy way out and argue that money should be spread around the big companies, because they are 'safer'. Fund laws and court rulings expect trustees to listen to their advisers, but they do not require those trustees to continue to use unacceptable advisers. In the United States and increasingly in Britain and elsewhere, there are financial advisers (including some at big and well-known banks and brokers) who are happy to take on portfolios without South African links and be judged on their performance. If present advisers are unwilling to do this, then trustees should simply change them.

The UK Trades Union Congress, in its *New Guidelines on Disinvesting in South Africa*, stresses that as many banks and insurance companies have links with South Africa, this means many pension funds will have investment advisers with at least indirect South African links: 'It is highly unlikely that financial institutions with significant links themselves with South Africa will recommend disinvestment to pensions fund trustees.' Therefore, 'change your investment adviser if it has major South African connections'.[27]

26   Will Industry Stop without South African Minerals?

South Africa's significance to the rest of the world is as a major producer of minerals. Apologists for South Africa have claimed that without its minerals Western industry would grind to a halt. The reality is somewhat different.[1]

South Africa produces an unusually wide range of minerals. In part this is because of the geology of the region, which is what attracted the mining engineers in the first place. But South Africa's attractiveness as a source of minerals has much more to do with the apartheid system, which provides the hundreds of thousands of cheap black workers necessary to do the work of extraction. The massive profits generated by South African mines led the large mining houses to concentrate their exploration and development there. Thus South Africa is much better mapped and the reserves better known than almost anywhere else in the world; other countries have significant reserves of the same minerals, but lower potential profits have resulted in less exploration. This also means that South Africa is an important supplier of minerals where it has no particular geological advantage. Indeed, some mines still operate in South Africa which would be totally uneconomic anywhere else in the world.

For most of the minerals exported by South Africa there are large numbers of other producers, and prices are generally depressed. In these cases, the total loss of South African supplies, due to sanctions or revolution, would make no difference. This includes coal, iron, asbestos, uranium, copper, nickel, lead, zinc, tin, and even diamonds.

For five types of minerals, however, South Africa is the world's first or second producer and supplies at least one third of Western world consumption (see Table 1 on p. 244). These are manganese, vanadium, chromium, platinum group metals and gold. The first three are all essential to the steel industry, while platinum is vital as a catalyst for oil refining and for emission controls of cars. Thus these are strategic minerals, and it is sometimes claimed that the loss of South African

Table 1: **Key South African minerals**

	Chromium (total Cr)	Ferro-chromium	Manganese ore	Ferro-manganese
Percentage of world production by:				
South Africa	31	31	15	7
USSR	35	15	36	31
South Africa share (%) of imports by:				
United States	54	63	28	45
EEC	51	39	44	52
Japan	45	63	49	0

	Platinum group metals	Vanadium	Gold
Percentage of world production by:			
South Africa	53	38	48
USSR	41	29	19
South Africa share (%) of imports by:			
United States	64		
EEC	47		
Japan	49		

Production figures are for 1984. South Africa and the USSR occupy first or second place for six of the minerals. For ferro-manganese, the USSR is number 1 and South Africa number 4. Import figures are for 1980–84 (US) and 1980–83 (EEC and Japan), and include both direct and indirect imports.

Source: *South Africa and Critical Minerals*, Open File Report 1976–86, Bureau of Mines, US Department of Interior, July 1986.

supplies would have catastrophic consequences for Western industry (and military capability).

In the rest of this chapter we will look at each of the five minerals individually. But it is necessary to make general points first about outside factors affecting their availability: the role of markets, the possibilities of substitution, the position of the Soviet Union, and the possible effect of a revolution.

Supply and demand

Metals are traded in various international markets. Attempts to control metals markets, either through cartels or through manipulation, have been notoriously unsuccessful. This is underlined by two recent and spectacular failures. In 1981 Nelson Bunker Hunt lost more than $1 billion in an ill-fated attempt to corner silver. And in October 1985 the International Tin Council (the tin producers' and users' cartel) failed in an attempt to keep prices artificially high and collapsed with debts of £900 million.

If a significant portion of the world's supply of a metal is cut off, market mechanisms come into play – the price jumps to two or three times the previous level. This in turn affects both demand and supply. Some users find alternatives, reducing demand. But, at the new higher price, increased recycling becomes practical and hoarded metal is sold at a profit. Metal held in government and private stockpiles is released to fill some of the gap. Production is increased to the maximum possible level with existing equipment, and if the price remains high long enough, new mines are opened. (With most metals, reserves have already been identified and it takes four or five years actually to open the new mine.)

The ability to substitute is usually underestimated. For example, chrome, manganese and vanadium are used primarily in alloys (known as ferro-alloys) to produce stainless, high-strength and other special steels. In some cases the specific chemical properties of a metal are needed to produce a special result. But in most cases at least one of the other steel additives can be used, for example molybdenum, nickel or titanium (or manganese, which we will see is not in short supply even without South Africa). For example, vanadium and molybdenum are often interchangeable. Vanadium is only used in significant amounts now because the molybdenum price jumped ten-fold in 1979; the price has now dropped and some re-substitution is already taking place. In some cases there is no one-for-one substitution and the replacement of a slightly different grade of steel may require minor design modifications, say to a machine tool; but the original grade of metal was most likely chosen on price grounds, and the re-design may also be justified in the same way. Finally there is substitution at a broader level: if stainless steel becomes more expensive, then some users will employ aluminium or plastics instead.

Thus the market mechanism tends to balance supply and demand. Exactly this occurred in the two recent cases where a major part of world production of a mineral was disrupted: in 1969, when a long strike in Canada cut off much of the world's nickel; and in 1978, when the Shaba wars cut off Zairean cobalt, which is more than half the world supply. In neither case did the supply cut-off cause the kind of disruption which apologists for South Africa claim will occur if sanctions are imposed. We will see below if this is true for the five key metals from South Africa.

Whom should we trust?

The role of the USSR is vital, because it is the alternative main supplier for all five metals. For Prime Minister Margaret Thatcher that is sufficient reason to oppose sanctions: 'To me it is absolutely absurd that people should be prepared to put increasing power into the hands of the Soviet Union on the grounds that they disapprove of apartheid in South Africa.' And she goes on to note that if sanctions pushed up mineral prices, that 'would have a fantastic effect on the economy of the Soviet Union'.[2]

These two points are diametrically opposed. As we have just noted, it is indeed true that sanctions would increase prices, and this would benefit the Soviet Union. Mrs Thatcher's second point is really a moral and political question. Is the USSR really an 'evil empire' which is so awful that it is better to support apartheid than do anything which might indirectly benefit the Soviet Union?

The first point is more serious, however. Despite extensive and increasing trade with the socialist bloc, the United States and its allies in NATO have defined the USSR as their main enemy. Is it safe to depend on the enemy for strategic minerals?

It should be stressed that the West is already heavily dependent on the USSR for a whole range of strategic minerals. This choice has been made on purely commercial grounds – these minerals are available from the USSR at a much lower cost than that of maintaining inefficient or difficult mines in the West. We have already decided that we will not hurt ourselves in order to hurt the USSR by not buying its minerals. In this case, profit has come before any mythical security risk. Thus one must be suspicious when Mrs Thatcher suddenly raises this argument about sanctions against South Africa, which she has stated repeatedly she does not want to impose.

In any case, there are three reasons to think that dependence on the USSR is safe. First, Mrs Thatcher has really answered her own criticism. The USSR is much more likely to want to earn extra profits by selling minerals than it is to want to cause trouble for the West by withholding them.

Second, the Soviet Union has always treated exports on a much more commercial basis than the USA; the USSR almost never manipulates them for political ends, in sharp contrast to the USA. The one exception was in 1948, when the USSR cut off supplies during the Berlin blockade crisis. But in the nearly 40 years since, the USSR has never done this again. This is due both to a rigid central planning system and to the USSR's continued need for dollars.

Third, and probably most important, the USSR would do unacceptable damage to its international image if it cut off supplies to the West. This is because the USSR would gain leverage purely because of sanctions against South Africa. If the USSR did try to use this leverage for political purposes, the sanctions against South Africa could be lifted and purchases made from there again. The USSR places a much higher value on its image in the Third World than does the USA; it wants to be seen as a supporter of liberation movements and socialism in the fight against imperialism and capitalism. It is therefore inconceivable that it would allow itself to be put into a position where it could be blamed for the lifting of sanctions, and thus for the weakening of the fight against apartheid. The USSR would be forced to supply the West with strategic minerals precisely to ensure that sanctions remain in force. Thus sanctions may give the USSR increased power, but it could not possibly use that power.

This leads directly to another factor affecting the supply of minerals: the level of unrest inside South Africa. In January 1986 the workers at Impala Platinum went on strike. Impala sacked the workers rather than negotiate. But it found, contrary to expectations, that it could not find skilled workers to replace the sacked men, and it had to rehire most of them. But production was disrupted for three months. This one strike reduced South Africa's platinum production by more than 10 per cent.[3]

Disruptions are bound to increase as black workers push harder to overthrow the apartheid regime. Mines are highly complex organizations which can very easily be disrupted by strikes and other action by workers. In particular, mines require constant maintenance; an extended strike can permit deterioration which closes part of a mine for a long period, or even permanently. Sabotage would have a similar effect. Finally, it should be noted that South African officials have threatened to cut off South African minerals, especially chrome, as a counter-sanction against the West if it should impose sanctions.[4] Dependence on South African minerals is dangerous on a purely practical level. The growing rebellion will increasingly disrupt those supplies. From a purely practical standpoint the USSR is probably a much more secure source of supply.

Ironically, the dependence on South African steel-making alloys has increased sharply in the past decade – the period since the Soweto uprising when the risks of instability there should have been clear. Plants have been closed in Western Europe and the United States with the loss of many jobs, while new ones have been opened in South Africa. This transfer has been supported by both trans-national companies and governments. For example, in 1978 the EEC agreed to a reduction in European ferro-chrome production; instead more ferro-chrome would be imported from South Africa, and it would be duty free instead of at the normal 8-per-cent rate.

It would be wise for Western governments and industry to begin now to urgently develop alternative sources of supply, and to investigate alternative materials. In many countries it is nationalized steel industries that have recently increased their dependence on South Africa for ferro-alloys, and they could be directed by governments to change that policy. In any case, precisely because governments consider these to be 'strategic minerals', they can already make directives to private importers about sources of supply.

Manganese and vanadium

Two of the key mineral imports turn out not to be significant at all. Three quarters of manganese is used as ferro-manganese in the production of irons and steels. Pure manganese is used in certain aluminium alloys, dry cell batteries, dyes and chemicals. According to a 1986 US government study,[5] in 1984 surplus world capacity was nearly one and a half times the total South African production, and a similar amount could be brought into production (largely in Australia) in one to two years. For a few particular uses, South African ferro-manganese has been essential. For example, 40 per cent of Norwegian imports from South Africa were manganese, because it had an unusually low phosphorus level which was required for certain kinds of very special alloy steels. Now, however, similar manganese is available from new mines in Brazil and Australia. Thus a total cut-off of South African manganese would have little effect.

Most vanadium is used as a hardening agent for steel, for example for oil pipe. It is also used with titanium in aluminium alloys for aircraft and as a catalyst in the chemical industry, especially to produce sulphuric acid. Vanadium consumption has fallen sharply in recent years. According to the same US government study, world-wide surplus capacity exceeds South African production. In addition, 'a disruption of South African vanadium supplies would have minimal domestic [US] impact initially because of substantial private stocks (equivalent to 21 months of 1984 domestic consumption)'.[6] Finally, it is possible in most cases to substitute molybdenum, of which the USA is the main producer.

Chromium

Roughly three quarters of chromium is turned into ferro-chrome for making stainless steel. The rest is used as pure metal, as chromic acid for chrome plating, and as chromite in foundry sand (for moulds for castings). South Africa is not an important supplier of chromium for any of the non-steel-making uses.

Ferro-chrome comes in three grades: charge chrome (containing about 55 per cent chrome), high-carbon ferro-chrome (roughly 5 to 8 per cent carbon), and low-carbon ferro-chrome (under 1 per cent carbon). Zimbabwe is a major supplier of the more expensive high- and low-carbon ferro-chrome. But South Africa supplies most of the cheaper charge chrome. Furthermore, the importance of charge chrome has increased substantially in the past two decades due to the development of the AOD (argon–oxygen decarburization vessel) furnace which uses the cheaper charge chrome to make stainless steel. Thus South African charge chrome has become central to world steel-making, and a cut-off of supplies could in principle cause problems.

What are the alternatives to South African charge chrome? First, it should be made clear that charge chrome is used purely because of price (determined by the workings of the metals markets discussed earlier). The AOD and other processes will use other grades of ferro-chrome, and there is no shortage of capacity to turn chromite ore into ferro-chrome. According to the US government study, surplus world chromite capacity is about 68 per cent of South African annual production. If the price rose considerably, new capacity equivalent to South Africa's total production would come on stream in three to five years. The same study noted that US consumption of 'new' chromium could be reduced by 30 per cent through improved processing to promote more efficient chromium use, and by increased recycling of stainless steel.[7] The price for stainless steel scrap is at present too low to encourage much recycling.[8]

A sudden cut in South African ferro-chrome exports would cause some disruption, particularly because stainless steel producers and users would have to modify the processes. Producers would have to use different grades of ferro-chrome, while users would have to substitute other types of steel or switch to plastics or aluminium. The loss of South African exports would obviously cause ferro-chrome prices to jump, which would impose some costs on Western countries. (It is unrealistic to expect sanctions to be completely free.) But the higher prices, combined with reasonable alternative supplies, would mean that market mechanisms should sort out ferro-chrome and steel supplies. Thus sanctions against South African chromium would not cause a crisis in the West.

There is one problem area. Zimbabwe now supplies 5 per cent of the world's chromium and accounts for 30 per cent of the non-South African surplus capacity (in part a hang-over from the days of Rhodesian sanctions). In recent years South Africa has frequently attacked Zimbabwe's rail links to the sea, and would be likely to step up those attacks if Zimbabwe became a major alternative supplier of chromium. If it succeeded in cutting off Zimbabwean supplies, this would increase the impact on the West. Thus a necessary part of a sanctions package, might be the provision of military and economic assistance to Zimbabwe to help it protect its rail links to the sea.

Platinum

There are six metals in the platinum group: platinum itself, palladium, rhodium, ruthenium, iridium and osmium. They are always found together in the same ore, but the proportions vary substantially. Nearly all platinum group metals (PGMs) are produced in South Africa and the USSR. In the USSR the ore is 70 per cent palladium and 20 per cent platinum, while in South Africa the proportion is reversed. Since platinum is by far the most important of the P G M s, this means that South Africa is the predominant world supplier (see Table 2).

Table 2: **Platinum group metals production**
(percentage of Western world supply, 1985)

	Platinum	Palladium
South Africa	85%	37%
USSR exports	8%	53%
Canada	5%	7%

Source: *Platinum 1986*, Johnson Matthey, London, May 1986.

Table 3: **Platinum consumption**
(Western world, 1985)

Autocatalyst	31%
Jewellery	29%
Hoarding	9%
Chemical	8%
Electrical	7%
Glass	5%
Petroleum	1%
Other	10%

Source: *Platinum 1986*, Johnson Matthey, London, May 1986.

Nearly half of platinum metal is used as catalysts, normally mixed with smaller amounts of other P G Ms. The most important use is in catalytic converters to reduce the harmful constituents of car exhausts. A catalyst is something which activates or speeds up a chemical reaction, but which is itself not consumed by the reaction. When hot exhaust gases pass by the catalyst, it assists a series of reactions which convert carbon monoxide to harmless carbon dioxide, hydrocarbons to water, and nitrogen oxides to nitrogen. Other platinum catalysts are used in oil refineries and in the production of nitric acid for fertilizer and explosives.

Other less important industrial uses are for the production of glass fibres and in various electronic components.

However, 38 per cent of platinum is used for jewellery or hoarded. Japan accounts for 83 per cent of platinum purchases for jewellery, which is also more than half of Japanese use of the metal. Until recently platinum was not hoarded like gold. Since 1981, however, Johnson Matthey and other platinum dealers have been promoting small platinum bars and coins as an investment. This has been highly successful (for them) and now accounts for 9 per cent of platinum use.

Of all the metals we are discussing, production of platinum is the most inelastic. Platinum is produced as a co-product with copper and nickel. Outside South Africa and the USSR, it occurs in small amounts compared with the copper and nickel, and it is their prices rather than that of platinum which determine production. Therefore even sharply higher platinum prices would increase production by only a few per cent, by making a few presently marginal small mines profitable.

However, there is substantial scope for recycling. At present prices it is not worth recycling car catalysts, although the equipment is available to do so. A further rise in prices would make this profitable (and would also generate substantial amounts of stainless steel from the cylinders which contain the catalysts). It is estimated that more than one year's South African platinum production is tied up in junked cars. In addition, perhaps half of the annual demand for car catalysts could be met by re-using the catalysts in vehicles scrapped each year.

What are the possibilities of reducing platinum use, especially if the price were to rise sharply? Unfortunately, many uses of platinum are not price-sensitive. Catalysts, for example, are a tiny part of the cost of any chemical process and are designed for optimum chemical efficiency almost independent of price. However, substitution is easier in the electronics industry. The US government study estimated that in the short term substitution and conservation could lower consumption of PGMs by 15 to 35 per cent, without imposing any constraints on car catalysts.[9]

On the other hand, jewellery use is sharply price-sensitive. When the platinum price doubled between 1985 and 1986, Japanese purchases for jewellery fell to only one third of the normal level. If prices went up further, consumption would continue to drop, and it seems likely that some people would sell jewellery to make a quick profit. (About five years' total South African platinum production is tied up in Japanese jewellery.)

Under fairly reasonable assumptions, world platinum demand would fall to about 45 per cent of present levels. Of this, about one third would be supplied by non-South African sources. Reserves and the backlog of car catalysts would meet the remaining gap for more than five years.[10]

This ignores one factor: hoarding. If platinum prices began to rise and seemed likely to go significantly higher, then the demand for small platinum coins and bars would jump. Since they already account for 9 per cent of consumption, this could be a significant and worrying factor. Indeed, through heavy promotion, South African-owned brokers could divert substantial amounts of platinum into private hands and away from critical industrial uses, helping to sabotage sanctions. This means that an essential part of any sanctions programme must also include:

A ban on any sales of platinum coins or small bars.

Such a ban must also include sales of 'bearer certificates' under which the broker holds the platinum bars in a tax haven such as Jersey or Switzerland, but the certificate shows ownership of the bars. These are already used to avoid value added tax (VAT) in Britain on the purchase of platinum bars, and could be used to avoid bans on buying and selling the bars.

On the other hand, the ban should exempt the sale of such bars to authorized agents for industrial purposes. Many people would sell their bars to take a profit caused by the sanctions-induced rapid price rise.

A tight enough ban on hoarding would stretch out reserves to fill the gap for more than seven years.[11]

The final step would be to reduce the use of platinum in car catalysts. There has always been a choice of technologies: it is possible either to produce less noxious exhaust or to clean up the mess afterwards. So far, the latter route has been taken, and the method chosen is to use complex catalytic converters to remove the noxious gases. But there are at least two alternatives. Other processes do exist to clean up exhaust, but so far these have not been commercially developed. The other choice is to create fewer noxious gases with the 'lean burn' engine, which mixes more air with the fuel. This leads to more complete combustion and thus less exhaust gases. This technology already exists; Ford, Toyota and Honda already produce cars with 'lean burn' engines. Until recently, however, the automotive industry concentrated on catalyst technology, which means it is much further advanced than improved engine design or other methods of cleaning up exhaust. Under government or consumer pressure, this could be reversed. Thus, linked to a sanctions programme should be:

Support for research and development into non-catalytic exhaust reduction systems.

'Lean burn' engines still require catalytic converters, but they use much less platinum. If 'lean burn' engines or other exhaust reduction systems were in general use in seven years, virtually the entire remaining shortfall would be accounted for. And seven years is more than enough time for their development.

In other words, using favourable but still reasonable assumptions, it is possible to do without South African platinum. This is, however, very different from the other metals we have discussed, where the market would take care of the problems. In practice, we have assumed a certain amount of government intervention, particularly to prevent further hoarding. It would also be useful if the user governments (particularly the EEC, United States and Japan) formed some sort of supply cartel to ensure that platinum in short supply was distributed to the most important users. This is done in time of war, and there is no reason not to do so in this case.

The final question to ask is: would South African platinum exports really be stopped by sanctions? If the platinum price rose to $1,000 or $2,000 per ounce, as it would be expected to do, South Africa would surely try to smuggle at least some platinum. Although South Africa would be tempted to withhold platinum as a form of counter-sanction, its own need for hard currency would outweigh any desire to create difficulties for the West.[12] South Africa's total production is only about 65 tonnes per year, which could be smuggled out in one jumbo jet. Smuggling would surely ease much of the remaining tightness of supply.

But that raises another point. The fear of the impact of sanctions, combined with speculation and hoarding, could push the price of platinum up so high that South Africa could well earn more from platinum smuggling than from ordinary sales. (If the price of platinum rose four-fold and South Africa sold half its production, its income would double.) Platinum is South Africa's *only* export for which this is true. Thus it is not clear that a platinum sanction would hurt South Africa. This means:

If sanctions are imposed in phases, a platinum ban should be the last step.

This is, in effect, a proposal that platinum could be one of only two exemptions to sanctions, at least in the short term. (The other would exempt Lesotho, and possibly Botswana and Swaziland, from applying sanctions – see the next chapter.) But this should not be taken as a licence to create a host of other exemptions – excuses can always be found to leave out this or that item, until so-called comprehensive sanctions become as leaky as those against Rhodesia.

The conclusion is that platinum *is unique*. South Africa provides such a high proportion of world consumption that, on its own, the market will not balance supply and demand in the longer term. Nevertheless, with a limited degree of government intervention, it is possible to get by without South African platinum.[13] But platinum sanctions have a low priority and, because of the inevitable smuggling, will not hurt South Africa. Thus a ban on South African platinum should only be imposed if sanctions have become so tight that smuggling can be controlled.

Gold

South Africa is by far the world's largest gold producer, and in recent years gold has accounted for between 42 and 48 per cent of total exports. Thus gold holds the key to any sanctions campaign – if it were possible to halt South African gold sales, that alone would break the economy. The gold price is also important and has varied widely since price-fixing ended in 1971. Between 1973 and 1978 it stayed between $100 and $200 per ounce. Then it jumped to its alltime high of $835 in 1980, quickly falling back. Since 1981 it has generally stayed between $300 and $450 per ounce.

If the price changes by just $50 per ounce, South Africa loses or gains more than $1 billion per year, equivalent to about 7 per cent of total exports. Thus a price near the all-time high would counteract all possible non-gold sanctions, while a price at the mid-1970s level would be equivalent to blocking half of the non-gold exports.

Gold's importance is entirely mystic. Gold has symbolized wealth for so long that it retains an essential psychological place in the world economic system. Only 15 per cent of annual gold production is used for practical purposes such as electronics and dentistry; just over half goes into jewellery and the rest is hoarded in other ways, particularly as bullion and coins. It is estimated that 80 per cent of all the gold ever mined still exists as some form of wealth storage. The level of official government holdings worldwide is 35,500 tonnes, of which 8,200 is held by the United States. By contrast, total world production is 1,400 tonnes per year and South African production about 680 tonnes per year. Consequently, there is no need for South African gold.

Major world currencies are no longer directly linked to gold, and, officially at least, gold plays a very minor role in the world monetary system. It is supposed to be only a reserve against the total collapse of the international financial system. But gold holdings are self-perpetuating; the volume held is so much larger than production or consumption that it will retain its 'value' only so long as not enough is sold to flood the market and cause the price to collapse.

Undoubtedly, the best way of putting pressure on South Africa would be for the United States, alone or in cooperation with other governments, to sell enough gold to depress the price substantially. But is it possible? There is clearly a fear that any tampering with the gold price would break the spell surrounding gold and possibly devalue reserves forever. So far, central banks have tended to keep the normal price within a narrow band, buying gold 'cheap' when it falls toward $300 and selling to take profits when it rises above $425. They will be reluctant to use gold as a weapon against South Africa. However, in order to minimize South African profit while not hurting themselves:

At the very least, central banks should ensure that gold remains near the bottom of the normal price range.

But there is another factor which needs to be taken into account. Precisely because gold has so little monetary value and earns no interest (unlike, for example, bonds), some central banks would like to reduce their gold holdings if they could do so in a controlled way without lowering the price. For example, the US Reserve Bank showed its keenness to run down reserves by stressing its willingness to supply gold for the new US Eagle coin.

This leads to a proposal from Peter Robbins, a London metals dealer, and Ian Lepper, a financial analyst. They suggest two linked actions:

A ban on all imports of newly mined South African gold.

The release from national reserves of a quantity of gold equivalent to that which would normally be imported from South Africa.

A group of countries would announce their intention to release their gold on to the market in a controlled way. This would prevent speculators from pushing up the gold price if sanctions were threatened or imposed. The advantage of this is that it does not need total international agreement, simply the agreement of a few of the nine biggest holders of gold (USA, IMF, West Germany, European Monetary Fund, Switzerland, France, Italy, the Netherlands and Belgium). For example, the Netherlands could play a leading role. And it would be to their advantage, because it would permit these countries to convert some of their useless gold reserves into income-earning reserves. This ensures a low but steady gold price.

The other half of the proposal involves sanctions, which admittedly cannot be enforced. But the proposal takes this into account. Robbins and Lepper argue that every gold ingot is clearly labelled as to source and date, and the trade in gold is closely regulated. Thus the main gold dealers would not handle illegal new South African gold. But chemical analysis will not show the origin of refined gold, nor could new South African gold be distinguished from old. Thus South Africa would simply mould the gold into counterfeit ingots – for example, presenting it as older South African ingots. However, this means that sanctions-busters would have to be found who would filter large quantities of illicit gold on to the market. For this they would charge a substantial fee.

By announcing that they would supply the gold previously supplied by South Africa, the new selling countries would keep the price low and steady. If significant amounts of South African gold found their way on to the market, this would cause a glut which would sharply depress the price of gold. Thus sanctions-busting would not be in the interests of the main gold-traders, who would want to enforce the embargo as a way of keeping the price up. This, in turn, means that the sanctions-busting fee would tend to increase – perhaps to as much as $100 an ounce.

The beauty of the proposal is: (1) it is in the interests of some central banks who want to sell gold anyway; (2) it would be in the interests of the main gold-dealers to limit sanctions-busting in order to keep the price up; and (3) the more South Africa succeeds in selling, the lower the gold price goes, cutting South African earnings as well as raising the sanctions-busting fee South Africa would need to pay.

Whatever other actions are taken, it is also necessary to stop the sale of *all* gold coins, not just Krugerrands. This is because the relatively small amount of gold traded, compared to production and stocks, means that medium-sized sales and purchases can have a significant effect on the price within the now accepted range. In particular, gold going into coins can push up the price. In normal years about 200 tonnes of gold is made into coins and medals. In early 1986 Japan bought 220 tonnes to mint a gold coin to mark the sixtieth anniversary of the accession of the Emperor Hirohito; this purchase was large enough to help push the gold price up to nearly $440 in mid-1986, before it began to fall again.

The increasingly widespread ban on Krugerrands, the South African gold coins, is politically important, and has been so successful that South Africa has stopped minting Krugerrands. But the practical reality is that South Africa can still sell all the gold it produces, and that the promotion of gold coins of any sort increases gold consumption and thus the price. Canadian Maple Leaves and US Eagles may contain no South African gold, but their widespread production and promotion still pushes up the price South Africa receives for its gold.

Conclusion

Unquestionably, industry will *not* grind to a halt without South African minerals. Claims to the contrary are merely excuses not to impose sanctions. Indeed, only two minerals, chrome and platinum, will cause any difficulties at all. With chrome, there will be some disruption, but market forces should quickly balance supply and demand.

With platinum, some government intervention will be required – at least to ban the sale of small bars and coins, perhaps to allocate supplies, and possibly to promote development of 'lean burn' engines. Sufficient platinum is available for all essential uses. But the impact of the higher price means that South Africa could earn substantial amounts from smuggled platinum, defeating the purpose of the ban. Thus a platinum sanction should be left until last, and then introduced only if it can be enforced.

On the other hand, gold provides an ideal opportunity. Forcing the gold price down would hit South Africa hard. Even if governments are unwilling to do so, at the very least they should sell enough gold to keep the price near $300, the bottom end of the current range, which would reduce South Africa's earnings. This would be a practical action which could be taken by a few countries, such as the Netherlands and the oil exporters. What is particularly important, it would not require international agreement because it would not require very large sales, and because it would not push the price so low as to trigger large-scale buying. It would be an ideal first step, which if it worked could lead to other coordinated actions to depress the gold price further. The next step could be the ban on new South African gold and the agreement to sell an amount equivalent to that normally sold by South Africa.

27 *Other Excuses*

When faced with the serious prospects of sanctions, some businesses and individuals show an unprecedented concern for the well-being of black people in Southern Africa. Surely, they say, we can help them more if we stay and continue to profit from apartheid? And if we don't, surely others will? Black South Africans have made their views clear by showing unmistakable support for sanctions, despite the fact that it is illegal in South Africa to advocate sanctions. This has been discussed earlier in the book and will not be reviewd again. In this chapter we will look at three other arguments against sanctions.

What about the neighbouring states?

South African officials often point to the potential harm sanctions might do to South Africa's neighbours. (See map on p. 94.) There are nine majority-ruled states, which together form the Southern African Development Coordination Conference (SADCC). Of the nine, two (Angola and Tanzania) have no economic dealings with South Africa, while two others (Mozambique and Zambia) have only limited trade. South Africa provides about one third of the imports for Zimbabwe and Malawi, and more than half their overseas trade passes through South African ports. Finally, the three tiny states of Botswana, Swaziland and Lesotho, with a combined population of only three million, are members of a customs union with South Africa and are closely integrated with it economically. Lesotho is a special case: it is totally surrounded by South Africa, and more than half its employed adults work in South Africa, particularly in the gold mines.[1]

The impact of sanctions on the nine neighbouring states must be divided into three different cases: (1) indirect effects of sanctions imposed by other states; (2) direct effects of the nine imposing sanctions; and (3) retaliation by South Africa.

If sanctions were imposed by South Africa's main trading partners but not by the neighbours, and if South Africa did not retaliate against the neighbours, then sanctions could only be beneficial. Those goods which the neighbours buy from South Africa (and which South Africa could no longer make because of sanctions) could easily be purchased elsewhere, often at a lower price. Furthermore, there would be major advantages. Weakening South African military capacity would reduce the number of raids on the neighbours. Some of the firms withdrawing from South Africa might invest in the neighbours. For example, Coca-Cola is to move its concentrate plant from South Africa to Swaziland. Steel, textiles, coal, metals, and agricultural products now bought by the industrialized countries from South Africa could be bought from the neighbours instead.

It is usually assumed that at least some of the neighbouring states would not be expected to impose sanctions.[2] It is only South Africa's main industrialized trading partners that have the economic importance to make sanctions effective. The neighbours' tiny trade is a relatively small proportion of South Africa's total trade and would have little impact even if it continued. They could be exempted from having to impose sanctions – so long as they did not increase their trade and become sanctions-busting conduits.

But what would happen if the neighbours did impose sanctions, or if they did not, but South Africa imposed counter-sanctions against them? Assuming a total embargo and thus a total closure of the border, there would be four problem areas.

First, Lesotho is totally surrounded by South Africa – an island of majority-rule in an apartheid sea.

Second, Lesotho is dependent on its miners in South Africa for much of its income. Mozambique, Botswana and Swaziland also have miners in South Africa.[3]

Third, Botswana, Lesotho, and Swaziland (BLS) are dependent on South Africa for oil, electricity, some food and most consumer goods. These could all be replaced given enough time, although the position of Lesotho is particularly difficult as its trade would have to pass through South Africa. South African firms have extensive investments in BLS and Zimbabwe, which might create problems. But Zimbabwe and Malawi, despite the large imports from South Africa, would not suffer seriously from a border closure.

The fourth problem is transport. Several rail lines in the neighbouring states have been closed by repeated attacks by South African commandos and South African-backed guerrillas. This destabilization means that Zimbabwe, Malawi, Botswana, Swaziland and Zambia are partly dependent on South African ports and railways. However, rehabilitation of railways and ports in Mozambique and Tanzania means this dependence will be considerably reduced during 1987.

Most of the neighbouring states could impose sanctions. But Lesotho is totally dependent on South Africa, and physically surrounded by it, so it seems nonsense to ask Lesotho to impose sanctions. It is also unrealistic (due to their dependence on South Africa) to expect Botswana and Swaziland to impose all sanctions – and unnecessary, because their trade with South Africa is so tiny. Thus there should be an exception, and the neighbours need help:

Lesotho, and perhaps Botswana and Swaziland, should be exempted from applying sanctions (so long as they do not become sanctions-busting channels). Help should be given to the neighbouring states to assist them to reduce their dependence on South Africa.

The question of South African retaliation is much more serious. South African destabilization of the neighbouring states has cost them more than £10 billion ($15 million) and 100,000 lives since 1980.[4] Transport links have been a particular target, precisely to increase dependence, which can then be used as an argument against sanctions. South African attacks close railways in Mozambique and Angola, so Zambia, Zimbabwe, Malawi and Swaziland are forced to ship cargo through South Africa. Then Pretoria uses this forced dependence to claim that the neighbours really deal with South Africa by choice, while at the same time threatening that if sanctions are imposed it will retaliate by disrupting traffic. Indeed, South Africa has repeatedly imposed its own sanctions by delaying traffic for Zambia, Zimbabwe and Botswana, especially in 1981 and 1986. So South Africa uses a curious circular argument: sanctions should not be used to end destabilization, precisely because destabilization has made the neighbours dependent on South Africa.

Inevitably, as sanctions are imposed, South Africa will retaliate against its neighbours. This retaliation is likely to take three forms. First, it will surely hold Lesotho hostage, probably closing the border (as it did for a month in early 1986) and expelling the migrant miners in an attempt to starve it into submission. This might occur even if Lesotho were exempted from sanctions, and might necessitate an airlift similar to that used to supply Berlin in 1948.

Second, South Africa might cut off electricity supplies to Mozambique, Lesotho and Swaziland. It might also attack oil supplies in BLS (as it has in the past) in an effort to prevent them from developing alternative supplies.

Third, South Africa would surely step up military attacks and other destabilization in the neighbouring states. It would particularly try to attack railways, in an attempt to force the neighbouring states to use South African railways and thus break sanctions. Thus it is clear that:

The neighbouring states need economic and military help to resist South African retaliation.

One estimate is that economic aid of £1,870 million ($2,800 million) would be required over several years.[5] This is not a huge sum – a bit more than one year's foreign aid to the SADCC states. It is also small compared to the cost of destabilization already. Two comments by leaders from the region make their view clear. SADCC's chairman, the Botswana Vice-President Peter Mmusi, said simply: 'When we join the campaign for sanctions, we know they will impose hardships on us. We accept such hardship, as a woman accepts the pain of labour, in the belief that it will bring forth new hope.'[6] And in a speech on 15 June 1986, Prime Minister Robert Mugabe of Zimbabwe specifically rejected the argument that sanctions should not be imposed because they will hurt the neighbours: 'We are already suffering. How much more can we suffer?' he asked. 'We support sanctions because it will shorten the time that we must suffer.'

Won't someone else just take our place?

To be most effective, sanctions should be universally applied. In practice, they are not. For example, as the major US computer companies have pulled out, some Japanese and European companies have expanded to fill the gap. Isn't that a danger with all sanctions: as one company or country pulls out, another will take its place?

It is important to distinguish between South Africa's exports and its imports. South Africa is a producer of primary products such as minerals and fruit for which the world market is glutted; there is no need to buy South African coal instead of US or Australian coal, for example. South Africa's friends, such as Taiwan and Israel, are small and can only take up a tiny proportion of South African exports. Thus to sell its products, South Africa will have to cut its prices drastically to make sanctions-busting worth while. This in turn sharply cuts its income – which is exactly the goal of sanctions. (Gold and platinum, the possible exceptions, were discussed in the previous chapter.) This sort of sanctions-busting will also be politically unacceptable in some countries. For example, Japan has imposed a partial ban on imports from South Africa, and its Ministry of International Trade has asked importers not to undermine the sanctions being imposed in the United States and Europe.[7] In other words, Japan is not prepared to end imports of coal and other materials, but these will not be increased to take up the slack caused by sanctions elsewhere. Indeed, there seems little likelihood of any major country stepping in to buy South African exports which are boycotted by other countries.

As was already noted (see Chapter 23), selling to South Africa will be much more competitive. For a price, South Africa will be able to purchase many of the foreign goods it wants. Most companies will sell so long as it is legal. Sanctions-busting channels and front companies in third countries will be very useful for illegal sales. Imposing sanctions does not necessarily mean that someone else will take your place. But controlling South Africa's exports is clearly easier.

For both imports and exports, official government bans are essential. And these must be backed up by effective sanctions monitoring. But in practice the central role will be played by trade unions, shareholders and campaigning groups. They will have to put pressure on governments to impose bans, and then monitor the sanctions once they are imposed. And they will have to take direct action, partly out of self-interest. As we noted above, dependence on South Africa is highly risky; for a firm to increase its dependence by stepping in to fill the gap left by a departing company involves a foolhardy increase in risk. This is not in the interests of either workers or shareholders; they will have to make known their objection to the company's putting their jobs and profits at risk. Similarly, sanctions-busting is clearly immoral, and those companies which do try to fill gaps should be a special target for pressure groups. This leads to two sanctions priorities:

South African exports should be the first target for sanctions.

Unions and campaigning groups should give priority attention to companies that break sanctions or that replace others imposing sanctions.

Aren't codes of conduct better than withdrawal?

It is sometimes argued (for example by some of the people quoted in the first half of this book) that transnational companies (TNCs) are 'progressive forces' in South Africa which help to advance reform.

Instead of withdrawing, it is said, they should set an example as progressive employers. The EEC Code of Conduct, the US Sullivan Principles, and codes in Australia and Canada are voluntary guidelines intended to promote this role. They set standards for adequate pay, desegregation of the workplace, equal pay for equal work, job training and advancement, improved education and social facilities, and trade union recognition.

Beneath the rhetoric about helping to end apartheid, TNCs had two reasons to introduce codes. First, and most important, they hoped that codes would pre-empt demands that they withdraw. Second, it was hoped that under the codes a group of privileged, middle-class workers would be created, and that this group would defend the presence in South Africa of the TNCs.

The codes clearly have improved the lives of some workers. Nevertheless, they are now widely rejected on two grounds. First, they have failed even in their own terms to make significant changes. And second, at best they make life under apartheid more palatable for a few black people, but do nothing to end apartheid.

About 350 companies are covered by codes, and they employ under 200,000 black workers – about 2 per cent of the black workforce.[8] Thus only a tiny minority benefit from codes. Roughly half these workers are employed by British firms. The Ethical Investment Research and Information Service studied the returns of the 135 British companies and found that only five paid all black workers the EEC's target minimum wage of R525 (£165, $235) per month. Indeed, 78 per cent of the firms pay minimum rates 'significantly below' the target. It also appears wages have not kept up with inflation. Equal opportunities and training have not had much effect either, and company reports give 'the general impression of blacks getting the worst jobs (and still not a fair proportion of them)'.[9] Even many unskilled jobs are still effectively reserved for whites.

The Sullivan Principles are a code of progressive employment practices first set out by the Reverend Leon Sullivan, a black Baptist minister from Philadelphia, in 1977 (see also Chapter 19, pp. 166–7). They have been increasingly adopted by US companies as a way of staving off disinvestment, but have been no more successful than the EEC codes in improving the situation of black workers. Training for sales and professional positions is still mainly for whites; indeed the proportion of blacks being trained for such jobs is actually decreasing. Seven years after the introduction of the Sullivan Principles, more than two thirds of those companies still reported that not even one of their white employees was being supervised by a black employee.[10]

Black workers report that many companies covered by the EEC code or Sullivan Principles are still anti-union. It seems that only a minority of firms recognize an independent black union; some have sacked union members for striking and there have been bitter confrontations. The EEC code explicitly says that workers should be free to 'join the trade union of their choice'. But some British companies have informed police and other authorities about the identities of trade union activists, according to officials of South Africa's Metal and Allied Workers' Union (MAWU).[11] This inevitably means that some will be detained under emergency regulations. 'The various codes of conduct . . . have been an abject failure,' comments MAWU's Bernie Fanaroff. 'They cannot deal with the sophisticated union-busting tactics of the transnationals, nor the disputes which result.' And he adds: 'It has to be accepted that transnationals are here to exploit the markets and the labour conditions. They have not come here with the objective of improving the living conditions of the people.'[12]

Proponents of the TNCs argue that foreign investment creates black jobs. In its 1985 call for disinvestment, the South African Council of Churches 'concludes from the evidence placed before it that foreign investment does not necessarily create new jobs and that the contrary is often the case because new investment is frequently in the form of sophisticated technical equipment'. This is confirmed by the most recent Sullivan report, which showed that companies which had signed the Sullivan Principles were increasing their numbers of white workers and cutting back their black workforce.[13]

Thus codes have made little real change to the working lives of black workers. At the same time, TNCs which have signed the codes do nothing to challenge apartheid outside the workplace; indeed a common 'social' project is supporting black schools which are directly part of the state's dual education system.

Some code-signers actively support the apartheid system. They provide fuel, equipment and strategic technology to the government and the military. They have other military links as well. Some continue to pay the salaries of white staff who are on military duty, although a few (particularly Swedish) firms have been forced by anti-apartheid pressure to stop doing this.[14] Many firms are required by law to have their own white militia which has been given counter-insurgency training and which will not only protect plant but also can be used in military actions.[15]

Some of these companies have actively supported South African sanctions-busting, for example of the oil embargo. The US Fluor Corporation was the main contractor for the Sasol plants. The British ICI is part owner of AECI, which is currently working on a massive synthetic fuel project called by the prestigious *Financial Mail* 'a kind of life-jacket designed to rescue South Africa from increased energy sanctions'.[16]

Some companies boast of the help they give South Africa. Siemens talks of its 'total commitment to South Africa' and how the West German parent gives 'unconditional support' to its South African subsidiary. In particular, Siemens is helping South Africa to produce computers locally – a key sanctions-busting technology. The Swedish Fagersta provided modern stainless steel technology which won an export award from State President P. W. Botha. Inside South Africa, the Swedish firm ASEA advertises itself with the slogan 'Can you possibly get more South African?'[17]

The history of General Motors in South Africa and of GM's involvement with the Sullivan Principles is an important example of the problems and limitations of codes. According to the London *Financial Times*, 'GM has been one of the staunchest supporters of the pro-South Africa group of US companies that have argued that wisely used investment in South Africa can be a powerful force for change.'[18]

GM was an early proponent of the Sullivan code, and Sullivan himself was taken on to the GM board of directors. Yet just when GM was adopting the code and stressing its desire to improve the position of its black workers, it was also taking action to support the apartheid state. Two documents written in 1977 by GM South Africa's managing director were later leaked.[19] They outline procedures to contain 'industrial disruption and civil unrest'. These would involve the all-white 'GM Commando' which the firm is required to establish under South African law. In its 'assumptions', GM states that such conflict would be racial, with whites acting to contain black unrest. In a specifically racist assumption since proved false, GM assumed that blacks could not sustain their struggle for any length of time because of their 'lack of purpose'. The company goes on to accept that if unrest did continue, vehicles it was producing 'may be taken over for civil defence purposes' and that there would be a military presence in the factories to ensure production: 'It would be fair to assume that under conditions of national emergency, the major elements of this industry would be taken over by an arm of the Ministry of Defence.' Nevertheless, GM would continue operations unless restrictions interfered with profitability. Finally GM stressed the importance of continuing to supply vehicles to the military, because any refusal 'might be interpreted as reflecting doubt on the motives of the company'.

Indeed, the tactics of the company seem clear – military support for the apartheid state combined with amelioration of the worst conditions of black workers. As time passed, even the Reverend Sullivan began to realize that his Principles were not affecting apartheid itself. In 1984 he added a new series of principles which required companies abiding by the code to 'support the ending of all apartheid laws' and to use their 'influence' to help black business and encourage other firms in South Africa to follow the Principles. The uprisings which started in late 1984 and which still continue convinced Sullivan that even this was not enough. In May 1985 he set a deadline, and argued that if by May 1987 'apartheid is not actually and in fact statutorily abolished as a system, and blacks do not have equal political rights and full citizen rights, I would call for the total withdrawal of all US companies and a total economic embargo of the United States against South Africa'. A year later he called on companies to 'practice civil disobedience against all apartheid laws'.[20]

At first GM followed this line. In early 1986 it openly challenged the policy of beach segregation in Port Elizabeth (see Chapter 19, p. 169). Soon after, it decided to stop supplying vehicles to the police and military. Then, in October GM pulled out.

But the method of the withdrawal raised major questions. Employees were not consulted at all about the withdrawal, and no provision was made for them, provoking a major strike. The management, still US controlled, simply sacked the strikers. And it called in the security forces who wielded rifles and sjamboks (whips) to evict strikers staging a sit-in. The National Automobile and Allied Workers' Union made clear that 'the action by the workers is not aimed at preventing the Americans from leaving'.[21] Rather, it was a reaction to the way GM simply made a deal with the managers, without ever talking to the workers. (See Chapter 2, pp. 34–6.)

GM sold its South African branch to its managers – with a firm agreement that it could buy it back later if it wanted to. And it actually sent R 100 million ($45 million) to South Africa to pay off company debts, so the new owners could start with a clean slate. In addition GM will continue to supply $100 million worth of components a year from Germany and Japan. Thus, the 'withdrawal' is token at best. Its only effect has been to withdraw the limited Sullivan Principle protection from its staff, without reducing GM profits or support for the apartheid government – hardly the action of a company genuinely concerned about the welfare of its workers, as it claimed when it promoted the Sullivan Principles. Will GM, as a staunch backer of the Reverend Sullivan, cut off all economic links and stop supplying its former subsidiary if blacks do not have 'equal political rights' by May 1987?

Codes of conduct have failed to speed the end of apartheid. As the *Wall Street Journal* commented, 'It is widely recognized that the US presence has failed to improve conditions beyond the workplace and beyond the 96,000 people (1 per cent of the work force) that US companies employ.'[22] And it hasn't done much for them either.

The flow of goods and money to South Africa can be restricted only by plugging as many leaks as possible.

Undoubtedly the most serious leaks are through officially encouraged loopholes in sanctions legislation. These are often consciously constructed by governments which accept sanctions only under popular pressure, but which in fact still oppose them. The EEC provides three examples. (1) When in September 1985 it agreed to a 'cessation of oil exports to the RSA', Britain soon announced that it interpreted this to mean only crude oil, and that refined oil products would still be sold. (2) Similarly, the 1986 ban on 'iron and steel' imports from South Africa has been interpreted by some states to mean a ban on pig iron but not on iron ore. (3) Finally, uniquely among measures imposed by international agencies, the EEC sanctions apply to South Africa but not to Namibia, despite the fact that Namibia is illegally occupied and administered by South Africa. This allows Namibia to be used as a sanctions-busting route for oil, investment, etc.

Still another kind of loophole is to write legislation that applies to governments, but not to nationalized and parastatal industries.

Just what are 'arms'?

The most serious loopholes are in the arms embargo. One sort relates to so-called 'dual purpose' equipment. Another involves the recipient of the equipment.

Many items are 'dual purpose': lorry parts can go into both civilian and military vehicles, computers have a wide variety of uses, and so on. Western exports to the socialist bloc are covered by the CoCom list, under which exporters are effectively required to show that goods have no possible military use. Exports to South Africa are controlled by the opposite principle – goods can be sold to South Africa so long as they have a possible civilian purpose. Thus helicopters are sold to the South African police for 'traffic control' and are then used against uprisings in the townships. Light aircraft are not even covered by the regulations, yet the South African military writes openly about using U S Cessna aircraft for low-level reconnaissance and to control ground fire. Similarly, motor vehicles are not covered by the rules, and Perkins (Canada), Daimler Benz (West Germany), Fiat (Italy), British Leyland (U K), and Nissan (Japan) have all provided technology, components or specialized vehicles for the military.[1] Centurion tank engines were sold to South Africa, supposedly for vehicles to haul coal across the desert, although none of South Africa's coal deposits are near a desert.[2] And so on through hundreds of other cases.

Two radar sales show just what a gaping loophole this is. Britain gave Plessey permission to sell an A R 3 D radar system to South Africa, supposedly for civil air traffic control. But Plessey itself describes the A R 3 D as a system for tracking enemy aircraft and automatically choosing the missile or other weapon to shoot it down. Its range is 500 km (300 miles), which means it can track aircraft in the neighbouring states; it must have tracked the plane of Mozambique's late President Somora Machel en route to its mysterious crash (see Chapter 11, p. 108). Britain used just this system in the Falkland Islands to track Argentine bombers and select weapons to destroy them.[3] Similarly, Marconi was given an export licence to sell £5 million worth of electronic equipment to update an S 247 radar, again allegedly for civilian air traffic control. Two years later photographs said to be of this radar appeared in the official journal of the South African Defence Force with the caption: 'A Marconi radar at Northern Air Defence Sector, Devon – an intricate part of the fighter control tracking system.'[4]

It is in fact so easy to sell military hardware to South Africa that one route for smuggling such items to the socialist bloc is to export them legally to South Africa first! The U S Commerce Department licensed the sale to South Africa of advanced Digital Equipment Corporation (D E C) Vax 11/782 computers, which cannot be sold to the U S S R. In at least one case, a computer arrived in South Africa and was then sent on by the importer to the U S S R. It was seized in November 1983 in transit through Sweden. In a subsequent investigation, the U S Department of Defense said that the Vax 11/782 is 'state-of-the-art computer hardware' with 'heavy military value'.[5]

The other loophole relates to the recipient of goods. Computers which cannot be sold to the government or to Armscor, the parastatal arms manufacturer, can be sold to private companies which serve primarily as Armscor contractors. The USA is sending plane-loads of weapons to South Africa, apparently claiming them to be exempt from the embargo because they are intended for South African-controlled Unita forces fighting in Angola. With these loopholes, it is surprising that the arms embargo works as well as it does.

Clearly sanctions campaigners must monitor loopholes closely. They must read the details of any legislation and force governments to publish clear guidelines. Where loopholes are obvious or discovered later, campaigns to close them are often more important than pressing for new sanctions.

Sanctions-busting, monitoring, and enforcement

Actual sanctions-busting provides a growing flow of goods. A variety of tricks are used. False labelling is the most common – changing the country of origin to say that steel comes from Mozambique instead of South Africa, or labelling a crate of military equipment for South Africa as if it were office equipment. Third parties can be particularly important. For trade in both directions, many goods are sold first to a safe third country and then sent on to the final destination. In particular, significant amounts of military technology sold to Israel have shown up in South Africa. Free and transit ports are also used for trans-shipments.

But means are available to investigate sanctions-busting. Customs records often give adequate details of what the goods are and of their country of origin. A sanctions monitoring unit which just checked customs records and normal reference sources could sharply cut sanctions-busting. For example, standard military reference books[6] will show the military applications of some allegedly civilian equipment.

Mislabelling can also be combated. A quick telephone call or check in an industrial directory will show that Swaziland does not manufacture matches or produce wine, and thus such goods labelled 'Made in Swaziland' are almost certainly South African.

Minerals are South Africa's most important export and can be easily controlled. The world's minerals have been studied in detail; most international shipments come with a document showing chemical composition, trace elements, contaminants, and so on. For a particular mineral, these vary widely around the world, so they can be used to identify the country of origin and often the mine. If there is any question that a mineral may be from South Africa, then the importer should be required to produce the chemical and physical analysis report and thus demonstrate convincingly that it is not from South Africa. If there is doubt about the validity of the analysis, a new one can be done with modern automated equipment for a few hundred pounds. In general, trace elements are most common in the raw ore – there should be no dispute about coal, iron ore, manganese, asbestos and certain others. As the ore is processed – chrome into ferro-chrome, copper into wire bars, etc. – some trace elements are removed and detection becomes harder. But the buyer must be able to identify the plant where the metal was processed, and could be forced to demand a pre-processing chemical analysis to demonstrate country of origin.

A few sanctions-busters have been caught. There have been convictions for illegal arms trading with South Africa in West Germany, Denmark, Britain and the USA. In the West German case, managers of the Rheinmetall company were jailed for selling arms, ammunition and a complete ammunition-making plant to South Africa.

But the reality is that enforcement is normally very weak, especially compared with enforcement of bans on trading with socialist countries. Western security services monitor trade with the east very closely. And they can quickly crack down on trade with Nicaragua, Libya, Cuba and others seen as enemies of the United States. By contrast, Western security services still have close ties with their South African counterparts. The 1986 US sanctions law allows continued intelligence collaboration. This is important because US security services monitor the ANC and pass information on to South Africa. (This has gone on for a long time – it was a CIA agent who infiltrated the ANC and in 1961 fingered Nelson Mandela.) Not surprisingly, Western security personnel consider the South Africans as colleagues who are badly treated by their political masters, and thus they do not oppose trade with South Africa. In any case Western security services are rarely instructed to enforce sanctions against South Africa. There seems to be a lack of the essential political will required to make sanctions monitoring effective.

The USA clearly has that political will with respect to computers – where some destinations are concerned. Consider the way in which the Vax computers were stopped in transit on their way from South Africa to the Soviet Union; that meant the US security services had been keeping a very close watch on South African trade, yet they never questioned the export to South Africa of a sophisticated state-of-the-art military computer.

Similarly, the USA has tried to go far beyond the CoCom agreement and exert control over British universities. It insisted that universities which bought US supercomputers must sign an agreement that no one from a Soviet bloc country (or several other countries) would be allowed to use the machines or obtain research results from them.

The CIA has been given the responsibility for ensuring that British computer companies do not break US embargoes, and it has allegedly broken into company offices to steal documents.[7]

The USA also displayed that political will in the cases of Cuba and Rhodesia. For example, the repeal of the Byrd Amendment in the United States in 1977 meant a ban on Rhodesian chromium. As noted in Chapter 22, the US government took the policy change seriously. It imposed a requirement that importers of stainless steel and related products demonstrate that they had taken action to exclude Rhodesian chromium. And imported South African chromium was tested to ensure that none had come from Rhodesia. The Rhodesians themselves admitted that this killed their chromium market.

When the USA imposed its embargo on Cuba it denied export permits to dozens of companies which traded with Cuba. Sanctions rules applied not only to US companies but to any foreign company which had more than 10 per cent of its equity held by a US company. The USA blacklisted any ships that carried cargoes to or from Cuba, and President Kennedy encouraged maritime unions to boycott ships on the government list – a far cry from the court action taken against dockworkers who tried to boycott ships from South Africa.

Even when governments accidentally catch companies that are breaking the sanctions against South Africa, the affair is sometimes hushed up, with the company agreeing to pay a fine in exchange for no publicity. In Britain this is called 'compounding'. In 1981 a company was secretly fined £193,000 for smuggling £2 million worth of arms to South Africa. And more recently a company was dealt with in the same way for sending 140-mm howitzers to South Africa (probably for use by South African-controlled guerrillas in Mozambique and Angola); the cargo was labelled as agricultural machinery.[8] Yet one study of Rhodesia sanctions showed that publicity is 'the single most important factor'. This is because 'public image is important and to be publicly accused of contravening the Rhodesian sanctions is not regarded as being beneficial for that image'.[9]

Enforcing sanctions against South Africa requires some of the imagination that the U S A and Britain have used against Libya. Despite British efforts at a boycott, Libya was able to use intermediaries to buy two second-hand Airbuses from British Caledonian Airways. But the planes remained grounded for many months. The Libyans could not obtain insurance because most of the world's aviation insurance is handled by Lloyd's of London, which at the request of the British government refused to insure the planes. And the planes require a monthly update on ground beacon locations, etc., for their flight management system. The data cassettes are available from only two firms, one in the U K and the other in the U S A, which refused to supply them.[10] This kept the planes grounded for some time. It is sad that the U S A and Britain do not treat South Africa with the same seriousness as they treat Libya and Cuba.

In practice, much of the investigation and exposure of sanctions-busting is done by non-governmental groups. Trade unions have played a key role. For example, dockers and shipworkers exposed illegal arms shipments in Britain, Antigua, Denmark and elsewhere. Trade unions in sanctions-busting firms have also tipped off the anti-apartheid movement; it is the workers who know the true nature and origin or destination of goods.

Perhaps the most dramatic enforcement has been by the Finnish Transport Workers' Union (A K T), which has imposed an effective and total ban on trade between Finland and South Africa, aided by the fact that all Finnish dockworkers belong to A K T. With help from unions in other countries, they caught companies trying to evade the ban and threatened to boycott all their foreign trade unless they stopped dealing with South Africa. Soon after the boycott started in October 1985, Finland's trade with Botswana, Lesotho and Swaziland (B L S) jumped ten-fold. Some of this may have been B L S exports previously handled by South African marketing boards, but most was probably sanctions-busting. So the A K T now issues special 'licences' for Lesotho wool and other goods which can be shown to be genuinely from B L S. Licensed goods can still be imported, but all non-licensed goods are assumed to be South African and are banned.[11]

The Shipping Research Bureau in Amsterdam has been able to identify the tankers and sources of oil for about half of South Africa's imports.[12] Many of the ships were owned by British, Norwegian and

German firms. Oil came from countries which supposedly enforce the embargo, including Saudi Arabia and Oman. The Shipping Research Burea depends on dogged investigation, particularly the combing of shipping records, as well as information from workers in ports and on ships. Security agencies in the United States and USSR could trace and identify those ships easily, using existing spy satellites. But if they do, nothing is said or done about it.

The British Anti-Apartheid Movement, and the World Campaign Against Military and Nuclear Collaboration with South Africa, based in Oslo, scour military journals and press cuttings and have documented numerous breaches of the arms embargo. Some are patently obvious. Abdul Minty, Director of the World Campaign, cites the case of the 16 British-made Buccaneer SMK50 aircraft which are flown by the South African Air Force. These aircraft were supplied twenty years ago and are wearing out: significant quantities of spare parts are needed to keep them in the air. Only two air forces in the world still fly Buccaneers – those of Britain and South Africa. It is inconceivable that the British government and aircraft industry cannot easily find out who is supplying those spares.[13]

The importance of the work of trade unions and non-government organizations is in demonstrating the hypocrisy of governments. With meagre resources they expose sanctions-busting which the professionals have apparently missed. Publicity is their strongest weapon. But they are also important in giving concrete support to those political leaders in various governments who want to impose sanctions but are resisted by the civil servants. Thus sanctions enforcement should remain a two-pronged effort:

Governments must tighten laws against sanctions-busting, and must establish sanctions monitoring units.

Indeed, it would also be useful to establish special sanctions-busting prosecution units. But, at the same time:

Non-government organizations monitoring sanctions must be given more support, in both money and information, and be encouraged to co-operate with government monitoring and prosecuting units.

Finally, there is a serious problem that in many countries trade unions are restricted by laws on secondary boycotts, confidentiality, etc. This means that they may be acting illegally when they expose sanctions-busting. Thus:

There should be legal exemptions to permit and encourage trade unions to enforce sanctions and expose sanctions-busting.

Withdrawing without withdrawing

It is not just governments that try to take measures which look like sanctions but in fact are not. Companies under pressure from protest campaigns, disinvestment and consumer boycotts have developed a wide range of tricks. The most common is to be seen to be withdrawing from South Africa without doing so in practice.

This can be seen by looking at three very different types of withdrawals from South Africa that occurred in October and November 1986. When Eastman Kodak pulled out, the US firm announced that it was to shut down its RSA operations and would bar the export of any of its photographic and computer products to South Africa. Clearly this is a total withdrawal.

In a middle position is Barclays Bank. It sold its interest in the South African Barclays National Bank to the Anglo American Corporation of South Africa. Barclays is to take out of South Africa roughly £80 million from the sale, and the South African bank will not be able to use the Barclays name. Nevertheless, the UK bank will continue to provide training and technology to its former subsidiary. The British bank will also remain correspondant bank, and will continue to provide credit for British trade with South Africa.

At the other end of the scale are IBM and General Motors (GM). They sold their South African subsidiaries to the present management. But far from taking money out of South Africa (as Barclays is), IBM and GM sent more money into South Africa to provide their managers with the money for the buy-out. IBM and GM continue to supply their former subsidiary, and have retained the right to buy it back when the political situation improves.[14] South African managers describe such changes as 'cosmetic' – taking the name off the door and off the products without making any practical difference.[15]

British companies, such as Standard Bank, do not even go that far. They have increased the number of shares in their South African subsidiary and sold all of them locally, not buying any themselves. This money is used to expand the South African company; the British parent now owns a smaller part of a bigger company. It allows the British parent to claim that the South African firm is no longer a subsidiary, but merely an 'associate' which it does not control. But in practice all the old technical and managerial links remain and little has changed.

Such pseudo-withdrawals do have useful propaganda value, because they show the continued pressure on South Africa. And they have some practical value, in that they may limit the flow of capital and new technology. But the impact has been watered down through a continued long-term commitment to supply the South African market, at least indirectly. Thus pseudo-withdrawals should receive limited praise as a useful first step, and as a sign that a company is susceptible to pressure. But then the pressure should be increased to force a real withdrawal. In particular, companies which carry out pseudo-withdrawals should still be subject to disinvestment. Anti-apartheid groups have taken a strong stand on this. Furthermore, US disinvestment laws usually apply to companies 'doing business in or with' South Africa. As a Los Angeles city official said, the GM and IBM pseudo-withdrawals 'do not get them off the hook'.[16]

29 *Which Sanctions?*

Sanctions against South Africa are neither free nor easy. They have a cost, although it is not excessively large. Some fears, such as those over disinvestment and some minerals, are totally baseless. Other sanctions will cost some jobs, and there could be limited disruptions due to temporary shortages of chromium and platinum.

Supporters of the present regime in Pretoria make much of potential job loss in Europe, Japan and the USA. In fact they exaggerate that potential loss, giving figures as much as ten times as high as is likely to be the case. Yet they say little about the substantial job loss which has already taken place as companies move production to South Africa and close factories in Europe and the USA, and as South African destabilization cuts the ability of the neighbouring states to buy goods from the Western industrialized nations.

Even looked at in a crass and pragmatic way, sanctions are the cheaper alternative for those in the West imposing them – for workers and consumers as well as for companies and governments. Sanctions mean a temporary halt to buying South African fruit, coal and chromium, as well as to selling machinery to South Africa. But an extended war inside South Africa would devastate that economy, leading to a much longer disruption of the trade in those same commodities.

In the same way, sanctions will temporarily increase the suffering of black people in Southern Africa. But these same people say they accept this as a necessary cost of ending the much greater suffering caused by apartheid. As was shown in Part 1, black leaders inside South Africa and in the neighbouring states have stressed the importance of sanctions to help them in the struggle to overthrow apartheid. They believe sanctions will work, and they have repeatedly urged the rest of the world to impose them as a concrete and directly useful act of solidarity.

Sanctions will not be quick or easy. It will be several years before even effective sanctions bite hard enough to force white South Africa to the conference table. Initially, sanctions might cause a mini-boom inside South Africa, as industry gears up to produce some things that are now imported; indeed, foreign investors have already aided South Africa to do this in some areas. Some sanctions-busting is also inevitable. Nevertheless, South Africa is extremely vulnerable and sanctions can be made to work – especially acting in parallel with the growing liberation struggle inside South Africa.

No easier alternative has been found which can work. Deep discussion, 'constructive engagement', and the odd slap on the wrist have strengthened white resistance rather than encouraged change.

Goals and objectives

If sanctions are to be imposed, it is necessary to reiterate the goals and objectives. The overall political goals are:

● The end of apartheid in South Africa.
● Independence in Namibia.
● Democratic rule and 'one person one vote' in both countries.

The two overlapping strategic goals, as set out in Chapter 24, are:

● To convince white South Africans that it is in their own interests to negotiate a prompt and peaceful hand-over of power.
● To reduce the ability of the white minority to suppress the black majority.

This in turn leads to three tactical objectives:

1. Denial of essential items – weapons, oil, technology, skilled people, etc.
2. Imposing economic strain and cutting off foreign exchange: reducing exports and imposing a high 'apartheid tax' on sanctions-busting imports and exports.
3. Hitting white morale through the economic squeeze and with sports, cultural and other boycotts.

Clearly these overlap. For example, if there is no foreign exchange to buy consumer goods whites find essential, then white morale will suffer.

The position now

Sanctions have moved ahead rapidly, even during the few months of the writing and researching of this book: days before the final manuscript was completed, Barclays announced its partial withdrawal from South Africa, marking the success of a 17-year campaign. The oil embargo is effective enough to cost South Africa substantial amounts of money. The arms embargo is partly effective, and there is growing resistance to purchases of arms from South Africa. Cultural and sports boycotts are quite tight. Three countries which were medium-sized trading partners of South Africa – India, Finland and Denmark – now have a total ban on trade. The United States has imposed the tightest bans of any major trading partner, cutting off imports of South African iron, steel, coal, farm products and textiles, as well as imposing various other restraints. New outside investment in South Africa has virtually ceased, due to a combination of government and pressure group action in many countries and the decline of the South African economy, which makes new investment unprofitable anyway. Nearly 200 companies have pulled out and no longer have staff or direct investments in South Africa. Disinvestment is also growing – literally billions of pounds' and dollars' worth of portfolios have some restrictions on investing in South Africa-linked companies.

But this remains only a beginning. The EEC and Japan have imposed only token sanctions; US sanctions hit only a small part of its trade with South Africa. Re-investment of profits and general trading with South Africa continues largely unchecked; the South African government and military can still obtain most items they deem essential, while the only export really suffering so far is coal. And the wave of US disinvestment is, in large part, bogus, because most companies maintain the same commercial links as they did before. Talking about sanctions, Christo Wiese, Chairman of Pepkor, South Africa's second-largest clothing and footwear manufacturer, commented: 'South Africans have come to accept that the bark may be worse than the bite.'[1]

People's sanctions

With governments reluctant to impose and enforce sanctions, and companies unwilling to end their dealings with apartheid, ordinary people have been forced to take the initiative. 'People's sanctions' are some of the most common anti-apartheid actions. And anti-apartheid groups have put pressure on governments and companies.

The most common 'people's sanction' must be refusal to buy South African goods. Organized boycotts of Outspan oranges have been going on for nearly three decades. More recently the approach of this sort of campaign has broadened so that canteens and cafeterias in hundreds of schools, universities, companies, town halls and even government departments do not sell South African fruit and vegetables. Many government bodies and universities also refuse to buy South African goods. Textiles are a growing South African export, but Christo Wiese admits that in Britain the 'Made in South Africa' label on his clothing is now causing problems.[2]

The refusal to sell goods and services to South Africa is also important. There too people have taken action. As long ago as 1970 Neil Wates, who created one of the most successful building companies in Britain, refused to expand to South Africa. He visited to see for himself and wrote on his return: 'The parallel between Hitler's treatment of the Jews in the 1930s and South Africa's treatment of the blacks today became daily more obvious to me. Just as I think with hindsight it would have been totally wrong to connive at Nazism in those days, so also do I think that we should do nothing that would help perpetuate apartheid.' And he concluded: 'The idea of doing business in South Africa is totally unacceptable to me'.[3] But few firms agreed with Wates, and not many have refused to enter South Africa or have withdrawn on moral or political grounds.

More recently workers at a small British computer company, DarkStar Systems, decided to refuse all further orders from South Africa. Director Robert Sather explained: 'DarkStar's exports to South Africa are not large, and we are aware that their suspension will be at most a minor irritant to some South Africans. However, a concerted boycott by a large portion of the computer goods community would have an immediate and serious impact on South African industry.'[4]

Individual and group action of this sort does reduce South African exports and imports. Many small actions combine to form a rising wave. Such actions do have some practical effect – in particular they do increase the 'apartheid tax'. But the main importance of 'people's sanctions' is the publicity they generate. In the country where the action is taken they play a vital role in keeping apartheid in the public eye and showing that individuals can do something. And inside South

Africa black people see such 'people's sanctions' as an important mark of solidarity with their struggle, while white South Africans see each small action as another brick in the wall of their isolation.

Nevertheless, the overall effect is small – it is the transnational companies and not individual workers and shoppers that control South African trade. The real need is to put pressure on governments and companies to act. This is done best through organizations – trade unions, anti-apartheid movements, and special campaigns like those against Shell and Barclays. Organized action can cut South African trade and can move corporations and governments.

Trade unions have refused to handle South African goods and have organized boycotts. For example in the USA, textile workers organized an effective campaign against South African-made children's clothes. The strike at Dunne's Stores in Dublin (see Chapter 21, p. 201) brought immense publicity. The *Irish Times* in its regular column on produce reported 'a high level of consumer resistance' to South African fruit.[5] Eventually the Irish government banned South African fruit and vegetables.

Some trade union action has been remarkably successful. A prime example is the ban on trade between Finland and South Africa enforced by the Finnish Transport Workers' Union (AKT). (See Chapter 28, p. 275.) Firms trying to evade the ban were dealt with firmly. For instance, when AKT discovered that two companies had shipped paper to Hamburg, where it was re-shipped to South Africa, this was publicized and a total boycott of the offenders' foreign trade was threatened. Both firms then pledged to ensure that none of their paper would go to South Africa, even indirectly. The ban has been so successful that Finnish trade with South Africa in 1986 was less than 5 per cent of the 1985 level.

Putting on pressure

Few trade unions on their own can close down an entire country's trade with South Africa. Normally this requires government action. But few governments – or corporations, or university canteens for that matter – act against South Africa on their own initiative. They act only when pressed by the organized Anti-Apartheid Movement (AAM). Two important points have emerged from AAM and trade union experience so far.

First is the key role of publicity in keeping apartheid and sanctions in the public eye, stressing that people outside South Africa need not stand idly by as the South African army and police kill innocent children in the townships. Regular pickets outside the South African embassies in Washington, The Hague, London and elsewhere draw attention to the issues. So do the shanty-towns built on some university campuses in the United States. It is particularly important that any sanction, such as a disinvestment, or banning Outspan from a canteen, be given maximum publicity – to maintain the overall sanctions momentum.

The second point to note is the extremely varied nature of the actions that have been taken. Apartheid's tentacles reach everywhere, providing ample opportunity for action. South Africa has been expelled from conferences of therapists, veterinarians and numerous other occupations. Cities all over North America and Europe have stopped buying South African goods. Sweden and Ireland may be relatively tiny trading partners for South Africa, but they have proved to be important for high technology: Sweden is the eighth most important supplier of technology[6] to South Africa, while Ireland is becoming an important source of computers. This provides obvious foci for campaigns.

Looking at the bottom line

Probably the most important and effective campaigns so far have been directed at corporations, to force them to stop selling South African products, to withdraw from South Africa, and to stop making loans to South Africa.

At their most successful, these are organized national or international campaigns. The two most prominent are those against Shell and Barclays Bank. Such campaigns try to make it more nuisance than it is worth to remain in South Africa and Namibia. They have three direct goals: to cost the company money through lost business (preferably more than it earns from RSA), eventually to depress the share price, and to create 'hassles' for the management.

The Royal Dutch / Shell group is an obvious target on several grounds. It is one of the largest oil companies in South Africa. Although Shell denies sanctions-busting, substantial quantities of oil find their way from Brunei Shell Petroleum, via intermediaries, to the Shell South Africa refinery in Durban.[7] Shell supplies the military with fuel, as do all the oil companies in South Africa. At the same time

Shell is also a major coal mine operator in both the United States and South Africa, and there have been lengthy strikes at its mines in both countries. The South African National Union of Mineworkers (NUM) has appealed for international action against Shell, and the United Mine Workers of America are coordinating the Shell campaign in the USA.[8] The international campaign involves consumer boycotts, shareholder action and disinvestment. Royal Dutch/Shell earns substantially more in the United States alone than in South Africa, and the campaigners' hope is that if its US and European profits can be cut enough, Shell will withdraw from the South African market as the cheaper alternative.

Disinvestment (divestment in the USA) and boycotts have been the main weapons. Pension and other funds are asked to sell shares in firms linked to South Africa, and to make that sale publicly known. The goal is to create bad publicity for a company by stressing its South African links. Eventually, if enough funds refuse to invest in South Africa-linked shares, this will limit their market and depress their price. One form of pressure may be exerted by shareholders who can ask questions at annual company meetings and otherwise hassle the management.

Boycotts of firms active in South Africa are of growing importance. Many universities and some cities, including San Francisco and Birmingham (England), have restrictions on some purchases of goods from firms with South African links. Birmingham's policy is to not place contracts with 'any person carrying on a trade, business, or profession in the Republic of South Africa'.[9]

Such pressure can be highly successful, as the Barclays withdrawal showed. In the USA, Bell and Howell cited the combined pressure of boycott and disinvestment as its reason for withdrawing from South Africa. The Swedish stationery company Esselte also pulled out after a boycott. Other major companies, including Fluor and Shell, have publicly stated that, whatever their political views, it is the 'bottom line' that counts; their main obligation is to their shareholders and if US profits are too badly hit by boycotts, they will be forced to withdraw from South Africa.[10]

The problem with boycotts and disinvestment is that literally thousands of companies have some link with South Africa (see Table 4). Some, like Shell and IBM (even after its formal withdrawal), play key roles in the South African economy. In other cases a firm may simply be a subsidiary of a company which has another largely independent

Table 4: **Transnational corporations with interests in companies in South Africa**

Home country	Total companies	Companies in strategic sectors
Australia	24	12
Austria	2	1
Belgium	6	3
Canada	20	11
Denmark	2	0
Finland	1	0
France	20	11
West Germany	142	88
Hong Kong	1	1
Italy	7	5
Malaysia	1	0
Netherlands	17	7
Norway	1	0
Portugal	1	1
Spain	1	0
Sweden	18	12
Switzerland	32	18
UK	360	186
USA	352	157
TOTAL	1008	513

Corporations are listed if they hold, either directly or indirectly, more than 10 per cent of the equity of subsidiaries, associates or affiliates in South Africa, or if they are parties to joint ventures in South Africa. The total figures are as of 15 December 1986; the strategic figures for 1983.

Sources: total figures: *Transnational Corporations in South Africa and Namibia: United Nations Public Hearings*, Vol. 1 (UN Report ST/CTC/68, 1986), as updated by the UN Centre on Transnational Corporations; strategic figures: *Policies and Practices of Transnational Corporations Regarding Their Activities in South Africa and Namibia*, UN Report E/C.10/1983/10/Rev.1.

subsidiary in South Africa; boycotting the local subsidiary might hurt local workers without seriously hurting the parent company. Also, trying to boycott large numbers of firms at the same time could lead to confusion and disruption, as well as mitigating the overall publicity effect.

Clearly the goal is to break all links with all companies in the UN lists of firms active in South Africa (see Bibliography, p. 376). But if this is not to be done all at once, it is possible to establish a hierarchy:

- Start with companies that are already subject to international campaigns, such as Shell.
- Next target the other companies which are most important *to* South Africa. Typically these will be the ones with the largest sales to South Africa or the most employees inside South Africa. Some people have aimed at those firms which have the biggest proportion of their capital, staff or profits in South Africa, but this tends to miss out the big companies like Shell. It is better to follow the line of some church groups and the TUC, and mark out a list for priority action based on their importance to South Africa (see p. 289).
- Link action to the struggle inside. Within the group of target firms, pay special attention to companies which are having disputes with their workers and where trade unions inside South Africa have asked for support.
- At a time when sanctions are still inconsistently applied by different countries, it is essential that top priority be given to exposing and stopping any company or agency which steps in to replace another firm which has been forced to withdraw because of sanctions or other anti-apartheid pressure. This includes European and Japanese computer companies stepping in when US firms withdraw.
- Do not accept withdrawals which are in large part bogus, such as those by IBM and GM. They continue to supply the apartheid state, even if they have technically withdrawn.
- Action should be directed as much as possible at the parent company, and not initially at local subsidiaries who have little influence on the parent.
- Disinvestment should also include sales of any direct holdings of South African shares and bonds. Many local authority and trade union pension funds have already done this, often quietly in

response to the early phase of the disinvestment campaign. Nevertheless, foreign holdings of South African shares remain high, particularly in well-known mining companies like De Beers, Anglo American and Impala. In all, 16 per cent of South African mining shares are held in the USA and another 13 per cent elsewhere, particularly Britain.[11]

The goal is to put pressure on firms. Joint priority must be given to the potential effectiveness of the actions and the importance of companies to South Africa. Thus if a pension fund decides on disinvestment and has big holdings of both Shell and BP (quite common for UK funds), then Shell should be sold first on the grounds that there is now an international campaign against Shell.

Similarly, Consolidated Goldfields is the biggest British employer and sixth largest UK investor in South Africa. A major British subsidiary is Amey Roadstone, a construction company which depends on government contracts for roads and the like, and is thus more sensitive than some to pressure, especially from local government. Therefore a secondary boycott campaign has been organized against Amey.[12]

An important consideration for a boycott is the importance of the local market compared with that in South Africa. The *Financial Times* noted the 'South African worry about what will happen if one of the main Japanese companies has to choose between losing markets in the US or continuing to sell to South Africa'.[13]

Based on these principles, various lists of priority companies have been drawn up. In Britain the Trades Union Congress (TUC) has called for immediate disinvestment of an 'inner circle' of six companies – Barclays, Consolidated Gold, Standard Chartered, RTZ, Shell and BP – followed by the 14 other largest employers in South Africa[14] (see Table 5). The TUC also points out that 'subsidiaries in South Africa of BTR, Rowntree-Mackintosh and Shell have ruthlessly sought to break independent trades union organisations'.[15] The UK Anti-Apartheid Movement in January 1987 published a target list of 20 companies 'whose operations are so important to the fabric of the economy that their presence is directly prolonging the existence of apartheid'. AAM includes GEC and Plessey, who are accused of breaches of the mandatory arms embargo.

In the United States a group of 17 Protestant denominations and 220 Roman Catholic orders and dioceses are working through the

Table 5: **British companies targeted for disinvestment**

Company	TUC inner circle	One of top 20 employers	AAM target	Strategic sector	'Ruthlessly' anti-trade union
Barclays	x	x	x	x	
Cons. Goldfields	x	x	x	x	
Standard Chartered	x	x	x	x	
RTZ	x	x	x	x	
Shell	x	x	x	x	x
BP	x	x	x	x	
BAT		x		x	
BET		x	x	x	
BOC		x	x	x	
BTR		x	x	x	x
Courtaulds		x		x	
GEC		x	x	x	
ICI		x	x	x	
Lonrho		x	x	x	
Northern Engineering		x		x	
Pilkington		x		x	
Unilever		x	x	x	
Great Universal Stores		x			
Metal Box		x			
Trafalgar House		x			
Plessey			x	x	
Hill Samuel			x	x	
NatWest			x	x	
STC			x	x	
Thorn EMI			x	x	
Norwich Union			x		
Rover			x	x	
Rowntree-Mackintosh					x

Sources: *Beating Apartheid* and *New Guidelines on Disinvesting in South Africa*, Trades Union Congress, London, 1986; *Allies of Apartheid*, Anti-Apartheid Movement, London, 1987.

Table 6: **US companies targeted for disinvestment**

Company	ICCR 'dirty dozen'	One of top 10 US employers	Strategic sector	Bogus withdrawal
Control Data	x		x	
Burroughs	x		x	
Citicorp	x		x	
Mobil	x	x	x	
Texaco	x		x	
Chevron	x		x	
Fluor	x		x	
Ford	x	x	x	
Newmont Mining	x	x	x	
IBM	x		x	x
GM	x		x	x
Shell*	x		x	
US Steel		x	x	
US Gypsum		x		
Goodyear		x		
Allegheney		x	x	
R. J. Reynolds		x		
Johnson & Johnson		x		
3M		x	x	

* Royal Dutch/Shell is not a US company, but it is included in the ICCR list because shares are held by a number of US investment funds and because it is the subject of an international campaign.

Sources: Interfaith Centre on Corporate Responsibility, American Committee on Africa.

Interfaith Centre on Corporate Responsibility to target a corporate 'dirty dozen': IBM, Control Data, Burroughs, Citicorp, Mobil, Texaco, Chevron, Fluor, Shell, Ford, General Motors and Newmont Mining.[16] And they have published a list of '100 top US corporations in South Africa' for action after the dirty dozen.[17]

Taking action

The rest of this book is a menu of possible actions. It explains each action, sets out its purpose, discusses possible problems and then lists

Table 7: **South Africa's Foreign Trade, by country** (1985)

Country	Exports from RSA			Imports to RSA			Total Trade		
	R mn	$ mn	£ mn	R mn	$ mn	£ mn	R mn	$ mn	£ mn
USA	3,041	1,388	1,071	3,178	1,450	1,119	6,219	2,838	2,190
Japan	2,829	1,291	996	2,280	1,041	803	5,109	2,332	1,799
West Germany	1,258	574	443	3,807	1,738	1,340	5,065	2,312	1,783
UK	2,124	969	748	2,772	1,265	976	4,896	2,235	1,724
Netherlands	1,367	624	481	457	209	161	1,824	832	642
Switzerland	1,319	602	464	477	218	168	1,796	820	632
Italy	1,023	467	360	720	329	253	1,743	796	614
France	614	280	216	1,041	475	367	1,655	755	583
Belgium	634	289	223	408	186	144	1,042	476	367
Botswana*	830	379	292	137	62	48	967	441	340
Zimbabwe*	263	194	143	264	195	144	526	389	288
Hong Kong	627	286	221	159	73	56	786	359	277
Lesotho*	692	316	244	15	7	5	708	323	244
Swaziland*	470	215	165	143	65	50	613	280	215
Taiwan	281	128	99	317	145	112	598	273	211
South Korea*	281	128	99	281	128	99	562	256	198
Australia	245	112	86	253	115	89	498	227	175
Spain	318	145	112	180	82	63	498	227	175
Canada	204	93	72	267	122	94	471	215	166
Israel	267	122	94	116	53	41	383	175	135

Country	Exports from RSA			Imports to RSA			Total Trade		
	R mn	$ mn	£ mn	R mn	$ mn	£ mn	R mn	$ mn	£ mn
Sweden	47	21	17	288	131	101	335	153	118
Malawi*	136	124	81	21	19	13	157	143	94
Zambia*	156	135	78	3	3	2	159	138	80
Turkey	287	131	101	6	3	2	293	134	103
Denmark	175	80	62	115	52	40	290	132	102
Norway	67	31	24	190	87	67	257	117	90
Argentina	21	10	7	197	90	69	218	99	77
Austria	36	16	13	136	62	48	172	79	61
Ireland	88	40	31	74	34	26	162	74	57
Brazil	35	16	12	125	57	44	160	73	56
Finland	12	5	4	123	56	43	135	62	48
Mozambique*	116	53	41	4	4	2	120	57	43
Portugal	84	38	30	35	16	12	119	54	42
Chile	48	22	17	70	32	25	118	54	42
Sri Lanka	51	23	18	27	12	10	78	36	27
Greece	69	31	24	7	3	2	76	35	27
New Zealand	20	9	7	27	12	10	47	21	17
Venezuela	29	13	10	0	0	0	29	13	10
Peru	19	9	7	4	2	1	23	10	8
Uruguay	4	2	1	14	6	5	18	8	6

Mexico	10	5	4	6	3	2	16	7	6
Iceland	3	1	1	13	6	5	16	7	6
Colombia	12	5	4	1	0	0	13	6	5
Ecuador	12	5	4	1	0	0	13	6	5

Except where noted by *, figures are based on official South African trade statistics for 1985 for the Southern African Customs Union (SACU), which also include Botswana, Lesotho and Swaziland (BLS). BLS account for only 1 per cent of total SACU imports and 5 per cent of SACU exports (largely Botswana diamonds). South African trade data excludes gold and some strategic commodities, particularly arms. Thus trade with some countries as reported by South Africa is significantly smaller than trade as reported by the countries themselves.

The figures for each country have been converted at the average rate of exchange for the year of the data, and countries are listed in order by total trade in $ US. For 1985 the average rates of exchange were: R1.00 = $0.4564 = £0.3521.

South African data does not include trade with other African states or with South Korea, which has been calculated as follows:

South Korea: RSA data gives 'Oceania' which has been taken to be South Korea.

Zimbabwe: official government figures for 1984.

Malawi: official government figures for 1983.

Zambia: official government figures for 1982.

Mozambique: official government figures (RSA exports 1985; RSA imports 1982).

BLS: most recent figures for total trade (B and S government 1985; L, IMF, 1985) combined with most recent data for proportion of trade with RSA (B, 1984; L, 1979; S, 1982; from J. Hanlon, *Beggar Your Neighbours*, CIIR, London, 1986).

Table 8: **Main components of trade for principal trading partners**

%	Main goods from RSA	customs code	%	Main goods to RSA	customs code
United States (1985)					
27	Platinum		10	Digital computers, digital and office machines	
9	Precious and semi-precious stones		4	Aircraft parts	
6	Diamonds		4	Mechanical shovels	
s	Uranium compounds		2	Chemical mixtures	
s	Metal coins				
5	Ferrochromium and chrome ore				
3	Manganese and compounds				
s	Iron and steel				
Japan (1985)					
s	Sugar	C17	6	Iron and steel	C73
3	Salt, cement, lime	C25	3	Tools	C82
18	Metallic ores	C26	17	Machinery	C84
23	Coal, etc.	C27	13	Electrical machinery	C85
3	Inorganic chemicals, uranium	C28	38	Vehicles	C87
2	Wood	C44	4	Optical and photographic	C90
3	Wool	C53			
28	Precious metals and stones	C71			
s	Iron and steel	C73			
West Germany					
6	Fruit	C08	2	Organic chemicals	C29
14	Coal	C27	4	Resins and plastic	C39

s	11	Precious metals and stones	C71	3	Iron and steel	C73
s	7	Coins	C72	31	Machinery	C84
s	11	Iron and steel	C73	14	Electrical machinery	C85
	12	Copper	C74	21	Vehicles	C87
				4	Optical and photographic	C90

United Kingdom

	10	Fruit	C08	4	Beverages	C22
	3	Prepared fruit	C20	6	Resins and plastic	C39
	14	Metallic ores	C26	24	Machinery	C84
	4	Coal	C27	11	Electrical machinery	C85
	5	Wool	C53	9	Vehicles	C87
s	2	Iron and steel	C73	4	Optical and photographic	C90
	13	Unclassified	C99	6	Unclassified	C99

Netherlands

	9	Fruit	C08	10	Organic chemicals	C29
	5	Salt, lime, cement	C25	6	Resins and plastic	C39
	13	Metallic ores	C26	17	Machinery	C84
	25	Coal	C27	7	Electrical machinery	C85
s	10	Inorganic chemicals, uranium	C28	5	Optical and photographic	C90
	4	Organic chemicals	C29	6	Unclassified	C99
s	5	Iron and steel	C73			

Switzerland

	32	Fruit and vegetables	S05	7	Organic chemicals	S51
	17	Non-metallic minerals	S66	20	Specialized machinery	S72
	28	Non-ferrous metals	S68	9	Industrial machinery	S74
	10	Electrical machinery	S77			
	6	Instruments	S87			

%	Main goods from RSA	customs code	%	Main goods to RSA	customs code
Italy					
3	Metallic ores	C26	4	Resins and plastic	C39
14	Coal	C27	37	Machinery	C84
3	Hides, leather	C41	14	Electrical machinery	C85
3	Wool	C53	6	Vehicles	C87
67	Precious metals and stones	C71			
s 2	Iron and steel	C73			
France					
7	Fruit	C08	9	Iron and steel	C73
s 38	Coal	C27	32	Machinery	C84
18	Inorganic chemicals, uranium	C28	18	Electrical machinery	C85
8	Wool	C53	4	Vehicles	C87
5	Precious metals and stones	C71			
s 7	Iron and steel	C73			
Belgium					
6	Coal	C27	5	Organic chemicals	C29
81	Precious metals and stones	C71	6	Resins and plastic	C39
			23	Machinery	C84
			7	Electrical machinery	C85
Hong Kong (1985)					
31	Coal	S322	9	Cotton fabrics	S652
4	Vegetable oils	S423	5	Telecom. equipment	S764
5	Paper	S6411	16	Watches and clocks	S885

	6 Precious stones	S667	12 Toys and sports equipment	S894
	16 Iron and steel bars	S673		
	6 Iron and steel plates	S674		
Taiwan (1985)				
	29 Minerals		27 Textiles	
	40 Metals		22 Machinery	
South Korea (1985)				
	14 Animal products		42 Chemical products	
	12 Chemical products			
	11 Paper			
	17 Metals			
Australia				
s	16 Fish and shellfish	S03	37 Cereals	S04
	12 Fertilizers	S56	12 Animal fats and oils	S41
	9 Paper	S64		
	9 Textiles	S65		
s	11 Iron and steel	S67		
Spain				
	6 Hides and skins	S21	15 Textile yarn	S65
	8 Textile fibres	S26	7 Non-metallic minerals	S66
	9 Metallic ores	S28	9 Industrial machinery	S74
	43 Petroleum products	S33	9 Electrical machinery	S77
s	15 Iron and steel	S67		

	%	Main goods from RSA	customs code	%	Main goods to RSA	customs code
Canada (1985)						
s	12	Fresh fruit		47	Sulphur	
s	12	Sugar		4	Fertilizers	
	22	Metals ores		5	Nickel	
s	12	Iron and steel		5	Mining machinery	
Israel (1982)						
	13	Coal		17	Fertilizer	
	18	Processed grain		5	Resins and plastics	
	46	Iron and steel		14	Machinery	
				11	Electrical machinery	
				11	Optical and photographic	
Sweden						
s	28	Fruit and vegetables	S05	9	Paper	S64
s	27	Iron and steel	S67	6	Iron and steel	S67
	20	Non-ferrous metals	S68	11	Power-generating machinery	S71
				14	Specialized machinery	S72
				18	Industrial machinery	S74

% = Percentage of the country's purchases from RSA or sales to RSA.

s = Total or partial sanction or embargo has now been placed on this commodity.

Sources: Eurostat, OECD, and South African and national data. Figures given are for 1984 unless otherwise noted.

Customs codes: various countries use different commodity classification systems. Where possible, chapter or division codes have been given:

S = SITC = Standard International Trade Classification

C = CCCN = Customs Cooperation Council Nomenclature

countries or other groups which have already imposed such sanctions. The hope is that within this framework any government, council, trade union or pressure group can find some appropriate action to take against South Africa.

The overall goal must be, as the Reverend Leon Sullivan made clear, 'a total economic embargo'. And as Malcolm Fraser, a former Prime Minister of Australia and member of the Commonwealth Eminent Persons Group, warned: 'This is no time for symbolic measures – measures of substance are needed urgently . . . History and recent experience indicates that the South African government does not respond to reason or diplomacy, but that it does respond to pressure, including external pressure. Such pressure is required now.'[18]

Directory of Sanctions

The following list contains more than 50 actions. Some are formal sanctions which can be taken only by national governments. But most are suitable for local councils, trade unions, pension funds, pressure groups and individuals. Indeed, those groups are forced to act precisely because of the unwillingness of governments to impose comprehensive mandatory sanctions. The list shows that a remarkable range of actions has already been taken and that there have been some major successes; it also shows key areas where little has been done. But the main purpose of this directory is not to tabulate past efforts – it is intended to be a handbook that provides the basic information for anyone who wants to help to impose sanctions against apartheid South Africa.

The actions in the directory are classified as follows:

1. **TOTAL BOYCOTT**
2. **BAN ON SALES AND TECHNOLOGY TRANSFER TO RSA**
   2.1 Total ban
   2.2 Arms
   2.3 Oil
   2.4 Nuclear
   2.5 Computers
   2.6 Other high technology and licences
   2.7 Other sales
   2.8 Services
   2.9 End export support
   2.10 Regulation and information
   2.11 Enforcement
3. **BAN ON PURCHASES FROM RSA**
   3.1 Total ban
   3.2 Agricultural products

3.3   Industrial minerals and steel
3.4   Precious metals, coins and diamonds
3.5   Purchases of RSA arms
3.6   Other industrial products
3.7   Purchases in RSA
3.8   Purchases from RSA-owned companies
3.9   Protest action and secondary boycotts
3.10 Enforcement and information
3.11 Enforcing UN Decree No. 1

4. **FINANCIAL BANS**
   4.1   Total investment ban
   4.2   New investment ban
   4.3   Total loan ban
   4.4   Prohibition of some loans
   4.5   Prevent IMF loans to RSA

5. **COMPANIES**
   5.1   Withdrawal from RSA
   5.2   Disinvestment/divestment
   5.3   Shareholder action
   5.4   Shadow annual reports and other protest action
   5.5   Boycott campaigns to force company withdrawal
   5.6   Boycott campaigns against banks
   5.7   Boycott campaigns against companies serving RSA
   5.8   Campaigns against funds holding RSA-linked shares
   5.9   Ban on take-overs or investments by RSA-owned companies

6. **OTHER TRADE AND ECONOMIC ACTION**
   6.1   Selling off gold
   6.2   Cutting air and sea links
   6.3   Limiting travel and tourism
   6.4   Ban on recruiting
   6.5   Ending double taxation agreements
   6.6   Post and telecommunications bans

7. **RETALIATION**

8.   SOCIAL AND POLITICAL ACTION

8.1   Diplomatic relations
8.2   Requirement of visas for South Africans
8.3   Sports and cultural boycotts
8.4   Scientific and professional boycotts
8.5   Expelling RSA from international organizations
8.6   Exposing RSA-linked individuals

9.   POSITIVE MEASURES

9.1   Codes of conduct
9.2   Assistance to South Africans
9.3   Support for SADCC
9.4   Promotion of anti-apartheid struggles at home

For each action, the following information is given (where appropriate):

Explanation: Just what the particular sanction involves.
Purpose: Why the sanction is imposed.
Problems: Factors which make it difficult to impose the sanction, or which make it less effective.
Side-effects: Difficulties caused by the sanction in South Africa or to those imposing the sanction.
Loopholes: Gaps in the normal formulation of the sanction which make it easy for South Africa to bust it.
Priority: How important this action is, and which aspects of the sanction should be stressed.
Exemption: Any commonly agreed view that a sanction should not apply to, or be applied by, some group or country.
International organizations: Calls by the EEC, UN Security Council, Commonwealth, OAU and OPEC for the sanction to be imposed. Only calls which have some force of law or consensus have been included; simple anti-apartheid and sanctions resolutions have not been tabulated.
Action: Who has imposed the sanction, and details of what they have done.

The following abbreviations and terms have been used for countries and international organizations:

EEC = European Community = Belgium, Denmark, France, Greece, Ireland, Italy, Luxemburg, Netherlands, Portugal, Spain, UK, and West Germany.

Frontline states = Angola, Botswana, Mozambique, Tanzania, Zambia, and Zimbabwe.

Nordic = Denmark, Finland, Iceland, Norway, and Sweden.

OAU = Organization of African Unity

OPEC = Organization of Petroleum Exporting Countries

RSA = Republic of South Africa

SADCC = Southern African Development Coordination Conference = Frontline states plus Lesotho, Malawi, and Swaziland. (All SADCC states except Malawi and Tanzania border RSA and/or Namibia.)

Parastatal covers any company controlled by the government. This includes nationalized industries, joint ventures, nominally private companies in which the government has a controlling interest (either a large portion of the shares or a so-called 'golden share'), and state-run marketing boards.

1. TOTAL BOYCOTT

Explanation: No financial, trade, cultural or diplomatic links with RSA. Ban on RSA goods (except personal items). RSA aircraft not permitted to overfly or land. RSA ships not permitted to call. National ships and aircraft not allowed to go to RSA. Restrictions on post. South Africans not allowed entry unless known opponents of apartheid.

Purpose: To completely isolate RSA.

Priority: High. Other actions in this list need be considered only because most countries will not break all links.

International organizations: OAU

Exemptions: In Africa, the OAU accepts that the SADCC states (and Cape Verde) can continue to have links with RSA, for historical and geographical reasons. The Commonwealth accepts that 'adjustments' will be necessary in sanctions to take account of the SADCC states.

Action: India is the only major state to break links with South Africa and impose a total boycott. (This was done in stages between 1946 and 1963.) Cyprus, Singapore, Malaysia, Jamaica and various others broke links in the 1960s.

Most OAU members (except the neighbouring states, Malawi, Zaire and Cape Verde) never established links with RSA and officially impose a total ban. The socialist bloc also declares a total boycott against RSA. In practice there is limited trade between RSA and some OAU and socialist countries.

Although they have not imposed a total boycott, a series of actions by Denmark and Finland brings them closer to a total boycott than any other Western industrialized nations.

2. BAN ON SALES AND TECHNOLOGY TRANSFER TO RSA

The South African economy is unusually open, and dependent for its survival on massive imports and exports. Sanctions in this section try to prevent key goods, technologies, and services from reaching RSA. (Bans on finance and capital flows are dealt with in section 4.)

2.1 Total ban

Explanation: (1) Complete national blockage to stop all types of goods and services from going to the RSA. This includes licences and technology transfer. (2) Alternatively, governments may impose more limited bans, particularly prohibiting parastatal companies from dealing with RSA.

Purpose: To strangle the economy; RSA could not for long survive comprehensive blocking of goods and services from abroad.

Problems: Some sanctions-busting is inevitable. Because exporting is so competitive, and exports of manufactured goods hard to monitor, sellers to RSA are often willing to break sanctions. By contrast, RSA primary product exports must compete with those from many other countries, and there is less reason for buyers to break sanctions. Thus sanctions-busting will be more effective with respect to RSA imports from abroad than for RSA exports. Firms have already established sanctions-busting channels to ensure a flow of essential goods to RSA.

Side-effects: Most sanctions also hurt the black people in South Africa, but this has been accepted as a necessary price to end apartheid.

Priority: Higher in certain areas than others (see below). In general, because of the problems of sanctions-busting, bans on purchases from RSA should be given priority over bans on sales to RSA.

Action: Total boycott states (see item 1) plus Denmark and Finland. Danish 1986 law bans imports and exports of 'any kind of goods and services'. Finland's Transport Workers' Union (AKT) has banned all imports and exports of RSA goods; this has been given tacit government approval.

No country has imposed a general export restriction on its parastatals that does not apply to private companies. (Some have imposed import restrictions – see 3.1.)

The Nordic states and Brazil have policies to reduce trade with RSA.

2.2 *Arms*

Explanation: Ban on the sale of arms, ammunition and military equipment to RSA, as well as equipment to manufacture these things. Also includes some restrictions on vehicles, aircraft, ships and other equipment which can be used by the military and police. Various types of military cooperation are also banned. (See also 2.4 and 2.5.)

Purpose: To deny the white minority the ability to suppress its own majority, to occupy Namibia, and to attack the majority-ruled neighbouring states. Despite its claims, RSA is not self-sufficient in weaponry; an effective arms embargo would have a dramatic effect.

Problems: Arms salesmen are frequently willing to bust sanctions. Israeli non-adherence to the arms embargo creates particular problems.

Loopholes: The very narrow definitions in the UN's mandatory arms embargo (see **International organizations**, below) means that much of the equipment actually used by the police and military in the townships and neighbouring states is not covered. A particular problem is caused by so-called 'dual-purpose' equipment – items which have both a civilian and a military use. Thus British radar systems used to support air raids on neighbouring states were permitted because they are also used for civilian air traffic control.

In particular, Western countries do not treat R S A as strictly as they treat the socialist bloc. The N A T O countries plus Japan have an export control mechanism for arms sales to socialist states. This is CoCom (Coordinating Committee for Multilateral Export Controls), which has a detailed list of strategic commodities which cannot be exported to East bloc states. 'Dual-purpose' is interpreted by Western arms-exporting countries in totally opposite ways with respect to R S A on the one hand and the socialist bloc on the other. In practice, the main arms-exporting countries say that items may be sold to R S A so long as they have a possible civilian use. Under CoCom rules items may not be exported to socialist states if they have a possible military use, or even if they are civilian technologies which strengthen a socialist state's strategic capacity.

Other loopholes relate to the way regulations are often framed in terms of end user rather than type of equipment: (1) The export of dual-purpose equipment to R S A is permitted if ordered by a firm other than the police or military. But it is impossible to prevent the later transfer of that equipment, which can be commandeered and that action kept secret under R S A law. (2) Equipment may be sold to military contractors such as the Council for Scientific and Industrial Research. (3) It is difficult to prevent third countries re-exporting equipment to R S A, particularly as part of a larger system. Indeed, U S rules actually allow this in some cases if the equipment is less than 20 per cent of the total being sold.

Priority: Top. Special attention should be given to closing loopholes and achieving a change to the CoCom approach.

International organizations: (1) This is the only mandatory U N sanction. Resolution 418 (1977) was adopted unanimously by the Security Council, which declares in it that 'the acquisition by South Africa of arms and related material constitutes a threat to the main-tenance of international peace and security'. Therefore it 'decides that all states shall cease forthwith any provision to South Africa of arms and related material of all types, including the sale or transfer of weapons and ammunition, and spare parts for the aforementioned, and shall cease as well the provision of all types of equipment and supplies and grants of licensing arrangements for the manufacture and development of nuclear weapons'. The Security Council 'calls upon all states' to review existing contractual arrangements and licences relating to the manufacture and maintenance of arms, ammunition, and military equipment and vehicles 'with a view to terminating them'. Note that in diplomatic jargon 'decides' means a mandatory ban, while the weaker 'calls upon' denotes a voluntary ban.

In approving Resolution 418 the Western powers were unwilling to make mandatory the much broader voluntary embargoes contained in Resolution 282 (1970). This 'calls upon all states' to stop the supply of all spare parts and 'vehicles and equipment for use of the armed forces and paramilitary organizations of South Africa'. It also calls for 'revoking all licences and military patents' granted to the RSA government or RSA companies to manufacture arms, ammunition, aircraft, naval craft and other military vehicles. Finally, Resolution 282 calls for an end to military training for members of the RSA armed forces and an end to 'all other forms of military cooperation'.

(2) The EEC ministers agreed on 10 September 1985 to 'a rigorously controlled embargo of arms and paramilitary equipment to the RSA', a 'refusal to cooperate in the military sphere', 'freezing of official contacts and international agreements in the sporting and security spheres', and the 'cessation of exports of sensitive equipment designed for the police and armed forces of the RSA'. EEC regulations apply to RSA but not RSA-occupied Namibia.

(3) The Commonwealth heads of state on 20 October 1985 agreed 'the strictest enforcement of the mandatory arms embargo' and 'an embargo on all military cooperation with South Africa'.

Action: Tight bans are imposed by the total ban states (see 2.1), the Nordic states, Netherlands, Japan, Ireland, Australia and Brazil. Sweden's export ban is very broad, including photographic equipment, navigation equipment, helmets, etc. Denmark and the Netherlands also ban their nationals and companies from transporting arms to RSA. Australia bans the sale of any product known to be of use to the security forces. The French ban includes paramilitary and riot control equipment.

Virtually all states say they abide by the mandatory UN ban, but they set their own definitions. The USA's is one of the most important. In 1977 it backed the UN mandatory arms embargo by banning the export of anything on the Munitions List, the official directory of 'arms, ammunition, and implements of war'. In 1982, as part of its policy of 'constructive engagement' with RSA, the USA began to permit the export of some of these items; in 1984 licences were issued to export $88 million in Munitions List items to RSA, largely data-encoding technology, navigation gear and image intensifiers. The 1986 law which overrode President Reagan's veto again banned Munitions List sales to RSA.

This still does not cover most dual-purpose equipment, which comes under other US export licensing provisions, and is still not regulated. (Except for some computers, discussed further in 2.5 below.) In the early 1980s the USA exported computers and other equipment to subsidiaries and contractors of Armscor, the South African armaments corporation; the USA also sold 2,500 electric shock batons to a private RSA company.

Finally, it should be noted that some bans on military cooperation (for example by the USA and UK) exempt links between intelligence-gathering services. Other national bans on police cooperation (say by the UK) apply only to the national government and do not extend to local police forces and private companies.

2.3 Oil

Explanation: Ban on the sale and transport of oil and oil products to RSA.

Purpose: To affect the RSA economy through its high dependence on imported oil, either by causing a serious shortage or by raising the price and imposing an 'apartheid tax' on fuel.

Problems: The present world oil glut ensures some sanctions-busting. Local production capacity plus sanctions-busting makes it virtually impossible to cut off oil supplies. But sanctions do raise the price (see Chapter 22).

Loopholes: (1) Swap arrangements (see below). (2) Sales of oil on the high seas and through third parties. (3) Some countries permit sales of refined products (as distinct from crude oil). (4) The EEC ban applies only to RSA, and not RSA-occupied Namibia.

There are two forms of 'swap arrangement', under which either markets or cargoes are swapped. This permits the sale of embargoed goods, and works where there is a generally accepted cartel, as with oil. In the first form, if company A is not permitted to sell to R S A but wishes to retain a long-term right to its share of the market, it makes a deal with company B which *is* permitted to sell to R S A. Under the deal, company B temporarily takes company A's share of the South African market, and in exchange temporarily swaps an equivalent market somewhere else in the world. The second form involves the swap of a cargo, typically on the high seas. If a company wishes to sell oil to R S A but only has embargoed oil, say from the North Sea, it will swap a cargo of North Sea crude for a cargo of oil which is not subject to an embargo.

Priority: Enforcement

International organizations: O P E C, E E C, Commonwealth

Action: All significant oil producers say they abide by an oil embargo, although the rules vary. The U S A, Canada (voluntary) and Australia ban the sale of crude oil and refined petroleum products. France bans export or re-export of 'petroleum fuels'. But the U K bans the export only of crude oil from its sector of the North Sea, and continues to sell refined products to R S A. Norway bans the sale of crude oil and gas only; Norwegian gas has been legally sold to the U K for processing and sale to R S A.

Apparently no country bans swap arrangements. A number of countries only restrict the sale of oil they produce, not oil from elsewhere.

Denmark prohibits its ships or nationals from transporting oil or oil products to R S A. Norway requires its ship operators to register any calls in R S A.

2.4 Nuclear

Explanation: Ban on technical support, services (such as enrichment and reprocessing), sales of equipment, and sales of enriched uranium to both civilian and military nuclear industries.

Purpose: The South African nuclear industry has been developed entirely through foreign support, and is still dependent on it. R S A probably has nuclear weapons capability, and sanctions could prevent the development of nuclear bombs and missiles. Nuclear power is being developed for electricity-generating as a way to bypass the oil embargo, and thus is a target as part of an energy boycott.

Problems: (1) Israel has nuclear capabilities and will not join any embargo. (2) Historic (and totally unnecessary) dependence on Namibian and South African uranium by several states has caused close links to develop between the RSA and the European nuclear industry. (3) Evidence that RSA has tested a nuclear weapon is limited, making it difficult to use this as an argument against nuclear collaboration.

Loopholes: (1) Some bans only limit military nuclear cooperation, yet there is substantial overlap between civilian and military. (2) Some bans only apply to new collaboration, permitting existing contracts and support to continue. (3) The EEC ban applies only to RSA and not to RSA-occupied Namibia.

Priority: Politically important because nuclear issues generate publicity. But the RSA nuclear capability is probably less important than other areas of technology and arms, so nuclear issues do not have as high a priority. Within this, the stress should be on enforcement of the ban on new collaboration.

International organizations: (1) UN Security Council Resolution 569 (1985) 'urges' the 'prohibition of all new contracts in the nuclear field'. (2) The EEC (10 September 1985) agreed to a 'prohibition of all new collaboration in the nuclear sector'. (3) The Commonwealth on 20 October 1985 agreed on 'a ban on new contracts for the sale and export of nuclear goods, materials, and technology to South Africa'.

Action: Because RSA has not signed the Nuclear Non-Proliferation Treaty, the USA has long-standing restrictions. Under an executive order, President Ronald Reagan on 9 September 1985 banned 'exports of nuclear goods or technology to South Africa'. The 1986 law bans the export to RSA of 'special nuclear material or sensitive nuclear technology', as well as items of 'significance for nuclear explosive purposes'.

The EEC bans new collaboration, and France requires all nuclear equipment exports to be licensed. Nordic states, Japan, Australia, New Zealand and Austria also ban nuclear collaboration.

2.5   Computers

Explanation: Ban the sale of some or all computer hardware and software.

Purpose: Computers are central to the administration and enforcement of the apartheid system. They are also vital to the modernization of both the military and industry and to RSA's ability to withstand sanctions. Yet RSA has no indigenous computer industry, so halting the transfer of computers and computer technology would be a blow to white efforts to maintain apartheid.

Problems: Computer software can be sent over telephone lines and would be difficult to ban.

Loopholes: (1) Most bans relate to specific agencies, so computers can be purchased by other bodies and then leased to prohibited agencies. Only those parts of the Council for Scientific and Industrial Research (CSIR) engaged in weapons research are banned from receiving US computers, so other sections of the Council can obtain the computers to be used by all of CSIR. (2) There may be sales via third countries (so bans by countries which do not themselves produce computers are also important).

Priority: (1) In general, the priority is to block RSA exports (so that it will not have the money to pay for imports). But computers, arms and oil are the three RSA imports which are vital and which can be stopped – thus they rate a high priority. (2) Computers also rate a high priority because little has been done to restrict computer sales, and RSA is computerizing as quickly as possible in expectation of sanctions. CoCom rules apply to computers for the socialist bloc and could be extended to RSA.

International organizations: (1) UN Security Council Resolution 569 (1985) 'urges' a 'prohibition of all sales of computer equipment that may be used by the South African army and police'. (2) The Commonwealth on 20 October 1985 agreed on 'a ban on the sale and export of computer equipment capable of use by South African military forces, police, or security forces'.

Action: The USA and Canada ban computers for the police and armed forces, as well as agencies which enforce apartheid. According to the US Department of Commerce this is most of the government (including the Ministry of Education), Armscor and its subsidiaries, part of the CSIR, and all police and military forces. These bodies accounted for at least 30 per cent of US computer sales to RSA before the restrictions were imposed (see the *Financial Mail*, Johannesburg, 27 September 1985).

Japan, Austria, UK, France, Australia, New Zealand, Ireland and the Nordic states restrict the supply of computers to the police and armed forces. The EEC ban on 'sensitive equipment destined for the police and armed forces' clearly includes computers, but the EEC does not prohibit sales to RSA-occupied Namibia.

General trade bans (see 2.1) include computers. But no other countries ban all computer sales.

Computer hardware and software are particularly susceptible to action by individual companies or their workers and trade unions. For example, the staff of DarkStar Systems in Britain decided to refuse all further orders from RSA.

2.6 *Other high technology and licences*

Explanation: Restrictions on the transfer of technology, either specific machinery or patents and production licences.

Purpose: To prevent the modernization of industry and the military and limit the ability to resist sanctions.

Problems: This is an area where some sanctions-busting is inevitable.

Action: The Nordic states have agreed to discourage technology transfer; in particular, Finland has decided that 'no patents or production rights may be given to South Africa'. Sweden has banned the assignment and lease of patents and manufacturing rights to RSA companies. India's total ban thwarted an attempt to transfer radio technology to RSA in the 1960s.

2.7 *Other sales*

Explanation: Specific bans on other classes of goods.

Purpose: General pressure on RSA economy. Because much of RSA machinery is imported, a ban on the sale of spare parts to RSA could be very disruptive. Similarly, despite continued attempts to increase local content, many RSA industries are dependent on imported components and raw materials; without these some firms would grind to a halt.

Problems: (1) Sanctions-busting is easy, especially for small or commonly available spares. (2) In practical terms it is probably easier to press for a total trade ban than for a complex package restricting some sales to RSA but permitting others.

Action: Italy restricts the export of civilian aircraft. No other government has tried to ban categories of exports other than arms, nuclear, oil and computers. But some individual firms have banned the sale of their products, especially as part of a withdrawal from South Africa (see 5.1). The cultural and academic boycotts (see 8.3 and 8.4) block the export of some books, films, etc.

2.8 Services

Explanation: Prohibitions on the provision of services (as distinct from goods).

Purpose: RSA is dependent on foreign financial, information, transport, repair and maintenance services. Cutting these can affect industry and the military, and can also increase the cultural isolation of white South Africa.

Problems: People who provide services will sometimes go to great lengths to break sanctions if the price is high enough. Financial and information services can be provided electronically and are easy to conceal.

Side-effects: As for the cultural boycott (see 8.3) it is sometimes argued that blocking information prevents South Africans from reading about criticisms of apartheid and alternatives to it. There are two responses to this. First, most information is used to maintain apartheid. Second, RSA censorship through various laws and government control of radio and TV means that the white minority regime largely (albeit not totally) controls what information can be distributed inside the country. Thus it is better to use external information channels such as the BBC World Service, the ANC's own radio, etc.

Exemption: The neighbouring states can be permitted to provide non-essential services (such as news reports).

Action: Service bans have been imposed by individual companies and trade unions. Some companies which have withdrawn from RSA no longer service machinery there. British Library staff refuse to process requests for information from RSA, and a similar ban has been proposed in Australia. The British National Union of Journalists calls on members not to supply material to the South African Broadcasting Corporation (because it can be distorted and misused), and recommends that members in Britain not write for RSA publications (except for those known to oppose the government).

2.9   End export support

Explanation: Terminate anything that encourages sales to RSA, including export credits, export credit guarantees and insurance, export promotion, and participation in trade fairs.

Purpose: (1) To discourage private companies from selling to RSA. (2) To force RSA by ending export credits to pay cash rather than paying after some months. This worsens RSA's cash flow problems, exacerbating the effects of other financial squeezes (see 4.3). Thus this is another 'apartheid tax'.

Loopholes: (1) Bans are often voluntary and poorly enforced. (2) Bans sometimes apply to the government but not to government-funded trade promotion agencies. (3) Bans on loans (see 4.3) often exempt export credits.

International organizations: (1) UN Security Council Resolution 569 (1985) 'urges' the 'suspension of guaranteed export loans'. (2) The Commonwealth on 20 October 1985 agreed on 'no government funding for trade missions to South Africa or for participation in exhibitions and trade fairs in South Africa'. On 5 August 1986 the Commonwealth mini-summit (with Britain dissenting) decided on 'the termination of all government assistance to investment in, and trade with, South Africa'.

Action: Finland has banned export credit and export credit guarantees. Australia, Austria, Canada, New Zealand and Norway have banned export credit guarantees and insurance. Netherlands and West Germany have banned medium- and long-term export credit guarantees. Ireland has restricted export credits. The Nordic states do not provide government export credits.

The Nordic states ban trade promotion. Australia, Ireland and New Zealand prohibit any government assistance (including help and information) for export to RSA, prohibit government involvement with trade missions, and bar trade offices in RSA; Australia closed its trade mission in RSA. Canada has ended facilities for sales to RSA which were available under its export development programmes. Japan does not promote trade with RSA.

The 1986 US law says that no government funds may be used 'for any assistance to investment in, or any subsidy to trade with, South Africa, including but not limited to funding for trade missions in South Africa and for participation in exhibitions and trade fairs in South Africa'.

The UK accepts the narrow Commonwealth ban on 'no government funding for trade missions' and trade fairs, and a subsidy of roughly £180,000 per year has been ended. But it continues to promote exports to RSA and support trade missions to RSA in other ways. The British Overseas Trade Board (part of the Department of Trade and Industry) stresses that it is free to provide help 'for business visitors to the [RSA] market whether they go as individuals or members of a group', and that the British Embassy in Pretoria will continue to assist visiting trade missions.

2.10 Regulation and information

Explanation: Licensing, and requirements to report, used to restrict and monitor the flow of exports to RSA.

Purpose: To show what goods are being exported to RSA, as a first step toward a ban.

Priority: Useful where it is politically difficult to obtain a ban.

Action: Finland, Sweden and Norway require export licences for all trade with RSA. Norway requires that its tankers report any calls at RSA ports. Swedish and Finnish licences are published, making it much simpler for trade unions and anti-apartheid groups to put pressure on companies.

The October 1986 US law contains a clause ordering the President of the USA to conduct a study on violations of the arms embargo, 'including an identification of those countries engaged in such sale or export, with a view to terminating United States military assistance to those countries'.

2.11 *Enforcement*

Explanation: Legal and other actions to stop the breaking of agreed embargoes, particularly of arms and oil.

Purpose: To curb sanctions-busting.

Problems: Many laws relating to secrecy, limiting trade union action, etc., make it difficult for individuals and groups to enforce sanctions.

Priority: High, to expose government duplicity in agreeing to sanctions and then failing to enforce them. Publicity is particularly important. Further support is essential for non-government organizations which already monitor sanctions.

Action: Legal action against individuals breaking the arms embargo has been taken by the governments of the USA, UK, Sweden, Denmark, Netherlands and West Germany. (In the UK, anti-smuggling actions by customs authorities are kept secret if the guilty party agrees to pay a fine.) However, trade unions, particularly of dockers and seafarers, have been much more important in stopping and exposing illegal arms shipments.

The leaks in the oil embargo have been regularly exposed by the Shipping Research Bureau in Amsterdam, with extensive help from trade unions. The United Nations General Assembly voted in November 1986 to establish an 11-member inter-governmental group to monitor the oil embargo.

The World Campaign Against Military and Nuclear Collaboration with South Africa (in Oslo), the United Nations Centre Against Apartheid, journalists and anti-apartheid movements in many countries have played key roles in exposing sanctions-busting.

Finnish workers have enforced their own embargo, and enforced Finland's licensing rules, with the cooperation of trade unions in other countries.

---

3. BAN ON PURCHASES FROM RSA

South Africa is dependent on a high level of exports to pay for its imports of essential goods. Experience of sanctions elsewhere is that while it is often hard to block the target country's imports, it is easier to block its exports and thus cut off the money with which it pays for those imports. Bans in this section all aim to do that.

3.1 *Total ban*

Explanation: Complete ban on the transport, purchase, and sale of RSA products. Import bans can be imposed by a national government. Sale and purchase bans can be imposed by governments, local councils, chains of shops, trade unions and a variety of other organizations.

Purpose: To deny money to the South African economy.

Problem: National legislation sometimes prevents local government and trade union action.

Side-effects: (1) If effective, such bans would put miners and farm labourers in RSA out of work. But in general such bans have a harsher effect on the white community, which is the real target of sanctions. And tens of thousands of miners and labourers are already being put out of work by mechanization; thus not imposing such bans does not necessarily save jobs. (2) It is sometimes argued that some RSA commodities are essential, and that banning them will put people out of work in Europe, Japan, and the USA. In general this is not true (see Chapters 25 and 26), but one specific case is dealt with below in item 3.4. Indeed, bans on RSA items are a good sanction to aim for because they often *create* jobs in the country that imposes the ban.

Loopholes: Third-party transactions of various sorts provide the main route for sanctions-busting. This includes directly fraudulent actions like re-labelling and re-invoicing. But it also includes direct loopholes, such as sending semi-finished RSA goods to another country for completion.

Priority: Top.

Exemptions: The SADCC states are often exempted from purchasing bans. Their purchases are small compared to those of RSA's main trading partners and their trading patterns were imposed by the former colonial powers; therefore the primary responsibility for imposing sanctions rests with the industrialized states.

International organizations: UN Decree No. 1 For the Protection of the Natural Resources of Namibia permits the seizure of any 'animal resource, mineral, or other natural resource produced in or emanating from the Territory of Namibia' (unless production permission has been granted by the UN Council for Namibia, but such permission has never been given).

Action: Bans on all imports from RSA have been imposed by the total boycott countries (see item 1) plus Denmark and Finland (in the latter a trade-union-imposed ban is accepted by the government). In early 1987, Norway is expected to ban all South African goods except manganese. Bermuda agreed a total ban on RSA goods, but the UK Prime Minister, Margaret Thatcher, refused to allow this British colony to impose the ban.

The USA bans the import of a broad range of items from RSA parastatals. The 1986 law specifies that 'no article which is grown, produced, manufactured by, marketed, or otherwise exported by a parastatal organization of South Africa may be imported into the United States'.

Canada, Australia and the Nordic states do not permit the government or government agencies to buy South African goods. In Ireland the Ministry of Health and all government health agencies do not buy South African goods.

In October 1985 Sweden 'urged' importers to find non-RSA sources of supply, 'called the attention' of companies to Decree No. 1 and 'recommended' that they respect it.

At local level, hundreds of councils and other bodies have acted. In the UK the 'model' or 'Sheffield' declaration is gaining wide acceptance. In part it commits the council to 'cease the purchase of any goods originating from South Africa and Namibia'. At least 70 local councils including Manchester have adopted the Sheffield declaration and banned purchases of RSA products, though sometimes only if non-RSA items are not much more expensive – typically the limit is 10 per cent – than RSA goods. At least two health authorities (North West Thames Regional and Brent District) also ban RSA goods.

In the USA, one state (Maryland) and a number of cities (including Chicago, Boston, Los Angeles and New York) restrict RSA and Namibian products. Outright bans vary, and include: (1) complete bans, (2) bans subject to competitive tendering laws, and (3) bans unless no non-RSA product is available or the ban would cause undue financial harm. Others ban the purchase of RSA goods unless the alternative is a certain amount (typically between 5 and 10 per cent) more expensive.

Elsewhere there are a variety of local boycotts. In Ireland several councils, including Cork, have signed the Sheffield declaration and banned RSA goods. Many Norwegian municipal councils have agreed a similar declaration. In the Netherlands 50 councils, including Arnhem, do not buy South African goods. In Canada the Province of Ontario bans all R S A goods in provincial institutions.

Consumer and trade union pressure has forced a number of individual shops and chains to stop selling R S A goods. In Britain these include the Co-op, Fine Fare, Hepworth, Next, Richard Shops, Littlewoods, British Home Stores, Argos, and Harris Queensway. In the U S A the biggest chain to ban R S A goods is Winn-Dixie.

The Irish Transport and General Workers' Union (I T G W U) and the Irish Distributive and Administrative Trade Union (I D A T U) have taken a different approach which effectively accomplishes the same end. They have gained agreements from Mirror Mirror, Berni Inns, Thomas Carlisle (Harp) and others that members need not handle R S A goods, and that individuals cannot be questioned about this when they are hired (to prevent employers discriminating against people who will not handle R S A items). Clearly it will be easier for the shops and restaurants not to sell R S A items than to have some items which only some of the staff will sell.

Counter-action: It is sometimes argued that national legislation preempts local legislation, and thus local authorities are not permitted to impose their own stronger bans. It is also argued that bans on R S A goods violate competitive bidding requirements and other requirements to purchase the cheapest goods. To meet problems like this, Sweden has passed a special law permitting local and county councils to boycott R S A goods.

The U S sanctions law said that there could be no deduction in public funds and that 'no penalty may be imposed by the federal government by reason of the application of any state or local law concerning apartheid to any contract entered into by a state or local government' until 1 January 1987. But the U S Department of Transportation (D O T) said that after that date it would cut off funds to local projects in cities with anti-apartheid selective buying laws because such laws violate competitive bidding guidelines. Undoubtedly the D O T action will be tested in court.

Similar action has been taken in the U K. Birmingham City Council requires all its contractors to specify that no R S A goods will be used; the British government would not agree to this, and Birmingham gave up responsibility for the maintenance of national motorways in the city rather than change its standard contract. A bitter eight-week strike was unsuccessful in trying to force Portsmouth District Health Authority to stop buying R S A tinned fruit for its hospitals; the health authority said it was not allowed to impose such a buying ban.

3.2   Agricultural products

Explanation: Ban on some or all farm products. Usually includes processed products as well, in particular tinned and dried fruit, sugar, wine and sherry, and wool.

Purpose: Agricultural exports are an important foreign currency earner for R S A. White farmers are the mainstay of the National Party and thus the white minority regime, so agricultural exports hit a politically important group.

Side-effects: (1) Black job losses in R S A (although there is some job creation in other countries). (2) For a few items such as fresh grapes at a few times of the year, alternative supplies are more expensive.

International organizations: (1) The Commonwealth mini-summit on 5 August 1986 agreed (with Britain opposed) on a ban on the import of 'agricultural products'. (2) U N Decree No. 1 (1974) for the Protection of the Natural Resources of Namibia prohibits the processing, sale or export of any 'animal resource'; in practice this applies mainly to karakul (Persian lamb) pelts.

Action: The U S A, Australia, Canada, New Zealand and the Nordic states all ban R S A agricultural products, although definitions vary. Norway bans wine, fruit and vegetables. Ireland bans only fruit and vegetables. The U S law is very broad, banning any 'agricultural commodity, product, byproduct, or derivative thereof', and any 'article that is suitable for human consumption'. Most Canadian provinces (where liquor sales are a provincial monopoly) do not sell R S A wine and sherry.

One ban is indirect: the Irish ban only remains in force so long as fruit and vegetables are produced using prison labour. Japan reduced imports when R S A would not permit Japanese sanitary inspectors to work in R S A and check citrus fruit before it was sent to Japan.

In the Netherlands the main wholesale auction firms have stopped handling R S A flowers because of a fear of protests, and because similar flowers are available from Zimbabwe. All major Dutch shop chains do not sell R S A fresh or tinned fruit, which has halved Dutch fruit imports from R S A.

3.3 Industrial minerals and steel

Explanation: (1) Bans on materials related to the steel industry: iron ore, various ferro-alloys, pig iron, and steel. (2) Bans on uranium, sometimes only on Namibian uranium. (3) Bans on coal, asbestos and a variety of common metals.

Purpose: Industrial minerals are R S A's second most important export (after gold) and thus an essential source of money to pay for imports.

Problems: Although ores can easily be identified as to source, this becomes harder after the ores have been smelted or processed. For example, it is impossible to tell if a piece of stainless steel contains chromium from R S A. Also mineral shipments can be doped or mixed to conceal the R S A origin. This means sanctions against minerals must be coupled with enforcement procedures which require clear documentation and analysis reports on the original ore.

Side-effects: Limited disruption to stainless steel production and some slightly higher prices (see Chapter 26).

Loopholes: (1) Bans on 'iron and steel' usually include only pig iron and steel, and exclude iron ore and ferro-alloys. (2) Bans usually only refer to direct imports from R S A, and do not include products from third countries containing banned R S A minerals.

International organizations: (1) U N Decree No. 1 (1974) for the Protection of the Natural Resources of Namibia bans the mining, processing, and exporting of any Namibian mineral. Any such product, and any ship or vehicle carrying it, can be seized (although this has never been done). (2) The Commonwealth mini-summit on 5 August 1986 agreed (with Britain opposed) to 'a ban on the import of uranium, coal, iron and steel'. (3) The E E C agreed on 16 September 1986 to ban the import of iron and steel.

Action: *Pig iron and steel bans*: Canada, E E C, Japan, New Zealand, Australia, Hong Kong and U S A. Austria states that it will follow the E E C policy but has not yet done so.

Ores and ferro-alloys: The Swedish government has recommended that industry stop buying R S A minerals, and there has been some shift.

Uranium: Canada, Netherlands, and New Zealand. Canada has also banned the processing of Namibian uranium for third parties. Japan bans the import of uranium from Namibia but permits the import of R S A uranium; the Japan Anti-Apartheid Movement reports that illegal imports of Namibian uranium are made. The U S A bans uranium ore and uranium oxide from R S A and Namibia, but not uranium hexafluoride.

Coal: Total national bans by Sweden, Canada, Denmark (imposed before total import ban), New Zealand, Australia and U S A. Four countries have parastatal bans, but permit private imports of coal: U K (Central Electricity Generating Board does not use R S A coal), France (parastatal coal and electricity companies), Ireland (Electricity Supply Board and other parastatals) and Netherlands (parastatals). Sanctions cut R S A coal exports by £30 million in 1986, according to official R S A figures.

3.4 *Precious metals, coins and diamonds*

Explanation: (1) Bans on the import of gold, platinum and diamonds. (2) Bans on the import and sale of gold coins and platinum coins and small bars.

Purpose: To cut off R S A's most important source of revenue.

Problems: (1) The mystic significance of gold in the world monetary system makes it unlikely that central bankers will permit gold sanctions. (2) The central control of the world diamond market by De Beers (part of the Anglo American Corporation of South Africa) makes diamond sanctions unlikely. (3) Diamonds, as well as gold and platinum coins, are easily concealed and smuggled.

Side-effects: Platinum is the one mineral of which R S A supplies genuinely are important. Cutting them off would cause substantial price rise, could cause some disruption, and would demand government intervention in the markets.

Loopholes: It is difficult to distinguish R S A gold and platinum from that produced elsewhere. Furthermore, such large quantities are hoarded outside R S A that it is impossible to distinguish recently exported gold, platinum and diamonds from those same materials exported before sanctions were imposed. Thus it is virtually impossible to develop the sort of control mechanisms available for other materials.

Priority: (1) In general low, because of the difficulties involved. In particular, as platinum is the one mineral for which a ban could cause some disruption, any sanction involving platinum should be left for last (and thus should only be part of *comprehensive* sanctions).

(2) Bans on Krugerrands and other R S A gold coins also have low priority because they have little practical value (although they do have publicity value). Krugerrands are simply replaced with non-R S A gold coins, and the increasing demand for any gold coins pushes up the price R S A receives for its gold. A ban on all gold coins would be more useful, but is probably too hard to impose.

(3) High priority should be given, however, to a ban on the retail sale of all platinum coins and small bars. The market for such coins and bars is not yet large, but it is growing and it would disrupt any attempt to regulate platinum supplies, should R S A platinum not be available (either because of comprehensive sanctions against R S A or due to counter-sanctions by R S A). Such a ban should include all platinum bars and coins, not just South African ones, and should include trading in certificates showing ownership of platinum bars and coins which are physically held in another country.

(4) High priority should also be given to the development of 'lean burn' engines and non-catalytic exhaust systems, in order to reduce the need for R S A platinum for catalytic converters to clean car exhausts. This means anti-apartheid organizations should build links with environmental and green groups to push governments and the E E C to support research and to legislate on car emission in such a way as to encourage 'lean burn' engines in preference to catalysts.

International organizations: (1) The Commonwealth (20 October 1985), the E E C (16 September 1986) and the U N Security Council (Resolution 566) all call for a ban on Krugerrands and other R S A gold coins. (2) U N Decree No. 1 covers Namibian diamonds.

Action: *All gold coins*: Ireland and France. *R S A gold coins – mandatory*: Australia, Austria, E E C, New Zealand and Sweden. *R S A gold coins – voluntary*: Canada, Norway and Japan. The E E C ban applies only to RSA and not to RSA-occupied Namibia, and permits the continued circulation of Krugerrands sold by South Africa before 31 October 1986. *Other items in this category*: no bans.

3.5 *Purchase of RSA arms*

Explanation: Ban on the import of RSA-made weapons, arms, ammunition, paramilitary equipment, military vehicles, etc.

Purpose: The RSA attempt to develop an indigenous arms industry (and thus beat the mandatory arms embargo) is extremely expensive, and is possible only if RSA can defray some of the cost by exporting arms. The embargo is intended to prevent this.

Priority: High, in part because RSA has not yet become a major arms supplier. Thus the need is to prevent a planned export growth rather than stop an existing trade.

International organizations: (1) UN Security Council Resolution 558 (1984) 'requests all states to refrain from importing arms, ammunition of all types, and military vehicles produced by South Africa'. (2) The Commonwealth (20 October 1985) agreed to 'a strict and rigorously controlled embargo on imports of arms, ammunition, military vehicles and paramilitary equipment from South Africa'. (3) The EEC (10 September 1985) agreed to 'a rigorously controlled embargo on imports of arms and paramilitary equipment from the RSA'.

Action: Widely agreed, including by USA, EEC, Nordic states, Canada, Australia and New Zealand.

3.6 *Other industrial products*

Explanation: Bans on RSA textiles, vehicles and other manufactured goods.

Purpose: Because the black majority inside RSA has been kept so poor and thus cannot afford to buy many goods, RSA must export some of its industrial products to gain the economies of scale needed for local production. RSA industrial exports are relatively minor, but they are important both as an earner of foreign currency and as a help to the development of local, sanctions-busting industry.

Action: The US Congress banned RSA textiles (after President Reagan tried to increase the RSA quota by 4 per cent). In Britain there has been an attempt to boycott the Ford P100 pick-up truck, which is made in RSA and exported to Europe. But there are no other bans on RSA manufactured goods.

3.7 Purchases in RSA

Explanation: Restrictions on purchasing goods in South Africa, as distinct from buying RSA-made goods (see 3.1).

Purpose: To reduce direct dealings with the apartheid state.

Exemption: RSA's neighbours.

International organizations: The Commonwealth mini-summit on 5 August 1986 agreed (Britain opposed) to 'a ban on all government procurement in South Africa'.

Action: No country that does not already have a broad ban on RSA goods has imposed such a ban. Some have taken individual steps, for example Zimbabwe is to refine its own gold instead of sending it to RSA for processing. Some aid donors including Sweden and the Netherlands restrict or ban the use of aid funds for purchases in RSA.

3.8 Purchases from RSA-owned companies

Explanation: Prohibits purchases from, and contracts with, subsidiaries and associates of RSA firms both inside RSA and in other countries.

(An alternative sanction attempts to block RSA firms from acquiring or setting up businesses outside RSA [see 5.9]. Also note that boycotts of RSA-owned companies are distinct from boycotts against transnationals active in RSA [see 5.5] and boycotts of goods produced in RSA [see 3.1–3.7].)

Purpose: RSA companies have become major investors outside RSA, in part as a way of getting money out of RSA. Anglo American is now a genuinely transnational corporation and the other large RSA monopoly groups have also made purchases in Britain, the USA, Brazil and Canada. This sanction is aimed at the operations of those firms outside RSA. It is intended (1) to put pressure on RSA firms;

(2) to prevent RSA firms gaining influence in countries trying to impose sanctions; and (3) to prevent RSA firms from developing sanctions-busting routes.

Problems: In some areas, particularly in Southern Africa, RSA firms dominate the economy and there is little choice but to deal with them.

Side-effects: In most cases, the RSA company has bought an already operating company. This means that British or Canadian staff suddenly find themselves working for an RSA firm and have no choice in the matter. Sanctions against such firms can harm local workers who have no influence over the RSA parent.

Loopholes: (1) It is not always easy to identify RSA ownership. Barlow Rand, for example, holds some companies through a Dutch subsidiary. (2) Bans often talk of 'majority-owned RSA companies', yet the RSA parent often controls a firm without owning 50 per cent of the shares – see note below. (3) Bans rarely block third-party transactions, so there is nothing to stop the RSA-owned firm passing the goods to a non-RSA-owned firm and then on to the person imposing the sanction.

Note: Defining ownership or control is not always straightforward – it depends on whether the definition is based on strict majority ownership or on effective control. Consider Consolidated Goldfields (ConsGold), which is officially a British firm. It owns 48 per cent of Gold Fields of South Africa (GFSA). This unquestionably gives it control of GFSA because most other shareholdings are widely dispersed and thus ConsGold is assured of a majority at any company general meeting. But because it only owns 48 per cent (rather than 50 per cent), GFSA is an 'associate' but not a 'subsidiary' of Cons-Gold. This means that although ConsGold is by far the largest British employer in RSA, it is not required to produce detailed reports under the EEC code of conduct (see 9.1). But the picture is even more complicated, because Anglo American Corporation of South Africa owns 27.8 per cent of ConsGold – 11 times as much as any other single shareholder. And Anglo owns 20 per cent of GFSA. Anglo has become sophisticated at controlling associated companies without having majority ownership, and many writers on the RSA economy argue Anglo effectively controls both ConsGold and GFSA. In practice ConsGold ought to be considered both a major UK employer in RSA and RSA-dominated or controlled; yet if definitions are based on 'majority ownership', as they often are, then on strict technical grounds ConsGold is neither a big employer in RSA nor RSA-owned.

Priority: Relatively low, because of: (1) difficulties in imposing the sanction, (2) possible side-effects, and (3) the low probability of influencing RSA-owned companies. Bans on goods from RSA (see 3.1–3.7) and from transnationals in RSA (see 5.5) have a much higher priority. Sanctions against RSA-owned companies should be imposed only with the agreement of the local workers and trade unions involved.

International organizations: The Commonwealth 5 August 1986 mini-summit agreed (with Britain opposed) to 'a ban on government contracts with majority-owned South African companies'.

Action: Australia does not give any construction contracts or any other contracts over A$20,000 to majority-RSA-owned firms, nor does it provide them with industrial assistance grants and export assistance. Canada bans government contracts with majority-RSA-owned firms. The Industrial Irish Development Authority does not provide grants and other incentives to RSA firms, although the Shannon Free Airport Development Company does.

3.9 Protest actions and secondary boycotts

Explanation: A wide variety of actions to disrupt the shipment and sale of RSA goods.

Purpose: (1) To cut off such goods where official bans do not exist. (2) To give publicity to the continued sale of such goods.

Problems: Individual actions are much less effective that direct official bans.

Priority: Important where other actions are not available, especially to gain publicity as part of a campaign for a boycott.

Action: The most common action is for trade unions to encourage their members to delay or to refuse to handle RSA goods. Dockworkers in Australia hold up RSA cargo sufficiently often for shipping companies to have imposed a 15 per cent surcharge on the RSA–Australia run to cover delays in Australian ports. There was a combined Nordic trade union ban on RSA cargoes in November and December 1985. In 1985 some Canadian unions (with government acquiescence) refused to unload RSA steel in Canada. Actions which did not have official approval included a refusal to unload RSA coal at Swansea (Wales) in March 1986, blockades of RSA cargo in San Francisco in March 1986 and for 11 days in 1984, and a refusal to unload Outspan oranges in Bordeaux (France) in September 1985 (some oranges were also thrown overboard or painted red). In 1985 French trade unionists dumped two tonnes of RSA coal outside a government office.

The International Mineworkers' Organization (which includes the South African National Union of Mineworkers) on 23 November 1986 called on trade unionists to refuse to handle RSA coal.

In Britain the National Union of Seafarers has banned all RSA goods from ferries between Scotland and the Shetland and Orkney islands. The National Union of Public Employees and the Civil and Public Services Association both encourage members not to handle RSA goods, for example in canteens. In some instances contracts with RSA firms have been indefinitely delayed, and passport applications from RSA-dual nationals have not been processed. Also in the UK, ACTT members at Grampian TV refuse to transmit commercials for Outspan fruit and other RSA produce.

Canadian protest groups used boats and dockside pickets to protest at the monthly arrivals of Namibian uranium.

There have been frequent campaigns against RSA fruit and other products in supermarkets. Some have involved direct action such as filling supermarket trolleys and then leaving them at the check-out. In Britain protesters in a small 'bloodspan' campaign allegedly sprayed RSA fruit with human blood.

Often firms which stock South African goods or which are involved directly in South Africa are less socially aware in other ways too, sometimes having bad labour relations or polluting the environment. Campaigns which combine several issues can be more effective because they involve more people. For example, a highly successful joint campaign against Winn-Dixie stores in ten southern states of the US focused both on selling South African goods and on discrimination in hiring and promotion.

3.10 Enforcement and information

Explanation: Various actions to enforce existing bans or to provide information about the importation of RSA goods. Import licensing and country of origin labels are particularly important.

Purpose: (1) To support campaigns for new sanctions. (2) To enforce existing embargoes.

Problem: A recent EEC ruling may mean that member states can no longer require that goods carry a label showing the country of origin. This would make it much harder to identify and boycott RSA goods.

Priority: (1) It is important to develop government and non-government sanctions monitoring agencies to check on compliance with the new bans on importing coal, fruit and vegetables, iron and steel, etc. (2) Identification of RSA goods is the first step to any campaign, so country-of-origin labelling must be supported. In Europe it is important to ensure that countries modifying their law to correspond to the EEC ruling still require labels on South African goods.

Action: Sweden and Finland require that all imports from RSA have a special licence, and lists of licences are published. Britain and some other countries require that clothing, other manufactured goods, and packaged goods clearly identify the country of origin. Loose produce must sometimes be identified by country of origin.

In Britain, country-of-origin labelling requirements will be repealed in 1987. At the time of writing it was not clear what form the replacement would take. UK officials believe it would be acceptable to require country-of-origin labels on goods from outside the EEC, which would include RSA, but the anti-sanctions lobby may try to prevent this.

Import bans are relatively new and no agencies yet exist to monitor or enforce these sanctions.

3.11 Enforcing UN Decree No. 1

Explanation: Seizure of Namibian produce including diamonds, uranium, other minerals, and karakul pelts. This is authorized under UN Decree No. 1 For the Protection of the Natural Resources of Namibia.

Purpose: To enforce what are effectively existing economic sanctions against R S A-occupied Namibia.

Problem: Legal status of Decree No. 1 has never been tested.

Action: None, although there have been demonstrations against the sale of Namibian uranium and karakul in London and elsewhere.

The U N Council for Namibia is expected to bring a court action in the Netherlands against Urenco, the joint British–Dutch–West German company which enriches Namibian uranium.

4. FINANCIAL BANS

One of the principal objectives of sanctions is to reduce R S A's access to foreign capital. Bans in this category are intended to directly interdict vital financial flows. All R S A sources stress that foreign capital is essential for development; the effect of even partial financial sanctions was an outflow of R 9.5 billion between July 1985 and June 1986. (See also 5.1.)

4.1 Total investment ban

Explanation: Law or regulation banning all investment in R S A, including re-investment of profits. Not only does this prohibit transfer of capital, it also blocks transfer of equipment and the local purchase of new capital goods.

Purpose: (1) To increase the outflow of capital from R S A. (2) To throttle R S A industrial and military development.

Side-effects: Hitting the economy does hit black as well as white living standards, but this is widely accepted as necessary to end apartheid.

Priority: Very high.

Loophole: Investment via third countries.

International organizations: The Commonwealth mini-summit, on 3 to 5 August 1986, called (Britain opposed) for 'a ban on new investment or re-investment of profits earned in South Africa'.

Action: Japan is the only major country with a total investment ban (dating from 1968). But Japan permits its companies to have offices in RSA, and to transfer technology. Furthermore investment is in fact made via third countries, particularly the USA.

At the time of writing no Commonwealth member had actually followed the August 1986 recommendation, although New Zealand and Canada have announced voluntary bans. They and Australia say they will impose a full ban.

4.2   New investment ban

Explanation: Law or regulation banning new foreign investment in RSA, but permitting re-investment of profits and renewal of existing equipment. Sometimes loans to the private sector are considered as investments and sometimes they are treated separately (see 4.3 and 4.4).

Purpose: To slow the expansion of the RSA economy.

Side-effects: It is sometimes alleged that new foreign investment creates jobs and improves the living standards of black people in RSA, and thus that an end to investment will reverse this. In practice, few are helped at best, and much new investment is for mechanization which actually reduces jobs.

Loopholes: (1) Most new investment has already stopped due to the collapse of the RSA economy, so in many cases a ban on new investment simply recognizes a decision businesspeople have already taken. (2) Re-investment of profits that would have been repatriated is effectively new investment and permits industrial modernization. (3) Under the guise of simply replacing worn out machinery, much more modern equipment is often installed. (4) Companies bypass the investment ban by leasing new equipment to their RSA subsidiaries. (5) Companies invest via subsidiaries in third countries such as Britain. (6) EEC bans do not apply to RSA-occupied Namibia, which could become a conduit for funds.

Priority: High, but pressure should be maintained for a full investment ban.

International organizations: (1) UN Security Council Resolution 569 (1985) 'urges' no new investment. (2) The EEC (25 September 1986) has banned new investment.

Action: Sweden, Denmark and Finland have the tightest bans – no new investment, no expansion of RSA subsidiaries or associates, no leasing, and no new investment via third parties. Because investment is defined in terms of acquisition of machinery and other 'fixed assets', rather than transfer of funds, this also blocks some re-investment of profits.

In some respects the Swedish law comes close to a total investment ban. In particular, Swedish companies in RSA require governmental permission even to replace worn-out equipment (and then this is conditional on the new machinery not increasing production capacity). During 1985 and 1986 permission for even such limited investment was not granted to any company. On the other hand, the tightest aspects of the Swedish law apply only to RSA subsidiaries of which the Swedish parent has more than 50-per-cent ownership or in which it 'alone has a controlling influence'. Thus major firms like Atlas Copco (which owns 22 per cent of its RSA associate) and ASEA (24.9 per cent) are exempt from the re-investment restrictions.

Denmark allows investment 'to maintain a commercially sound operation'.

The EEC bans new direct investment, which includes 'new or increased participation in new or existing undertakings', establishing or extending branches, establishing new undertakings, and 'loans for a period of more than five years, which are made for the purpose of establishing lasting economic links'. The ban includes new acquisitions of share and loan capital as well as inter-company and branch–head-office transactions. But the ban does not include 'direct investment made with a view to maintaining the level of existing economic activity', nor does it cover portfolio investment and normal trading activity. EEC sanctions do not apply to South African-occupied Namibia, so new investment there is still permitted. France had already imposed a ban on all new investment in RSA 'in any sector and on any terms whatsoever' before the EEC decision.

The USA bans new investment but specifically permits re-investment of profits and investment needed to allow an RSA subsidiary or associate 'to operate in an economically sound manner, without expanding its operations'.

Countries with weaker bans include: Austria (no new investment by parastatals, although Austria has said it will eventually adopt the EEC sanction), Australia (parastatals) and Norway (no foreign currency allocations for investment).

4.3   Total loan ban

Explanation: (1) Ban of all loans to the R S A state, parastatals, private firms and individuals. Includes ban on 'rolling-over' loans (renewals of existing loans when they fall due). (2) Ban on the purchases of and trading in bonds, both state and parastatal (such as those issued by Escom – Electricity Supply Commission).

Purpose: To withhold from R S A shorter-term foreign capital, which has been increasingly used to replace long-term investment (which had already been reduced).

Problems: The 1985 repayments freeze shows that the R S A government is prepared to prevent the repayment of loans which are not rolled over. Indeed, it might give preference for repayment to banks prepared to roll over expiring loans. Thus banks are locked in.

Loophole: The internationalization of finance makes it very easy for loans to be made indirectly and covertly. Regulations may be required to block such devious loans.

Priority: Very high.

Action: No country has specifically imposed a total ban on loans.

4.4   Prohibition of some loans

Explanation: Ban on all new loans, or on certain categories of new loans, such as those to the R S A government and parastatals. Rolling over old loans can be conditional.

Loopholes: As for 4.3. Also, partial and conditional bans are much harder to enforce. It is generally felt that R S A was let off too easily by the banks in the 1985/6 debt renegotiation.

Priority: High, although total ban preferred.

International organizations: The Commonwealth (3–5 August 1986) called (Britain opposed) for 'a ban on all new bank loans, whether to the public or private sectors'.

Action: The U S A and the Nordic states ban all new loans. (Sweden still permits loans for less than two years, but not to the government or parastatals.) Australia, Japan, Ireland and the Netherlands have effective voluntary bans on new loans. The E EC new investment ban includes 'long-term loans of a participatory nature'.

Bans on new loans to the R SA government or its agencies have been imposed by New Zealand, Canada (voluntary) and the U K (only loans by government).

Short-term trade credits are exempt from most bans, as are loans which would allegedly be of direct benefit to black people. The U S A permits new loans and new investments 'to a firm owned by black South Africans'.

No country has required that political conditions be imposed on the rolling over of loans.

Many individual banks have imposed their own bans, in response to disinvestment and other pressure, as well as to the worsening economic climate and the debt moratorium which clearly makes R S A a bad risk. Before the broader U S ban (imposed 2 October 1986 over President Reagan's veto), more than half of the 105 largest U S banks had banned loans to the R S A public sector and at least 30, including Bank of America, had banned all new loans. Some, including Chase Manhattan Bank, in 1985 even refused to roll over outstanding loans, and it was this which triggered R S A's September 1985 default. (Chase, in turn, was responding to pressure from New York City – see 5.6.)

4.5   *Prevent I M F loans to R S A*

Explanation: In I M F meetings, vote against new credits to R S A.

Purpose: The February 1982 loan by the International Monetary Fund (I M F) bailed out the apartheid state when commercial lending was already restricted. This sanction would ensure this does not happen again.

Action: Nordic states and U S A have said they will oppose any new loan to R S A. Ireland, Greece and a number of other countries opposed the 1982 loan. U S opposition alone is effectively enough to block future loans, so it is highly unlikely that R S A will obtain any new I M F loans.

5. COMPANIES

South Africa is dependent on money, technology, machinery, inputs and skilled people from abroad. These are normally provided by private companies rather than government. So a key area of sanctions is to cut private-sector links with South Africa.

5.1 Withdrawal from RSA

Explanation: (1) *Full withdrawal* involves cutting all links with RSA, including trade (sales to RSA and purchases from RSA), services, licences, franchises and investment – including in particular the sale of subsidiary and associate companies in RSA. (2) *Equity withdrawal* is selling all holdings in subsidiary and associate companies, but not ending trade and licence links. (3) *Partial withdrawal* involves reducing a company's holding in an RSA subsidiary or associate but retaining some ownership. (Note that loans are covered in section 4.)

Terminology: The term 'disinvestment' is sometimes used for this, especially in the USA and RSA. We reserve the terms 'disinvestment' and 'divestment' for the sale of shares in RSA-linked companies (see 5.2), and use 'withdrawal' for companies pulling out of RSA.

Purpose: To deprive RSA of money, technology, etc., thus meeting all three tactical objectives.

Side-effects: (1) Potential loss of jobs in RSA. This has been accepted as a price that must be paid to end apartheid. (2) Potential loss of rights provided under codes of conduct. But if withdrawing companies are genuinely concerned about their workforces, special provisions can be made. (3) Loss of profits to companies. (4) After majority rule, companies that withdrew will be at a disadvantage in comparison with those that did not. Official policy in Sweden is that it is 'valuable that some Swedish companies retain a foothold in the South African market pending the abolition of the apartheid system'.

Loopholes: Partial and equity withdrawal are often cosmetic changes that do not actually end company links with RSA.

Priority: (1) The emphasis should be put on those firms which are most important to the maintenance of apartheid, and/or which are subject to national or international campaigns. (2) Pressure should be maintained on firms which make bogus partial and equity with-drawals.

Action: Since 1980, nearly 200 corporations have disposed of their South African equity interests. More than 90 US companies have withdrawn, including four among the top 15 US investors or em-ployers in RSA: IBM, GM, GE, and Coca-Cola. More than half the withdrawals, including most of the biggest ones, are only equity withdrawals; there are often special agreements to continue to supply former subsidiaries, and sometimes to re-purchase them at a later date. On the other hand, on 19 November 1986 Eastman Kodak an-nounced a total withdrawal; it said it would shut down its RSA opera-tion and halt the supply of all products – largely photographic supplies and computer systems. Other withdrawals come close to total. AT&T will continue to offer the standard long-distance telephone service, but will not provide new services such as data transmission; AT&T computers may not be sold in RSA and AT&T has stopped the purchase of platinum and palladium from RSA. CBS will not supply records once existing contracts expire. Few firms have provided protection for workers, although Coca-Cola left behind $10 million for trust funds.

Forty UK firms have made equity withdrawals since 1980, in-cluding Barclays, Associated British Foods, McAlpine, Crown House, Reed and Smiths. Partial withdrawals include Standard Chartered, Hill Samuel, Prudential, Turner & Newell, Metal Box, BET, ICL, Northern Engineering, Cadbury Schweppes, and Blue Circle.

At least a dozen Canadian firms have withdrawn, including Bata, the world's largest shoemaker. Two New Zealand firms, South British Insurance and New Zealand Insurance, withdrew after a lengthy pro-test campaign. Another 30 firms from other countries have also pulled out since 1980, including Jardine Matheson of Hong Kong. One partly RSA-owned firm has also withdrawn – Philbro-Salomon, the US-based banking and commodity trading group which is partly owned by Anglo American Corporation of South Africa.

5.2 Disinvestment/divestment

Explanation: Sale of shares in companies which have links with RSA. Disinvestment is usually done in association with shareholder action (see 5.3) and boycotts (see 5.4 to 5.6); sometimes disinvestment is threatened unless a company withdraws by a given date. Criteria for the selection of companies for disinvestment vary: (1) The strongest criterion is that the company does business *in or with* South Africa. In this case total withdrawal is required for a firm to be exempted from disinvestment. (2) A weaker criterion is that it has investment, loans, or offices in South Africa; this is known as 'South Africa-invested' (SAI) and simple equity withdrawal will exempt a company. (3) Still weaker criteria include investment in a strategic sector, failure to comply with a code of conduct, failure to recognize black trade unions, or making a major contribution to the maintenance of apartheid.

Disinvestment always includes the sale of any direct RSA holdings – shares in RSA-registered companies and in RSA bonds. Banks which make loans to RSA are also subject to disinvestment.

Purpose: (1) To press the company to withdraw from RSA (see 5.1) or stop making loans to RSA (see 4.3). (2) To educate the public through publicity about disinvestment. (3) To show solidarity with the black majority in South Africa. (4) To uphold a moral duty not to profit from apartheid.

Problems: Sympathetic shareholders normally own too small a proportion of shares to affect share prices, so secret disinvestment has little effect. But combined with boycotts and public announcements of disinvestment, the 'hassle factor' and bad publicity for the company is sometimes enough to precipitate withdrawal.

Loopholes: Often only SAI firms are disinvested. This means that companies like GM and IBM, which still have licence or franchise agreements with their former subsidiaries, are no longer subject to pressure.

Priority: (1) Top priority should be given to the sale of direct portfolio investment in RSA – that is, South African bonds and shares in RSA-registered companies. (2) The next priority is those transnational companies with the most important South African links, those which have carried out bogus withdrawals, and/or those which are subject to campaigns. Companies should be chosen for their importance to South Africa, rather than for South Africa's importance to them; criteria like percentages of assets or profits from South Africa often miss key firms. (3) Priority should be given to publicizing disinvestment or threats of disinvestment.

Exemptions: News-gathering organizations (TV, newspapers, etc.) which maintain staff and offices only for that purpose.

Action: In the USA, $230 billion in investment funds are subject to some restriction (equivalent to 10 per cent of the total value of shares on the New York Stock Exchange); at least $30 billion worth of shares in companies with South African links have been sold or are scheduled for sale. The largest sellers are the California Public Employees' Retirement Fund and Teachers' Retirement Fund ($11 billion), the University of California ($3 billion), New Jersey state pension funds ($4 billion) and Minnesota Board of Investment ($1 billion). By late 1986, 19 states, 85 cities and counties, more than 100 schools and universities and at least 60 religious bodies had imposed South African restrictions on investments. Several corporate pension plans offer South Africa-free options.

US churches, working through the Interfaith Centre on Corporate Responsibility, have targeted a 'dirty dozen' corporations for priority action. After that they propose disinvesting a list of what they define as the '100 top US corporations in South Africa'.

In Britain, between £6 billion and £10 billion in funds are affected by restrictions on South African links. At least 40 local authority pension funds have imposed restrictions or disinvested, as well as five church groups including the Church of Scotland and the Methodist church. The National Union of Teachers disinvested in the 1970s; APEX, the National Union of Seafarers and several other unions have done so more recently. Because of trade union pressure, the Post Office–British Telecom pension fund has imposed limited South African restrictions. Both the Trades Union Congress (TUC) and many local authorities have called on pension funds to disinvest from the 20 largest employers; the TUC also urged trustees to start with the 'inner circle' of UK companies: Barclays, Consolidated Gold, Standard Chartered, RTZ, Shell, and BP. The UK Anti-Apartheid Movement has targeted a slightly different list of 20 'allies of apartheid' (see Table 5, p. 289).

There has been some disinvestment in other countries as well. Canada's largest Protestant denomination, the United Church of Christ, sold £14 million in RSA-linked shares; McGill, York, Dalhousie, and Windsor Universities have disinvested. In Ireland, Trinity College, Dublin, and various religious bodies have disinvested. In the Netherlands, the joint Protestant churches are disinvesting and have appealed to their members to do so as well; some Dutch trade unions and the largest trade union federation, FNV, have disinvested.

Counter-action: Some US companies, including Marathon Oil, have stopped educational grants and scholarships to universities refusing to hold investments in the firms because of their South African links.

5.3 Shareholder action

Explanation: Shareholders (either individuals or institutions such as pension funds) sponsor resolutions or ask questions from the floor at corporation annual general meetings. Typically, such resolutions call on the corporation to withdraw totally from RSA, stop selling to the RSA government or military, or abide by a code of conduct. This action often precedes disinvestment or is part of a larger coordinated campaign.

Purpose: (1) To press the company to change its policy on RSA. (2) To publicize the role of the company in RSA.

Problems: RSA resolutions rarely gain a majority vote. (In contrast, shareholder resolutions in areas such as infant foods, political contributions and union recognition have been more successful because they gained support from mainstream investment funds.)

Priority: Because of the low rate of success, shareholder action is only suitable as part of a larger campaign, or where it is impossible to push immediately for disinvestment.

Action: In the USA, hundreds of resolutions on RSA have been submitted, particularly by churches. Apparently only one has actually won: a New York City Employees' Retirement System resolution asking Pizza Inn to sign the Sullivan Principles received 68 per cent of the shareholder vote in 1986. But South Africa resolutions regularly receive more than 10 per cent of votes and help to create a climate of opinion against corporate involvement in RSA. It is agreed that shareholder resolutions do force management to justify, and thus sometimes re-think, their RSA policy. Shareholder action is considered to be one of the reasons why a number of large corporations have agreed to equity withdrawals, and why others have stopped loans or signed the Sullivan Principles.

In some instances, resolutions have been withdrawn in exchange for partial corporate agreement – for example a resolution asking J. P. Morgan to stop loans was withdrawn when it agreed to restrict loans.

In Britain, resolutions are regularly put and questions asked at annual meetings of high-priority companies, particularly Barclays, Shell and RTZ, but none has been successful. The TUC calls for shareholder action by pension funds in parallel with disinvestment. Shareholder action has also been tried in the Netherlands, West Germany and Canada. In New Zealand shareholder action and protests at company meetings helped to persuade two insurance companies to withdraw from South Africa.

5.4 Shadow annual reports and other protest action

Explanation: (1) A 'shadow' board of directors is created, which publishes its own annual report for a corporation, stressing the links with RSA. Usually linked with disinvestment, shareholder action and boycotts (see 5.2, 5.3, 5.5 and 5.6).

(2) Other protest action ranges over the whole normal spectrum from leaflets to pickets and sit-ins.

Purpose: To provide additional publicity against key target corporations.

Side-effects: Concentrated anti-company publicity has triggered some illegal action, particularly attacks on Shell petrol stations in the Netherlands, Denmark and Norway.

Action: Shadow reports are regularly published on Shell, RTZ, Barclays, and Dresdner Bank. Shell has been a particular target of more general protest action; for example TransAfrica, which organized the year-long series of arrests at the South African Embassy in Washington, also organized a sit-in at the Shell office in Washington.

5.5 Boycott campaigns to force company withdrawal

Explanation: Refusal to buy the products or services of companies with investments in, or which trade with, RSA. (Banks are discussed in 5.6.)

Purpose: (1) To put pressure on companies to withdraw. Profits from the US or UK are often much higher than those from RSA, and thus a successful boycott can make withdrawal a 'rational' business decision. (2) To publicize the role of companies in supporting apartheid.

Side-effects and problems: Purchasing bans can hurt innocent local workers of the company, who have no involvement in setting corporate policy. Trade union cooperation is essential to avoid a backlash and unfavourable publicity. Because of the impact on workers, boycotts are usually restricted to certain companies which are the object of a larger campaign, such as Shell. The Interfaith Centre on Corporate Responsibility in the USA targets a 'dirty dozen' for shareholder action, and if that fails to change their policy, ICCR proposes boycotts and disinvestment of those 12.

Priority: High, especially for corporations which are the target of coordinated campaigns.

Action: Some boycotts have already been successful. In the USA, Bell & Howell cited the fear of a boycott of its textbooks and school materials as a major reason for its withdrawal from RSA; Coca-Cola was clearly influenced by the fear of a consumer boycott. In Sweden in 1985 school pupils and teachers boycotted Esselte, the educational materials supplier and 'Letraset' producer. In early 1986 it sold its RSA subsidiaries.

Shell is the target of the biggest current international campaign, with strong union backing inside and outside RSA. Sales of Shell petrol (gasoline) and other products in the USA and elsewhere have been affected. Some Shell petrol station operators have switched to other brands, or asked Shell to pull out of RSA. So far Shell remains unmoved.

In the USA, the state of Maryland and at least 30 cities have restrictions on purchases from RSA-linked firms. San Francisco does not purchase from RSA-linked firms for items over $5,000, so long as there is an alternative source and there is no significant financial loss. Others (such as Howard County, Maryland; Alameda County, California; Washington, DC; and Chicago) give an advantage (typically between 5 per cent and 10 per cent) to non-RSA-linked firms in competitive bidding. That means corporations without RSA connections can win contracts even if their prices are slightly higher than those of RSA-linked corporations. In August 1986 the Fluor Corporation lost a $2.5 million contract with Los Angeles because of its RSA links. New York City gives a 5 per cent advantage to firms which do not deal with the RSA military or police. (Note that there are disputes with the US government over this – see 3.1.) Several municipalities in the Netherlands, including Arnhem, boycott RSA-linked firms.

In Britain, Rowntree-Mackintosh has been subject to a low-level campaign in solidarity with strikes in RSA; some councils and student unions have banned the sale of Rowntree sweets and other products. In France a boycott has been launched against the (40-per-cent state-owned) Total oil company.

5.6 Boycott campaigns against banks

Explanation: (1) Withdrawal of accounts and an end to the use of other financial services (e.g., investment management) of banks which lend to RSA. Usually combined with disinvestment (see 5.2) and publicity (see 5.3). (2) Other limited bans, including refusal to accept cheques drawn on key banks. (3) Bans are also sometimes imposed on banks which sell Krugerrands.

Purpose: To put pressure on the banks to end lending (see 4.3) and to withdraw as corporations (see 5.1).

Priority: High. Especially after the success of US campaigns and the subsequent 1985 debt moratorium, it is essential that banks do not resume lending, and impose strict political conditions on the re-negotiation of existing loans.

Action: Campaigns against banks have been one of the most visible and successful types of action. One of the first was the Boycott Barclays campaign, which began in the UK in 1969. Barclays was chosen because its RSA subsidiary was the largest bank in RSA. Intensive activity by the National Union of Students and End Loans to Southern Africa meant that by 1985 only 17 per cent of new student accounts were at Barclays, compared with 27 per cent in 1983. Campaign tactics have included publicity, pickets of local branches of Barclays, student unions not accepting Barclays cheques, and Barclays being denied facilities given to other banks (such as use of mailing lists). As well as individuals, many local councils, colleges, churches, trade unions, associations and charities (including Oxfam) closed Barclays accounts with an annual turnover of £7 billion. Outside Britain, Nigeria withdrew government accounts from Barclays in the 1970s and gradually nationalized the bank there because of its RSA links. There were Barclays campaigns in Australia and Ireland as well.

Finally, after 17 years, Barclays announced on 24 November 1986 that it would do an equity withdrawal. Basil Hersov, Barclays RSA Chairman, admitted that 'political pressures on Barclays plc to withdraw from South Africa finally became irresistible'. Commentators agreed that a key element in the decision to withdraw was that Barclays wanted to expand into the USA, and boycotts would have made this impossible.

The UK Anti-Apartheid Movement (AAM) was not satisfied with Barclays' partial withdrawal. It noted that Barclays was still heavily involved with South Africa. It is maintaining links with its former subsidiary that go beyond those of a simple correspondant bank, including an agreement to continue cooperation on technology and training. Furthermore, Barclays has £700 million in outstanding loans to RSA (mostly to its former subsidiary). AAM has not suspended its boycott, but decided to suspend publicity campaigns against Barclays for six months (until mid-1987) to try to gain concessions on three points: (1) the rapid repatriation of the sale price, (2) a harder line on debt re-scheduling and roll-overs, and (3) an end to correspondant bank links.

With Barclays' partial withdrawal, AAM has made Shell its main target. However, the 20 'allies of apartheid' which are also subject to boycott campaigns include four banks: Barclays, Standard Chartered, Hill Samuel, and National Westminster.

Boycott campaigns were a major force in the decisions of US banks in 1985 to stop new loans to RSA. (See 4.4 for more details.) Several US cities have bans on dealing with any bank which gives loans to the RSA government or which sells Krugerrands. In February 1985 Citibank ceased all lending to the RSA public sector when the New York City pension fund threatened to withdraw its $20 billion investment portfolio from the bank's management. More than 20 churches, as well as other organizations, have closed their accounts at Citibank – in part because Citibank is the only US bank with a subsidiary in RSA. Some cities' bans on RSA-linked banks are tied to a disinvestment policy.

The Netherlands had the first major success, when all the major banks agreed to no-loans policies in the late 1970s. In West Germany Dresdner Bank has been chosen for a campaign by the Protestant Women's Association and the German Anti-Apartheid Movement

(AAB) because it was the lead bank in loan consortia, and because of its heavy involvement in Namibia; seven other banks have been targets of lesser campaigns. Several church groups and the World Council of Churches (WCC) have closed accounts at Dresdner.

In Switzerland the WCC has called on its members to cease doing business with three major banks (Union Bank, Swiss Banking Corporation, and Credit Suisse), and a few have done so; the International Labour Organization (ILO) and the Lutheran World Federation have also taken this action. Campaigns against banks are also under way in France (where government-owned banks have lent to RSA), Belgium, Italy, Canada and Austria.

The Norwegian bank Kredittkassen stopped selling Krugerrands at the time when church organizations were threatening a boycott.

5.7 *Boycott campaigns against companies serving RSA*

Explanation: Boycotts against advertising agencies, law firms, consultants, lobbyists, etc., which do work for the RSA government, RSA firms (particularly parastatals), and bantustans.

Purpose: To further isolate RSA. In particular, to attack agencies linked to RSA propaganda.

Problems: Only works if the company is large enough to have other accounts which are more important than RSA, or is susceptible to pressure in some other way. Furthermore, RSA can simply switch to another company which can be pressured less easily.

Priority: High if there is an easy way to bring pressure against a particular company. Otherwise low.

Action: The largest law firm in Washington, DC, dropped South African Airways as a client one week after law students at Yale, Harvard and New York University announced a boycott.

5.8 *Campaigns against funds holding RSA-linked shares*

Explanation: Action to press large investment funds to disinvest.

Purpose: (1) To encourage disinvestment and thus company withdrawal from RSA. (2) To generate publicity.

Problems: Relatively indirect – pressing A to press B to withdraw.

Priority: High, to force disinvestment by large local authority, church, pension and other funds.

Action: Universities and local councils normally disinvest only when they are pushed to do so by local activists. This always involves publicity, in the local press and elsewhere; sometimes it involves sit-ins, pickets, etc. Campaigns continue in many places. One of the largest is to force the Church of England to disinvest from 65 RSA-linked companies (including £18 million in Shell).

5.9 Ban on take-overs or investments by RSA-owned companies

Explanation: (1) Ban on an RSA-owned or -dominated company purchasing control of a local company, or opening a new subsidiary or associate. (2) Protest action to prevent such an investment.

Purpose: The biggest RSA companies are all expanding abroad (see Chapter 8, p. 83). Anglo American Corporation of South Africa is one of the biggest foreign investors in the USA, Canada, Brazil and elsewhere. The Rembrandt group, through Rothmans's and its links with Phillip Morris, has extensive tobacco interests in 100 countries; it also controls the Carling O'Keefe brewery group in Canada and various other companies. Barlow Rand and Liberty Life both purchased major British companies in 1984 and 1985. These firms have five reasons to expand abroad: (1) normal capitalist expansion abroad (in part because the apartheid-constrained market is too small); (2) acquisition of sanctions-busting conduits such as shipping and trading companies, as well as factories to use RSA-made components; (3) an attempt to control non-RSA production of key minerals in an attempt to make sanctions harder and sanctions-busting easier; (4) an attempt to gain a foothold and credibility abroad, perhaps as a way of influencing government and other businesses not to put pressure on RSA; and (5) partial withdrawal from the doomed apartheid economy.

The purpose of any action to prevent RSA firms moving abroad is to counter all of these points. There is both a moral and a practical argument that these companies have grown fat on profits from the low wages of apartheid, and that they should not now be allowed to run away from the problems they have created. Also, the growing importance of RSA companies in areas that will be vital for sanctions – like oil and metals trading – could sabotage sanctions programmes, and thus RSA involvement must be restricted.

Action: No country specifically bans take-overs or investments by RSA-owned or -dominated companies, although Australia has banned investment by the RSA government and parastatals. (However, there are a growing number of bans on dealing with majority-RSA-owned companies – see 3.8.)

At least one expansion by an RSA firm was blocked by trade unions and anti-apartheid campaigners, when Raymond Ackerman's Pick 'n' Pay company was blocked from opening hypermarkets in Australia in 1985.

6. OTHER TRADE AND ECONOMIC ACTION

6.1 Selling off gold

Explanation: (1) Large sales of gold by the big powers, particularly the USA and/or USSR, to depress the gold price. Or (2) smaller sales to keep the gold price at the bottom of its normal range and to provide supplies in the event of restrictions on RSA gold sales.

Purpose: To cut RSA earnings sharply. Cutting the price to $100 per ounce would be equivalent to blocking nearly all of RSA's other exports.

Problems: (1) The mystic significance of gold in the world monetary system means many bankers would be reluctant to manipulate the price. (2) Large gold sales would require an unprecedented level of international cooperation (not least between the USA and USSR) for all countries to agree to purchase no more gold than was needed for normal consumption. Otherwise some countries could take advantage of the depressed price, buying gold at the artificially low price and selling when it was allowed to return to its normal price. Indeed, if such purchases were large enough it would sabotage the whole exercise by keeping the gold price up. (This would not be a problem with smaller gold sales.)

Side-effects: During the period when the gold price was kept low, many countries would find the value of their reserves depressed.

Priority: This one sanction would be more powerful than any other, but it also presents more problems, especially because the role of gold in the world monetary system is so unclear. Thus high priority should be given to continuing discussion and analysis of this sanction.

Action: None.

6.2 Cutting air and sea links

Explanation: Bans on: (1) South African Airways (SAA) overflying and landing; (2) the RSA shipping company (Safmarine) entering ports; (3) national shipping and air lines calling at RSA ports; and (4) foreign shipping and air lines which also serve RSA (linked to oil embargo – see 2.3). Also (5) trade union bans on, and disruptions of, SAA, Safmarine and RSA cargoes.

Purpose: (1) Primarily political, to reinforce the isolation of RSA and make it difficult to travel and ship goods, and thus hit at white morale. (2) Hit the earnings of RSA shipping and air lines. (3) Disrupt and restrict sanctions-busting.

Problems: It can sometimes be very difficult to discover whether a ship has called at RSA. Ships are sometimes re-named in transit, calls at RSA ports are not recorded, etc.

Loopholes: (1) Flags of convenience can be used by both national and RSA shipping lines to avoid sanction laws. (2) Air traffic to RSA may be diverted to neighbouring states which are not asked to impose the ban, particularly Botswana, where the airport is close to the RSA border. (This loophole may be acceptable, as it would allow Botswana to earn money, and would force South African travellers to pass through a successful majority-ruled country.)

Priority: Priority should go to the prevention of sanctions-busting. (1) Monitoring organizations (like Shipping Research Bureau) should be expanded. (2) Trade unions should be encouraged to monitor trade and expose sanctions-busting, and be given legal support where needed. (3) Laws should apply to all nationals and all subsidiaries of national companies, to prevent the use of leased ships and airliners and flags of convenience.

Exemption: States neighbouring RSA. The OAU also exempts Cape Verde, which is the only African transit point for SAA. It would be far better to organize an international fund to provide the $5 million per year that Cape Verde earns from SAA, and then to end this exemption.

International organizations: (1) UN Security Council Resolution 566 (1985) 'urges' the 're-examination of maritime and aerial relations with South Africa'. (2) The Commonwealth mini-summit (5 August 1986) agreed (Britain opposed) on 'a ban on air links with South Africa'.

Action: India, the socialist bloc and all mainland African countries (except the SADCC states) do not grant SAA overflight or landing rights. The USA and Australia have cancelled SAA landing rights and prohibit national carriers from flying to RSA. Denmark, Norway and Sweden stopped their jointly owned Scandinavian Airlines System (SAS) from flying to RSA, thus cutting all links. The Seychelles revoked SAA landing rights in 1980. Canada, Japan, Finland and New Zealand, which did not have direct air links with RSA, have prohibited any future links; Canada bans air cargo as well as passenger flights. The Spanish airline Iberia has ended its flights to Johannesburg, although SAA still flies the route.

Canada, Japan and Australia have closed SAA offices in their country; New Zealand has stopped the national airline from acting as SAA agent. Ireland closed the Aer Lingus office in Johannesburg in the 1970s.

Japan has instructed its government officials not to use SAA.

In September 1985 Rome airport ground staff refused to handle SAA aircraft, forcing the cancellation of several flights. Dockers have disrupted RSA ships and cargoes in several ports.

Finland has broken all maritime links with RSA. Danish-controlled ships are prohibited from carrying oil or oil products to RSA. Norwegian oil tankers must register any calls at RSA. The city council of Wilmington (Delaware, USA) has decided that the port of Wilmington shall accept no ships off-loading cargoes from RSA.

Saint Lucia bans all air and sea links with RSA.

SAA still flies to: UK, Netherlands, Greece, Belgium, West Germany, Portugal, Spain, France, Austria, Italy, Switzerland, Brazil, Hong Kong, Taiwan, Israel, Zimbabwe, Zambia, Botswana, Cape Verde, Malawi, Mozambique, Mauritius, Reunion, and the Comoros.

RSA still has direct (non-SAA) air links with: Congo (Brazzaville), Zaire, Swaziland, Lesotho and Kenya.

6.3 Limiting travel and tourism

Explanation: Measures which block South Africans from travelling abroad and/or prevent people from going to RSA. These measures include both travel restrictions and bans on travel promotion. (See also visa restrictions – 8.2.)

Purpose: (1) To further isolate white South Africans and thus hit morale. (2) To cut the revenue earned from tourists visiting RSA. (3) To make it more difficult for RSA sanctions-busters and security agents to travel.

Loopholes: (1) Travel via third countries (which does at least make travel more difficult, and thus partly fulfils the purpose). (2) Many bans are only voluntary and not fully respected.

Priority: To enforce and strengthen existing bans.

International organizations: The Commonwealth mini-summit agreed (5 August 1986) on 'a ban on the promotion of tourism to South Africa'. (In contrast to the other measures in this package which the UK opposed, Britain agreed to a 'voluntary ban'.)

Action: Canada and the UK have 'voluntary' bans on tourism promotion, but the meanings are very different. After the announcement of the bans, advertising which promoted tours to RSA appeared in both the Canadian and the British press. This was publicly criticized by Canadian Foreign Minister Joe Clark and the RSA tourist office in Canada was closed. By contrast, the UK adverts drew no comment from the UK government.

Ireland closed its tourist office in RSA. Australia closed the RSA tourist office in Australia. New Zealand has stopped the government tourist offices from selling tours to RSA. The Dutch airline KLM has stopped promoting travel to RSA, but refuses to end its flights there.

In Ireland, Trinity College, Dublin, University College, Dublin, and RTE (state radio and television) will not give leaves of absence or finance for staff to go to RSA.

The Norwegian development agency (Norad) does not permit staff in Southern Africa to go to RSA on holiday.

6.4 Ban on recruiting

Explanation: Prevent R S A recruiting skilled people abroad.

Purpose: Because the apartheid education system gives such poor training to black people, there is a severe shortage of skilled technicians, computer programmers, etc., and R S A has become dependent on immigrants. By recruiting whites abroad, R S A maintains white dominance and continues to avoid the need to train black people. A ban on recruiting challenges this directly. It also starves the economy of essential skilled people.

Action: Italy closed the R S A recruiting office and discouraged emigration. Some magazines (such as *New Scientist* in the U K) and newspapers (such as all three Irish national dailies) do not accept R S A recruitment advertising. Many councils ban R S A recruiting literature from libraries and other facilities. Because of student pressure, some universities ban R S A recruiting.

6.5 Ending double taxation agreements

Explanation: End agreements with R S A under which a national or company of one country working in another country need pay taxes in only one country, not both.

Purpose: Double taxation agreements are quite common and intended to make it easier for companies and individuals to work abroad. When a country ends such an agreement with R S A, it means that its companies and nationals are at a disadvantage working in R S A as compared with other foreign countries (and thus have less incentive to work there), and that R S A companies and nationals are at a disadvantage in the country imposing the ban compared with companies and nationals of other foreign countries. The purpose is to impose a financial penalty on job and business links with R S A, in the hope of reducing these.

Problems: R S A tax law has automatic double taxation provisions. Thus a country ending a double taxation agreement earns somewhat more tax revenue, but there will be relatively little effect on companies and individuals.

Priority: Low, because of ineffectiveness.

International organization: Commonwealth mini-summit on 5 August 1986 (Britain opposed).

Action: U S A, Canada. R S A still has full double taxation agreements with Botswana, Gambia, West Germany, Israel, Lesotho, Malawi, Mauritius, Netherlands, Seychelles, Sierra Leone, Swaziland, Switzerland, Tanzania, Uganda, U K, Zambia and Zimbabwe.

6.6 Post and telecommunications bans

Explanation: Halting letters, telephone calls, telexes, etc., to and / or from R S A.

Purpose: Cut links.

Problems: Often criticized because it blocks the free flow of information, and because traditionally post is not disrupted even in wartime. But South Africa already censors both incoming and outgoing post, seizing a wide range of material it does not approve of on political grounds.

Action: Nigeria bans post from South Africa. Action has been taken by trade unions in various countries. Finnish, Norwegian and Australian workers blocked post to R S A in November 1985. Greek workers stopped manually connected telephone and telex links for five days in March 1986.

7. RETALIATION

Explanation: This covers all possible actions against firms and governments which break sanctions, or which refuse to impose them.

Purpose: Secondary actions to enforce or encourage boycotts.

Priority: Should be much higher than it has been, because sanctions-busting will become increasingly important.

Action: The most dramatic retaliation was the August 1986 boycott by 32 countries of the Thirteenth Commonwealth Games in Edinburgh, in protest against British refusal to accept the proposed Commonwealth sanctions package. Threats have been made (for example by Zimbabwe) to deny landing rights to airlines which serve R S A, but this has not been done yet.

8. SOCIAL AND POLITICAL ACTION

Explanation: Various sanctions which do not have a direct economic effect on RSA, but which isolate it and hit white morale.

8.1 Diplomatic relations

Explanation: A variety of measures ranging from a complete break in diplomatic relations to the expulsion and/or withdrawal of various attachés.

Purpose: (1) Further isolation. (2) By cutting the RSA diplomatic presence, reduce the opportunities for RSA to spy on (and attack) exiles and organize sanctions-busting.

Loopholes: (1) Bans usually affect a post rather than a person, so that diplomats and spies can still be sent simply by changing their titles. (2) A refusal to grant new accreditation, as distinct from an expulsion, allows the present RSA official to remain in place.

International organizations: (1) The EEC agreed on 1 September 1985 to the 'recall of military attachés accredited to the RSA, and the refusal to grant accreditation to military attachés from the RSA'. (2) The Commonwealth mini-summit agreed on 5 August 1986 (with Britain opposed) on 'the withdrawal of all consular facilities in South Africa except for our own nationals and nationals of third countries to whom we render consular services'.

Action: Many countries have never had diplomatic relations with RSA, including all the total-boycott states (see item 1). In 1985 and 1986 Argentina, Denmark, Panama and New Zealand cut diplomatic relations (at all levels) with RSA. Officially Japan has diplomatic relations with RSA only at consular, not ambassadorial, level, but it always appoints as consul someone of ambassadorial standing.

The Australian and Canadian consulates in RSA will not issue tourist or business visas – RSA tourists and businesspeople will have to apply at Australian and Canadian consulates in third countries. Australia also expelled four RSA diplomats, while Canada cancelled the non-resident accreditation of four RSA attachés: those for science, mining, labour and agriculture.

South Africa closed its consulate in Norway after a series of demonstrations in Oslo which included the burning of coffins in front of the Consulate.

EEC members have withdrawn military attachés from RSA. France, Spain, Belgium and Luxemburg went further than the EEC agreement and also expelled the RSA military attaché; UK, West Germany and Italy have allowed the present RSA military attaché to stay. (At least five other countries still station military attachés in RSA and/or accredit an RSA military attaché: Bolivia, Malawi, Paraguay, Taiwan and Switzerland.)

RSA still has diplomatic missions in the following 24 countries: *Europe*: Greece, Switzerland, West Germany, Belgium (plus special representation to the EEC), Netherlands, Finland, UK, Portugal, Spain, France, Italy, Sweden and Austria; *Americas*: Paraguay, Brazil, Bolivia, Uruguay, Canada, Chile and the USA (and the UN); *Asia and Pacific*: Australia, Israel and Taiwan; *Africa*: Malawi.

8.2   Requirement of visas for South Africans

Explanation: RSA requires visas for visitors from all countries except the UK, Ireland, West Germany and Switzerland. By contrast South Africans can enter many countries without visas. Making this requirement would restore the balance.

Purpose: (1) To make it more difficult for white South Africans to travel, and thus stress their 'pariah' status. (2) To make it easier to control visits by sportspeople and others (see 8.2 to 8.4 below).

Priority: Important for control of sanctions-busting.

Action: Many countries already require visas. The Nordic states, Australia, Austria, Belgium, Luxemburg, Netherlands and Spain have introduced visa requirements.

In addition, many states use visas to impose certain criteria on visits by South Africans. Finland only grants visas to known opponents of apartheid and Denmark is very restrictive. Many states will not grant visas for South Africans to participate in sporting and cultural events. On the other hand, Sweden still allows RSA tourists and business-people (although not for trade promotion) and permits South Africans to attend some international conferences.

8.3   Sports and cultural boycotts

Explanation: Breaking all sporting and cultural links with RSA by: (1) preventing RSA sportspeople and entertainers from competing and performing abroad; (2) preventing sportspeople and entertainers from going to RSA; (3) limiting books, tapes, films, TV programmes, etc., going to RSA; and (4) carrying out secondary actions against people and groups violating the boycotts.

Purpose: Isolation of white South Africa.

Problems/Side-effects: Also limits information on alternatives that is available to relatively progressive South Africans. This leads the British Publishers' Association (BPA) to argue that the free passage of books is 'essential to the education and freedom of those who are oppressed'. Furthermore, it argues that no distinction should be made and all books allowed to RSA, because 'even the most popular works contain ideas'. Author Art Spiegelman, who tried to block his Holocaust book *Maus* from being distributed in RSA (see also Chapter 13, pp. 126–70), disagrees. He thinks the publishers are concerned more with profits than morals: 'They're talking about jogging books, dieting books, and sex and violence for white housewives. They're talking about business as usual with criminals' (*Observer*, London, 23 November 1986). The other factor is that genuinely anti-apartheid books are often banned by the government; even with the best intentions it is largely the jogging and dieting books that are allowed through.

Exemption: (1) South African refugees are always exempt from boycotts. (2) Progressive theatre and arts groups, such as the Market Theatre of Johannesburg, are normally permitted foreign tours. (3) Political literature in support of the struggle can clearly be sent to RSA. (4) It is sometimes accepted that books directly relating to the problems of Southern Africa can be sent to RSA. Sometimes also books considered to be subversive of white rule are exempted, but this remains subject to debate.

International organizations: The UN Security Council, EEC and Commonwealth all call for sporting and cultural links to be discouraged and restricted.

Action: Undoubtedly these are the most widely practised and most effective sanctions to date.

The 1977 Gleneagles Declaration, calling on Commonwealth members to take 'every practical step to discourage' sporting contacts with RSA, was one of the first internationally agreed sanctions. Most countries now restrict sporting links; it is a newsworthy event when a South African athlete tries to compete abroad, while foreign sportspeople require massive fees to go to RSA (and even then, few do). RSA has been expelled from virtually all international sporting bodies and events, including the Olympic Games.

Many countries, including the Nordic states, Japan, Brazil, Netherlands, Austria and Spain, use visas to prevent RSA sportspeople and entertainers from visiting. 'We do not allow South African sporting organizations to come here, even though there is no visa requirement,' according to the Irish Foreign Minister.

Preventing sportspeople and entertainers from going to RSA is more difficult. The United Nations Special Committee Against Apartheid publishes lists of sportspeople and entertainers who go to RSA (see Part 2 Bibliography) and this is widely used as a basis for retaliatory action. The Sheffield Declaration adopted by many local councils in the UK and Ireland says that people on the UN lists should not be allowed to use council-run facilities. Some councils in the Netherlands, including Amsterdam, impose a similar ban. Austria, Ireland and many local councils do not give grants or other public funds to sports bodies which maintain links with RSA. Many sporting bodies (like the New Zealand Rugby Football Union) will not select for national teams athletes who visit RSA. Many teams won't play against athletes who have visited RSA; in 1985 the England B Cricket Tour was called off after Bangladesh and Zimbabwe both refused to play when the team included four players who had been to RSA. As part of the boycott, some teams (such as Derbyshire County Cricket Club) and local councils have gone further and also ban RSA goods and advertising from their sportsgrounds.

In the entertainment and cultural sector trade unions have played a key role. The UK actors' union Equity had a ban on members performing in RSA; this was overturned by the courts, but the union maintains a widely accepted recommendation not to go to RSA. The UK Musicians' Union has a ban on providing music for RSA; this meant that TV coverage to RSA of the 23 July 1986 Royal Wedding was cut off whenever union musicians were playing. Also in the UK, the Marshall Cavendish publishing company agreed with the National Union of Journalists that South African price-lines would not be printed on new partworks. The company also agreed to full union consultation on any proposed publishing launches in South Africa. Many playwrights, including John Mortimer, Alan Ayckborn and Robert Bolt, will not allow their plays to be performed in RSA. Where possible, performers have stopped their TV programmes and films being shown in RSA; *Dallas* was taken off TV screens there. Where long-term contracts make this impossible, some performers still make a gesture: the stars of TV's *Cagney and Lacey* give their RSA royalties to the ANC.

Unions can also help to enforce boycotts against people who perform in RSA. In Norway the broadcasting unions forced the cancellation of TV coverage of a concert by Cliff Richard and Shirley Bassey, then on the UN list.

In Ireland there have been demonstrations outside concerts by singers on the UN register; several agreed not to go to RSA again (and have thus been taken off the register).

8.4 Scientific and professional boycotts

Explanation: Break all scientific and professional links with RSA by: (1) prohibiting South Africans from attending conferences abroad; (2) not attending conferences in RSA; (3) expelling RSA from international scientific and professional bodies; (4) libraries and other bodies refusing to send information to RSA; and (5) journals refusing to publish scientific papers from RSA.

Purpose: (1) Restricting the flow of scientific and technical knowledge that will help sanctions-busting as well as industrial and military development. (2) Socially isolate white South Africans.

Problems: (1) Much scientific research is published in open journals. (2) A false tradition that science is 'neutral' means that many scientists feel they are 'above' politics and boycotts.

Priority: High. Scientific research is vital to military development. Yet RSA has a limited scientific capacity (both because of its size and because of the apartheid education system). Thus RSA is highly dependent on outside scientific and technical expertise, and it is possible to hit key industrial and military development through a scientific boycott.

Exemption: Work on post-apartheid RSA.

Action: Increasingly South Africans are banned from international conferences. For example, in September 1986 the World Archaeological Congress in Southampton (UK) and the International Federation of Information Processing (IFIP) in Dublin (Ireland) refused to accept South Africans. In August 1986 South Africans were barred from the World Congress on Diseases in Cattle in Dublin. The International Congress of Occupational Therapists (in Denmark in June 1985) and an international conference marking the 400th anniversary of the death of Sir Philip Sidney (in the Netherlands in September 1986) were cancelled rather than allow South Africans to attend.

Three factors have been important in decisions such as these. First, increasing numbers of countries – particularly the Nordic states and many Third World countries – will no longer participate in conferences attended by South Africans. On quite practical grounds, the quality of the papers presented at a conference is higher if RSA is excluded, because so many people will not attend if South Africans are present.

Second, the policies of the host cities are important. Both Southampton and Zutphen (site of the Sidney meeting) have taken strong anti-apartheid stands and decided to cut all links with apartheid South Africa; an international conference is one of the places that such a decision can be made to stick. The Lord Mayor of Dublin had said he would boycott the IFIP conference if South Africans were not barred.

Third, the role of trade unions is critical. Ultimately it was the support of the Irish Congress of Trade Unions that made the difference at the Dublin IFIP conference – the Communications Union of Ireland, the Federated Workers' Union, and the Union of Professional and Technical Civil Servants all promised action if South Africans attended.

Visa restrictions can be used even where conference organizers want to include RSA. For example, Australia refused to grant visas to South African police who wanted to attend the International Police Conference in October 1986. The Nordic states also restrict visas to South Africans who want to attend conferences.

RSA has been expelled from a number of international scientific bodies, including the World Federation of Mental Health. Many professions are now curbing joint recognition of qualifications: for example, the Royal Institute of British Architects (RIBA) no longer 'recognizes' the architecture degrees of three RSA universities on the grounds that insufficient progress has been made in the admission of black students. Students from schools with 'recognized' degrees do not need to sit the RIBA examination.

Various actions have reduced foreign representation at RSA conferences. The International Conference of High Speed Photonics in Pretoria in September 1986 was boycotted by several countries, including Sweden, Australia, Finland, India, Ireland, Pakistan, China and the USSR. In part this was because the official subject of the conference included military use of high-speed photography. The UK government stopped government scientists from attending, but only after the issue was raised in the press. In the end, only 15 non-South Africans attended. A coordinated campaign also cut foreign attendance at a conference on radiation waste in Cape Town the same month.

Many international exchange programmes with RSA have been terminated. For example, Austria has stopped its student exchange programme. The Netherlands has stopped providing funds for students to go to RSA and no longer helps them find places there.

8.5   Expelling RSA from international organizations

Explanation: Eject RSA from international economic and technical organizations.

Purpose: Further isolation.

Action: RSA has not participated in the UN General Assembly since 1974. It has been expelled or forced to withdraw from many organizations, including the International Red Cross; UN Economic, Scientific and Cultural Organization (UNESCO); International Labour Organization (ILO); UN Food and Agriculture Organization (FAO); and World Meteorological Organization. Its role has been curtailed in the World Health Organization (WHO) and UN Environment Programme (UNEP).

However, RSA remains in a number of bodies, some of which are of key political or economic importance. It is a member of the World Bank (IBRD), International Monetary Fund (IMF), International Finance Corporation (IFC) and International Development Association (IDA). It is a member of many UN bodies: International Civil Aviation Organization (ICAO), International Telecommunication Union (ITU), Universal Postal Union (UPU), World Intellectual Property Organization (WIPO), UN Conference on Trade and Development (UNCTAD), UN Children's Fund (UNICEF), UN Development Programme (UNDP) and UN Industrial Development Organization (UNIDO).

RSA is also a member of the African Postal and Telecommunication Union (APTU), Commonwealth War Graves Commission, Intergovernmental Committee for European Migration, Intergovernmental Oceanographic Commission (IOC), International Bureau of Weights and Measures (BIPM), International Hydrographic Organization (IHO), International Institute of Refrigeration, International Lead and Zinc Study Group, International Sugar Organization, International Telecommunications Satellite Organization, General Agreement on Tariffs and Trade (GATT), International Vine and Wine Office (IWO), International Whaling Commission, International Wheat Council, International Wool Study Group, International Commission for the Conservation of Atlantic Tunas, International Commission for the South-east Atlantic Fisheries, International Commission on Large Dams, International Radio Consultative Committee (IRCC), International Seed Testing Organization, International Standards Organization (ISO), and International Office of Epizootics.

RSA is still a member of the International Atomic Energy Agency (IAEA). It has not attended an annual conference since 1979, when its credentials were rejected, but it still has access to IAEA facilities. At its 3 October 1986 annual meeting in Vienna, the IAEA voted 66 to 26 to call on the IAEA governors to 'consider recommending' the suspension of RSA – but the entire Western bloc voted in favour of continued RSA membership.

RSA groups have been expelled from a wide range of international organizations. For example, because of its racist policies, the all-white South African Typographical Union has been expelled from the International Graphical Federation.

8.6 *Exposing RSA-linked individuals*

Explanation: To identify publicly prominent people with RSA links, and expose them to protest if they do not break those links.

Action: Various individual actions. In Bermuda, there was a sit-in at the office of a local barrister who is a senator and a director of Minorco, a key Anglo American subsidiary. In Canada, York University removed from its Board of Governors Sonia Bata of the Bata shoe company, which then had several factories in RSA and the bantustans.

9. POSITIVE MEASURES

Included in this section are all measures which do not put pressure on the white minority government, but which support black people and the anti-apartheid struggle in other ways.

9.1 Codes of conduct

Explanation: Rules for foreign private companies operating in RSA, which set minimum standards for wages, integration, social facilities and recognition of trade unions.

Purpose: (1) To improve the lot of those black people who work for transnational corporations. (2) To provide a model for RSA companies. (3) To show that apartheid is not necessary.

Problem: Codes have not had the intended effect of provoking change outside the workplaces covered, nor have they been all that successful in improving the lot of the workers concerned.

Loopholes: (1) Many codes are voluntary. (2) The EEC code does not require public reporting, so compliance often cannot be checked.

Priority: Low, due to ineffectiveness.

Action: EEC, USA, Canada and Australia have codes of conduct. In the USA, the Sullivan Principles call for non-segregated eating, 'comfort' and work facilities; equal employment practices; equal pay; training for non-whites 'in substantial numbers'; increasing the number of black people in management and supervisory positions; spending 'to improve the quality of employees' lives outside the work environment in such areas as housing, schooling, recreation, and health'. Companies are also called upon to 'support the recension [revision] of all apartheid laws'; support black business and push RSA companies to follow the Sullivan Principles; practise corporate civil disobedience against all apartheid laws; and use company financial and legal resources to assist blacks in the equal use of all public and private amenities.

The EEC Code states that workers must be allowed to choose their own trade union and that these should be recognized; firms using migrant labour should regularly renew contracts and make it easier for families to live nearby; pay must be above the 'supplemented living level', as set by the University of South Africa (UNISA); there must be equal opportunities and equal pay for equal work; training should be given 'if possible'; supervisory and management jobs must be 'open' to black employees; company funds should be used for insurance, health, education, housing, transport and leisure facilities; workplaces, canteens, education and sports facilities should be desegregated; and black business should be encouraged through sub-contracting.

9.2 *Assistance to South Africans*

Explanation: Financial and other help to South Africans struggling against apartheid, both inside and outside RSA.

Ostensible purpose: To help those suffering most from apartheid.

Actual purpose: The hidden reasons are often different. Assistance to South Africans is often given: (1) as an alternative to sanctions, (2) to identify future leaders and win their allegiance, through scholarships and grants, and (3) to gain influence with the anti-apartheid movement in the hope of being able to affect the direction of the struggle.

Problems: (1) The RSA government does not permit money to be given directly to those who are most active against apartheid, like the United Democratic Front (UDF). (2) Few governments will give help to those who are actually doing the fighting – the guerrillas of the ANC (African National Congress), PAC (Pan Africanist Congress), and SWAPO (South West African People's Organization). Money is normally restricted to education and welfare, which is necessary for refugees but is of limited help to the armed struggle. (3) Financial assistance has not prevented the RSA government from detaining many key activists, often precisely those in 'non-violent' organizations assisted with foreign funds. (4) With the sudden rush to pour money into RSA, there has been difficulty finding suitable recipients and competition to fund favoured groups.

Priority: In general, low, as large amounts of money are now flowing. However, black trade unions do need more support, especially from other trade unions.

Action: The UN, Commonwealth, USA, EEC, Nordic states, Canada, Australia and other countries and organizations have pro-grammes to support churches, education groups and other (as the EEC calls them) 'non-violent anti-apartheid organizations'. They also support refugees outside RSA. Australia specifically assigned to refugees the money it had previously used to fund a trade mission in RSA.

Under the various codes of conduct, many transnational corpora-tions have established social and educational funds.

Trade unions have increasingly been supporting their counterparts inside RSA with funds, publicity for detained leaders, and other solidarity activity. Some support is channelled through the Inter-national Congress of Free Trade Unions (ICFTU). The British Trades Union Congress (TUC) has a programme of support which also includes pressure on UK companies active in RSA to improve the condition of workers there. The TUC and ICFTU try to develop links between similar sorts of workers (say car-workers in the UK and RSA); individual UK unions are urged to 'adopt' detainees from their counterpart unions.

9.3 Support for SADCC

Explanation: (1) Development and other assistance to the SADCC states. (2) Transfer to SADCC of quotas and investment removed from RSA. (3) Military help to resist RSA aggression.

Purpose: The nine majority-ruled states which are neighbours of RSA and form the SADCC group have come under increasing attack. RSA's destabilization has cost more than £10 billion ($15 billion) and 100,000 lives in the SADCC states. They are victims of apartheid, but they also serve as a model of an alternative society. Assistance helps them survive the South African onslaught, ensure they are not harmed by sanctions, and helps them develop as a viable multi-racial alternative to apartheid.

Problems: (1) RSA destabilization creates problems. Companies withdrawing from RSA tend not to invest in the neighbouring states because destabilization has reduced their commercial potential. Some countries are reluctant to commit money and technicians to development projects for fear that RSA will attack them. (2) Governments are more willing to give development than military assistance.

Priority: High, because (1) RSA is attempting to hold the neighbouring states hostage as a way of holding off sanctions, and (2) the link between apartheid and the crisis in the neighbouring states has not been fully made, and some countries (notably the USA) have been supporting RSA actions against the SADCC states.

Action: The Nordic and EEC anti-apartheid programmes have special provisions for supporting the SADCC states. The Nordic states have given strong support to SADCC since its founding in 1980.

US legislation does not include support for the SADCC states; in addition, the RSA sugar quota was given to the Philippines rather than an SADCC sugar producer. Furthermore, the USA is supporting RSA attempts to overthrow the government of Angola (an SADCC member).

The Swedish government recommended to its shipping companies in October 1985 that they should refrain from stopping at RSA ports and call at SADCC ports instead.

The Non-Aligned Movement at its summit in September 1986 established a fund to assist the Frontline states and the liberation movements of South Africa and Namibia.

9.4   Promotion of anti-apartheid struggles at home

Explanation: Actions to strengthen the anti-apartheid movement and raise the consciousness of both politicians and ordinary people.

Action: Literally thousands of different activities, only a few of which can be listed here. Regular demonstrations have taken place outside the RSA embassies in Washington, London and The Hague. Mass rallies and petition campaigns have now involved hundreds of thousands of people. In many countries people are increasingly realizing the importance of joining the organized Anti-Apartheid Movement (AAM). For example, AAM membership in the UK jumped 70 per cent during 1986.

In Norway 80 per cent (364 of 454) of municipalities have taken some kind of stand against apartheid.

In Britain 120 local councils have taken some anti-apartheid action; in the USA hundreds of councils, including those of nine of the ten top cities, have taken some action. As well as engaging in disinvestment and buying boycotts, many declared their areas 'anti-apartheid zones'. Bristol (UK) commissioned a special 'apartheid audit' to find out just what its RSA links were. Dozens of councils carried out publicity campaigns in libraries, in schools, using council magazines, through newspaper advertising, etc. Sometimes this has been linked to anti-apartheid weeks. Many towns now have buildings, gardens and streets named after South African resistance leaders, particularly Nelson Mandela. Some cities, such as Glasgow and Aberdeen, have given Mandela the 'freedom of the city'. In London a statue of Mandela is displayed in a prominent place in front of a major concert hall.

Universities have given Winnie Mandela, Archbishop Desmond Tutu and others honorary degrees. Opponents and victims of the apartheid state have won many national and international awards.

MPs have formed anti-apartheid organizations, including the Association of West European Parliamentarians for Action Against Apartheid (AWEPAA), the Latin American Inter-Parliamentary Congress on South Africa, and Parliamentary Action for the Removal of Apartheid (PARA) in India.

Trade unions are playing a major role. In Britain the Trades Union Congress (TUC) has produced an anti-apartheid cinema commercial (in the UK, such an advertisement is considered 'political' and thus cannot be shown on TV). Thirty-eight national trade unions, representing 93 per cent of TUC membership, have affiliated to the AAM. Several unions and trades councils have distributed anti-apartheid leaflets and booklets. The National Union of Journalists (UK and Ireland) distributed a leaflet to members advising them not to write articles with unchallenged statements by the RSA government, and to ensure that if a report from RSA is censored that this be stated.

Artists and performers have gone further than simply boycotting RSA. Many have performed at Anti-Apartheid events, and there have been several records supporting the liberation movement. In 1985 more than 50 rock, rap, reggae, pop and jazz stars, brought together by rock musician 'Little Steven' Van Zandt as Artists United Against Apartheid, made the *Sun City* record, which promoted the boycott as well as raising money for apartheid's victims. (See the associated book, *Sun City*, by Dave Marsh, Penguin, 1985.) In Scotland a number of artists got together to produce a cassette, *Freedom is Coming*. And the

Welsh Language Society produced a record which makes links between oppressed peoples in South Africa and elsewhere in the world. The title, which translated as *Buffalo Soldiers of Wales*, is *Galwad ar Holl Filwyr Byffalo Cymru.*

Bibliography: Part 1

Short titles are used in the Notes where appropriate; other abbreviations used are shown here in parentheses.

Books, reports and other single publications

Davenport, T. R. H., *South Africa: A Modern History*, 2nd edn, Macmillan, London, 1978
'Disinvestment', Special issue of *Leadership* magazine, Johannesburg, June 1985 ('Disinvestment')
Documents, see *United States and South Africa*
FAC I, II and Observations, see House of Commons
Hanlon, Joseph, *Apartheid's Second Front*, Penguin, Harmondsworth, 1986
Hanlon, Joseph, *Beggar Your Neighbours*, CIRR/James Currey, London; Indiana University Press, Bloomington; 1986
Horrell, Muriel, *Laws Affecting Race Relations in South Africa 1948–1976*, South African Institute of Race Relations, Johannesburg, 1978 (*Laws 1948–76*)
Horrell, Muriel, *Race Relations as Regulated by Law in South Africa 1948–79*, South African Institute of Race Relations, Johannesburg, 1982 (*Laws 1948–79*)
House of Commons: Sixth Report from the Foreign Affairs Committee, Vol. I, HC 61–I, London, 1986 (FAC I)
House of Commons: Sixth Report from the Foreign Affairs Committee, Vol. II, HC 61–II, London, 1986 (FAC II)
House of Commons: Sixth Report from the Foreign Affairs Committee: Observations by the Government, Cmnd. 9925, London, 1986 (FAC: Observations)
Laws 1948–76, see Horrell
Laws 1948–79, see Horrell
Lodge, Tim, *Black Politics in South Africa since 1945*, Ravan Press/Longman, Johannesburg and London, 1983
Myers, Desaix, *US Business in South Africa*, Indiana University Press, Bloomington, 1980
Omond, Roger, *The Apartheid Handbook*, 2nd edn, Penguin, Harmondsworth, 1986
Orkin, Mark, *The Struggle and the Future: What Black South Africans Really Think*, Ravan Press, Johannesburg, 1986
Rees, Mervyn and Chris Day, *Muldergate*, Macmillan, Johannesburg, 1980
Schlesinger, Arthur, *Robert Kennedy and His Times*, André Deutsch, London, 1978
Slabbert, Frederik van Zyl, *The Last White Parliament*, Sidgwick & Jackson, London, 1985 (LWP)
South Africa 1985, Official Yearbook of the Republic of South Africa, Department of Foreign Affairs, Pretoria, 1985 (*Yearbook 1985*)

Stuart, Kelsey, *The Newspaperman's Guide to the Law*, 2nd edn, Butterworth, Durban, 1977

Survey of Race Relations in South Africa, South African Institute of Race Relations, Johannesburg (*Survey*, various editions)

United States and South Africa: US Public Statements and Related Documents 1977–1985, Office of the Historian, Department of State, Washington, DC, 1985 (*Documents*)

Walshe, Peter, *Church versus State in South Africa*, C. Hurst & Co., London, 1983

Yearbook 1985, see *South Africa 1985*

Other Sources: newspapers, news agencies, magazines, journals, radio and television stations

Argus, the, Cape Town
Associated Press (AP)
Beeld, Johannesburg
Business Day, Johannesburg (*BD*)
Cape Times, Cape Town (*CT*)
Capital Radio, Umtata
Citizen, the, Johannesburg
City Press, Johannesburg (*CP*)
Daily Dispatch, East London (*DD*)
Daily Telegraph, London (*DT*)
Die Burger, Cape Town
Eastern Province Herald, Port Elizabeth (*EPH*)
Echo, the, Durban
Evening Post, Port Elizabeth
Finance Week, Johannesburg
Financial Mail, Johannesburg (*FM*)
Financial Times, London (*FT*)
Gaborone Radio, Gaborone
Guardian, the, London
Guardian Weekly, Manchester
International Herald Tribune, Paris (*IHT*)
Mbabane Radio, Mbabane
Mbabane Television, Mbabane
Mozambique Radio, Maputo
Namibian, the, Windhoek
Natal Mercury, Durban (*Mercury*)
Natal Witness, Pietermaritzburg (*Witness*)
New Statesman, London
New York Times
Observer, the, London

Pace, Johannesburg
Pan-African News Agency (PANA)
Post, Johannesburg
Pretoria News, Pretoria
Radio Freedom, Addis Ababa
Radio Havana, Havana
Rand Daily Mail, Johannesburg (RDM)
Reuter
Sechaba, London
South African Digest, Pretoria (*SAD*)
South African Press Association (SAPA)
South African Radio, Johannesburg (SA Radio)
South African Television, Johannesburg (SATV)
Sowetan, the, Johannesburg
Star, the, Johannesburg
Sunday Standard, Nairobi
Sunday Star, the, Johannesburg
Sunday Telegraph, London
Sunday Times, Johannesburg (*ST*)
Sunday Times, London
Sunday Tribune, Durban (*Tribune*)
The Times, London (*Times*)
Washington Post, Washington DC (*WP*)
Weekly Mail, Johannesburg (*WM*)
Work in Progress, Johannesburg (*WIP*)
Writers' News, London
Zambian Radio, Lusaka
Zimbabwe Radio, Harare

Notes: Part 1

Chapter 1

1. *Survey* 1959–60, p. 54
2. *Survey* 1973, p. 184
3. *Survey* 1972, p. 220
4. *Survey* 1973, p. 186
5. *Survey* 1972, p. 220
6. *Survey* 1972, p. 221
7. ibid.
8. *Survey* 1973, p. 187
9. Stuart, *Newspaperman's Guide to the Law*; *Laws* 1948–79; *Survey* 1982
10. *CP*, 21 September 1986
11. *Argus*, 13 August 1986
12. *WP*, 3 January 1985
13. Reuter, 20 March 1986
14. Reuter, 2 April 1986
15. SAPA, 2 April 1986
16. SA Radio, 4 April 1986
17. SA Radio, 7 April 1986
18. *Argus*, 4 April 1986
19. Reuter, 11 April 1986
20. *SAD*, 11 April 1986
21. SAPA, 26 May 1986
22. *Sunday Standard*, 27 July 1986
23. Reuter, 18 August 1986
24. ibid.
25. SAPA, 21 August 1986
26. *CT*, 8 September 1986
27. Reuter, 23 May 1986
28. *Tribune*, 31 August 1986
29. *SAD*, 29 August 1986
30. *Star*, 13 December 1985
31. Reuter, 16 April 1986
32. *DD*, 4 October 1986
33. Radio Freedom, 7 August 1986
34. Radio Havana, 18 June 1986
35. Radio Freedom, 1 August 1986
36. Radio Freedom, 6 August 1986
37. *Guardian*, 22 September 1986
38. Radio Freedom, 3 October 1986
39. FAC II, p. 8
40. FAC II, pp. 109–11
41. FAC II, p. 9
42. FAC II, p. 10
43. *Sowetan*, 25 July 1986
44. *Namibian*, 26 September 1986
45. *Pace*, October 1985
46. *Post*, 27 July 1986

Chapter 2

1. *RDM*, 22 March 1985
2. ibid.
3. *ST*, 29 September 1985
4. *RDM*, 22 March 1985
5. *Mercury*, 4 September 1985
6. *ST*, 29 September 1985
7. *FM*, 10 October 1986
8. *CT*, 2 December 1985
9. SAPA, 2 December 1985
10. *Guardian*, 2 July 1986
11. *Guardian*, 27 August 1986
12. *Witness*, 27 August 1986
13. *Argus*, 22 September 1986
14. *CT*, 31 July 1986
15. *FM*, 14 November 1986
16. *BD*, 31 October 1986
17. *Guardian*, 17 November 1986
18. *BD*, 31 October 1986
19. *CT*, 16 November 1986
20. ibid.
21. *Guardian*, 18 November 1986
22. *Guardian*, 19 November 1986
23. *Guardian*, 17 November 1986
24. *Guardian*, 20 November 1986

Chapter 3

1. *CT*, 28 June 1985
2. SAPA, 14 July 1986
3. *Pretoria News*, 10 September 1986
4. *Post*, 27 April 1985
5. *SAD*, 30 May 1986
6. *CT*, 9 July 1986
7. *Argus*, 24 July 1986
8. *Argus*, 20 March 1986
9. *SAD*, 26 September 1986
10. *EPH*, 27 June 1986
11. Myers, *US Business*, p. 51
12. ibid.
13. 'Disinvestment'
14. SA Radio, 3 May 1986
15. Text of Buthelezi speech
16. FAC II, pp. 97–8
17. ibid.
18. FAC II, pp. 72–3
19. FAC II, pp. 204–5
20. FAC II, p. 206
21. SAPA, 28 July 1986
22. FAC II, pp. 208–21

Chapter 4

1. 'Disinvestment'
2. ibid.
3. *Tribune*, 16 December 1985
4. *Sechaba*, September 1985
5. 'Disinvestment'
6. *Pretoria News*, 16 August 1985
7. *Sunday Times*, 25 August 1985
8. *Sunday Times*, 3 August 1986
9. *Sunday Times*, 25 August 1985
10. 'Disinvestment'
11. Orkin, *The Struggle and the Future*
12. *Sunday Times*, 25 August 1986
13. *Pretoria News*, 16 August 1985

Chapter 5

1. Walshe, *Church versus State*, pp. 192–3 and 197–8
2. *Survey* 1984, pp. 911ff.
3. *Star*, 12 September 1986
4. ibid.
5. *Star*, 17 March 1986
6. *Star*, 3 October 1985

7. *Yearbook* 1985, pp. 783ff.
8. *Evening Post*, 16 September 1986
9. *DD*, 28 July 1986
10. *Argus* and Reuter, 2 May 1986
11. *WM*, 9 May 1986

Chapter 6

1. FAC II, pp. 12ff.
2. Slabbert, *Last White Parliament*, pp. 130ff.
3. SAPA, 9 April 1986
4. *CT*, 31 February 1986
5. *CT*, 13 April 1985
6. *Star*, 17 September 1986
7. *IHT*, 4 June 1986
8. *Guardian Weekly*, 4 August 1985
9. 'Disinvestment'
10. ibid.
11. *Tribune*, 6 October 1986
12. *Mercury*, 12 June 1986
13. *Pretoria News*, 27 August 1986
14. 'Disinvestment'
15. ibid.
16. ibid.

Chapter 7

1. FAC II, p. 137
2. FAC II, pp. 146–7
3. Slabbert, *Last White Parliament*, p. 157
4. *Mercury*, 18 September 1986
5. SATV, 4 October 1986
6. *Sowetan*, 24 July 1986
7. *Citizen*, 5 March 1986
8. *ST*, 11 May 1986
9. Capital Radio, 13 July 1986
10. SAPA, 16 July 1986
11. *Star*, 11 June 1986
12. Slabbert, *Last White Parliament*, p. 157
13. *Star*, 13 March 1986
14. *Star*, 1 October 1986
15. SA Radio, 6 August 1986
16. SA Radio, 19 August 1986
17. *SAD*, 6 June 1986
18. SATV, 5 August 1986
19. AP, 18 August 1986
20. SATV, 12 August 1986

Chapter 8

1. SATV, 12 October 1986
2. *CT*, 4 July 1986
3. *WIP*, no. 44, September/October 1986
4. ibid.
5. ibid.
6. ibid.
7. Myers, *US Business*, p. 128
8. *ST*, 15 June 1986
9. Myers, *US Business*, p. 128
10. *CT*, 13 June 1986
11. Reuter, 6 August 1986
12. FAC II, p. 130
13. *BD*, 3 July 1986
14. SAPA, 13 August 1986
15. *Guardian*, 3 October 1986
16. *Guardian*, 7 October 1986
17. SA Radio, 9 August 1986
18. *Star*, 23 July 1986
19. *Argus*, 16 July 1986
20. *SAD*, 29 August 1986
21. SATV, 23 August 1986
22. *BD*, 4 September 1986
23. *DT*, 11 October 1986
24. *Star*, 16 October 1986
25. *CT*, 6 August 1986
26. SAPA, 23 July 1986
27. *Star*, 16 September 1986
28. SA Radio, 6 October 1986
29. SA Radio, 16 June 1986
30. *Argus*, 17 August 1986
31. *DD*, 18 September 1986
32. ibid.
33. SAPA, 9 August 1986
34. *Argus*, 26 July 1986
35. *Star*, 12 September 1986
36. *Star*, 25 June 1986
37. *Argus*, 23 July 1986
38. *Star*, 1 September 1986
39. *WM*, 29 August 1986
40. ibid.
41. ibid.
42. ibid.
43. *BD*, 5 September 1986
44. *CT*, 9 October 1986
45. *BD*, 5 September 1986
46. *FM*, 15 August 1986
47. Reuter, 14 May 1986
48. *FM*, 15 August 1986

Chapter 9

1. Orkin, *The Struggle and the Future*, pp. 18–19
2. ibid.
3. ibid.
4. *Argus*, 13 June 1986
5. *ST*, 6 July 1986
6. *DD*, 20 October 1986
7. ibid.
8. FAC II, p. 140
9. *DT*, 6 October 1986
10. ibid.
11. SA Radio, 27 June 1986
12. *FM*, 15 August 1986; SAPA, 5 August 1986
13. *Argus*, 10 September 1986
14. *Times*, 8 August 1986
15. *Star*, 15 September 1986; *Times*, 8 August 1986
16. *Star*, 15 September 1986
17. *SAD*, 9 May 1986
18. *Argus*, 27 April 1985
19. FAC I, p. xxii
20. FAC II, p. 44
21. FAC II, p. 176
22. FAC II, p. 181
23. FAC I, p. xxxv
24. FAC I, p. xxii
25. AP, 13 August 1986
26. FAC II, p. 10
27. Lodge, *Black Politics*, p. 202

Chapter 10

1. Gaborone Radio, 10 August 1986
2. ibid.
3. Gaborone Radio, 22 August 1986
4. ibid.
5. Reuter, 8 July 1986
6. SAPA, 10 July 1986
7. SAPA, 5 July 1986
8. *Citizen*, 4 July 1986
9. *BD*, 10 July 1986
10. SA Radio, 6 October 1986
11. *BD*, 10 July 1986

12. *Star*, 20 October 1986
13. Reuter, 6 November 1986
14. ibid.
15. ibid.
16. Mbabane Radio, 22 August 1986
17. Mbabane Television, 26 August 1986

Chapter 11

 1. Reuter, 6 August 1986; *Guardian*, 8 August 1986; *Times*, 7 August 1986
 2. Reuter, 14 April 1986
 3. SATV, 5 August 1986
 4. Zambian Radio, 26 August 1986
 5. SAPA, 6 August 1986
 6. ibid.
 7. Reuter, 11 August 1986
 8. SAPA, 6 August 1986
 9. Zambian Radio, 14 August 1986
10. *Star*, 13 August 1986
11. SAPA, 26 August 1986; SA Radio, 27 August 1986
12. Reuter, 11 August 1986
13. *Witness*, 5 August 1986; *Times*, 7 August 1986
14. *FT*, 9 August 1986
15. SAPA, 4 August 1986
16. *BD*, 4 August 1986
17. Table by Colin Stoneman in Hanlon, *Beggar Your Neighbours*
18. *Times*, 9 August 1986
19. SA Radio, 28 August 1986
20. ibid.; *BD*, 27 August 1986
21. Zimbabwe Radio, 2 July 1986; *CT*, 2 July 1986; Reuter, 6 July 1986
22. SAPA, 13 August 1986
23. *BD*, 12 August 1986; *ST*, 24 August 1986
24. *FT*, 9 August 1986
25. Zimbabwe Radio, 8 August 1986
26. *Survey* 1984, p. 832; Omond, *Apartheid Handbook*, p. 155
27. SAPA, 7 October 1986
28. SA Radio, 9 October 1986
29. SA Radio, 15 October 1986
30. SA Radio, 16 October 1986
31. Mozambique Radio, 3 July 1986
32. PANA, 12 July 1986
33. *EPH*, 11 August 1986
34. *Star*, 8 September 1986
35. *Star*, 26 May 1986
36. *BD*, 25 September 1986
37. *Star*, 6 September 1986
38. SAPA, 27 June 1986
39. SAPA, 1 August 1986
40. SA Radio, 13 August 1986
41. SATV, 13 August 1986
42. ibid.
43. *ST*, 24 August 1986
44. *Citizen*, 30 August 1986
45. *CT*, 20 September 1986
46. SAPA, 8 October 1986
47. SA Radio, 9 October 1986
48. Mozambique Radio, 8 October 1986
49. *Star*, 9 October 1986
50. *Star*, 10 October 1986
51. *Star*, 9 October 1986
52. ibid.
53. ibid.
54. *Guardian*, 1 September 1986
55. Reuter, 17 October 1986
56. Reuter, 21 October 1986
57. *Argus*, 25 April 1986
58. *BD*, 30 May 1986
59. *EPH*, 18 March 1986
60. *Argus*, 13 October 1986
61. *Star*, 12 September 1986
62. *Evening Post*, 22 May 1986
63. SAPA, 13 June 1986
64. *Star*, 8 July 1986

Chapter 12

 1. *Laws* 1948–79, pp. 146–7
 2. *Survey* 1959–60, pp. 227–38
 3. *Echo*, 18 September 1986
 4. *CT*, 13 September 1986
 5. ibid.
 6. ibid.
 7. *Star*, 3 October 1986
 8. *Guardian*, 9 October 1986
 9. *CT*, 9 October 1986
10. *CT*, 14 October 1986; *Argus*, 17 October 1986
11. *Argus*, 22 October 1986
12. *Argus*, 17 October 1986
13. *ST*, 31 August 1986
14. ibid.

15. *WM*, 19 September 1986
16. *Observer*, 24 August 1986
17. *Times*, 6 September 1986
18. *Observer*, 14 September 1986

Chapter 13

1. *Writers' News*, March 1984, p. 7
2. ibid.
3. *New Statesman*, 10 October 1986
4. ibid.
5. *BD*, 13 March 1986
6. *Writers' News*, March 1984, p. 7
7. ibid., p. 9
8. *BD*, 17 March 1986
9. Reuter, 11 April 1986
10. *Guardian*, 30 July 1986
11. *New Statesman*, 26 September 1986
12. ibid.
13. *New Statesman*, 10 October 1986
14. *Observer*, 23 November 1986

Chapter 14

1. *Survey* 1984, pp. 921–32
2. ibid.
3. Omond, *Apartheid Handbook*, pp. 71–4
4. ibid.
5. ibid.
6. *Survey* 1984, p. 921
7. *Laws* 1948–79, pp. 168–87
8. ibid.
9. ibid.
10. *Yearbook* 1985, p. 848
11. FAC II, p. 15
12. *Laws* 1948–79, pp. 168–87
13. ibid.
14. ibid.
15. *Survey* 1980, p. 588
16. *Laws* 1948–79, pp. 168–87
17. *Survey* 1980, p. 586
18. *Survey* 1982, pp. 584–8
19. *Survey* 1983, p. 638
20. ibid.
21. *Yearbook* 1985, p. 845
22. FAC II, p. 125
23. FAC II, p. 167

Chapter 15

1. Davenport, *South Africa*, p. 29
2. FAC II, pp. 174–5
3. *Survey* 1959–60, p. 275
4. *Survey* 1966, p. 112
5. *Survey* 1967, p. 86
6. *BD*, 26 May 1986
7. *CT*, 17 July 1986
8. *Times*, 2 October 1986
9. *Guardian*, 2 October 1986
10. FAC II, pp. 161 and 163
11. *Times*, 2 October 1986
12. FAC II, p. 164
13. FAC II, p. 166
14. FAC II, p. 170
15. FAC II, pp. 167 and 169–70
16. *CT*, 22 March 1985
17. *CT*, 12 December 1985
18. *Star*, 15 August 1986
19. *Guardian*, 21 July 1986
20. ibid.
21. *Guardian*, 8 July 1986
22. ibid.
23. *Evening Post*, 16 September 1986
24. *Times*, 8 May 1986

Chapter 16

1. *CT*, 2 April 1986
2. ibid.
3. *Times*, 14 July 1986
4. *DD*, 17 August 1986
5. ibid.
6. *Star* and *DT*, 11 July 1986
7. All the following quotes from Mrs Thatcher are from the *Guardian*, 9 July 1986.
8. *SAD*, 20 June 1986
9. SATV, 29 July 1986
10. *Guardian*, 24 September 1986
11. *Guardian*, 10 October 1986
12. ibid.
13. *Guardian*, 7 August and 9 July 1986
14. SA Radio, 4 August 1986
15. *CT*, 7 August 1986
16. *CT*, 25 June 1986
17. Zimbabwe Radio and Reuter, 3 June 1986
18. FAC I, p. xxvii

19. FAC I, pp. xxix–xxx; FAC II, p. 37; FAC Observations, p. 4
20. FAC I, pp. xxx–xxxiii
21. *CT*, 7 March 1986
22. *Guardian*, 31 July 1986
23. *Star*, 26 September 1986
24. *Guardian*, 5 August 1986
25. FAC I, p. xxx
26. *Guardian*, 8 October 1986
27. ibid.
28. Reuter, 21 October 1986
29. *Guardian*, 21 October 1986
30. FAC I, p. xxxi
31. *Guardian*, 31 October 1986
32. FAC Observations, pp. 5–6
33. ibid.

Chapter 17

1. *Survey* 1959–60, p. 281
2. *Survey* 1959–60, p. 276
3. *Survey* 1967, p. 87
4. *Survey* 1966, p. 86
5. Schlesinger, *Robert Kennedy*, pp. 743–9
6. ibid.
7. *Survey* 1967, p. 87
8. *Survey* 1970, pp. 70–1
9. ibid.
10. *Survey* 1972, pp. 116–20
11. ibid.
12. ibid.
13. ibid.
14. Rees and Day, *Muldergate*, p. 164
15. *Survey* 1977, p. 574
16. *Survey* 1977, pp. 572–3
17. *Survey* 1977, pp. 10 and 21
18. *Survey* 1977, pp. 574–6

Chapter 18

1. *BD*, 21 August 1985
2. Reuter, 20 August 1986
3. AP, 13 August 1986
4. *WP*, 16 August 1985
5. ibid.
6. Reuter, 21 July 1986
7. *WP*, 2 July 1986
8. *IHT*, 1 October 1986
9. Reuter, 7 August 1986
10. *Citizen*, 24 March 1986

11. *WP*, 21 July 1986
12. *WP*, 18 June 1986
13. *WP*, 30 July 1986
14. Myers, *US Business*, p. 135
15. *CT*, 6 February 1985
16. *BD*, 20 December 1985

Chapter 19

1. *WP*, 3 February 1985
2. *CT*, 28 July 1986
3. *CT*, 12 March 1986
4. *New York Times*, 17 January 1986
5. AP, 27 February 1986; SAPA, 26 March 1986
6. *BD*, 15 August 1986; *Sowetan*, 18 August 1986; *DD*, 3 October 1986
7. *Tribune*, 14 September 1986
8. *EPH*, 12 September 1985
9. Reuter, 23 May 1986; *BD*, 26 May 1986
10. Reuter, 17 October 1986
11. Reuter and AP, 20 October 1986
12. Reuter, 21 October 1986
13. *Guardian*, 21 October 1986
14. Reuter, 21 October 1986
15. *Guardian*, 22 October 1986
16. Reuter, 22 October 1986
17. ibid.
18. ibid.
19. Reuter, 18 October 1986
20. Reuter, 16 October 1986
21. *Guardian*, 20 October 1986

Chapter 20

1. All quotes from *WP*, 23 July 1986
2. *Guardian*, 23 July 1986
3. All quotes from *WP*, *Guardian*, and AP, 13 August 1986
4. *BD*, 15 August 1986
5. *Documents*, no. 38
6. ibid., no. 138
7. *CT*, 11 July 1986
8. *Documents*, no. 77
9. ibid., no. 68
10. ibid., no. 138
11. ibid., no. 161
12. ibid.
13. Myers, *US Business*, p. 135

Bibliography: Part 2

DISINVESTMENT/DIVESTMENT

General

Brooke Baldwin and Theodore Brown, *Economic Action Against Apartheid*, The Africa Fund (198 Broadway, New York 10038, USA), 1985 ($3). Excellent handbook on how to disinvest.

Amy L. Domini and Peter D. Kinder, *Ethical Investing*, Addison-Wesley, Reading, Massachusetts, 1984. For US investors.

Sue Ward, *Socially Responsible Investment*, Directory of Social Change, London, 1986. For UK investors.

Company lists

The United Nations Centre on Transnational Corporations (UNCTC) has compiled two lists. The larger is of all corporations holding, directly or indirectly, an equity ownership of more than 10 per cent in one or more affiliates in South Africa or Namibia. This is entitled *Transnational Corporations with Interests in South Africa or Namibia* and was published as part of the Public Hearings on the Activities of TNCs in South Africa and Namibia, held at the United Nations, New York, 16–20 September 1985. A shorter list of about half these corporations which operate in 'strategic sections of the southern African economy' is included in *Policies and Practices of Transnational Corporations Regarding Their Activities in South Africa and Namibia*, Report no. E/C.10/1983/10/Rev.1.

More detailed and complete lists have been produced for individual countries. These include:

UK: *UK Companies and their Subsidiary or Related Companies in South Africa and Namibia*, Anti-Apartheid Movement (13 Mandela Street, London NW1 0DW), September 1986 (£1.50).

USA: *Unified List of United States Companies with Investments or Loans in South Africa and Namibia*, The Africa Fund (198 Broadway, New York 10038, USA), updated edn., November 1985 ($7). To be updated in 1987 to include companies with franchises or licences but no investments.

Various shorter priority lists have also been published, including:

UK: *Allies of Apartheid*, Anti-Apartheid Movement (13 Mandela Street, London NW1

ODW), January 1987; and *Profiting From Apartheid: Britain's Links with South Africa*, Labour Research Department (78 Blackfriars Rd, London SEI 8HF), July 1986. Also 'Shame of UK Stake in Apartheid' in *Labour Research*, London, September 1985.

USA: *The Corporate Examiner*, Interfaith Centre on Corporate Responsibility (475 Riverside Drive, Room 566, New York 10115). Published ten times a year ($25 a year). The dozen priority companies selected by US churches are profiled in Vol. XIV, nos. 4, 5 and 6, 1985. Similar material is available in the *Divestment Resource Pack*, United Church Board for World Ministries (475 Riverside Drive, 16th Floor, New York 10115, USA; $7.50). A list of 100 top US corporations in South Africa has been published by the Churches Emergency Committee on Southern Africa (475 Riverside Drive, Room 612, New York 10115, USA).

Individual Companies

Barclays Shadow Report, published annually from 1981 by End Loans to Southern Africa (PO Box 686, London NW5 2NW; £1 each).

Shell Shadow Report, Embargo (PO Box 686, London NW5 2NW), or Holland Committee on Southern Africa (OZ Achterburgwal 173, 1012 DJ, Amsterdam, Netherlands), 1986. Also *Boycott Shell*, United Mine Workers of America (900 15th St NW, Washington, DC, 20005, USA), undated.

Consolidated Gold Fields – Partner in Apartheid, Counter Information Services (9 Poland Street, London W1), 1986 (95p).

Daimlers Rüstung für Südafrika, Eigenverlag, Stuttgart, 1982.

Dresdner Bank Shadow Report, Kein Geld für Apartheid (Siegesstrasse 9, 8000 München 40, West Germany), undated.

OIL EMBARGO

South Africa's Lifeline: Violations of the Oil Embargo, September 1986, Shipping Research Bureau (PO Box 11898, 1001 GW Amsterdam, Netherlands), September 1986; also several other reports from the same source.

ARMS EMBARGO

International Seminar on the UN Arms Embargo Against South Africa, London, 28–30 May 1986. Documents available from World Campaign Against Military and Nuclear Collaboration with South Africa (PO Box 2, Lindeberg Gaard, 1007 Oslo 10, Norway) or Anti-Apartheid Movement (13 Mandela Street, London NW1 ODW).

Gavin Cawthra, *Brutal Force: The Apartheid War Machine*, IDAF (64 Essex Road, London N1 8LR), May 1986 (£6).

NATIONAL REPORTS

UK

Richard Moorsom, *The Scope for Sanctions*, CIIR (22 Coleman Fields, London N1 7AF), 1986 (£3.95).

Barbara Rogers and Brian Bolton, *Sanctions against South Africa: Exploding the Myths*, Manchester Free Press, 1981.

Beating Apartheid, Trades Union Congress (Congress House, Great Russell Street, London WCIB 3LS), September 1986 (£2.50). Also from the TUC *New Guidelines on Disinvesting from South Africa*, October 1986.

Paul Snell, *The Apartheid Connection: West Midlands Companies in South Africa*, TURC Publishing (7 Frederick Street, Birmingham BI 3HE), June 1986 (£1.50). An excellent example of a regional report, identifying local links with RSA and targets for local campaigns.

A Tiny Little Bit: An Assessment of Britain's Record of Action against South Africa, Anti-Apartheid Movement (13 Mandela Street, London NWI ODW), 30 July 1986 (£1).

UK Companies' South African Pay and Conditions, Ethical Investment Research and Information Service (9 Poland Street, London WIV 3DG), June 1986 (£2).

Richard Moorsom, *Sanctions Against South Africa*, 2 volumes: 'A Background Report' and 'Statistics on South Africa's External Economic Relations', Oxfam Public Affairs Unit (274 Banbury Rd, Oxford OX2 7DY).

USA

Summary Chart on Public Fund Disinvestment, American Committee on Africa (198 Broadway, New York 10038; $1); regularly updated.

Richard Knight, *Computers in South Africa*, Africa Fund (198 Broadway, New York 10038; $2), 1986. Also Baldwin and Brown, listed above under 'Disinvestment/divestment'.

Elizabeth Schmidt, *One Step in the Wrong Direction: An Analysis of the Sullivan Principles*, Episcopal Churchpeople for a Free Southern Africa (339 Lafayette Street, New York 10012), 1985 ($1).

Austria

Walter Sauer and Theresia Zeschin, *Die Apartheid-Connection: Österreiches Bedeutung für Südafrika*, Verlag für Gesellschaftskritik, Wien, 1984; available from the Austrian anti-apartheid movement (Anti-Apartheid–Bewegung in Österreich, A 1061 Wien, Postfach 146).

Canada

Trafficking in Apartheid: The Case for Canadian Sanctions, SACTU Solidarity Committee (Box 490 Station J, Toronto, Ontario M4J 4Z2), 1985 (C$5).

Finland

Rauhan-Poulesta, monthly newspaper of the Finnish Peace Committee (Eerikinkatu 15–17 B 21, 00100 Helsinki). The October 1986 issue is a special one in English with news of the Finnish trade union imposition of sanctions.

India

Enuga S. Reddy, *India and the Struggle against Apartheid*, Hansib Publishing (139 Fonthill Rd, London N4 3HF, UK).

Ireland

Irish Anti-Apartheid Movement Annual Report, Irish AAM (20 Beechpark Rd, Dublin 18).

Japan

The Contradictions in Japan's Policies towards South Africa (in English), Japan Anti-Apartheid Committee (Room 306, Ebisu 4–5–23, Shibuya-Ku, Tokyo), 1986.

Netherlands

Nederland Investeert in Apartheid, FNV, Amsterdam, 1986.

Norway

'Økonomiske Sanksjoner mot Sør-Afrika' in *FAFO Rapport*, no. 61, August 1986 (FAFO, Lilletorget 1, 0184 Oslo 1).

Sweden

Svensk Teknologi till Apartheid, Isolera Sydafrika-kommitten (ISAK, Barnängsg. 23, 116 41 Stockholm), 1986. Also available in English as *Swedish Technology and Apartheid*.

The Swedish People's Parliament against Apartheid in Stockholm, 21–3 February 1986: Final Document. Available in English from ISAK (see above).

West Germany

Die Deutsche Wirtschaft und Südafrika, Christen für Arbeit und Gerechtigkeit weltweit (Obere Seegasse 18, 6900 Heidelberg), April 1986.

Banken und Apartheid, Anti-Apartheid Bewegung (Blüchestrasse 14, 5300 Bonn 1).

OTHER OFFICIAL UNITED NATIONS LISTS

Register of Entertainers, Actors, and Others who have Performed in Apartheid South Africa, UN Special Committee Against Apartheid, UN Document A/Conf.137/Ref.7, 29 April 1986. Regularly updated.

Consolidated List of Sportsmen and Sportswomen who Participated in Sports Events in South Africa from 1 September 1980 to 31 December 1985, UN Special Committee Against Apartheid, UN Document A/Conf.137/Ref.3, 22 May 1986. Regularly updated.

Eva Militz, *Bank Loans to South Africa from Mid-1982 to December 1984*, UN Document

A/Conf.137/BP.5, 29 April 1986. Published for the UN's World Conference on Sanctions Against Racist South Africa.

Sanctions Against South Africa: A Selective Bibliography, 1981–1985, UN Report A/Conf.137/Ref.1, 7 May 1986.

PERIODICALS

Anti-Apartheid News (13 Mandela Street, London NW1 0DW, UK). Ten times a year: £7.50 (UK), £10 (rest of Europe), £12 (elsewhere).

Facts and Reports (OZ Achterburgwal 173, 1012 DJ Amsterdam, Netherlands). Fortnightly press-clips on Southern Africa. $40 per year.

AWEPAA News Bulletin, Association of West European Parliamentarians for Action Against Apartheid (PO Box 402, 2501 CK The Hague, Netherlands).

Notes: Part 2

Chapter 21

1. Albert Luthuli, *Let My People Go* (Fontana, London, 1963), p. 185.
2. The EPG report was published as *Mission to South Africa* (Penguin, London, 1986). The quote is from p. 133 of this edition.
3. 'Investment in 1986', supplement to the *Financial Mail* (Johannesburg), 29 November 1985.
4. Motlatsi was speaking at the first annual conference of the International Mineworkers Organization, where IMO called for sanctions against South African coal (*Financial Times*, London, 24 November 1986).
5. *New York Times*, 16 June 1986.
6. *Guardian* (London), 17 September 1986.
7. For example, Resolutions 34/93A of 1979, 35/206E of 1980, 40/64A of 1985, and 41/35 of 1986.
8. Letter from the Institution of Professional Civil Servants section at the British Library Document Supply Centre to British Anti-Apartheid, 15 December 1985.
9. *Guardian* (London), 25 November 1986.
10. Head Office Circular No. 239/86, Barclays Bank (London), 14 July 1986.
11. *Financial Times* (London), 25 November 1986; 'The SA Connection', Phillips & Drew Banks Research (London), 12 August 1986.
12. *Guardian* (London), 25 November 1986.
13. Chairman Donald Frey quoted in the *Washington Post*, 8 February 1986.
14. Chief Executive John Wilson quoted in *Business Day* (Johannesburg), 9 July 1986.
15. Patrick McVeigh, *Out of South Africa: The Insight Study of the South African Divestment Movement*, Insight (711 Atlantic Avenue, Boston, Massachusetts 02111, USA), July 1986.

Chapter 22

1. *Guardian* (London), 9 July 1986.
2. Gary Clyde Hufbauer and Jeffrey J. Schott, *Economic Sanctions Reconsidered* (Institute for International Economics, Washington, DC, 1985).
3. All based on constant 1965 prices as calculated by the government and published in the *Monthly Digest of Statistics*. In part quoted by Duncan Clarke in 'Zimbabwe's International Economic Position', *Journal of Commonwealth and Comparative Politics*, March 1980.
4. Donald Losman, *International Economic Sanctions* (University of New Mexico Press, Albuquerque, 1979), p. 103. In the early 1970s, the rate of exchange was roughly: R$1 = US$1.75 = £0.80.

5. Martin Bailey, *Oilgate* (Hodder & Stoughton, London, 1979).

6. Losman, op. cit., p. 122.

7. E. G. Cross, 'Economic Sanctions as an Instrument of Policy, The Rhodesia Experience', a paper at the Economic Symposium, Salisbury 8–10 September 1980. Part of the paper was published in the *World Economy* (Oxford), March 1981.

8. In an interview by Elizabeth Schmidt, who has written several articles on the subject, including 'The Sanctions Weapon: Lessons from Rhodesia', *TransAfrica Forum*, Vol. 4, no. 1, Fall 1986; and others in *African Business* (London), September 1986, and *Guardian* (London), 1 August 1986.

9. Two different estimates are compared by Richard Moorsom in *The Scope For Sanctions* (CIIR, London, 1986), p. 41.

10. Paul Conlon, 'The Sasol Coal Liquefaction Plants', UN Centre against Apartheid Document 10/85 (October 1985), p. 40.

11. Speaking at a meeting at Vereeniging on 24 April 1986, quoted in the *Financial Times* (London), 1 May 1986, and elsewhere.

Chapter 23

1. *Guardian* (London), 3 October 1986.

2. US sanctions against Cuba will not be discussed in detail here. See, for example: Gary Clyde Hufbauer and Jeffrey J. Schott, *Economic Sanctions Reconsidered* (Institute for International Economics, Washington, DC, 1985); Donald Losman, *International Economic Sanctions* (University of New Mexico Press, Albuquerque, 1979); and Robin Renwick, *Economic Sanctions* (Harvard Studies in International Affairs No. 45, Centre for International Affairs, Cambridge, Massachusetts, 1981). The United States imposed comprehensive sanctions in a series of steps between 1960 and 1964, with the support of the Organization of American States, but not of the United Nations. Sanctions were lifted in 1975, but re-imposed by President Ronald Reagan in 1981. The sanctions were economically disruptive, particularly because Cuba could not sell its sugar to the United States, nor obtain spare parts for its US-made machinery. Cuba estimated the cost up to 1982 at $9 billion. But in 1960 the Soviet Union stepped in, agreeing to buy sugar and to supply Cuba with oil and other commodities. Soviet aid probably exceeds the damage caused by the embargo. The goal of sanctions was to destabilize the government of Fidel Castro, leading to his eventual overthrow. They clearly failed to achieve this. Losman comments: 'The embargo has been quite economically damaging, although much of its incidence has been shifted to the socialist bloc. Its political results, on the other hand, have been questionable.'

3. Richard Moorsom, *The Scope for Sanctions* (CIIR, London, 1986), p. 9.

4. Elizabeth Schmidt, 'Sanctions: The Lesson from Rhodesia', *AfricAsia* (Paris), August 1986.

5. Jim Jones, *Financial Times* (London), 24 October 1986.

6. *Financial Mail* (Johannesburg), 4 October 1985.

7. ibid., 20 September 1985.

8. ibid., 18 October 1985; *Standard Bank Review*, November 1985.

9. *The Effect of Sanctions on Employment and Production in South Africa* (FCI Information Services, Johannesburg, 1986).

10. *Star* (Johannesburg), 15 June 1986.

11. Losman, op. cit., p. 122.
12. Renwick, op. cit., p. 80.
13. In a paper, 'The Laager Economy and After', given at a conference at the University of York, 2 October 1986.

Chapter 24

1. It is not too early to ask about the criteria for lifting sanctions, and it is important to keep in mind the political goal. In Rhodesia, the minority government in 1978 tried to impose its own 'majority-rule' government which included only collaborators and excluded the main liberation movements. Ian Smith then asked the international community to remove sanctions. It was only the refusal to do this that forced Smith to go to Lancaster House and agree to genuine majority rule. The white minority in South Africa will surely also try to impose its own internal settlement and then say that sanctions should be lifted. Thus the conditions for lifting sanctions should be clearly defined in advance. I would suggest that all of the following should be satisfied: (1) Participation of the liberation movements recognized by the United Nations and the Organization of African Unity, namely the ANC, PAC, and SWAPO, in any negotiations for a settlement. (Sanctions should not be lifted until an agreement is signed.) (2) Unconditional release of all political prisoners, including ANC, PAC and SWAPO leaders. (3) Legalization of all political parties and the guarantee that they could participate freely and equally in any post-independence election.
2. *Mission to South Africa* (Penguin, Harmondsworth, 1986), pp. 133 and 137.
3. Sixth Report from the House of Commons Foreign Affairs Committee, Vol. II, HC 61–II (London, 1986), pp. 109–11.
4. *Guardian* (London), 9 June 1986.
5. *Financial Mail* (Johannesburg), 27 June 1986.
6. *Financial Mail* (Johannesburg), 4 October 1985.
7. For example, 'Cultural boycott strikes again', *Star* (Johannesburg), 20 February 1986.
8. *Observer* (London), 13 April 1986.
9. *Observer* (London), 14 September 1986. See also 24 August 1986.
10. Joseph Hanlon, *Apartheid's Second Front* (Penguin, London, 1986), p. 58.
11. *Mission to South Africa* (see n. 2 above), p. 140.

Chapter 25

1. *Guardian* (London), 26 June 1986 and 22 August 1986; *Sunday Times* (London), 29 June 1986.
2. *Trafficking in Apartheid* (SACTU Solidarity Committee, Toronto, January 1986).
3. The bulk of the Duport steelworks in Llanelli, including blast-furnace equipment, was sold to Iscor in 1981 for £3.7 million.
4. *The EC and Southern Africa* (May 1984), a newsletter produced by the Editorial Board of *Amandla*, Amsterdam.
5. *Financial Times* (London), 2 September 1986.
6. Very roughly, one man produces 1,000 tonnes of coal per year, and the EEC imported nearly 20 million tonnes in 1984, so this gives 20,000 jobs. Brian Bolton has calculated that ending fruit and vegetable imports to Britain would create between 1,500 and 2,000 jobs, particularly producing and packing apples. (Personal

communication. Bolton is co-author with Barbara Rogers of *Sanctions against South Africa: Exploding the Myths*, Manchester Free Press, 1981.) Britain accounted for 48 per cent of EEC fruit and vegetable imports from South Africa in 1985, so doubling this gives the figure for the EEC as a whole. In addition, of course, there are knock-on effects – jobs are created for agricultural and mining machinery suppliers, etc.

7. Richard Moorsom, *The Scope for Sanctions* (CIIR, London, 1986), pp. 69–86. Much of this section is based on Moorsom's work.

8. The main industry-by-industry studies are in Brian Bolton and Barbara Rogers, op. cit., and B. Rivers and Martin Bailey, *Britain's Economic Links with South Africa* (Christian Concern for Southern Africa, London, 1979). The Cambridge model is discussed by Donald Roy in a paper presented at a Fabian Society Conference in London on 11 July 1986. Because the Bolton/Rogers and Rivers/Bailey studies are based on a period when UK trade with RSA was substantially higher, I am using figures as corrected by Richard Moorsom.

9. Roy's study shows a particularly important point. A big loss if total sanctions are imposed is of unearned income from South Africa – profits and dividends to shareholders, interest payments, and income from property. In effect, the economy compensates for this lost unearned income, and it does so through increased earned income – by stepping up exports of goods. This creates jobs. Thus a *loss* of unearned income from South Africa actually stimulates the British economy.

10. *Guardian* (London), 28 November 1986; *Independent* (London), 13 January 1987.

11. Joseph Hanlon, *Apartheid's Second Front* (Penguin, Harmondsworth, 1986), p. 1; Joseph Hanlon, *Beggar Your Neighbours* (CIIR/James Currey, London, 1986), p. 270.

12. Some account must be made for the fact that exports to South Africa are more capital-intensive and involve proportionately fewer jobs than exports to South Africa's neighbours. See Donald Roy for an estimate.

13. *Beating Apartheid* (TUC, London, September 1986).

14. Two useful books on ethical investment are, for Britain, Sue Ward, *Socially Responsible Investment* (list from p. 29), and for the USA, Amy Domini and Peter Kinder, *Ethical Investing*. (See Bibliography, p. 376, for details.)

15. Although US and British law are different, the guidelines for trustees are almost identical. In the United States, the Employee Retirement Income Security Act (ERISA) of 1974 covers private pension plans, but its language is used in other laws as well. It says that a trustee shall act 'for the exclusive purposes of providing benefits to participants and their beneficiaries'. UK policy is defined by the Megarry decision, discussed below.

16. British policy comes from the 1886 court case Learoyd *v*. Whitley in which a judge said that the law requires a trustee to take the care that 'a man of ordinary prudence would exercise in the management of his own private affairs', except that the trustees must be particularly cautious over investments of a speculative character even if they would be purchased by 'businessmen of ordinary prudence'. ERISA says that a fund manager must invest as a prudent person who is acting in a like capacity and who is familiar with such matters.

17. In Britain the 1961 Trustee Investments Act states that trustees shall have regard to the need for the diversification of investments. ERISA specifies that assets be diversified so as to minimize the risk of large losses 'unless under the circumstances it is clearly prudent not to do so'.

18. Cowan and others *v*. Scargill and others (Chancery Division, Sir Robert Megarry V.-C.), *All England Law Reports (1984)*.

19. Definitions are important. In the United States the most common terms are 'South African-invested' (SAI) for companies with investments in South Africa or loans to the South African public sector, and 'South Africa-free' (SAF) for the non-SAI firms. But others look for a broader definition of companies doing any business 'in or with' South Africa. These could be called 'South Africa-linked' (SAL).

20. There are a variety of studies in the United States. One used the January 1980 *Standard and Poor's Stock Guide* and looked at companies with a rating of A− or better. It compared all 124 SAI companies in that group with the 124 largest SAF companies. Over the next five years, the total return (dividends plus price appreciation) on the SAF portfolio was 20.75 per cent, compared to 16.06 per cent for the SAI portfolio. This is a better performance of 29.2 per cent (Brooke Baldwin and Theodore Brown, *Economic Action against Apartheid*, The Africa Fund, New York, 1986). Note that I have calculated 'better performance' by taking the difference in return and dividing by the smaller return − in this instance:

$$(20.75 - 16.06)/16.06 = 0.292 = 29.2\%.$$

Another study looked at 152 SAI companies in the *Standard and Poor* 500 and compared them with the largest 152 SAF firms. For five years (apparently 1979–83 inclusive), the return on the SAI firms was 92 per cent and that on the SAF firms 160 per cent − a 74-per-cent better performance, and the highest in any of the studies (Wayne Wagner *et al.*, 'South African Investment', *Financial Analysts' Journal*, Nov.–Dec. 1984).

Two studies by fund managers covering longer periods and slightly different groups of stocks came up with similar results. The Boston Company compared portfolios of SAF and SAI stocks over the period 1973–83 and found a 17-per-cent better performance by the SAF portfolio. Trinity Management looked at somewhat different portfolios over 1974–82 and found the SAF performed 13 per cent better (Patrick McVeigh, *Out of South Africa*, Insight Report on Vital Industries no. 11, Boston, July 1986). These differences have continued up to the time of writing − between 1 January 1984 and mid-1986 the gap was over 25 per cent. (See Patrick McVeigh, op. cit., as well as *Issue Paper South Africa*, Good Money Publication, Worcester, Vermont, June 1986.)

There is only one good study for Britain, but it agrees with the US results. Ann Woodall completed an MA thesis in May 1986 for the City of London Polytechnic Department of Accounting and Finance. She looked at a portfolio based on all 505 companies in the Financial Times All Share Index, with companies included in proportion to their average value. This was compared with a similar portfolio of the 334 SAF companies. Over five years the first portfolio gave a return of 39.2 per cent, while the SAF portfolio grew by 42.1 per cent − a better performance by 7 per cent against a neutral portfolio. (This is in keeping with the US results, because the US studies compare SAF with SAI, whereas Woodall compared the broader SAF against the market. Replacing SAI shares with better-performing SAF shares will boost the performance of that portion of the total portfolio.)

21. How much power this gives local-authority fund trustees has yet to be tested in the courts, however.

22. Ann Woodall looked at this with respect to Britain, and found the difference relatively

minor. On a scale from 0 to 1, with 0 being immediately marketable and 1 meaning a sale requires three months or more, she found that the marketability of the market portfolio was 0.034, and that of the SAF portfolio 0.075 – a negligible difference in real terms. There are two higher costs associated with smaller firms. The reduced liquidity means that it may be necessary to pay a slightly higher trading commission. And the big stockbrokers tend to do less research on smaller firms, so the fund managers need to pay for this. But these extra costs are relatively small, and are more than compensated for by the higher profits. (See, for example, Patrick McVeigh, for actual costs of disinvestment for a $5.2 billion fund.)

23. In the United States in 1983, 37 per cent of *Standard and Poor* 500 companies were SAI, and they accounted for 46 per cent of the values of those 500 companies. The major withdrawals from South Africa in 1985 and 1986 would decrease this considerably, because of firms like GM and IBM. But using the broader definition of 'SAL' would increase this by including GM, IBM and others which have sold their South African subsidiary but are still trading with South Africa.

24. In the United States the variety of stock exchanges and very wide range of companies mean that a fund of any size can disinvest. For larger funds in smaller countries, avoiding SAL firms requires more planning and some overseas investment. In Britain funds over, say, £1 billion will be forced to place some money abroad in order to obtain wide enough diversification; in general, such investments are less risky than ones made in Britain, and it is possible to insure against undue risks caused by currency fluctuations.

25. *Sunday Express* (London), 24 August 1986.

26. In fact, many fund managers, on purely financial grounds, already do not buy SAI shares, but have not actually disinvested the SAI shares they already hold. Where large holdings are involved, disinvestment cannot be done quickly without incurring excessive costs. But if disinvestment is agreed, it is important to set realistic deadlines – otherwise the sales will be postponed indefinitely.

27. *New Guidelines on Disinvesting in South Africa* (TUC, London, 15 October 1986).

Chapter 26

1. This chapter was written with extensive help from Peter Robbins, a metals consultant who is the author of *Guide to Non-ferrous Metals* (Kogan Page, London, 1982).

2. *Guardian* (London), 9 July 1986.

3. *Financial Times* (London), 8 September 1986; Gail Levey, *Futures Research Quarterly Report: Precious Metals* (Shearson Lehman Brothers, New York, April 1986).

4. Such threats are usually denied afterwards. In one case, State President P. W. Botha said he had been misinterpreted (*Guardian*, London, 25 October 1985). But press references are frequent enough to suggest that at least some members of the South African government are considering this as a form of retaliation.

5. *South Africa and Critical Materials*, Open File Report 76–86 (Bureau of Mines, US Department of Interior, July 1986), pp. 34 and S–3.

6. ibid., p. S–3.

7. ibid., pp. 16–20 and 68. For example, there are new processes to produce stainless steel with half the present chromium content or even less.

8. The chromium itself is not recovered from the scrap; rather, the stainless steel is directly recycled, cutting the demand for new stainless steel.

9. *South Africa and Critical Materials*, p. 45.

10. Assume that the price of platinum rises high enough for there to be maximum recycling of car catalysts (thus demand for 'new' platinum is down by half, to 15 per cent of present total world demand), that old jewellery sales roughly match new purchases (meaning no demand for 'new' platinum), and that non-jewellery uses fall in line with US estimates (to, say, three quarters of remaining demand and thus 30 per cent of total demand). Then world platinum demand falls to about 45 per cent of present levels. Since non-South African producers supply about 15 per cent of current demand, there is a shortfall of 30 per cent. But we have old recyclable catalysts (say 100 per cent of one year's normal demand), plus reserves of perhaps 55 per cent of one year's normal use. (*South Africa and Critical Materials*, p. 45, estimates that private stocks are equal to 4.7 months' total US consumption. Assume this is also true of the rest of the world. The US strategic stockpile of platinum is 16 per cent of one year's world production. No other country is known to hold platinum reserves.) Together, then, this is enough to meet the shortfall for more than five years (155 ÷ 30 = 5.2).

11. At present hoarded metal amounts to only perhaps 30 per cent of one year's normal production, although much of this would trickle back on to the market when platinum bars and coins could no longer be easily bought and sold. More important would be the sudden end to the present hoarding of 9 per cent of consumption. Even if the ban were not perfect, and the amount hoarded stayed roughly constant rather than decreasing, we have still reduced total world demand to 36 per cent of normal, or only 21 per cent over non-South African supplies. Thus our 155-per-cent reserve would last for 7.4 years.

12. The *Financial Times* (London, 8 September 1986) commented that 'the South African government looks unlikely to react to any economic sanctions imposed by western countries by retaliating with restrictions on precious metal exports. South Africa needs the revenue too badly'.

13. Some brief comments should be made about other PGMs. Palladium is in surplus and it is widely believed that the USSR holds large stockpiles in order to keep the price up. However, rhodium could be a problem, because it is produced in quite small quantities. It comprises 8 to 12 per cent of normal car catalysts, yet forms only 3 per cent of non-South African ore. However, it is not used at all in the catalysts for 'lean burn' engines. So, in solving the platinum supply problem, the rhodium supply problem is automatically corrected. The other three PGMs are much less important.

Chapter 27

1. For more details, see Joseph Hanlon, *Beggar Your Neighbours* (CIIR/James Currey, London, 1986).

2. For example, the Organization of African Unity Resolution 734 (XXXIII) on sanctions includes the exemption clause: '. . . bearing in mind the current special difficulties confronting some independent states in southern Africa and Cape Verde, which are obliged to maintain some economic relations with the South African regime by virtue of historical and geographical circumstances.' The Commonwealth mini-summit in August 1986, which approved a series of new sanctions, also requested the Secretary-General 'to identify such adjustment as may be necessary in

Commonwealth countries affected by them'. This is interpreted to mean that there will be exemptions for the neighbouring states.

3. Mozambique still has some miners in South Africa. In October 1986 South Africa announced that it would no longer hire new Mozambican miners, nor renew the contracts of existing miners as is normally done every two years. This retaliation against US sanctions would have cost Mozambique at least $75 million per year, although it would also have removed the final economic link between Mozambique and South Africa (except for some electricity purchases). In fact, the mine-owners objected to losing the highly skilled and non-unionized Mozambican workers, and in January 1987 the South African government quietly backed down. There would be no new recruitment, but existing contracts would continue to be renewed.

4. Joseph Hanlon, *Apartheid's Second Front* (Penguin, Harmondsworth, 1986).

5. Joseph Hanlon, 'South Africa's Neighbours', paper given at a Fabian Society Conference, London, 11 July 1986.

6. Speaking at the SADCC annual conference in Harare, 31 January 1986.

7. *Financial Times* (London), 7 November 1986.

8. The non-white workforce is about 9 million (based on government figures cited in *South Africa to 1990*, Economist Intelligence Unit, London, March 1986, pp. 41–3).

9. *UK Companies' South African Pay and Conditions* (Ethical Investment Research and Information Service, June 1986, see Bibliography, p. 378).

10. Elizabeth Schmidt, *One Step in the Wrong Direction* (Episcopal Churchpeople for a Free Southern Africa, January 1985; see Bibliography, p. 378); updated in the *New York Times*, 17 January 1986.

11. *SouthScan* (London), 18 November 1986; *Independent* (London), 10 November 1986.

12. *Financial Mail* (Johannesburg), 11 October 1985.

13. *Insight*, Spring 1986; Franklin Research & Development Corporation, Boston.

14. *Sunday Tribune* (Durban), 14 September 1986.

15. *Transnational Corporations in South Africa and Namibia: United Nations Public Hearings*, Vol. 1, Reports of the Panel of Eminent Persons and of the Secretary General, UN Publication no. E.86.II.A.6 (New York, 1986), p. 15.

16. *Financial Mail* (Johannesburg), 9 November 1985.

17. *Financial Mail* (Johannesburg), 8 September 1985, 23 May 1986, and 20 June 1986.

18. *Financial Times* (London), 20 June 1986.

19. 'Contingency Planning by General Motors, South Africa', UN Centre Against Apartheid Notes and Documents 31/78 (September 1978).

20. *New York Times*, 27 July 1986.

21. *Guardian* (London), 17 November 1986.

22. *Wall Street Journal* (New York), 11 July 1986.

Chapter 28

1. *Transnational Corporations in South Africa and Namibia: United Nations Public Hearings*, Vol. 1, Reports of the Panel of Eminent Persons and of the Secretary General, UN Publication no. E.86.II.A.6 (New York, 1986), p. 77; *Guardian* (London), 23 October 1985.

2. Joanne Naiman, *et al.*, *Relations between Canada and South Africa*, Report 10/84 of the UN Centre Against Apartheid (August 1984), p. 17.
3. *Daily Mirror* (London), 19 September 1985.
4. *Observer* (London), 4 August 1985.
5. *Africa News* (Durham, North Carolina), 22 October 1984; 'The UN Arms Embargo and the USA', Paper C2 at the International Seminar on the UN Arms Embargo against South Africa, London, 28–30 May 1986.
6. Such as *International Defence Review*, *Jane's Defence Review*, and *Jane's Military Communications*.
7. *Guardian* (London), 15 May 1986, 22 August 1986 and 28 November 1986.
8. *Guardian* (London), 22 November 1986.
9. Harry Strack, 'The International Relations of Rhodesia under Sanctions' (Ph.D. thesis, University of Iowa, 1974).
10. *Independent* (London), 10 November 1986.
11. 'We do not want to harm the Front Line States – they have things hard enough already,' explained Seppo Antikainen, AKT Executive Secretary.
12. See *South Africa's Lifeline* (September 1986) and several other studies by the Shipping Research Bureau (see Bibliography, p. 377).
13. Noted in a statement of 9 April 1984 before the UN Security Council Committee Established by Resolution 421 (1977) Concerning the Question of South Africa.
14. *Financial Times* (London), 24 October 1986.
15. 'US Firms Keep a Foot in the Door', *International Herald Tribune* (Paris), 14 August 1986.
16. *Washington Post*, 24 October 1986.

Chapter 29

1. *Financial Times* (London), 22 October 1986.
2. *Financial Times* (London), 22 October 1986.
3. Quoted after his death in *The Times* (London), 23 October 1985.
4. *Guardian* (London), 20 November 1986.
5. *Irish Times*, 17 July 1986.
6. CCCN categories 84 and 85.
7. *Observer* (London), 2 November 1986.
8. UMW, 900 15th Street NW, Washington, DC, 20005.
9. *Financial Times* (London), 24 October 1986.
10. *New York Times*, 9 September 1986; *Facts and Reports* (Amsterdam), 24 October 1986, p. 10.
11. Some of this will be Anglo American's own offshore holdings.
12. *Britain's Partners in Apartheid* (Counter Information Services, 9 Poland Street, London WIV 3DG; 1986).
13. *Financial Times* (London), 24 October 1986.
14. *New Guidelines on Disinvesting from South Africa* (TUC, London, October 1986).
15. *Beating Apartheid* (TUC, London, September 1986).
16. *The Corporate Examiner* (Interfaith Centre on Corporate Responsibility, New York), Vol. 14 no. 4, 1985; updated by ICCR statement, 15 September 1986.
17. Statement from Churches' Emergency Committee on Southern Africa, New York, 22 August 1986.
18. *Observer* (London), 27 July 1986.

Index

church groups, 288–90, 338, 343, 362
Ciskei, 34, 37, 111
City Press, 37
Clark, Joe, 349
coal, 12, 77–9, 89, 137, 139, 150, 151, 153, 193, 198, 200, 202, 214, 243, 261, 263, 322
Coca-Cola (company), 172, 202, 261, 336, 341
CoCom (Coordinationg Committee for Multilateral Export Controls), 270, 274, 306, 311
Commonwealth: on sanctions, 77–80, 89, 105, 106, 107, 137, 141, 146, 149–50, 152–3, 194, 197–8; embargoes: agricultural products, 320, air links, 348, arms from RSA, 324. arms to RSA, 307, diplomatic relations, 352, culture, 354–6, finance, 314, 330–31, 333, gold, 323, oil, 309, sport, 354–6, tourism, 349, uranium, 321
Commonwealth Games Federation, 133
Communist Party, South African (SACP), 113–14, 179
Community Agency for Social Enquiry (CASE, 46–9, 84
computers, 196, 197, 199, 222, 267, 271–3, 310–12
conscription, 169
Conservative Party (CP), 65–7, 133
Conservatives for Fundamental Change in South Africa, 141–2
Consolidated Goldfields (company), 288, 326
'constructive engagement', 180–82
control of companies, 325–7, 345–6
Cooper, Saths, 28–9
copper, 102, 243, 273
Corwell, Allan, 104
COSATU, *see* Trade Unions, South African, Confederation of Council of Churches, SA (SACC), 47–8, 50–51
country-of-origin labels, 329
Counts, Cecilie, 179
CP, *see* Conservative Party
Crocker, Dr Chester, 68–9, 180–82
Cronkite, Walter, 179
Cronwright, Colonel Arthur, 67
Cross, Eddie, 207, 209, 215
Cry the Beloved Country (Paton), 61–2

Cuban intervention, 182
cultural boycott, 63, 124, 126, 127, 149, 196, 198, 199, 225, 280–81, 354–6
currency, foreign, 223–5; *see also* debts, foreign
Curry, David, 17
CUSA, *see* Unions of SA, Council of customs deposit, 103–4
Cyprus, 304
CZI, *see* Zimbabwe Industries

Daily News, 217
Daimler Benz (company), 235
Dallas (soap opera), 225–6, 356
DarkStar Systems (company), 282
De Beers (company), 97, 288, 322
debts, foreign, 74–5, 155, 210–11, 223–5
De Kock, Dr Gerhard, 75, 80–81, 212, 216
Denmark, 51, 199, 281, 304; *see also* Nordic States
desegregation, 128–9, 169, 177
destabilization, 102–17, 138, 236, 261–2, 279, 362
De Villiers, Dawie, 105
Dhlomo, Dr Oscar, 42
diamonds, 97, 110, 138, 214, 243, 322, 329
Diggs, Charles, 158
diplomatic relations boycott, 352–3, 356
disengagement, 17
disinvestment, 9, 14, 22, 28–9, 30–32, 37–44, 52–3, 65, 82–3, 194–5, 201–3, 237–42, 281, 285, 287, 289, 290, 336–9
divestment, 14; *see also* disinvestment
D'Oliveira, Basil, 128–9
double taxation agreements, 198, 200, 350–51
Duignan, Peter, 171
Duncan, Sheena, 50, 52
du Plessis, Barend, 74–5, 80, 216
du Plessis, Fred, 78
du Plessis, Piet, 18, 21, 76, 111
Durr, Kent, 76–7
Dutch Reformed Churches, 53

Eastman Kodak (company), 36, 277, 336
Economic Sanctions (Renwick), 217